The Year of Jubilo

The Year of Jubilo

A Novel of
the Civil War

HOWARD
BAHR

HENRY HOLT AND COMPANY
NEW YORK

Henry Holt and Company, LLC
Publishers since 1866
115 West 18th Street
New York, New York 10011

Henry Holt® is a registered trademark
of Henry Holt and Company, LLC.

Published in Canada by Fitzhenry & Whiteside Ltd.,
195 Allstate Parkway, Markham, Ontario L3R 4T8.

Library of Congress Cataloging-in-Publication Data
Bahr, Howard, 1946–
The year of Jubilo : a novel of the Civil War / Howard Bahr.—1st ed.
p.   cm.
ISBN 0-8050-5972-5 (alk. paper)
1. Mississippi—History—Civil War, 1861–1865—Veterans—Fiction.
2. Reconstruction—Mississippi—Fiction.   I. Title.
PS3552.A3613 Y4 2000
813'.54—dc21   99-088634

Henry Holt books are available for special promotions
and premiums. For details contact: Director, Special Markets.

First Edition 2000

Designed by Victoria Hartman

Printed in the United States of America

1   3   5   7   9   10   8   6   4   2

For Laura and Kathleen

Well, it must be now that the kingdom's coming,
In the Year of Jubilo.

—HENRY CLAY WORK

And as to you Death, and you bitter hug
of mortality, it is idle to try to alarm me.

—WALT WHITMAN
"Song of Myself"

The Year of Jubilo

June 1864

In the last week of May, Willy Landers passed his twelfth birthday, and on that day his mother presented him a pretty doorknob, broken from its shaft, that she'd found in the ruins of a burned house hard by the southerly road. He could not see the delicate flowers entwined on the cracked white curve of porcelain, but she told him they were there, and how they were pink and blue and yellow. He listened, and knew the gift was magic even before he closed his own hand around it.

In the days since then, he had carried his token everywhere, savoring the weight of it, and the coolness and smoothness of it. Sometimes he would speak to it, believing that deep inside lay a miniature realm where spirits dwelt who would listen. He could imagine them there, going about their business, recording all that he said in great leathern books like the ones he remembered in the courthouse when his father was clerk.

Willy Landers had been five years old when he lost his sight to the scarlet fever, so the images he relied on to give shape to the world were out of date. For seven years he had not seen the sky, nor any person, house, tree, fence—had not seen the rain nor the glitter of leaves nor the frost. He had these things in his memory, but he had changed many of them to suit his own sense (snow, for example, which he could hear falling softly on some winter nights, was golden; fire was a weaving, threadlike creature of silver), and he had never accounted for his own growth, so that people, to Willy Landers, were gaunt, towering things, and the rooms of his house were like great caverns.

He was compensated somewhat by a keen sense of hearing, of touch, and of smell, and these he used to illustrate his imagination. When a wren sang in her clarion voice, Willy saw her as a great bird with extravagant plumage, weighing down the branch where she perched. A hawk, on the other hand, which he never heard except in its distant keening, was small and fragile and shy. He would lay his hand on the rough bark of the oak that grew in the yard and allow the carpenter ants to crawl over his fingers. He would move his hands over the hard-packed earth until he found a feather, a leaf, a cob, a bit of stone, and his mind would fashion these things into shapes that pleased him. So he was content, and hardly missed the light.

On this sunny afternoon, a week after his birthday, Willy sat cross-legged in the yard, rubbing the doorknob against his cheek. Willy left the yard rarely, and never alone; it was a place he knew well, defined by the rough planks of the fence, with the big oak in the center and nothing worse to harm than the chickens that now and then pecked at Willy's bare feet. He liked the chickens but had missed them lately, had not heard their gabbling nor sensed the musty smell of them, and he thought he might ask Mother about it after a while. But for now he wanted to sit with the sun full on his face. He could hear a squirrel moving in the oak leaves, a woodpecker tapping, the dogs snoring under the porch. He smelled the mud of the road and the smoke from the fire under the great iron pot where his mother was washing clothes. His mother was singing to herself, and under her voice was the crackling and snapping of the silver fire. Then he heard the horses.

They were a great way off when he first noticed the sound; he could hear them drumming over the creek bridge where his father took him sometimes, then the muted thump of their hooves coming closer and closer on the road. Willy did not like horses. He remembered them as monstrous tall creatures with rolling eyes and stamping hooves, and whenever one would come around, his mother would warn him to stay away. Now here came a bunch of them, sure enough, and running.

"Mother?" he said, but his mother was singing and didn't hear.

He stood then, and turned his face toward the sound of the horses. He put all else out of the darkness behind his eyes and tried to imagine them running. He remembered the way they looked: their great long strides and their tails streaming out behind, heads tossing, the muscles moving in their flanks. Sometimes, he knew, men rode their backs, and perhaps men were riding these as they pounded up the road.

Closer they came, and closer. Now he could hear them breathing—a hack-hack sound as they ran—and the voices of men. And now Mother had quit her singing, though the fire still crackled.

Willy stood rigid in the yard, clutching the smooth, cool doorknob painted with flowers. He heard the horses stop outside the place where the fence was, a jangling and thudding and muttering so confused he could not begin to fashion a picture of it. He heard the door of the house open, heard his father's shoes on the porch; meanwhile the dogs were barking and howling, the horses blowing, and somewhere among it all the reedy piping of the bird his mother called a redwing. Then Mother was there, her hands rough and smelling of soap. *Get in the house* she said, her voice urgent, harsh. But Willy couldn't move. His mother stood behind him, her hands on his shoulders. Then Father was there, too. Willy had not heard him come, but knew he had by the smell of tobacco and shaving soap.

His father stood between them and the commotion in the road. *You all get in the house* his father said in the same voice, but Willy's mother only gripped him tighter. *No* she said. "No," said Willy.

The gate opened, creaking as it always did, and a man came in. There was a jangling about him, a smell of horses. The dogs were frantic in their barking now, and Father hushed them. Willy could hear their whining as they gathered close. The man spoke now, a pleasant voice. *Well, Simon*

He is a friend of Father's, Willy thought, and wondered why they were all afraid.

What you all want Father asked.

Other men were coming in now, shuffling, leather creaking, their pants legs whisking together. Their smell was sour, all sweat and horses and something the boy smelled on his father's breath sometimes. Willy's heart beat faster in the darkness as the sound of them made a circle all around, and their words came to him from here, from there: *Look at him—Who stepped in dog shit—Hey Lily how's the Judge—Damn it's hot*

Now Simon said the pleasant-voice man, *you know what we are here for It's been a long time coming but the day is here at last and you must answer for it You have hid behind the Judge's shirttail long enough*

Please Mother said. *We haven't ever hurt anybody*

Shut up Lily for God's sake Father said.

Show a little gratitude Simon said the pleasant-voice man. *She's the reason you have lasted as long as you have*

Solomon Gault said Mother, *You are not a soldier This trash is not soldiers How dare you*

Well there is no time for discussion in any case said the pleasant-voice man. *Sergeant Stutts*

Right here, Cap'n

A rustling then, a rattling of paper, then the pleasant-voice man: *Simon Landers you stand here convicted of high treason against the Confederate*

States of America during the time of war for which crime you will be hanged by the neck until you are dead God rest your soul   Signed this date Captain K S Gault, CSA—Sergeant Stutts take the prisoner

Now wait a minute hold on began Father.

No Mother cried. *You get out of our yard   This is our yard* and Mother's hands left Willy's shoulders then and he heard the rustling of her skirts as she moved, and the pleasant-voice man said *Goddammit*

Don't you Father said.

There was a sound Willy had heard before. He remembered a long time ago, back in the light, when he hit a little girl at the church and Mother said, Willy, don't hit the other children. Willy thought: That is the sound of hitting. Sometimes it came at night; Willy could hear it from his bed up in the loft. It was always followed by the sound of crying. Now he heard it, and heard it again: hitting, no crying like before but an animal snarling with his mother's voice. He moved toward the sound but the men were scuffling and Willy was pushed aside; he stumbled and struck the ground hard. He put his hands over his head as the noise and the voices closed around him. *She raked him good—Hold 'er Bill—Come on darlin   Ow son bitch she bit me   Looky there*

The men laughed, and under it his mother's voice snarling, and Father's voice saying *Don't now   Wait a minute   Let me talk*

And the pleasant-voice man: *No Simon you have done enough talking Goddammit get this woman off me*

His mother's voice rose in a long shriek then stopped all at once, and a sound then like when Father split a melon, and Father crying *Lily Lily*

At the sound of his mother's name, Willy struggled to his feet. He felt the doorknob in his hand, hot now from where he'd held it tight.

Aw, Cap'n, how come you done that   We might've had some sport—

"Mother!" cried the boy, and pushed into the men, flailing. They pushed him back, flung him to the ground again; he scrambled to his feet again, seeing the men as a high wall of long, leering faces, tall bodies with big hands. He drew back his arm and threw the doorknob as hard as he could toward the place where the faces were; he heard it strike, and a howl of pain. Now it's gone, he thought. Then he was struck himself, harder than his father ever did, and he reeled back, the lights sparkling in the dark.

Little son bitch—String him up too—Aw hell he's blind as a newt Look at him

Never mind the boy   I'll deal with him   Here   Stop that man Don't let him   Get hold of him can't you   That's it hold him   Get him over here

His father's voice, moving away among the shuffling: *No now boys   I swear to God   No don't do that   No please I*

More hitting, only like none he'd ever heard. Willy pressed his hands to his ears. The voices swirled around him, and the smell of the men. The dogs were barking again, roiling and lathering.

God damn these dogs—Well, shoot em if you don't like it—I ain't wastin powder on—God almighty Tom she's dead—Hell, it's still warm ain't it—I swear that Tom Beard would poke a snake wouldn't he

"Mother!" cried Willy. He was turning now, losing his father's voice among the voices swarming in his head, and the barking of the dogs, and the shuffling. Then he found his father's voice again, a long way off now. That is over by the oak tree, thought Willy. He knew the yard so well, and the sunlight, and the chickens.

Na na na said Father. *Plee plee don't*

Kick you son of a bitch—What's the matter Simon you ain't talking now

Let him down said the pleasant-voice man.

Aw Cap'n

Let him down I said   You think I came all this way just to hang him once

Willy had lost the place where his mother was. In his turning he had lost everything, and now he stumbled ahead, his hands outstretched, until he came up against the boards of the fence. The voices were behind him. He huddled against the fence where the grass was, time passing.

Burn it   Burn it all   I'll kill the man tries to bring anything out   The pleasant-voice man, only not pleasant now but shouting.

You want to th'ow em in there

Leave him right where he is   The pleasant voice again, like it was just talking. Willy could tell the voice was coming closer; he tried to burrow into the grass. *Cover up the woman   Shoot the dogs so they don't get her Leave the Judge something to bury*   Then the sound of shooting, yelping, the men laughing—then the voice, right in his ear: *Get up*

Willy felt himself lifted by the collar. It nearly choked him, and he coughed and put his hands back and grabbed the man's wrists, but the man dragged him along, moving toward a new sound, a new smell: fire, only not the fire under the pot, and not the one on the hearth. This was a fire turned loose, growling like an animal, and it smelled sharp, foul, like when they scalded the bristles off a hog. Willy saw the silver threads, thick as rope now, coiling toward the sky. Willy could feel the heat on his face. The voice came right in his ear again, whispering *You feel it   That's your house* then lifting to a shout: *Mount up   Lieutenant Beard*

Hey Cap

We camp at the Big Spring   See you are there by sundown
Too many voices now, shuffling, jangling, the horses stamping their hooves. Willy was choking, tried to pry the fingers from his collar but suddenly he was being dragged again, stumbling, pulled up, stumbling, pulled up, going toward the horses. He could hear the man breathing hard. Then the horses were going away, back down the road in the direction they'd come, and only one horse was left; Willy could hear it snort, heard the silky whisk of its tail. *Whoa you* the man said, and Willy thought If he gets up on the horse he will have to let me go, and then he thought If I can get back in the yard—but the man didn't let him go. Willy felt him rise, heard the leather creak in the saddle. Then the grip tightened and Willy was jerked off his feet and thrown across the back of the horse. He could feel the hair of the mane, and something hard pressed against his chest and shut off his breathing. He struggled, and the man pulled him off the hard place and Willy thought he was going to go off the other side, but the man had him tight by his suspenders now. *Come up* said the man sharply, and they were moving.

The hooves thudded under him, and clods of mud struck him in the face. He scrabbled for something to hold on to; his hands passed over the bristly hairs of the horse's shoulder, and he could feel the muscles moving under the hide. He finally found the man's leg, but he couldn't hold it. He cried out. They ran on, time passing.

Then they stopped. The horse was breathing heavy—*huff huff*—and Willy was wet with the hot sweat of him. For a moment, nothing happened. Then the man hoisted on Willy's suspenders and flung him off the horse. He seemed to fall a long way; he was shocked when he hit the ground. He was in grass. He could smell it, and hear the grasshoppers buzzing.

Willy rose to his feet, turning toward the place where the horse was breathing. Nothing happened. The saddle creaked. The horse stamped once, and off somewhere was the croak of a bird Willy knew was a crow. Then the voice came from somewhere up above, pleasant and unhurried as ever: *Your mother nearly clawed my eyes out* it said. *And your father Well it is useless to try to explain all that to you   Nevertheless I am inclined to be merciful   I have set you free   You may go now   You have all points of the compass to choose from   And if you should chance to meet anyone along the way which is unlikely you may tell them that Captain Gault paid a call   Can you remember that*

Willy made no reply. He wasn't listening to the voice anyway. After another moment, the pleasant-voice man said *Very well* and Willy heard the horse champing, the leather creaking, then the horse running again, through the grass that whispered with its passing. He could hear it a long time, and then he heard it no more.

Now the crow was talking somewhere, and the grass buzzed, but over these things lay a deep silence. For the first time in his life, Willy was alone. He stood a while longer, then knelt and began to move his hands over the ground. He crawled a little way, sweeping with his hands, until he found a clear place in the grass. Stones lay clustered here, smooth and round, and he chose one. This will be the doorknob, he thought. Then he stood up. He was dizzy for a moment, but the feeling passed. He lifted his face; he could smell the burning, but it seemed to come from all around, and he couldn't tell which way it was. He turned until he felt the sun on his face, and it was then he heard his mother. *Come this way* she said.

The sudden rush of joy was like a blow to him. "Mother!" he cried. He put out his hands and began to walk toward her voice. The crow was there too, talking. *This way, Willy* his mother said. She was moving away, and Willy knew he must follow.

In a little while, he was in the woods.

June 1865

· PART 1 ·

The Soldier
in the Wood

· I ·

Gawain Harper stood in the deep mud of the southerly road, listening.
To the west, just across the low ridge, he could hear the chuff of a
steam sawmill, the whine of the blade, and, when the blade was still, the
unhurried voices of men. Over these sounds, and through them, wove the
drowsy music of crickets in the grass, and a blue jay complaining. Gawain
found the jay in the green arch of the trees, bobbing up and down, running
through his litany of scorn. The bird was handsome in his black necklace
and blue frock coat, up there where the sun was. Soon another joined him,
then another, and in a moment half a dozen were jeering down at Gawain
Harper as if he were a snake or a tomcat or a raccoon come for robbing.

"Good God, boys," laughed Gawain, and jeered back at them.

In the road lay a fat, florid carpet bag and a U.S. bull's-eye canteen.
Gawain knelt, uncorked the canteen and drank. He could smell the water
as he tasted it—a sweet, dark odor like the inside of a gourd—and smell
the cork and the rust-spotted wool cover of the canteen. The tang of new-
cut pine from the sawmill reached him, the reek of mud and wet leaves and
the wood smoke drifting through the trees. He could smell the trees themselves: the cedars and pines, oaks and hickories, all second-growth timber
but already smelling old, as if they'd stood since the beginning of the
world. He imagined he could smell the very sunlight where it slanted
through the leaves, and breathe of the shadows, the blue sky and the
clouds that drifted overhead like little flags. And something else, too—
compounded of all the rest and better than them all, better than anything
Gawain Harper had ever smelled in his life. At first he could not put a
name to it. He looked around to see if he could find any one thing that
could give of such a smell, but nothing was there that wasn't there before.
He stood up and took off his hat and peered down the road, holding his
breath, watching. The road was empty. He was alone.

So that is it, he thought. *That is what freedom smells like.* And he was thankful he could smell all these things together.

He stood awhile longer, breathing the air that was already hot though it wasn't yet eight o'clock, and listening to the sawmill working over the ridge. Then, when he wanted to, he picked up his carpet bag and moved on, keeping to the edge of the road where the mud was not so deep.

✦　　✦　　✦

THE ROAD WAS changing with the season, though in many ways it still held the shape of spring, when it was churned by cavalry, deep-rutted by guns and limbers and the heavy trains of armies pursuing and pursued. Infantry had passed here too, and the mud still bore in places the prints—barefoot and shod—of men who had come this way, and some of these were dead now, and some were home, and some were traveling other roads homeward. But all this impress was fading under the rains, and soon the ruts and the marks of men would collapse little by little and dissolve into summer dust. Then whatever memory the road clung to would be gone as well, as if what had happened here had never happened at all. Such was the way of roads then, if not of those who journeyed them.

The night before, Gawain tarried in the house of a second cousin who lived just beyond the Cumberland County line. He passed the evening among women and children and dogs, all of them sitting on the gallery in the summer night, watching the fireflies lift their lanterns in the yard. The cousin himself, whose regiment ended up with the Virginia army, had not come home as yet, nor any news of him since the early spring; still, the sense of him was there—a dark, empty, yearning space he was, sitting with them on the broad porch among the creaking chairs. The women spoke of him only in the future tense: When he comes home. . . . When he fixes the well-house roof. . . . When he can plow or When he can clear new ground and What will he do to set things right now the negroes have run off. . . . And, Jamie, he will have something to say to you about the way you cut your hair, you mark my words, and Won't it grieve him to learn about Papa? and My, he won't know what to think, here is Tom growed a foot and wearin shoes in the summertime. Gawain listened and smoked and nodded his head, saying Yes, he'll be fit to be tied, and Yes, won't he though? and No, I can't imagine what he'll say to that, and never rising to the question the women would not ask, giving them nothing because he had nothing to give. He listened to them speak of the old pattern of life as if, just by talking, they could hold fast to it awhile longer. He supposed he would do the same thing himself, once he understood that it was really gone.

"How many them yankees did you kill, Cousin Gawain?" asked the least boy, his face earnest in the starlight.

Gawain flinched, then smiled at the lad. "Oh, hundreds and hundreds," he said. Then he showed them the powder grains lodged in his hand, and told something of his adventures, though not much. The women listened politely, and the children asked other questions that made him flinch, that might have led him to places he did not want to go again. So he told only a mild sketch or two—of a long march in the rain, of stealing a hog, of a snowball fight between brigades—things the cousin himself might tell if he were able to speak. And all the while Gawain imagined his cousin in the shadows, leaning against the balustrade, his eyes warning *I know what you want to tell, but you can't, you can't* and Gawain saying back *Don't worry, I will never tell* and trying to mean it.

Once, when they'd been quiet awhile, the cousin's wife reached across the little space between them and laid her hand on Gawain's wrist. "You know," she said, "Cumberland is burned since last summer."

He nodded. "We heard that. Somebody told it back in the winter when we got down to Tupelo. The whole square, they said, and the Academy, but not many houses."

"Not many," she said. "I supposed you ought to be ready, had it not come to you. There is a right smart of yankees there even now, but not the same ones who burned it."

"I am ready," Gawain said. "I expect it." That was a lie, though he did not know yet that it was. After a moment, he said, "My daddy's?"

The woman shook her head. "No," she said. "It stands yet."

"Thank God for it," said Gawain. Another quiet space then, while he formed the question, looked at it from all sides, then uttered it at last: "And Judge Rhea's?"

This time the woman sighed and did not answer right away, and for Gawain that was answer enough. His hands tightened on the arms of the chair, and even as they did so, the woman's hand tightened on his wrist. Hers was a small hand, but strong; Gawain felt the blunt nails dig into his skin. "Don't fret yourself over that," she said. "It was only just a house."

"Ah," he said.

"I was over there in April, found them all stayin at old T. J. Carter's house, who is Ida Rhea's cousin by marriage, I believe. Carter's boy was lost at—" She stopped, and moved her hand downward until it lay gently over Gawain's. "Oh, well," she said, "I don't need to tell you that."

"No," said Gawain. He searched his mind for the Carter boy's face, found he could not see it clearly. That was often the way with the dead.

After a moment, he asked the wife, "You saw them then? You saw the Judge and Miss Ida? Young Alex?"

"All well," she said. "Though the Judge has aged some."

He waited. He knew that she knew he was waiting. She wanted to hear him ask it—because she was a woman, and because he was a man and ought to ask it. Finally, he said, "And you saw Morgan? How does she fare?"

He could not see the woman blush in the darkness. "Very well," she said. "We took a stroll down by Leaf River. 'Twas the first warm day, and the old dogwoods in bloom, and the willows green, and the water high from all this rain. I recall we saw a martin scout, first one I saw this year. 'Twas pretty, Gawain. You'd of thought there'd never been a sorrow in this world."

Gawain stared out at the arabesque shadows in the yard, at the fireflies rising, blinking, illusive as the dream of two women walking among the delicate willows, clutching their shawls about them, watching the river. The vision came and went like the fireflies' light. He could not see their faces.

"She spoke of you," said the woman softly, and lifted her hand from Gawain's. "I can tell that, can't I?"

Gawain smiled himself then. "You can tell that," he said.

"She told how she had no word from you, nothing in a long time, since before you all crossed the river—where was it?"

"Florence, in Alabama."

"Yes."

Gawain lifted his hands, a helpless gesture. "I wrote her. After Nashville I wrote her, and down in Alabama."

"She had no word from you," said the woman again.

Gawain tried to remember what he had written. He could see himself sitting in the firelight, could see the page and the pencil moving. That was all.

"I think you ought to be ready," said the cousin's wife, touching his arm again. "She don't even know if you're alive."

"Good God," said Gawain.

They were quiet for a while. At last Gawain said, "Tell about the burning."

The old mother rocked forward, stabbing her pipe stem at the darkness. "Hatch!" she croaked.

"Beg pardon?" said Gawain.

" 'Twas that General Hatch, the cav'ry man, that done it. You ever hear tell of that General?"

"No, ma'am," said Gawain. "Was he a bad man?"

"Oh, a holy terror *he* was," said the old woman. "He chased the rebels clean out of town—we seen em come right by here, that damn peckerwood horse cav'ry, flailin the pitiful things they was a-ridin— I says to em, Where you think you goin? They holler, Gone to Texas, Granmaw!"

"My, how they flew!" said the oldest boy, the one who was wearing shoes now. "They horses was bony, all right."

"Hah!" said the old woman. "You couldn't of made a decent stew out the whole lot. Anyhow, they run off, and old Hatch turned his soldiers loose on the town—and a good many of em was these nigger soldiers, don't you know, all aflame with strong drink that he give em. They might near burnt ever goddamn thing."

"Now, Mama," said the cousin's wife.

"Rena Brown, don't tell *me*!" snorted the old woman. "And that General, they said he taken a armchair out the hotel and set right there and smoked a seegar the whole time."

"Well, I don't doubt it," said Gawain, though he did.

"Tell about the church, Granmaw," said the boy.

The old woman waved her arms. "Lord!" she said.

"Them yankees!" said the boy.

"What?" said Gawain.

"Why, that man told his soldiers to keep they horses right up in the Presbyterian church—had em right up in there, brought in forage and everything—and taken the organ pipes out and th'owed em in the street!"

"Who told you that?" asked Gawain.

"Why, lots of people. He kept em right up in there—"

"Was that before they burned the church, or after?"

"Well, they never burnt the *church*, goddammit," said the old woman.

"Mama!" said the wife.

"How'd they get em up the steps?" asked Gawain. "There is fourteen steps up to the front door of the Presbyterian church!"

"Well, I don't know—but they done it. They was all likkered up is how, I guess. It was them niggers."

"Well," said Gawain, and let it go. He had learned long since that the citizens could only be satisfied if the yankees who marauded them were aflame with strong drink, and perhaps it was just as well. How could any-one explain to them the random violence of a burning, or the joy that great acts of destruction brought to the soul? When a soldier, Gawain himself knew the exhilaration of torching a house, of watching the flames rise to his bidding, and in those moments (so frightening because they were so rational) he would gladly have burned buildings, towns, cities, whole civilizations—would have laid waste the earth with flames and artillery if he could. Such knowledge was not for the citizens—let them believe that only liquor brought ruin down on their heads.

But damn that business of horses in church! Gawain had heard that told in other towns time and time again, and it always irritated him. It seemed to Gawain that any intelligent person would be hard-pressed to imagine a more impractical place to keep horses than in a church, yet the citizens insisted that the yankees always kept them there. He had never heard of any *Confederate* cavalry keeping their horses in a church. But Gawain did not argue with the old woman. Horses in the Temple seemed to be a matter of theology with the citizens, so let them believe what they wanted, let them tell their tales, let them make whatever sense of it they could. Good God, let them hang their harps upon the willows and make their songs.

He looked again over the yard, into the thick, twinkling darkness of the summer night. Tomorrow he would see for himself. Tomorrow he would find Morgan. He tried to picture their meeting, tried to fashion it against the dark loom of the trees, out of the stars scattered in the infinite sky. But he couldn't. *It's all right,* he thought. *I am too tired now. Tomorrow is soon enough.*

"It ain't only the yankees that have played hell," said the wife suddenly. The bitter tone of her voice made Gawain look at her closely in the shadow of the porch.

"How do you mean?" he asked.

She took a long time answering. He could see her staring out into the yard, collecting her thoughts and arranging the pictures in her mind. Then she said, "When was the last letter you got from Morgan?"

He thought a moment. "Oh, way last June, I reckon. A long time."

"Did she tell about Lily?"

A dark thing moved across Gawain's heart, like a cloud covering the moon. Lily was the oldest girl, married to the circuit clerk, a man Gawain had never liked. Simon Landers was a vocal Unionist; the old Judge had disowned him and caused him to lose his position for it. But the man's politics were not the source of Gawain's dislike. He was small, petty, not worthy of Lily Rhea, though she clung to him fiercely. They had a boy, Gawain remembered. "No," he said at last. "No, she didn't."

The cousin's wife sighed, shook her head. "We had hard times out here in the country. There was some local men—rangers, they called themselves, though they were nothin but common peckerwoods too cowardly to go to the army—"

"That Simon Landers deserved hangin, the way he treated Lily," said the grandmother.

"*Hush,* Mama," said the wife. "I was comin to that."

"Oh, my God," said Gawain, rocking back in his chair.

"Yes, they hanged him," said the wife. "They burned the house, and . . . and they killed Lily in the yard." Her voice caught then. "Hard times, Gawain. She never hurt a fly."

Gawain rubbed his eyes. "How you know who it was?"

"Oh," she said. "I am told they left a paper pinned to Simon's shirt sayin what all they hanged him for. Treason, it said."

"Treason," said Gawain. "Damn."

"Never did find that boy of theirs," said the old woman. "Been a year now—hogs got him, I reckon."

"Mama!" said the wife. "Still, it's true. God keep him. So that was Lily, Gawain. Best you should know."

"Of course," said Gawain. "Who was their leader?"

"Man named King Solomon Gault, a big planter down in the Leaf River bottoms. He signed the paper, what I'm told."

"I have heard of him. Is he still around?"

The woman laughed bitterly. "Oh, yes. The rangers was whipped in a big fight up on the Tallahatchie in August, some of em was hanged. That's when Gault went to smugglin. He is the richest man around, I should say. You can't touch him. Still, it's a wonder the Judge ain't killed him."

"Maybe he will yet," said Gawain.

"Somebody will," said the woman.

The news about Lily Rhea Landers seemed to wear out their talk. In a little while, the young ones went off to bed, and the grown folks soon after. Gawain had not slept under a roof in a long while; he asked to sleep on the porch where he could see the road and the light of the stars. The wife brought him an armload of quilts.

" 'Tis cool enough," she said. "Maybe the bugs won't eat you alive. I wouldn't mind if you slept inside."

"I'll be all right," said Gawain. "I am obliged to you."

They stood shyly for a moment, facing one another across the pallet she had made on the rough boards of the porch. Out in the fields, a whippoorwill was calling, and a mockingbird perched high on the rooftree sang his melancholy nocturne. The liquid notes floated across the night, clear and sad.

"So much bad news, but I am glad you've come home anyway, Gawain Harper," said the wife at last. "So many haven't."

"He will come, Rena," said Gawain. "He is coming now, somewhere."

"You believe that?" she said. "Truly?"

"Yes," he said. In the dark shadow of the porch, he saw her shake her head. "Don't you?" he said.

She stepped across the pallet then, and touched his shoulder, and he felt the brush of her lips on his cheek. Then she was gone.

He was tired, but he did not sleep right away. It was the mockingbird kept him awake, he told himself, though he knew it wasn't the mockingbird. He lay under a quilt that smelled of wood smoke and home, and he studied the moving shadows that the leaves made. Nowhere among them could he find Morgan, nor even the two women walking by the river. And nowhere was Lily, dead and gone. But that was all right; shadows were not the place to look anyhow. In time he closed his eyes, and in time he slept. Then, deep in the night, he woke again to hear the geese passing overhead.

This was a late flock strayed from the big river far to the west, and voyaging long past the time for geese. All his life Gawain had marveled to see the geese moving like smoke across the stars, but tonight their mournful honking was the only evidence of their passing. Gawain imagined them in their long, wavering V's, following the rivers north. They were talking it over up there in the dark: joking, complaining, encouraging the stragglers, remembering other trips perhaps, and days spent among the marshes. Gawain smiled at the notion of geese talking, but that was the best way to think about it; the sound was too lonesome otherwise.

Then he thought about how it would be if he were a gray gander, and what he might see from aloft. He imagined the silence, the cool night air passing over him—and down below, the broad land revealed in starlight, crossed and recrossed by the thin, pale ribbons of roads—all of them leading somewhere, for somebody. And all across the earth the tiny, struggling figures of men caught up in a great migration of their own, all walking out of the long night toward a morning they had created for themselves from the darkness.

Gawain moved under the quilt, stretched his body and felt the muscles tighten in his legs. It was good to be there, drowsy and at peace, with the mockingbird singing and the whippoorwill querying away out in the overgrown fields, and his own people at hand to watch after him. Then he was dreaming again, and in the dream, a door opened somewhere, the hinges groaning softly, then the creak of a board, and a smell like soap, and the soft smell a woman has when she has been asleep for a while on a summer's night—something in the hair, the flesh gone warm with sleeping, a residue of dreams. He woke to the sound of her settling into the rocking chair by his head.

"Dell ain't comin home," she said. "He ain't ever comin home again."

"You don't know that," he said, turning his head a little. The moon had risen, and he could see her by the pale light of it; she wore a cotton gown washed to the color and thinness of smoke.

"I had a dream of him," she said after a moment. "Back in the early spring. In the dream, I couldn't see his face."

"Dreams don't mean anything," said Gawain, but she went on, her voice in a whisper: "Then last month, I saw him settin on the bed. He was gaunted, like you are. I woke up sayin his name, but he was gone. That was the last time he'll ever come. I know that."

"Rena, it's a long way from Carolina," he said.

She didn't answer, but began to rock slowly, a board creaking under the chair. In a moment, she said, "You don't mind, I'll set here awhile."

"No, I don't mind. It is a good sound."

The moon rose, the stars burned on without heat, and under them, the whippoorwill called, and frogs in the ditches, and the mockingbird sang. At last the night grew late, and all things fell silent, and mist rose from the fields, and the road lay white in the starlight. Gawain listened to the woman's rocking for a long time and found a comfort in it. When he slept, he dreamed of high places, and clouds feathering across the moon like geese. He woke at break of day, and she was gone.

At breakfast, she clattered pots and pans around the hearth and would not look at him. Then, when the children were gone out in the yard, and the old mother sat at the table muttering to herself, and Gawain had pulled on his coat, she turned to him. She had his canteen, filled with sweet spring water, and a bag of coffee, and four biscuits wrapped in a rag.

"This is for you, along the way," she said, and lowered her eyes.

"I am obliged to you," he said. "Rena—"

She shook her head to silence him. She was wearing her dress now, shapeless, of a faded brown, and her feet were bare. "Now, go on," she said.

So he went on his way, and they followed him a little distance up the road: the wife, the old mother, the three children, the dogs, a kitten, a hen—and the dark, empty shape of his cousin who was not home. Just before Gawain passed out of sight around a bend in the road, he looked back and saw them standing all together, the women's hands gathered in their aprons.

Now the sun was climbing toward the meridian, and the day promised hot and fair. It would be his last day on the road; when this sun went down he would be in Cumberland. The knowledge stirred in him a feeling he could not put a name to. After so long a time, he could not pretend to know what he felt about anything.

· II ·

Gawain Harper had just turned thirty-seven that beguiling afternoon in April 1862, when he and Sir Niles Reddick and young Tom Fitter, the mathematics professor at the Academy, presented themselves to the Confederate enrolling officers at the courthouse. Each of these gentlemen had delayed as long as he could, but now could delay no longer. They were among a dwindling minority of able-bodied Cumberland men who had resisted joining the service until the moment when their personal honor could no longer be sustained without it. Now they were tired of making excuses, tired of intellectual evasion, and they were especially tired of patriotic women. In the final tally, Gawain and Sir Niles and young Fitter joined the Confederate Army—would have joined any army that was handy, whatever its cause or banners—to escape the women of the town and their cold stares, their comments veiled behind fans and handkerchiefs, their pernicious habit of crossing the street whenever a robust civilian slunk guiltily by. Even Morgan Rhea—who, Gawain had supposed, was old enough to know better—was a little cool when he declared his lack of soldierly ambition. Though he hoped she would come around to his view, she never did, and Gawain had come to feel like a mewling dog in her presence. Moreover, her father, Judge Nathaniel Rhea—a fire-eating state legislator and among the first to raise the shrill cry of secession—made it plain to Gawain that no gentleman would keep himself out of the army at a time when the fate of his entire civilization hung in the balance.

Still Gawain had resisted. He was not *afraid* to go, he assured himself. He was sure he could endure the rigors of the field, was not unwilling to put up his life for a just cause. Yet he was not sure the cause *was* just, or even what it amounted to, or if it was worthy of the valuable commodity he represented in the great design. And anyway, he simply could not share in the sense of dark portent that drove so many in those days. What he knew of battles and the movement of armies he got from the newspaper,

and there it all seemed little more than a remote exercise. He understood
that men were killed—already there were Cumberland men who would be
seen no more—but these seemed to have disappeared not into death but
into some vast pen-and-ink rendering, where hundreds of men, all of
whom looked exactly alike, marched stiffly among puffs of smoke. He had
heard all the speeches, the rousing talk of adventure, honor, even the fun
to be had in making fools of the yankees. But Gawain was not a young
man any longer; his life was comfortable, suitably arranged, and it would
be a great nuisance to uproot everything for a few months' camping out.
As for civilization, Gawain could not see that it was in any real danger—
the war, he predicted sagely, would fizzle out by Christmas, the cosmic dust
would settle, and the politicians would return to their wrangling in distant
halls. And he was not afraid. He was definitely not afraid.

Then, after supper one evening in that early April of 1862, Gawain went
to call on Morgan Rhea. He presented himself to old Robert the Butler at
the door, then waited, standing on the gallery, studying the Lenten darkness. Soon the moon would rise and fill the yard with shadow; for now,
there was only the still night, and no voices in the grass, nor any sound
except the far-off barking of a dog. Gawain moved to the edge of the
gallery, put out his hand, palm outward, as if there were something in the
dark he might touch. But there was only the night, warm and empty, waiting for moonrise.

Presently, the door opened. Old Robert the Butler stood there again,
solemn and erect against the dim glow of the hall lantern. "Judge is home
from Jackson," he said. "He say to give you this." He held out a silver
tray; upon it lay a sheet of foolscap, folded and sealed with wax.

"I didn't ask for the Judge," said Gawain.

"You didn't know he was home either," said the old man.

Gawain took the paper. The seal was still warm. "So," he said. "I suppose—"

"Go on, Mist' Gawain," said the old man. "You won't ever get back
here if you don't start now." Then he closed the door.

Gawain walked the little way back to town and sat on a bench by the
courthouse and waited for the moon to come up. The square was mud in
this season—deep mud churned and mingled with the leavings of horses
and cattle. There were no trees, only the indistinct shapes of the buildings
that the trees had gone to make room for. In the center, the courthouse
stood utterly dark, silent, though in the cupola the great bell huddled,
waiting for the hour.

The moon rose. It was a big moon, and as it peered over the roofs of the
eastern row of buildings, the machinery in the cupola began to whirr and

mutter, and in a moment the bell struck eight o'clock. Gawain counted the strokes, and as the last one faded away he took the foolscap out of his coat pocket, turned it over and over in his hand and ran his finger across the seal. At last, when the square was lit by the moon and long shadows leaned from the buildings, he broke the seal and read.

> *Sir:*
> If you were welcome here, you would already have been admitted. Since you have not been, you may draw whatever inference seems appropriate. Perhaps one day you will conduct yourself in such a way that, should you live, you might be welcome even here. Until that time, I remain
>
> > *Very Respectfully Yours,*
> > *Nathaniel Rhea, Esq.*

When Gawain had read it twice, he fished in his waistcoat pocket for a lucifer match, found one, struck it against the iron leg of the bench and set the foolscap alight. In a moment, it was a rectangle of ash edged in scarlet; he let it go and watched it break up on the hard-trodden yard of the courthouse, watched the fragments drift away in the moonlight, driven by imperceptible currents in the air. He sat a while longer, then at last rose and moved across the moonlit square toward home.

◆　◆　◆

SO GAWAIN HARPER joined the Cause, whatever it might turn out to be, admitting to himself that he had no choice, and hoping he would at least have the consolation of fulfilling some unexpected destiny. He assured himself that something was happening he ought not to miss—an opportunity that would loom large in his personal history, more especially if he refused it. He recalled stirring words he'd read and taught: Shakespeare's *Henry V,* Lovelace, Byron, Tennyson's "Ulysses." He had believed in the words, secure in his lecture hall with all the world in order, and he tried to believe them now, in the springtime of his destiny. And why not? Why were the words ever made if they could not be believed? So Gawain told himself that afternoon, as he and Fitter and Sir Niles strolled down the leaf-shaded streets toward the courthouse. After all, it was too early for the ruined ones to have returned: the crippled and sick and blind who would come in time and tap their accusing canes on the sidewalks, whose voices might have whispered in his ear of the unthinkable possibilities that awaited him.

One of the enrolling officers was from the Twenty-first Regiment of Mississippi Infantry. This officer was appallingly young, but he had been in an actual battle and so was a veteran, and he already had the veteran's deep contempt for civilians. Nevertheless, he was courteous and persuasive (and he *did* look dashing in his uniform), so Gawain and his companions signed names in his book and, as if by magic, became privates in the Twenty-first.

Gawain looked at his name in the book. "There," he told Sir Niles. "That ought to satisfy the old son of a bitch."

The next morning, the new enlistees (there were more than a dozen, all looking a little sheepish) met at the ramshackle depot of the Mississippi Central Railroad, where a shy and inarticulate enlisted man—a corporal, they learned later—taught them how to stand in a line. That accomplished, they were free to bid farewell to their loved ones, and to the curious and the idle, while they waited for the train, which was, of course, late.

Gawain's Aunt Vassar was there, and his father, already befuddled by the fever spreading in his brain, and old Priam. They passed the time as if Gawain were only going up to Memphis on holiday, talking all around the reason for his leaving, not daring to look into the mystery that lay beyond the far curve of the railroad. Aunt Vassar told Gawain that she was proud of him, that she would send him a letter as soon as she knew his posting, and when he came back, my, what a grand Christmas they would have. Old Priam was solemn and decorous, standing among the white people with his buggy whip in the crook of his arm, guarding Gawain's valise and rolled umbrella. Gawain himself was deeply embarrassed and almost wished they had not come at all; nevertheless, he held his Aunt Vassar's hand for the first time in his life, could not seem to let it go even though he felt ridiculous. He kept thinking of his classroom at the Academy, how the sunlight was falling even then on the young faces, most of them glancing furtively out the window on this fine morning—and of old Professor Handback who would finish out the term for him, droning on through the spring in his moth-eaten frock coat, reading from his yellowed notes. How could that be happening now, apart from him? Gawain yearned deeply for that quiet, dust-smelling room with its dark wood. He would have walked home for dinner today, under the greening trees. He could see himself doing it so clearly that, for an instant, he believed there must be *two* Gawain Harpers, and one of them was getting the better situation. But he was the other one, that part of himself which, for reasons completely arbitrary, was having to turn its back on all that he had known.

Morgan was nowhere to be seen, which surprised him not at all—it was another bargain he had made. He had told her nothing of his enlistment, had not even seen her again to bid farewell. Let them find out on their own. In the end (he had to admit), simple perversity had led him to that evening call, and the same perversity now made him wish he'd acted differently. He kept searching the thin crowd, hoping she might show up and at the same time hoping she wouldn't. *Damn women anyhow,* he thought.

So he was relieved when the little teakettle locomotive hove into view from the south, bringing the waiting to an end. Gawain turned to watch the approaching engine and its three varnished yellow coaches, and again he had a feeling of dislocation, as if he were hovering in time. Gawain had been a brakeman on this road, not long after the rails were laid, and he knew the engine, knew the driver and the stoker, knew deep in his memory the clashing of the link-and-pin couplers as the slack ran out and the squealing of the brakes as the brakemen tied them down. Now he would board the yellow coaches and, among crates of chickens and greasy bundles, would ride off toward the war.

"Goodbye, my boy," said Aunt Vassar, patting his hand.

"Don't you be runnin no harlots up there," blurted his father who, it turned out, really did believe Gawain was going to Memphis on holiday.

"*Mister* Harper!" said his aunt.

"Goodbye, Aunt Vassar," said Gawain. "Goodbye, Uncle Priam—sure you don't want to go?"

Old Priam smiled gravely. "Hmmm," he said. "Naw, sir, I'd just leave a trail of broken hearts."

Gawain laughed in spite of the anvil set down on his heart. He approached his father, shook the old man's hand. "So long, Papa. I'll see you directly. I promise I won't run any harlots."

"What?" the old man said.

Aunt Vassar shook her head, reached out and touched Gawain's face so that he blushed. "Go on, now," she said. "You have your prayer book?"

The engine driver blew his whistle twice, the signal for departure. "Yes'm," said Gawain, "I have it."

"Don't forget to write every day," she said.

Gawain was about to reply when he saw Morgan. She was walking fast down the lane that led from the depot to the square, holding up her skirts, her face in a frown. She was all in white, though she was a widow and really too old to wear white, and it wasn't Easter yet. Some of the ladies saw her and whispered to one another behind their gloved hands.

Well, hell, thought Gawain. Here she was, and it was time to leave. Aunt Vassar caught Gawain's glance and turned. "Oh, my," she said. Then she squeezed Gawain's arm. "You didn't tell her you enlisted, *did* you," she accused.

Gawain clamped his jaws tight and shook his head.

"Well, you are not leaving 'til you speak to her," said Aunt Vassar.

All right, thought Gawain. *Fine. Just fine.* Then he quit thinking. He turned, slipped between the first and second coaches—there was slack, thank God—and pulled the pin from the coupling and dropped it between the wheels. He was out again in time to face Morgan Rhea.

Her face was pale, thin, pitted with smallpox scars, but still pretty. Her hair was dark, shot through with a little gray, though she was only thirty. Her hands were knotted tight in front of her, and when she saw Gawain, she speared him with her brown eyes.

"Well, this is a fine thing," she said.

The whistle blew again and steam shot from the cylinders. The driving wheels made a tentative turn.

"Now, Morgan—," began Gawain.

"No time for that," she said. "You have made me the fool, but what's done is done. Maybe you can still save yourself."

Behind them, the engine and the first car began to move. "Hey!" shouted the depot master. "Hold on there!"

"Tell me how to do it," said Gawain. They were close now, almost touching; he could smell the rose water on her. She opened her mouth to speak, but instead looked up the rails where the engine was chuffing away with only a third of its train. She smiled, then looked back at Gawain. He saw that, in spite of her smile, there was a shining in her eyes that might have been sorrow, regret, shame—who could tell?

"First," she said, "you must not blame the Judge. Do not carry that away with you. He is a hard man sometimes, but he has honor, and you must remember that."

"I bear him no grief," said Gawain. "I will remember."

"Second," she said. "Second, you must forgive me if I have sent you away to something . . . to—" Her voice broke and Gawain saw that she really was about to cry.

The engine had been halted at last and was backing. A brakeman had found the pin. Gawain took Morgan by the shoulders. "Understand me—," he began, prepared to lie, but she stopped him.

"I know you, have known all about you since I was in primer school. I know why you are going. So here's the third thing."

"What?" he asked, as the couplers clashed behind them.

She put the flat of her hand against his chest; he could feel something beneath it, pressing against him. He slid his hand beneath hers and closed it on the gutta-percha case—he knew what it was without having to look. "Now go on," she said.

The whistle blew again, petulantly. The coaches jerked forward. Gawain took her face in his hands and kissed her, feeling her tears on his cheekbone. She pushed him away then. "Go," she said.

Gawain cast around quickly, found Uncle Priam holding out his valise and umbrella. He swept them up. With his free hand, he swung up on the last coach as it rattled by, climbed the steps and leaned against the rail of the platform. He stood there until the white shape of her was gone, and Cumberland was gone, and nothing lay behind him but the bright morning woods and a haze of coal smoke.

✦   ✦   ✦

THEY TOOK THE Mississippi Central to Grand Junction, then changed to a Memphis & Charleston train crowded with soldiers and recruits bound for Corinth where the army lay. There they sought their regiment, which they found camped in a muddy field behind the railroad hotel. Gawain would never forget that first glimpse of his new life: the foul sinks, the mildewed tents, the pall of wood smoke from innumerable fires, the lean, bristly men who watched them in silence—who, most of them, were still glassy-eyed and half-mad from the Battle of Shiloh a few days before. He believed at that moment that he—Gawain Harper, standing in the mire, still clutching a valise and an umbrella—was unlikely ever to make a soldier, nor did he much want to be anymore, if he ever had.

Mister Julian Bomar, once the high sheriff of Cumberland County and now the regimental sergeant major, materialized before them.

"Well, well, well, well," said Mister Bomar, and from that moment Gawain Harper knew that all he could do was follow the colors of this regiment into the dark.

So follow them he did, under Bragg and Johnston and Hood. In the winter of '63, Gawain nearly died of pneumonia and was in hospital for a month or so, but for most of his service he was always present at roll call, and enjoyed good health and counted himself lucky, unlike young Fitter who had not even learned the manual of arms before the measles got him. He died in a fever, muttering Bible verses and logarithms and apologizing over and over to someone—his mother, they supposed—for drowning the cat in the cistern. They buried him at Corinth, in the muddy field behind the railroad hotel.

As time went on, Gawain discovered that the bourne of his endurance could be pushed far beyond anything he had ever imagined, and the knowledge gave him confidence and pride. He found to his surprise that he even enjoyed some of the life. He liked long marches in fair weather with the boys laughing and talking, or later, when they were tired, each man drawing into himself and plodding along in a comfortable, homey silence. He liked camp life when it wasn't raining, and the satisfaction that came from a well-executed drill. He enjoyed seeing his regiment, brigade, division in line, with the flags opened out overhead and the bayonets shining and the field officers out front on their restless horses. He liked wandering idly over the fields with his pards and, coming back, seeing the dingy shelter halves and smoky fires of camp. Most of all, he found comfort in his comrades, and humility and mercy and strength, too, as he came to know them, and depend upon them, and love them.

But there was the killing. One by one, the boys were left behind in the smoke while Gawain Harper went on. The last straw was at Franklin where so many were lost. Sir Niles Reddick disappeared there—simply vanished, as if he had never been at all. One minute he was at Gawain's elbow, going into the charge against the cotton gin—the next instant he was gone. Gawain never found him, though he searched that awful field high and low once the battle was done. After that, Gawain himself was finished, going through the motions of soldiering until he, too, should vanish and be no more.

Then, back in the first week of May, the remnant of the Twenty-first Mississippi allowed themselves to quit at last. They were down in the piney woods of south Alabama, on a futile march to join Uncle Joe Johnston (wherever he was; nobody seemed to know for sure), when a squadron of Federal cavalry swarmed down on them. The boys tried to form line of battle, but it was no use, and Gawain finally threw his musket down when he was nearly sabered by a zealous lad in an absurd, tight-fitting uniform with his cap affixed by its chin strap, riding the biggest horse Gawain had ever seen. At another courthouse, in a town he never knew the name of, Gawain Harper had signed his name again, to a parole this time—a document declaring that, though Gawain Harper was once an enemy of the United States, he was an enemy no longer. The parole now lay in his new carpet bag, which he'd bought as he passed homeward through the burned city of Meridian, Mississippi, along with a bottle-green frock coat (almost new) and a checkered waistcoat and breeches, and a broad hat of good Panama straw—all purchased with banknotes issued by the United States which, while he was still its enemy, Gawain had stolen from a waylaid Quartermaster's wagon on the advance to Nashville.

Gawain had kept his rusty bull's-eye canteen, but, into his new carpet bag, along with his treasured parole, he had emptied the contents of his old tarred haversack, the accumulation of three years of active campaigning: a rosary, a deck of cards with the Jack of Hearts forever lost, his *Book of Common Prayer*, an almanac for 1862, a tin cup and plate and a clever device with fork and spoon and knife all together, a blackened coffee boiler, a physic for headaches, a notebook and pencil, the Senior Warden's jewel from the traveling lodge of the Twenty-first Regiment of Mississippi Infantry, a pipe and pouch of tobacco and a dozen lucifer matches, a *Soldier's Song Book,* seven dollars U.S.—and a cracked ambrotype of Morgan Rhea in its gutta-percha case. These things, together with the coffee and biscuits his folks had given him, and the handkerchief from Rena, and the clothes on his back, were all he could safely say he owned this fine June morning, so close to home, after so long journeying.

Of course, he owned memory too, and one day this might prove to be his heaviest baggage. But not now. He had learned in these three years that sometimes it was all right to walk in the moment only, and that memory was merciful in this, at least: that now and then it gave way to music or to sunlight or to a little space when a man might walk along with nothing bad happening to him. Now he was forty, toiling up the southerly road, about to close the vast, complex circuit he had begun three years before. He walked along, thin of face, thin of hands, mostly bone now—*gaunted,* as his cousin Rena said. His mother, were she there to receive him, would not have known him at first, then would have set him down to a meal that most likely would have killed him; his sisters, could they see him, would have fluttered around him like doves, lamenting, but they were married and gone, one to New Orleans and one to Haiti, and only his father was left, and Aunt Vassar—and Morgan. Toward these, then, Gawain traveled, and whatever else awaited him. He walked along toward Cumberland, and for a little while he whistled a catchy French tune their fifer used to play, when they had a fifer.

◆　　◆　　◆

THE ROAD WAS bonny in all seasons, but never so much as in the first month of summer when the rains were still fresh on the earth and all was new and bright and delicate—in the time before the long hot days and the drought of August. In June the leaves did not curl or rattle; the wind made a soft sound among them, and their green was like the first green, as if these were the first leaves ever thought of. Alive with sap, the limbs and branches never creaked in their mournful winter way, nor broke themselves, nor seemed to mind the grapevines that looped among them. Along the road, in the ditches and fence rows, the rank grass, and Queen Anne's lace, and the lyre-leaf sage, and sumac; pink buttercups—every one, it seemed, with a laden bee sidling in and out—and wild morning glory, honeysuckle, trumpet vine (cow-itch, the old people called it), poke sallet gone to seed.

The road made its way by houses brooding in the shadow of great oaks, that lay at the end of cedar-lined walks laid in the herringbone style. Around many of these were neglected gardens with pools of foul dark water where egrets stalked; in the yards of all were the bloomless greens of daffodils past their prime, that not long ago had turned their faces toward the sun, and ancient blue irises just coming into their glory. In all these houses, Gawain Harper would have been welcomed had he wanted to call, and sometimes people waved at him from their galleries and shouted his name, or the name of someone they took him for. Once a lady made him stop and take a cup of cool water. And from each of these houses, invariably, a crowd of dogs sortied—some to bark, and some to fawn and cringe, and some to follow him down the road in a friendly way.

By cabins, too, the road passed—some of them empty, watching through the vacant eyes of their windows, and some of them still full of life: half-naked children playing in the swept dirt yard, and laundry on the line, and tame buttercups planted, and moonvine.

Gawain Harper took in all these things as he followed the southerly road. It all seemed familiar enough, seemed to fit neatly into the pattern of his memory—even in the changed places, as if some part of memory had adjusted itself, had already expected, say, those stark chimneys where a house used to stand. Yet, after a while, Gawain began to have the odd sense that he was walking through someone else's memory—not his at all, but some other's that had been told to him long ago, so often and so well that he had mistaken it for his own. The notion began to weigh on him— he did not want to feel like a stranger in his own land—and finally it aggravated him so much that he stopped in the road and lifted his voice.

"Now, this is nonsense," he said to the sky. "It's what you get for thinkin too much. It don't have to be so complicated, does it?"

The sky had no answer, nor did anything in the fields or woods around.

Gawain had a companion at that moment, a brown fyce the size of a possum, who had followed him from Mister Drew Whitfield's house. The dog sat gravely on his haunches, looking at him, cocking his head. Gawain looked around; they were at the edge of an old cotton field bright with sun and bordered by deep woods. Gawain looked down at the dog. "You want to tarry by the road awhile, eat a little biscuit?"

The dog stood and wagged his stump of a tail.

"All right, then," said Gawain.

The dog followed him into the field; they moved through the long grass to the edge of the woods, and there Gawain built an economical fire of branches. Soon, the tin boiler was filled with water and boiling, and Gawain added a palmful of the coffee he'd gotten from his cousin's people, and he thanked God for them, and for the coffee, and for the biscuits in the rag, and for all good things. Finally, when the coffee was boiled and poured into the tin cup, Gawain broke one of the biscuits and gave half to the fyce, who swallowed it in a single lunging bite. Gawain savored his own half, dipping it into the coffee, eating slowly.

In a little while, he took off his hat, slipped out of his coat and shoes and socks and rolled up his breeches (his legs were skinny and pasty white, and there was the red welt of a scar where a ball had barked him once) and strolled out into the field again. He found a bare tract of clay ground in the sun, and there he sat down, and filled his pipe and lit it, and drew his knees up and clasped them with his arms like a boy fishing. The dog came and circled once and lay down and soon was snoring, and around them the tall grass buzzed with sound and smelled hot like summer. Gawain breathed deep of it. "That is freedom," he told the dog.

He closed his eyes and felt the sun go deep inside him. He tilted his head, opened his eyes again and saw a heron passing over, bound for the Leaf River bottoms most likely, his broad wings beating a steady cadence, long legs stretched out behind.

On the ground were shards of flint and broken points—spearpoints and arrowheads and a knife that was almost perfect—a village site once upon a time, and here the pointmaker had squatted on his haunches, chipping away with a deer antler, muttering to himself. Gawain turned an arrowhead in his fingers and wondered what the fellow thought when he spoiled this one, wondered if the Indians had cuss words they could use on such an occasion, and if they didn't, how they got along. He wondered where the man's bones were now, or the dust of them, and what this place looked like back there at the first creak of time. Big timber for certain, and a complete, utter silence, and no sense of any place in the wide world but this one. People walked here then, believing the universe was in order—believing, no doubt, that they were the polished end of all creation and so would not be forgotten—unable to imagine the world without themselves in it. Well, that was all right, Gawain thought. That's what people did, even when they knew better.

✦　　✦　　✦

A HALF HOUR later, Gawain and the dog found themselves at a place called Wagner's Stretch, named for the family whose house had once stood impressively among the trees. The house had burned a decade before the war, set alight by discontented slaves. Old Wagner, who had discontented them, lasted most of that night sitting on the upper gallery in a rocking chair with a brace of pistols and a loyal boy to load and prime, until it finally occurred to the insurrectionists to burn the house down. The next day, a party of armed and mounted men hunted the Wagner negroes down with dogs, chasing them through the swamps and brakes like deer, and killed them every one, and burned their bodies among the ashes of the house. This was a haunted place ever since—Bad Ground, the Cumberland negroes called it—and men spoke of how chill the air was, passing here of a summer night, and of mysterious fogs that moved through the trees. The ruins of the house were hidden now among vines and creepers, among the dark cedars and the blackjack oaks, but every spring, a double row of daffodils appeared to mark the place where the front walk had been, the yellow trumpets pointing the way to nothing now.

He had never felt the legendary chill nor seen the ghostly fogs, but now, alone in the clear light of day, Gawain felt uneasy passing here. The dog felt it too, and stayed close beside.

"I'll tell you what I think," said Gawain to the dog, in a voice that was a little too loud. "I think it is not good for a fellow to be alone all the time."

In the woods, the shadows lay watching. Gawain thought he could see the chimneys of the old Wagner house, heavy with vines.

"No," he said, "too much time alone and you get to thinkin too much. I've found it so; yes, indeed, I have."

Here the trees crowded right up to the road and closed over it like a tunnel; there were no fields to open out, and the distant bend seemed to draw no closer however fast they walked, and somewhere a solitary crow was talking. *Haw, haw,* he said, in the gutteral tongue of crows. *Haw, haw.* The dog was panting now, and Gawain, for his part, found that he had no more to say. Though the mud dragged at his feet, he did not care to venture too close to the dark trees. *This is stupid,* Gawain told himself, yet he stayed in the middle of the road. He had never seen a ghost in his life, but no matter: in his view, dead people simply could not be trusted.

Even before the war, Gawain had seen a great many dead people. They died in accidents or were kicked by mules. They shot one another, they hanged themselves in barn lofts and attics and bedrooms, they caught the measles or the consumption or the milk leg or any of a thousand other afflictions of the flesh. They died in myriads from the yellow jack and took blood poisoning from the prick of a thorn. They died giving birth, the two souls, mother and child, passing each other in the darkness. Some, having lived long enough, simply quit breathing. When he was a boy, Gawain was often dragged to shuttered parlors or the candle-smelling gloom of churches where he was compelled to stand on tiptoe and peer into the face of a rouged and powdered doll-like thing stuffed uncomfortably into its narrow box. Such artifacts never bothered him; they were too far removed from light and air, from voice and movement, remote even from the grief that hung over them like the bitter smell of marigolds. They seemed to Gawain of no more substance than the dried cicada shells that clung to the bark of trees in August, empty and almost invisible, the living thing flown away.

But not all the dead were so tidy, and even those who were could not always be depended upon to remain calm. Gawain had seen these, too, before the war. A man hauled from Leaf River after two days in the water, an apparition like a swollen sausage, lips gone to the fishes, fingers to the snapping turtles, eyes like green muscadines. An engine driver flayed by the steam of a boiler explosion. A fellow student at the university burned to a shrunken black mannequin in a house fire. His Uncle Tom, dead of apoplexy, who cleared the room when he sat upright in his coffin and belched.

Then he went off to the war. In his first action, a minor skirmish on the retreat from Corinth, he was still wearing the clothes he'd left home in, but, in place of the umbrella, he carried a converted 1812 flintlock that sometimes fired and sometimes didn't. He had seen no casualties yet, but he knew people were killed in these affairs and was so scared that he was sure his heart would explode. He was in the rear rank, trying to make himself as small as possible, hiding behind the broad shoulders of the man to his front, when that gentleman took a ball in the forehead, splashing his brains into Gawain's face. Gawain dropped his musket and was wiping frantically at the mess, unbelieving, telling himself that such things simply did not happen, when the man turned and spoke to him. The sound was inarticulate, or of a language living men could not know, but it was speech, and Gawain sank to his knees as the man looked at him, his eyes bulging in their sockets but quick with outrage and accusation and surprise. Gawain could not have said how long the man stood there until he folded and fell to the ground like a bundle of rags, but it was long enough for Gawain to finally understand that sometimes the dead were a different kind of living thing. They could be *aware* somehow, and they could watch you—not from some distant place but from the cloudy eyes themselves. And somewhere deep in the cold lump of brain, or in the silent heart perhaps, a mysterious light burned on.

So he was afraid here, on the old Wagner's Stretch, even in the bright sunshine. *It is the aloneness,* he thought. Then he thought it was the weariness too, perhaps, or the strange silence along here where nothing seemed to live in the grass. It was the crow following through the trees. It was the strange vibration that violence left behind—the persistence of it in the air, as if only a slight tilt of the universe would bring it back again. Gawain made himself walk. He told himself that the dead were only dead after all, that whatever light may once have burned in them burned no longer, and they could do no harm. They would not rise to follow him down this road, gibbering of old violence, brushing his neck with their fingers. He made himself walk because he knew all about running, and just like in the old times if he ever once began to run—

Then, just like in the old times, he *was* running—running anyhow, in spite or reason and pride, and it seemed slow and hopeless, like running in a dream, like in the old times with the Federals hooting and cheering behind him and the balls humming around his ears and the little drawn-up place in the center of his back where the ball or the bayonet would go in if he didn't run fast enough—running in the impossible mud, awkward with the carpet bag in his hand and the canteen banging and his hat wanting to fly off, and trying not to trip over the dog who was running too. He ran a quarter of a mile before he stopped at last, just where the road began to curve. He was sweating and gasping for breath in the hot, still air, and he felt every inch the fool.

"I'll tell you," he said to the dog, who was panting in the grass, "It would kill a man to have to come home too often."

· III ·

Gawain had not seen Morgan Rhea since the morning three years before when he had boarded the cars to Corinth, so the image he had been carrying in his head was exactly that of the ambrotype she had given him. In the picture, she sat erect on a spindly chair, her dark hair pulled back from a face that was composed and thoughtful, her thin fingers clasped in her lap. While he was soldiering, Gawain had looked at that image so many times that he had difficulty seeing her in any other way, though he knew that somewhere in his memory she was moving, laughing, reclining, hopping with excitement, pointing, draping her hand over the back of a chair. Yet he could not reach these things, wherever they were; he saw her only as a slender, thoughtful woman seated before a ridiculous painted backdrop of what might have been willows, her hands forever joined in the lap of her voluminous dress.

Once, back in the winter on the Nashville campaign, he had found himself alone on picket. They were in Decatur, Alabama, waiting to see if the yankees would come out and fight so they could whip them and cross the river there. Gawain sat with his back against the frame of a deserted house, its weatherboards stripped for fires. The muddy yard, littered with stumps, was dismal in the pale twilight, and the air smelled of wood smoke, and somewhere a mule was braying, and the loom of the Federal earthworks was just visible at the end of the street. He was cold and would only get colder as night came. His nose was running, he had not eaten that day (though he was not hungry; he had long since quit being hungry) nor had he bathed in recent memory; his shoes were so thin he could identify leaves merely by stepping on them, and his breeches were stiff with mud, and he had fleas, and any moment the mean western yankees might sortie from their works and gobble him up. In that state he found himself yearning for Morgan Rhea in a way he had not done in months. The feeling came all of a sudden, rolling like a black fog over his heart, darkening the sky's last orange ribbon and deepening the cold beyond night. For a moment, he believed he could not bear it. He shut his eyes, and for another moment believed he could will himself across time and space, away from this wretched village and over the long hills and ridges westward toward the sun where she was. But when he looked again, he saw only the barren end of day, and beyond that tomorrow and tomorrow and tomorrow.

He scrambled to his knees then, fumbled at the buckle of his haversack, and drew thence the gutta-percha case that Morgan had pressed into his hand the day he left Cumberland. He opened it, and noticed for the first time that the image was cracked—a thin line down her face and between her breasts, from top to bottom of the plate. He could not say when he'd done it or how it could have happened, but there it was. He sat down again, cradling the picture in his hands, thinking *Of course it is broken, of course it is*—just like the letters he had lost. He had all her letters once, tied up with a piece of ribbon he'd found in an empty house, and in them he could hear her voice whenever he wanted—and he had lost them. One day they were gone, and with them her voice, and now her image was broken, and Gawain, in the last bitter fade of twilight, discovered he could no longer see her at all.

He would still look at the ambrotype every single day as the bloody winter passed into the last bloody spring of the war. But in that yard in Decatur, he put away once and for all the notion that he could see her, make her move, hear her voice—put away the idea that she was anything but a dream, something he had made up, patched together out of the sorry shambles of desire. She became an abstract like the dead used to be; a principle he had believed in once and didn't anymore, but that he still clung to anyhow, like honor, and love of country, and the regimental colors that tilted toward the dark.

The winter and spring brought terrible battles, defeat, the long retreat, surrender. But no more letters came, no voice out of the empty place that lay beyond the present moment. So he found it even easier to believe she was really a dream, or dead, or lost to him some other way, no matter. He was able to cling to that with a kind of satisfaction, growing used to the silence, ready for the time when he would be dead himself, and never sure that the moment had not come already.

Now suddenly he was free. He was alive after all, and unaccountably moving down the road that would take him home. So he pulled himself away from memory and saw the green woods again, and the gnats swirling in the shafts of sun, and heard again the towhee somewhere, and with him now a mourning dove, then another answering.

He stopped. There was the dog, gazing up into the branches of a sweet-gum where he had treed an old red squirrel fat on the spring bounty. The squirrel began to bark, and the dog watched him with interest.

He would have to believe again: that she was real, that somewhere up ahead she was moving through that very morning. He recalled what his cousin Rena had said, as if he were hearing it for the first time: She spoke of you. So Morgan Rhea did have a voice, even if he could not hear it, and she must remember.

But remember what? The Gawain Harper who had boarded the cars for Corinth with a valise and an umbrella? He had left her no image of himself save what she carried in her memory, so what did she see when she thought of him, if she thought of him at all?

"Hah!" he said, and laughed. He had come a long way from whatever it was she saw in her head; that much was plain at least. He would go and find out how far.

"Come along, dog," he said. "We goin to town."

The fyce did not want to leave the squirrel, but Gawain made him, and together they moved down the road. Gawain went quietly by old habit, watching, though he didn't have to now. Went quietly, he and the dog, so when they came around a bend, they spooked a horse standing there, a scrawny black gelding that, to look at him, shouldn't have had the energy to buck like he did and run off at the gallop, stirrups flapping, leaving his rider sitting in the mud. The dog took off after the horse, and Gawain looked at the rider. "Good God," he said.

"Good God yourself," said the man. "What you mean, ambushin me like that?" He began to pick himself up from the mud, and Gawain moved to help him.

"I wasn't ambushin," Gawain said, taking the man's arm.

"You ain't a robber, are you?" said the man. "For if you are, you have done run off the only thing I have worth stealin, and he ain't much, the son of a bitch. Throwin me in the road—the very idea. And after all we been through. I tell you, if I live a century I'll never figure out horses—they are crazy, ever one of em, through and through. I hope you ain't a robber—I have had my fill of—"

"Jesus and Mary," said Gawain. "Do I look like a robber to you?"

The man regarded Gawain with narrowed eyes. He was as tall as Gawain and as skinny, about the same age and with the same sunken face and bristly chin, but with long, greasy brownish-red hair that hung down over his collar. He wore a porkpie hat, still in place, and a dark butternut officer's frock coat, and checkered breeches tucked into his boots, and spurs, and a waistcoat with a thick watch chain, and a striped gingham shirt, and a cravat. The collar of the coat had a darker patch where the rank had been removed, but the right cuff bore an embroidered square-and-compasses, once gold but rusty now. He was all over mud, not just from the fall but from journeying too. "No," he said at last. "No, if you are a robber, you have not been a success at it." He put out his hand. "I am Harry Stribling," he said.

The two men clasped hands in the road. "Have you traveled long?" Stribling asked.

"Oh, a long time," said Gawain. "I am comin up from south Alabama, but my home is yonder, a mile or two, in Cumberland. And you?"

"Oh, a long ways. Truth to tell, though, I don't know where I'm goin. Just goin."

"Where is your home?" asked Gawain.

Stribling looked up the road. "Somewheres," he said. "Up yonder." Then he grinned. "Who knows?"

"Well," said Gawain, and let it drop. "You can come with me if you want. I am weary of solitude."

"Just so," said Stribling.

"I am sorry about your horse," said Gawain. "I will help you catch him, if that infernal dog ain't run him to Michigan."

"Oh, he won't need any catchin," said Stribling. "He is about used up and only did that because he's in a bad humor. We'll come upon him directly. Say, is that your bag in the road?"

Gawain nodded and picked up the carpet bag. They began to walk, Stribling limping a little. "You hurt your leg in the fall," said Gawain.

"No," said Stribling. "I got shot once, is all. It's nothin."

"Ain't it hard to walk?" asked Gawain.

"No, I prefer to walk. Fact of the matter is, when I get wherever it is I'm goin, I intend to do nothin *but* walk for the rest of my natural life. I am through with horses forevermore."

"You were a cavalryman. I have often heard them say such things."

"Indeed."

"I was in the infantry," said Gawain, "and I have *walked* all I care to."

"How will you get around then?"

"I intend to *stroll*," said Gawain. "Everywhere."

"Of course," said Stribling.

They talked awhile, telling their regiments and campaigns, finding places where the complicated arcs of their lives had crossed. Stribling had been with Chalmers and had operated in this very country, on this very road in fact, and had been in many of the fights Gawain had, and some that Gawain never heard of: Brice's Crossroads, for instance, and Harrisburg.

For his part, Gawain could claim the Atlanta campaign, which Stribling had missed. Then Stribling told how he'd been a captain once, but when he was paroled, the Federal officer made him remove the rank and buttons from his coat. Gawain said they let him keep his buttons, and he hadn't any rank anyhow, so that was all right.

"Where is your coat, then?" asked Stribling.

"I got shut of it," said Gawain. "Give it to a nigger when I bought this one."

Stribling laughed. He started to speak, then shook his head and laughed again.

"What?" asked Gawain.

"Just funny to think about," said Stribling. "About everything that's happened, and that's all it has come to."

"Yes," said Gawain. "Ain't it funny."

They walked in silence for a time, thinking about everything that had happened and what it had all come to. Then Stribling spoke again.

"What's your line? I mean, when you are home. Was home, I mean."

"Ah," said Gawain, and now he laughed. "I am—was—a professor of literature at the Cumberland Female Academy—which, I understand, is no more. And you?"

"Oh, I used to practice the law, had a newspaper for a while over in Alabama when the war came. At present I am . . . a philosopher."

"I would not think there'd be much call for that these days," said Gawain.

"Nor a professor either," said Stribling.

"Indeed," said Gawain Harper.

They talked along, and in a half mile or so they came to the horse cropping weeds by the roadside, the dog lying at his feet.

"Told you," said Stribling.

The horse rolled his eyes as Stribling approached, and sidestepped until Stribling took up the trailing reins. "You sorry, vile, ungrateful son of a bitch," said Stribling as he stroked the horse's bony nose. The animal wore a McClellan saddle and an army headstall with "U.S." rosettes. Behind the cantle were a blanket roll and a pair of saddlebags. "He is called Xenophon," said Stribling.

"That seems a good deal of a name for such a horse," said Gawain.

"Why I call him Zeke," said Stribling. "Come along, Zeke." He began to walk, holding the reins, and the horse came along behind, and the dog rose and followed the horse, and Gawain followed them all up the southerly road.

◆　　◆　　◆

PILGRIMS THEY WERE, and for a little while longer they could shape whatever possibilities they wished about the moment toward which they journeyed. The road led to places they had known once, that they believed they knew still. If they could only get there, they would not be strangers— the illusion would fold in on itself, collapse into the vacuum of the lost years and prove itself only an illusion after all. But the road, for all its relics, told them little, really; it was only a suspension, its lights and shadows hovering at the margin of time, and for this little while they moved like figures in a dream. At their backs lay the old world they had known, remote now as the valleys of the moon, to which they could never return no matter how much the old people spoke of it. Perhaps they wouldn't even if they could, for they had seen that old world doomed by its own essence; it had thrust them into the dark adventure, had been consumed and left them with little but the taste of ashes for their trials. And now the dark adventure was itself finished, more or less; quieter at least, no longer so immediate, though they would never be done with it altogether. Nor understand it either, for if their purpose was clear to them once, too much had happened for it ever to be clear again. Yet they would come to understand this much, long hence: that the adventure was a destination of its own, perhaps the only one they'd been born to, and wherever they traveled afterward would be less search than wandering.

But that was in time to come. Right now, Gawain Harper and Harry Stribling had no real sense of their own history, no more than the high geese traveling across the stars. They were too busy: they were spared of death, so must once again pay the tally for living; free, so they were indentured to tomorrow. It was the same tomorrow Gawain had seen long ago in the winter twilight, only now it was not so simple. Now it was a tangle of possibilities at which they could only wonder, like children in a magic wood. And wondering, they would have to yearn once more.

Gawain Harper could not speak for his companion, but for him the yearning grew more intolerable at every step. Getting closer made it so, he supposed, but that understanding gave no comfort. The feeling had withdrawn into a region below his heart and lay there like a coiled worm, gnawing at him. Harry Stribling was telling a story about the last time he and Zeke had been on this road; Gawain tried to listen, and at the same time wished he had a bayonet to prod the whole entourage along toward Cumberland. Then, suddenly, Gawain decided he could not go on at all. "Hold on," he said.

"What?" said Stribling.

Gawain moved to the roadside and sat down in the weeds.

"You gone get red bugs, doin that," said Stribling.

The dog came and sat down next to Gawain and looked at him. In a moment, Stribling dropped the horse's reins and came and squatted on his haunches, the leather of his boots creaking.

"What's the matter, boy?" said Stribling. "You sick?"

Gawain nodded.

"Well," said Stribling, "likely you got the dysentery."

"No," said Gawain. "No, it ain't the dysentery."

Stribling plucked a weed, put the stalk in his teeth. He looked up the road. Presently, he said, "You ever in all that time come home on a furlough?"

Gawain shook his head.

"Me neither," said Stribling.

"Look here," said Gawain. "I will show you somethin." He opened his bag, rooted around inside, came out with the gutta-percha case. He handed it to Stribling, who took it without question, opened it, looked for a long moment. "My, my, my," he said at last, in a tone that suggested approval, envy, even a hint that, given the chance, Stribling would steal this prize for himself: the immemorial response of a soldier presented with any image, letter, token of another's sweetheart, wife, sister, daughter—no matter how appalling.

"Her name is Morgan," said Gawain. "I have not laid eyes on her in three years."

Stribling closed the case, touched it reverently and gave it back. "So now you are afraid," he said.

Gawain shrugged. "I don't know what I am."

Stribling stood, his knees popping. "Ah, me," he said. "You ever ride a horse before?"

"Only when pressed," said Gawain.

"Well, what you need is to get up on old Zeke, and I'll whack him on the behind, and you'll be home just directly—then you'll see there ain't nothin to be afraid of."

"Oh, man," said Gawain. "You don't—"

"Bah!" said Stribling. He drew his watch out, looked at it, pocketed it again. "Be dinnertime before long. She'd be sittin down at table, look up, see you standin there in the doorway—" He turned, frowning. "Say, she ain't dead is she? Or married? Same thing, of course—"

"No," said Gawain.

"Then get up," said Stribling. "You think she'll be any less stranger to you than you are to her?"

"She don't even know if I'm alive or not," said Gawain. "What if she—" He stopped, and opened the case and looked at the image, and shut it again. "Jesus Christ," he said.

"You didn't finish your thought," said Stribling.

Gawain shrugged, shook his head.

"Then I will finish it for you," said Stribling. "What if she ain't the one in the picture anymore? That's what you're afraid of mostly, ain't it?"

"I don't know," said Gawain. "Maybe. I can't . . . I can't seem to *see* her anymore. I—"

"Well, you never will, sittin in the weeds," said Stribling. "Now quit bein so pitiful and let us be gone. Anyway, it's likely she never *was* the one in the picture— God only knows what you've made her out to be these last years."

"Well," said Gawain, and hoisted himself out of the grass. "I suppose I am bein pitiful."

They went on, and Stribling talked of how you could make things out to be something they weren't, especially people, especially women, and illustrated his point with colorful anecdotes from his own experience, until Gawain said, "Well, you *are* a philosopher, ain't you?"

"Only an apprentice," said Stribling. "There is one or two things I ain't figured out yet. Gravity, for instance."

"Gravity?"

"Yes," said Stribling. "I don't believe in it."

"Be damned," said Gawain.

Presently they came to an open space; ahead they could see a paling fence rambling by the road, a fence that was whitewashed once, but in bad repair now.

"Well, we are gettin ever closer," said Gawain. "There is the old grave-yard by the Mount Zion church."

The church itself came in view, a gray, weathered affair with tight-shuttered windows and a leaning bell tower that had never harbored any-thing but wasps. In the graveyard, a saddled mule stood ground-tethered, head bent in boredom. When Zeke whickered, the mule looked up, then bent its head again.

"There is a fellow diggin a grave all by himself," said Stribling. "A sor-rowful duty. I remember—"

"Hold on," said Gawain. They stopped in the road and watched the man; he was deep in the earth so that only his shoulders and head were visible, and the rising and falling of his shovel. He was gray and old, but his naked arms and shoulders were wiry, taut of muscle like a young man's. He glistened with sweat.

"Well, I'll be damned," said Gawain. "I reckon some things don't change." He put down his bag and walked to the fence and leaned his elbows on it. Stribling followed, and tied Zeke to one of the palings. The dog slipped through the fence and went over to the mule and lay down.

"Friend of yours?" asked Stribling.

Gawain laughed. "Oh, that is old Dial Ethridge. He is diggin up his father-in-law again."

"Say it ain't so," said Stribling.

"Well, it is so."

"Well, now, listen here—," began Stribling.

"Never fear," said Gawain. "Somebody always comes along to stop him—like us—though once he did actually hove out the old man onto solid ground. Nobody could figure out how he did it—he's in a pneumatic coffin, you see—old Waddell, I mean—mighty heavy. He—"

"But why does he do it?" asked Stribling.

"It's always his wife Lonny drives him to it. She is a terror, and he does it for revenge. You ought to see her—stout as a barrel, with a mustache. Good God."

"Well, still—," said Stribling.

"See here, Dial!" said Gawain, lifting his voice. "You can't be diggin up Mister Waddell. You come up out of there!"

The old man ceased his shoveling and squinted into the glare. "Who is that? Gawain Harper?"

"Yessir," said Gawain. "And this is my friend Harry Stribling."

The old man clambered out of the hole like a spider. He held the shovel at port arms. "Where you been?" he demanded.

"Well, I been off at the war," said Gawain.

"Oh, you have, have you?" said the man. He lowered the shovel. "What you doin right now?"

"Well, right now we are walkin to Cumberland. You—"

"Never mind," said the old man. "You come up here, help me get this out."

"Ah, me," said Gawain. He eased himself through a gap in the fence.

"Here! Where you goin?" said Stribling.

"Goin to fill up that hole again," said Gawain. "You don't have to come if you don't want to."

Stribling shook his head and followed through the gap. When they got to the grave, Gawain and Stribling peered within. Old Dial Ethridge had uncovered the coffin; the top was scarred with the marks of his shovel. Through the murky glass window, they could make out the pale oval that was the face of the departed. It was framed in muttonchop whiskers and seemed to be scowling.

"Look at the stone," said Gawain.

Stribling knelt by the headstone and brushed his fingers over the writing there:

J. Vincent Waddell
Born in Delaware, 1775
Died Cumberland, Mississippi, 1855
He Feared God Above Many

"That is a peculiar sentiment," said Stribling. "I may have to philosophize on that later."

"Well, I wish you would," said Gawain. "I have never made any sense out of it." Then Gawain made the old man sit down on the mound of dirt and lectured him on the sacredness of the grave and other proprieties. Soon, to Gawain's dismay, the old man burst into tears.

"You have no notion," the old man said. "You all got no idee what I go through. She ere a demon, boys—ever little thing she is on me like a ballface hornet—and I ain't seen her teats in a generation—not that I'd want to, understand, but it ere the principle of the thing, you see. God knows, it's little enough I ask out of life."

Stribling knelt by the old man and patted his knee. "Now, now," he said.

"*You* understand, don't ye?" sobbed old Dial Ethridge. "You a man of sensibility—I can tell by lookin at ye."

"Surely," said Stribling. He patted the old man again. "Did you ever think of just knockin the dog shit out of her?"

The old man let out a howl. "Lonny!" he wailed.

"Well, good God," said Stribling.

While the old man sobbed, Gawain went to the grave and contemplated the face of the dead man through the glass window of the casket. J. Vincent Waddell had died of apoplexy ten years before; now here he was, still in his old-fashioned collar and cravat, his cheeks still rouged, his hair brittle and white and grown long as a woman's. His eyes were squinched up, as if he were bothered by the light.

"By God, I am tired of lookin at dead people," said Gawain.

"Well, quit lookin at em then," said Stribling.

"Well, they keep showin up."

Old Dial Ethridge was snuffling now, and muttering to himself. Stribling patted him on the back, came and stood by Gawain and looked down into the grave. After a moment, he said, "Well, I am ready to philosophize now."

"Proceed, then," said Gawain.

Stribling knelt, and shoved his hat back on his head, and gathered a handful of dirt clods. He began to drop them one by one onto the window of the casket.

"You are goin to break that sure," said Gawain. "Then we'll all be sorry."

Stribling ignored him. He went on dropping dirt into the grave until the window was covered and the face of J. Vincent Waddell could be seen no more. Then he stopped and dusted off his hands. He looked at Gawain. "Here is my philosophy, and you may take it or leave it as you will." He paused again; he stood up, and with the side of his boot raked a shovelful of dirt into the grave, then another and another. The dirt rattled on the iron coffin, and Stribling went on kicking at the dirt, and all at once he seemed to be in another place entirely. Finally Gawain said "Harry!" and he stopped, breathing hard, the sweat running down his face, his eyes narrowed and fixed on the distant line of the woods. He was quiet for a moment; when he spoke at last, his voice was steady, though it might have been himself he was talking to.

"Maybe you have noticed," he said. "You can't raise the dead, no matter how hard you try. You can't fetch em back again, you can't fix em nor make em answer for anything." He looked at Gawain now, his eyes still narrow and glittering. "You know what they are? They are holes in the universe for a little while, and then they close up again, stoppered with dust. This one here, all these—" He waved his hand to take in the mossy headstones leaning in the sun.

Stribling looked off toward the woods again. A cloud shadow fled across the land; when it passed, the sun seemed brighter than ever. A bold mockingbird came and perched on the headstone, close enough for Harry Stribling to touch him. The bird flicked its tail and watched them. Finally, Stribling spoke again, and his voice was quiet now. "It ain't the dead that keep showin up—it's the ones we used to be. A lawyer, a professor, a girl in a picture." He nodded toward old Ethridge. "That feller there, who was young and in love with a girl once, who has a mustache now. That's who we keep seein. They seem mighty real, don't they?"

Gawain nodded. "Mighty real," he said.

"Yeah," said Stribling. He picked up a handful of dirt and crumbled it into the grave. "They *were* real, too. Once." The mockingbird hopped down, snatched up a fat worm that Stribling turned up, flew away and disappeared into a cedar tree. "But not anymore, Brother Harper," said Stribling.

"You think I don't know that?" said Gawain.

"I think maybe you think you do," said Stribling. He wiped his hand on his breeches leg. "I'll remind you of it, directly we get to Cumberland. I been there since you have, remember. Now, let us get this poor bastard covered up again and get on down the road. It's gettin on to dinnertime."

They took turn about with the shovel, and after an hour they had J. Vincent Waddell at rest in the earth once more. When the grave was finished and tamped down, they were all three drenched in sweat, and covered in mud, and hungry. The sun was high now, and the day was beginning to merge into the peculiar suspension of a summer afternoon. The birds were quiet, and clouds were gathering like sheep. They rested in the shade of a hickory tree and divided, among themselves and the fyce, the remaining three biscuits in Gawain's bag, and emptied his canteen.

"Well, we'll make a gallant spectacle comin into town," said Gawain, scraping at the mud on his shoes. "I am muddy, I stink, I am hungry unto death. Makes me homesick for the army."

Stribling laughed. "Let me get my pistol, go off a ways and empty a cylinder at you—then you'd be *right* at home."

"Hah," said Gawain. He looked at the old man then, who was sitting with his head between his knees. "Old Dial," said Gawain, "you ain't said much lately. How is it with you?"

The old man looked up, his eyes red and bleary, his face streaked with sweat and grime. "I'm sorry, boys," he said. "I been too much trouble for ye."

"Nonsense," said Gawain.

"No, it's the God's truth," said the old man. He slowly unfolded himself from the ground and walked off a little and stood with his hands in his pockets, gazing across the burying ground. He was still shirtless, and now, in his weariness, he seemed frail and very old. His bones showed through his sunburned skin; his stringy gray hair was plastered to his skull, and his single gallus looped down like a vine. After a while, he turned, looked at them, shrugged his thin shoulders. "I promise I won't try to dig him up no more," he said.

"I am glad to hear you say that," said Gawain. "It never made a great deal of sense anyhow."

"No," said the old man, "I suppose it didn't." He looked at the sky, his face twisted as if he might cry again. But he didn't cry. "I am obliged for the biscuit," he said. "I been too much trouble for everybody." Then he turned and began to walk toward his mule.

"Well, old Dial," said Gawain after him. "You go on and make peace with Miss Lonny if you can."

The old man stopped, turned again. He looked at Gawain for a long moment, then shrugged again. "I can't," he said. "She died last winter, of the blood poison. Then I had a dream last night—she was right there, except when I put out my hand, she warn't. I don't know. Sometimes I hear her in the crows, too. It was her I meant to dig for, but I got . . . I got confused. I thought it was another time, I reckon. I don't know. Anyway, it don't matter now."

Gawain and Harry Stribling sat quietly, their backs against the hickory tree, while old Dial Ethridge mounted his mule and rode away. They could see him get smaller and smaller until he was a speck against the treeline, and then he was gone.

· IV ·

Gawain Harper thought it odd that the road was so empty, and he remarked on the fact to Harry Stribling. They were walking again, side by side, the horse and the little fyce following behind.

"Well, where would the people have to go, if they wanted to go somewheres?" said Stribling.

"Well, I don't know," said Gawain. "Seem like *somebody* ought to be passin. Used to be—"

"'Used to be,' hell," said Stribling. "This ain't 'used to be.' How many times I got to tell you?"

"Well, surely, but—"

Stribling laughed. "What if there ain't any town? What if, when we get there, everbody's gone—nothin but old ashes with vines growin in em, weeds, black crows roostin in the chimneys and everthing still and solemn. What then?"

"You ought not to say that," said Gawain. "That ain't so."

They went on in silence a little way until Stribling spoke again. "No, I ought not to of said that."

"Perhaps it is just the way of philosophers," said Gawain.

"Hmmm," said Stribling. "I'll tell you, pard—maybe I ought to take up another line of work."

"Well, what would you do? Be a lawyer again?"

"No, no—I am a Christian now, since the war."

"Well, you could start a newspaper again. No doubt Cumberland will need one. You could—"

"No," said Stribling. "I am hampered by principles now, so that avenue is closed as well."

"The clergy, then," said Gawain.

"Hmmm," said Stribling.

They were coming into the Leaf River bottoms now, the road winding down out of the hills. This had been cleared country once, but the woods were taking it back: sweetgums, sycamores, lots of willows, scrub oaks with their ugly, stubby leaves knotty with galls. Not many cedars in this bottomland, for which Gawain was thankful. He marveled at the growth—three summers, and already the old cotton rows were hidden under the leaves and brush and rank grass. He had hunted birds here once in distant autumns, following the dogs through the brown stubble of cotton and the feathery broomsage. Now it would be deer country again, or pretty soon anyway, if somebody didn't get to work on it.

He was thinking hard on these things, his mind wandering further and further from the road and the bright noon, so when he heard the gunshot, he didn't know if it was real or something out of his memory—either way, the sound was already past when he found it in his head. "Did you hear that?" he said.

"Yes," said Stribling. "*Some*body's around besides us, anyhow."

"It wasn't a rifle," said Gawain.

"No. A fowling piece, I guess."

As if in confirmation, another shot came to them, flat and hollow, muffled by the woods. *Picket firing,* thought Gawain, not in words but as a shape, a picture. He pushed it away.

"Now, there's a pleasant novelty," said Stribling.

"What's that?" said Gawain, startled.

"Why, to be able to speculate on a gunshot in the woods and not take it personal."

Gawain looked at his companion. "I was just thinkin the same thing," he said.

"Were you?" said Stribling. "Well, I am not surprised, given our late profession."

"It wasn't any profession."

"Pastime, then," said Stribling. "A diversion."

"Wasn't that either," said Gawain.

"What was it then? It had to be something."

"Yes," said Gawain. "The longest dream I ever had, and the worst. Or maybe not. Maybe this is." Gawain stopped, tangled up in his own thinking. "I don't know what it was."

A cardinal lit by the roadside ahead, then flicked away. Gawain saw the red slash against the leaves, heard his fretful chipping.

"By and by, maybe we can figure it out," said Stribling. "It all had to mean something—I'd give worlds to know myself."

"I imagine a good many would," said Gawain.

"Such a long way we've come," said Stribling.

Yes, thought Gawain. *Such a long way.* Gawain felt the road under him, heard the old, comfortable sound of the horse plodding behind. The afternoon closed around them, the long grass full of voices. Suddenly, overhead, the cardinal sang:

Free-dom, *Free*-dom, *Free*-dom, *Free*—

Gawain stopped, looked up. He heard the bird again:

Free-dom, *Free*-dom—

"What?" said Stribling, stopping too.

"Listen. Listen at that redbird."

Free-dom, *Free*-dom, *Free*-dom, *Free*—

Stribling cocked his head. "He's calling for his lady," he said. He looked at Gawain. "They mate for life, you know." Then he frowned, as if listening to another voice. Gawain watched him.

"Did you hear?" Gawain asked, after a moment.

Stribling held up his hand; at the gesture, the bird ceased calling, and even the murmuring in the grass seemed to pause, waiting. The horse lifted his head, ears tilted. The dog watched them all, cocking his head just as Stribling had. Then the empty place passed, and the world began to turn again. Stribling lowered his hand. "Sorry," he said. "What was you sayin?"

"The bird," said Gawain. "Did you hear him? It sounded like—"

"No," said Stribling. "Not the bird."

The horse moved restlessly; Stribling spoke to him and rubbed his nose, all the while watching down the road. "I know this place," he said. He nodded. "That bridge yonder."

Stribling went on stroking the horse's nose, talking to him, while Gawain stared in wonder at the bridge. It seemed to have appeared out of nowhere, emerging from a line of sycamores Gawain now understood to be a stream bank; it was a narrow span of weathered gray planks, serene, drowsing in the dappled sunlight. The road led down to it in a gentle fall, then, at the far end, curved away into a dense wood. Gawain had not thought of the bridge until this moment; he had merely expected it to be there, and now it had caught him by surprise. They were close now, only a half mile or so from town.

"Why, that is Leaf River bridge," said Gawain. "Wonder why the yankees didn't burn it."

"I crossed it three times," said Stribling. "First time was at a walk, northbound. Second time was at the full gallop, southbound, and a dicey piece of work it was, too, with those other fellows on our heels. Then the last time going north again, ambling along, in no particular hurry to catch anybody. I wondered at the time why they didn't burn it; I suppose they didn't care if we caught them or not." Stribling laughed then, and pushed his hat back on his head. "It is the only intact span I have seen in years—I might have to burn it myself."

"I understand," said Gawain. "But do it from the other side, if you will."

"Surely," said Stribling. "I—"

The horse jerked at the reins, wanting to back up. "Easy," said Stribling.

"What's the matter with him now?" said Gawain.

"He's a horse is what's the matter with him," said the other.

"Well, they are crazy all right," agreed Gawain. He did not like the horse to be so nervous all of a sudden.

"Do me a favor, sir," said Stribling.

"All right."

"Open that offhand bag for me, would you?"

"Surely." Gawain set his carpet bag in the road, ran his hand down the horse's sweaty neck then moved aft, his hand touching the horse all the while. When he reached the saddlebag, he unbuckled it and looked at Stribling.

"Now hunt around in there and fetch my pistol. Be careful—there's some old underdrawers in there, too."

Gawain frowned, started to speak, but Stribling shook his head. Gawain reached into the bag and felt the cool flank of the pistol right away. He brought it out: a '49 Colt's Pocket Model, capped and loaded. He handed it butt-first to Stribling. "Here," he said.

"Thank you," said Stribling, and tucked the piece into the waistband of his trousers. He was watching down the road again, his left arm wrapped around the horse's nose, the fingers of his right hand tapping the butt of the pistol. The horse was still, but for a quivering in his flanks and his breathing. Meanwhile the fyce had trotted a few yards ahead and pointed his muzzle at the woods. Again the woods and the grass fell silent, and the sunlight seemed empty, and the leaves of the trees grew still.

"Hush," said Stribling. "See the dog yonder."

The fyce was creeping. His back was bowed, and the hair on it bristled; he lifted each foot with infinite care, as if he were walking on glass. His lip was curled, and he was moving toward the almost seamless wall of a stand of poplars grown thick in the bottomland.

"Watch it," said Stribling. "Watch the—" And that was all because the horse squealed and reared then, cutting at the air with his hooves, and Stribling ducked and almost lost the reins. But he held on, cursing, at the same time trying to shuck out of his frock coat. Then the horse reared again but lost his footing and slipped in the mud, landing hard on his side with a *whoof!* of air, and Stribling had his coat off and wrapped around the horse's head and pulled the pistol from his belt.

"Gawain!" he said, and flung the pistol at Gawain Harper, who caught the piece awkwardly between his hands, the muzzle pointed at his stomach—

"Jesus," said Gawain, and fumbled at the pistol, turning at the same time toward the trees.

The hounds came silently out of the grass in perfect harmony. Black they were, and long-legged, with great triangular heads creased down the middle, and long pink tongues flecked with slobber. Their muscles rippled like rope under the taut black hides. Their smell exploded over the road, and the fyce yelped and curled his lip. When he shot forward, the two hounds split apart, and the smaller one, the bitch, hesitated, offered her flank, and the fyce went for her. He bit, but his teeth closed on the empty air. The fyce whirled, but too late. Then the bite came, hard, at the base of his neck, and the sound like a stick breaking.

✦   ✦   ✦

WHEN HE SAW what the hounds were up to, Gawain cocked the pistol. He lay the bead on the center of the big one's head, the one that was circling, and pulled the trigger, and heard the dry snap of the hammer.

"Shoot em both, Gawain," said Harry Stribling, holding the horse's head. "You can get their names later." But Gawain didn't hear; he had already snapped the pistol again and now he was watching the big hound move fast, close his jaws on the fyce's neck and shake him once and fling him into the grass, then turn, both of them, and grin at him, tongues lolling, sliding apart again.

"Shoot, goddammit!" said Stribling, but Gawain wouldn't shoot again. He could hardly see now, and he knew what that was about—the red light breaking behind his eyes, like when you looked at a fire at night then looked away, and the breath coming in quick gasps, and the trembling, and the calm. That's how it had been, always—something he had learned, come to depend on: the calm, the quiet place he moved in. He could not have done it otherwise, all those times when he could see their faces, their hands, some odd detail of their dress—a button, a certain cut of jacket, a corps badge or set of chevrons, a ragged cuff—as they came out to meet him in the smoke, or recoiled behind their works, or ran before him. So he moved toward the big hound, wanting to kill it, wanting to lay the pistol barrel across the broad, creased head as many times as it would take to crack the bone, splinter it, make the pink froth spill between the jaws. From far away, he heard Stribling say his name, but he was watching the hounds' dull eyes, the lips curl over the yellow teeth and the coarse, bristling hair. The animals crouched—still silent, not a sound had they made since they came sliding out of the grass—then a voice that was not Stribling's voice but that of another: "Don't be doin that."

The voice brought him up, made him aware again. From the corner of his eye he could see Stribling and the horse; he could see the hounds crouching low, their eyes just over the tassles of the grass, and the jeans breeches, wet to the knees, of the man who had spoken. Gawain raised his eyes, blinked, the breath still coming quick so a moment passed before he could speak. Then he saw the man's face, swollen, peeling red, his mouth opening and closing as he breathed, and the red, peeling hands, and the muslin shirt worn to thinness and soaked with sweat, and finally the fowling piece, held together with wire, thrown casually over his forearm, the barrel steady and in a line with Gawain's eyes.

"Your dogs killed that little fellow," Gawain said.

"They's dogs," said the man. "They'll do that."

A powder horn hung from the man's shoulder by a leather thong, and a shot pouch, and a goat bladder of water. From his waistbelt, a brace of squirrels dangled head-down. One of the squirrels moved its paws lazily in the air, as if reaching for something.

Gawain studied the man. His eyes did not seem to blink, nor to be looking anywhere in particular. The face was empty of expression. Gawain moved a little to the side, watched the shotgun barrel follow him. It was a single-barrel gun, the muzzle worn from much shooting. The hammer was cocked; Gawain could see the little copper gleam of the percussion cap.

"I know you," said Gawain. "You and your goddamned dogs."

"Pardon me, gentlemen," said Harry Stribling. "You reckon I can unwrap this horse's head? He is gettin my coat all full of slobber."

The man looked up, as if noticing Stribling for the first time. "You askin me?" he said.

Stribling spoke to the horse, then pulled the coat away and stroked the horse's nose. Zeke rolled his eyes and snorted, but he stood fast, his feet planted stiffly in the road. All his near side, and the saddle and stirrup leather and saddlebags, was coated in mud from his fall. "Now then," said Stribling. He looked at the man. "You might want to point that gun some other way."

The man nodded, but he did not move the gun.

"You know," said Stribling, "it really is bad judgment to shoot squirrels in the hot summertime. They get the fever."

"Don't say," said the man.

"Yes, indeed," said Stribling. "I'd be real careful, I was you. Real careful."

They stood in silence for a moment: the three men, the dogs, the horse. It was hot and still, the air heavy now and smelling of pine. The birds were quiet, taking their midday rest. Then the man nodded again, as if he'd digested the advice Stribling offered. He said, "Yonder's the river; you ought to cross it now, go on to town if that's your notion."

"Gawain, let's be goin," said Harry Stribling.

But Gawain was moving slowly, looking at the trees, moving between the two dogs where they lay in the grass. He stopped then, looked down at the fyce. The dogs watched him, making no sound.

The fyce lay with his teeth bared and his eyes open, intact save for the odd twist of his neck. Already the fleas were leaving him; Gawain could see them moving under the bristly hair. He nudged the carcass with his foot, then looked at Stribling. "Would you care to offer a philosophy?" he said.

"No," said Stribling.

"That's too bad," said Gawain. Then his eyes lit up with remembering, and he turned once more to the stranger. "Molochi!" he said. "Molochi Fish!"

The other turned his swollen mask to Gawain, mouth opening and closing, eyes dead and lidless, as if in parody of his own name.

"You still hire out to the paterollers, Molochi?" asked Gawain, moving a little to the side while the eyes followed him. "Still hire out for Constable John Talbot?" He waved the pistol at the dogs. "That was all a long while ago, Molochi—these must be the pups of the one caught young Peter. My, that was a day."

Molochi Fish blinked at last. He worked his mouth and spat. "Ain't any paterollers since they freed the niggers."

Gawain slapped a palm to his forehead. "Of course! I just can't get it in my mind, been gone so long. They freed the niggers, Molochi, and there you have it. And Mister John Talbot?"

The man spat again. "Dead," he said.

"Ah, me," said Gawain. "What a good and righteous man he was, and now he sleeps with the angels. My, how the world goes and leaves us behind."

He turned to Stribling then, who was still watching, whose face still brooded in the shadows of the moving leaves. "Now Harry, this is Molochi Fish who used to be our hero in the old times, but has lost his situation now the niggers are free and the town constable is out of office—life's incumbent, you might say."

"A pleasure, I'm sure," said Stribling.

Gawain tucked the useless pistol into his waistband and squatted amiably beside the body of the fyce. Stribling watched him. Molochi Fish seemed not to see him at all.

"Now, Harry," said Gawain, "old Molochi here reminds me of the days when we had a little nigger we named Peter. He was sweet and harmless as a bird, but simple-minded, don't you see. My daddy, oh, how he loved young Peter—taught him to read and cipher, if you can imagine such a thing, and bought him a goat once that pulled a red wagon, and told me I could only ride in it if Peter said I could."

"I am glad to hear it," said Stribling, rubbing his leg. "Maybe we could—"

"Now, I am tellin a story," said Gawain, waving him off. "I have to tell you about my dear daddy first. He was always a good man, except sometimes things would happen inside his head. He wasn't mean by nature, but when a spell came on him, his eyes would go empty and bulge like grapes, and he would have to hurt somebody. So he'd hunt for a fault until he found it, then he'd come for anybody handy—hunt us through the house and yard—and we would all hide and hope he'd find Peter first, which he generally did because Peter didn't have sense enough to hide. God damn, that was noble of us, don't you think?"

"I wish you all'd go on," said Molochi.

"One day," Gawain said, "the old man was in a fit, and he caught me playin with some lead soldiers on the porch. He snatched me up by the collar and laid into me with his cane, when young Peter came around the porch and took up a flower pot and broke it across the old man's head. Jesus, what an eruption. Then Peter ran away."

"Gawain—," began Stribling.

"Of course, Papa went to Constable John Talbot, and Constable John Talbot went to Molochi Fish because that's what you did when you had a runaway nigger. Daddy made me ride behind him on the horse, and I was there when the dogs . . . when the dogs caught the boy in a corncrib. You remember that, Molochi? You remember that, goddamn you!"

Gawain was shaking now. He stood up and wiped his eyes with his shirtsleeve. "I ought to kill you," he said. "I could do it, easy."

Molochi blinked and raised the shotgun.

"Maybe this pistol won't snap the next time," said Gawain. He shook his head. He could feel the veins in his temples filled to bursting, and black spots moved before his eyes and danced against a curtain of red. "Ah, shit," he spat. "Ah, shit." He sat down again, the pistol in his lap. He pressed his palms to his temples. "Oh, Lord, oh, Lord," he said.

Harry Stribling came and took the pistol out of Gawain's hand and tucked it away in his pocket. The dogs rose, menacing, but Stribling looked at them, and they lay down again. Then Stribling came to Molochi Fish and pushed the shotgun barrel aside. "Mister Harper had a choice to make," he said. "If he'd chosen wrong, he'd be dead, and so would you, for I'd of killed you myself."

Molochi Fish backed up a step. The dogs came and stood behind him, close to his legs.

"Maybe one day you can pay him back for choosing right," said Stribling. He looked up the road then, toward the bridge and the woods beyond. The wind was rising in the trees, and he could smell rain coming. When he turned back again, Molochi Fish was gone.

· V ·

When Molochi Fish left the two strangers on the road, his idea was to go home and forget about them. He had gone a quarter mile into the woods before some impulse turned him back, and in a little while he was moving up the bank of Leaf River toward the gravelly ford. From there, he could watch the bridge and see when the strangers crossed it.

A big moccasin was on the gravel bar, in the cool mud just outside the willows. Molochi could smell the snake before he saw it: a smell like stagnant water and rotting leaves. The dogs smelled it, too, and wanted to go after it, but Molochi heeled them with a harsh, bitten sound that they knew was the last command before a beating. Man and dogs passed within two feet of the snake. It was an old one and had no pattern now, so that it might have been only a darker shadow save for its bulk, piled in thick, muscular folds in the lee of a driftwood log. The scarred end of its tail began to vibrate as the man and the dogs passed; the broad, wedge-shaped head arced slowly, watching as the man knelt in the grass, and the dogs lay down behind him. After a moment, the snake rested its head on the black, mossy scales of its body and watched with its lidless eyes.

Molochi Fish did not give a goddamn about the snake; he was interested only in the two men who were on the bridge now. He squatted on his heels, the fowling piece across his thighs, and watched them down the shadowed tunnel of the trees. He wanted to remember them, to etch them deeply into his recollection.

The gnats swarmed around him. They were at the eyes of the dogs too, but the dogs remained still, only flickering an ear now and then, or shaking their heads. Molochi knew they would not move.

The dogs, as Gawain had suspected, were the pups out of the bitch that had run the little nigger boy down. The bitch had been but a pup herself then, striving to make her place in the pack. Surely he'd had a pack then:

ten, sometimes fifteen dogs that he trained with nigger clothes and nigger hide and blood when he could get it, that could run all night and bite broomsticks in half. He remembered them not as individual dogs but as a dark roiling mass of tails and ears and glistening teeth moving through the deep shadows of the trees or over open ground in the moonlight.

Now only two dogs remained. Their dam was one of the few dogs he remembered outside the anonymous crowd; she had been his favorite, and he had felt something when he had to put her down with the rest. He had put them all down, all but these two, when the yankees came, when the niggers were freed. He had cut their throats one by one so as not to waste powder and shot. The bitch, he remembered, seemed to know what he was about; she crouched at the end of her tether, snarling at him. She bit him hard in the forearm before he could get hold of her muzzle and pull her head back and draw the knife across her. He saved some of her blood in a little bottle, but after a while it dried up and he threw it away.

The men on the bridge were talking. He could not hear the words, but he heard their voices. One was sitting on the bridge rail with his back turned, the other was leaning on the rail, looking down at the water. Molochi Fish did not wonder what they were talking about, nor what the Harper boy was seeing in the waters of Leaf River. He only watched them, feeling nothing, thinking nothing. He could hear the harsh sound of his own breathing. The gnats lapped at the raw skin of his face.

When he was three years old, Molochi Fish had been boiled alive. It was hog-killing time on the old Pershing place where his pap was overseer, and a great pot of water had been set on a fire and boiled to singe the bristles off the hogs. Into this pot Molochi's mother had dropped him. He knew at the time that she did it on purpose, but never had he questioned why—not then, and not twelve years later when he pushed her into the machinery at the gristmill. It never occurred to him that people had to have reasons for doing things. However that may be, he remembered sinking in the boiling water, drawing it into his lungs. He remembered crawling out, remembered walking through the niggers who fled from him, remembered their wailing and their upflung hands. He was seeking his mother, walking with the skin looping down in ribbons from his outstretched arms, making sounds with his mouth though he couldn't breathe, seeing though he couldn't see—until he found her, praying, reaching up her hands toward the sweet blue sky. She often prayed, he remembered. She was praying when he dropped her down the shaft at the mill.

Now, by the gravel bar, Molochi touched his face. His fingers came away wet. He wiped them on his breeches and squinted toward the bridge, where the one fellow, the one with the horse, was mounting up. In a moment, the bridge was empty. Molochi rose stiffly, and the dogs rose with him. At the movement, the old snake lifted its head, showing his dingy white mouth. But Molochi Fish and the dogs had already passed and vanished into the trees.

· VI ·

Lieutenant Colonel Michael Burduck had not been in Cumberland long when he heard the story of old man Wagner and his rebellious slaves. As soon as duty permitted, the Colonel rode out to Wagner's Stretch in company with Mister George Boswell, a citizen who knew every detail about life in Cumberland County since the dawn of time—about the Indians, the early settlers, the planters, the scofflaws—and who could recite the generations of families many residents had never known or long since forgotten. Mister Boswell was an older man, not much interested in the larger questions that had troubled the country for the past four years, and he was happy to find the Colonel so interested in local history. For his part, the Colonel found Mister Boswell congenial company and a mine of social information. The man's one drawback, in the Colonel's view, was his smoking. Mister Boswell smoked a pipe during all his waking hours, and for tobacco he used the leaves of certain woodland plants that he collected himself. He claimed that an old Chickasaw had taught him the blend; whatever its origin, the smoke from Boswell's pipe had a reek that carried for miles, that could hardly be tolerated in the open air, and indoors not at all. Beyond this, Mister Boswell was a kind and accommodating man beloved by all.

Mister Boswell showed the Colonel around the site of the old Wagner place, pointed out the vine-grown ruins of the house, described in vivid detail the events of that terrible night when Wagner sat on his gallery and reaped what he had sown. The tale was instructive, Boswell said, because it illustrated the way a man could shape his destiny out of the choices he made. The Colonel agreed, though for him the incident worked on another level as well. Old Boswell told him how the blacks called this Bad Ground—as well they might, Burduck thought. The Colonel had crossed a lot of bad ground in latter years: places which, if there really were ghosts, would be restless to the world's end. But in this place, Burduck thought, the ghosts were not just those of men, white or black, nor the violence only that of a night's bloody deeds. The old Wagner place, he thought, was a grand metaphor.

Colonel Burduck was a West Pointer, class of '50, who ended the war commanding a battalion of regular United States Infantry. Months before the surrender, the Colonel brought his battalion, two batteries of regular artillery, and a company of Ohio cavalry down from Memphis to guard the line of the Mississippi Central Railroad, the Federals having learned at last that they could claim no Southern ground unless a national soldier was actually standing on it with his bayonet fixed. They had fought no end of minor skirmishes with the rebels, and now, in this June of '65, they were handily in place to enforce the mandates of a victorious government. Burduck had expected a great deal of trouble, but found to his surprise that the citizens of the neighborhood were by and large more preoccupied with trying to figure out what had happened to them than in brooding about their defeat. In fact, for Burduck and his men—all veterans, all weary—their duty had proven so far a welcome respite from the rigors of the long war. True, the country was in ruins and stank of ashes, but this sojourn along the railroad promised to be the best of their military lives. Rations were plentiful, Burduck and his staff were quartered in a fine house in Cumberland, the troops had spanking new Sibley tents with stoves and plank floors, and there were no generals.

Still, Burduck could not forget that he was in the enemy's country. He had been too long under arms to have any illusions about the nature of the people among whom he dwelt, and over whose conduct he had some measure of control. He was not surprised, for example, to find that the women were the most intractable of his subjects, and the least amenable to his presence. They would sniff haughtily at the Federal soldiers, and would cross the street to avoid contact, and, early on at least, were openly insulting. This behavior did not set well with Burduck's Regulars, many of whom were rowdy Western lads whose return salvos were neither subtle nor genteel. Burduck himself was amused by the situation, and generally he allowed his soldiers to handle it themselves, as long as the skirmishing was verbal. Still, the women rankled, and Burduck suspected that, if there was a fuse anywhere, it might well be lit by the womenfolk.

Colonel Burduck's interest in the Wagner episode grew out of the fact that he had fought against, and now policed, a culture that had once championed human slavery. Burduck knew that slavery was not a paramount issue among his Western troops and colleagues; never had been, even in the fervent days of the war's beginning. Burduck himself, a New Yorker and presumably in philosophical harmony with the powerful East, had never been an active abolitionist. He was, after all, an officer of the United States, and his first duty was to the Union.

Nevertheless, the moral question of slavery had informed his conduct as a soldier in war and now captured his attention as a guardian of the peace. Beyond annihilation, no culture died easily, he knew. Indeed, much of this one might never die of its own accord. How could these rebels not see? he asked himself when, on idle afternoons, he would ride out to the old Wagner place. There he would tether his horse and stroll among the ruins, poking at the old ashes where fragments of bone still lay. He would sit and ponder the vines that grew over the chimneys and ask himself: How could they not see?

✦　　✦　　✦

ON HIS SIXTEENTH birthday, Michael Burduck signed as an ordinary seaman on the United States sloop *Nimble,* his elder brother John commanding. Two days later, they made sail for Africa, there to lurk for outbound slavers off the coast.

They passed the Montauk light just at daybreak; young Burduck stood at the rail and saw the dark shape of the lighthouse against the thin pink line of the coming day, the beacon glimmering on a sea so calm it could hardly be distinguished from the sky. He watched the light until it was no more than a firefly, then gone beyond the edge of the waking earth. Beneath him the sea, still dark, churned in the ship's passing, and Burduck heard in its whispering the promise of all his dreams.

They made the crossing. The salt wind blew from the rim of the world and filled the sails, and the canvas groaned and swelled toward unimaginable places, driving them down the long passage. The taut lines vibrated, the deck rose and fell, the cries of men aloft floated down like the cries of gulls, and under the keel the deep water slid green and dark and full of mystery. Some nights the moon threw a ribbon on the water while the stars burned in their ancient constellations; they read the stars, and the stars told their place upon the sea, and by day the sun at meridian never failed them. By the sun, by the moon and stars, they passed over the waters.

The *Nimble* took her station two days out from the Guinea coast, and for a fortnight tacked a long figure eight under the Atlantic sun. Then, on the fifteenth day, the lookouts cried a prospect, hull down and beating north under all her sails. The *Nimble* gave chase; it was no contest, and the capture was made within the watch.

The prize turned out to be a sorry thing, a slatternly old bark of mildewed canvas and weathered boards, manned by Dutchmen and Frenchmen and strapping big blacks whose bodies glistened in the sun.

When the *Nimble* bore down on her, she ran a British ensign the size of a courtyard up her mast, but no matter; the Americans took her anyway. A brave moment ensued then, like a vivid painting: the sleek and dangerous *Nimble* with her guns run out and Marines in the rigging; the guilty ship hove to, fat and wallowing in the swells; and between the two vessels a pair of fast cutters knifing the foam, their oars dipping and flashing, and Captain Burduck himself standing in the bow of the lead boat in frock coat and sword and pistol.

Boarding was tricky, for a rope ladder was the only accommodation the bark would offer, and she was rolling badly. Nevertheless, young Burduck made the leap, catching the ladder at just the right moment and clambering up as the ship heeled away. When he arrived on deck, he found his brother and the boat crew, armed with pistols and carbines and cutlasses, facing a semi-circle of strange, whiskery men, the ship's company. They were not armed, but they were sullen, not even talking among themselves, and watchful. Even young Burduck could discern that these men owned secrets they did not wish brought to light.

"Which of you is Master here?" inquired Captain Burduck.

A short man in an old-fashioned coat and absurd, piratical boots rolled forward. He began: "You are aware that this is Her Britannic Majesty's—"

Captain Burduck held up his hand. He said: "Quite right, sir—keenly aware, deeply aware. We salute Her Majesty, and all that, and invite you to please open that hatch yonder and let's get on with it."

The bark's Captain made a gesture. "Impossible," he said.

"Very well," said Captain Burduck, and nodded, and two of his own men took hold of the hatchway and banged it open and stood aside.

All the sailors who stood nearby moved away when the smell came. It was a palpable cloud rising from the hatch, extract of sweat and fear and excrement and the sweet reek of the lately dead, and the rust of chains, and the dripping of old wood, and vomit, and the rutting that will happen anywhere, even in hell. This foulness coiled out of the open hatch, and the sailors moved away, and the bark's Captain snorted and stepped back among his crew.

"Fetch a lantern," said Captain Burduck.

Someone brought a bull's-eye lantern, lighted, and Captain Burduck took it and moved to the open hatchway and paused.

"Go ahead," said the bark's Captain. "Have a peek, now that you're here."

Burduck turned and looked at the man. He set the lantern down carefully and drew his pistol. He crossed the little way to where the bark's

Captain stood grinning and slammed the barrel of the pistol across the man's cheek and laid it open to the glistening bone. The man sank to his knees and covered his face with his hands. Captain Burduck knelt beside him. "Oh, I have seen all this before," he said. "However, I will improve the occasion by instructing the nation's youth." He stood, turning, searching the faces of the men. "Burduck!" he said.

"Sir," said young Michael Burduck, stepping forward.

Throughout the trip, Captain Burduck had paid little attention to his younger brother, a fact for which Michael was grateful, for he had no desire to be treated any different from the rest of the crew. Now the two brothers stood only a few feet apart, and for the first time some old signal of their common blood passed between them. The Captain did not touch his brother, but his eyes betrayed him. At last he gestured with the pistol. "I want you to take that lantern and go below," he said. "Go all the way down, lad."

Young Burduck looked toward the black square of the open hatch. Around him, the men were silent, even the slaver captain, who had pressed a filthy rag against his cheek. After a moment, he turned back to his brother the Captain. "Aye, sir," he said.

He took up the lantern in which a short taper burned fitfully; in the bright sunlight, he could hardly see the flame. At the hatch coaming, he stopped. In his right hand, he still carried his pistol—until that day he had never held one, and it felt awkward and heavy in his hand. He slipped it into his belt, then stepped over the hatch coaming and onto the ladder that slanted away into the dark, into the smell. He made a step down, and another. The smell grew stronger, and with it the feeling that he was not alone in the hold. Something waited, holding its breath, watching without sound. The ladder was slippery and wet, and he had to move slowly. Halfway down, the lantern began to gutter for want of air, and in a moment it went out entirely and only a shaft of sunlight remained to give shape to the regions below. Young Burduck stopped, struggled with the urge to turn back up the ladder into the light. Then he filled his lungs, shut his eyes, and moved slowly down, feeling his way. He counted five more steps, then opened his eyes.

He saw a carpet of prone bodies, dark and glistening, chained together throughout the hold. He heard the shifting of iron links and the querying clicks of dry tongues and the rattle of pent breath, and the groans of men straining to rise who could not rise, and the popping of stiff joints as hands reached upward. And the eyes then, all turning toward him with the glossy brightness of boiled eggs, blinking in what, to them, was a flood of light.

"My Christ," said Burduck aloud, and dropped the lantern, and for answer rose a sudden gabble of voices: pleading, angry, afraid, or not even voices at all but the utterance of every dark thing that ever visited him in dreams. He cried out again. He felt he might pitch forward among them. Then he fled.

In the sunlight again, he fell to his knees and retched. No one spoke, no one laughed. In a moment, his brother the Captain knelt beside him, touched him then, a hand in the small of his back. "Well done," the Captain said. Then, in a voice almost a whisper: " 'Tis a hard thing, lad, but you must bear it. You must not forget it. Not ever."

Young Burduck, in his shame, was silent. In that moment, he hated his brother for giving him the responsibility of remembering. He had witnessed a great sin—but he understood already that a greater sin lay in forgetting. He rose from the deck and moved unsteadily to the bulwark; he grasped it tightly to keep his hands from trembling. Behind him he heard the voices of men, the harsh voice of his brother giving orders, the protests of the slaver crew. Over these he heard the old ship's groaning; she had not ceased, and Burduck knew she would not until her keel touched the bottom of the sea. Then, looking out, he saw the broad waters, endless and indifferent, stretching away toward tomorrow.

✦ ✦ ✦

THIS JUNE MORNING, not long after daybreak, Colonel Burduck had ridden alone to the Wagner place. His mind was restless, and he needed a place to hide for a time before the clerks and the orderlies and the petitioning citizens got to him. He tied his horse far back among the old outbuildings and, after checking for snakes, sat down in his usual place, on an overturned cookpot that, with its four stumpy legs, always reminded him of a dead hog. He had brought a lap desk with the idea of working up some correspondence, but he only sat quietly, listening, alone in the still morning. After a while, he found a stick he had whittled the day before, and with it began to scratch in the mud at his feet. He drew a star, a sun, a moon, and around these he drew a circle. He tapped his stick in the dirt. In the trees around, the birds sang; Burduck had never learned one bird from another, but he liked their singing. He could smell the damp leaves and a faint tinge of wood smoke.

Burduck stood up, restless, and then he noticed an odd thing. He bent and picked up a Henry cartridge from the ground. It had not been here yesterday. He was pondering it when he heard someone in the road.

From this place, the Colonel could observe the road with little chance of being seen himself. Often he watched people passing alone or in parties, afoot or mounted, sometimes driving a bony cow or a goat or a hog. This wayfarer was a lanky fellow in civilian clothes, with a carpet bag and a little dog. They were stopped, and the man was lecturing the dog, who seemed to listen intently. Burduck was sure that the man, for all his dress and baggage, was an ex-soldier; he could not have said how he knew, only that he did. Most of these rebs traveled in their rags of uniform, their blanket-rolls and haversacks slung about them, sometimes barefoot, always hungry. The roads were full of them these days, now that some time had passed since the last of them had surrendered. Not many were outfitted like this one, and not many would be conversing with a dog. Peculiar behavior, even for a rebel, the most peculiar species Burduck had ever known.

Burduck knew he ought to question the man, examine his parole and all that, but he couldn't bring himself to do it. For one thing, the fellow seemed harmless enough—most of them were—and Burduck trusted his own instincts. For another, he simply did not feel like busying himself at the moment. Besides, Burduck thought, the sight of a Federal Colonel popping out of the brush was likely to give the man apoplexy. Let him go home, then. The troops would examine him.

Burduck tossed the Henry cartridge into the brush and thought no more about it. Instead, he considered the man in the road and tried to imagine what he was feeling, or trying not to feel. Behind that lad stretched a vast ruin to which he could not return; ahead, over the Leaf River bridge or farther along the road, a great mystery lay waiting, a world he would not know and in which he would have little say. Burduck shook his head. He could not imagine himself in such a circumstance. Well, the rebels had no one to blame but themselves; let them puzzle it out as best they could. Were it not so much trouble, Burduck would have liked to accost this fellow and drag him by the collar to the vine-choked scattering of ashes that had once been a house and say to him, Do you see? Do you see now?

He would not do such a thing, of course, but the impulse was strong enough to propel Colonel Burduck toward the road where the returning soldier had moved on. Overhead a crow muttered in the trees—Burduck knew a crow anyway, though he hadn't much use for them—and the small birds sang, and some of the night voices still lingered in the grass. When he came to the road, he hesitated. He did not wish to appear the fool, and he really did not care to frighten the man, but after a moment he left the brush and stepped out into the mud of the road. The wayfarer was a hundred yards away now, walking briskly, the dog trotting along beside. Then, as Burduck watched, the man began to run.

✦ ✦ ✦

AFTERNOON, AND THE rain was coming again as it had every afternoon for a week now. The bright sun of morning was diminished to a
pearly light, and people in Cumberland looked to the western sky where
the darkness gathered. They watched the lightning flicker, heard the sullen
mutter of thunder beyond the western ridges, and not a few of them
remembered artillery, whether they wanted to or not.

Two soldiers stood on the portico of the Shipwright house, just south of
the square. The older one, Sergeant Raphael Deaton, was sergeant of the
guard today. He smoked a cunning clay pipe carved in the likeness of a
buxom Indian maiden. The younger man, Tom Kelly, worked an enormous
wad of plug tobacco in his cheek. Both men wore the dark frock coats and
sky-blue trousers of the Regular infantry, and forage caps still adorned
with the acorn badge of the old Fourteenth Corps with whom they had
served throughout the late war. Both leaned on their long Springfield muskets in the casual way of veterans.

"See here, young Kelly," said Rafe Deaton. "Since when did you take up
chawin anyhow?"

Kelly spat a long, careful stream of ambure toward the porch steps.
"Oh, days and days ago," he said, wiping his mouth on his coat sleeve. "I
am cultivatin my vices in hopes I might be a sergeant one day."

"Commendable," said Rafe. "Does Darlin Annie know about it?" The
reference was to Kelly's wife in Kentucky, upon whom he lavished a touching and, in Rafe Deaton's view, unaccountable devotion.

"Lord perish the thought," said Kelly. His face softened. "Reckon what
she is doin now?"

Rafe snorted. He had heard the same question a thousand times.

"It ain't funny," Kelly said.

"You're right," said Rafe. Then he asked, as he always did, "Well, what
do you *think* she's doin now?"

Kelly thought a moment. "Well, I expect she's makin dinner about
now," he said. "I can see her same as if I was there. She is rollin out biscuits, and there is . . . a *ham*. And some collards. It's hot as everything in
the kitchen."

"My, my," said Rafe. The vision reminded him that he had not eaten
since early morning, and now it was afternoon. He found himself thinking
of a girl he had never seen, her hands white with flour, in a kitchen full of
sunlight. He shook the image away. "I tried chawin once," he said. "Made
me sick as a dog."

Kelly spat again. "It does me, too, if the truth be known," he said.

"Well," said Rafe, "you will have to get shut of that chaw now, and look to your post. You might try standin at attention."

Kelly fished the wad out of his jaw and flung it off the porch. He straightened, and brought his musket to support arms. Even with the bayonet fixed, there was plenty of room under the tall portico. "Where is the good Colonel this day?" he asked.

"I'm sure I don't know," said Rafe. "The Colonel don't inform me of his whereabouts. Perhaps you would like to quiz Captain Bloom on the subject?"

The reference to their company commander made Kelly shudder. "Lord perish the thought," he said.

"I thought not," said Rafe, and turned away.

The other shifted uncomfortably. "Sometimes I wonder if he is well, Rafe. The Colonel, I mean."

The sergeant was about to go down the steps. Now he stopped, turned again. "Be careful what you say, young Kelly."

"Oh, well," said the other. "I don't mean nothing. Only—"

Rafe crossed the porch again. He reached out, his musket in the crook of his arm, and straightened Kelly's coat under his cartridge-box belt, and closed an errant button. "Only, what?" he asked. "You think the Colonel's about to lose his judgment again?"

Kelly shrugged. "I seen it happen once."

"So you did," said Rafe. "So did we all. Now, be a good lad and don't fret yourself about it. Look to your post."

"All right," said Kelly. "Say, if it rains, will you bring my poncho?"

"Oh, surely," said Rafe. "I would not have you die of consumption and leave Miss Annie to the clutches of a scoundrel like myself."

"What do you mean by that?" asked Tom Kelly.

"Oh, nothin, lad," said the sergeant, and laughed. He crossed the porch, went down the stairs, and picked his way across the mud of the yard to the road. He, too, would have liked to know where Colonel Burduck was. The battalion was still spread up and down the railroad, and no doubt the Colonel was off to see about things. On the other hand— *But never mind,* he thought quickly. And anyway, wherever the Colonel was, there was nothing that he, Sergeant Rafe Deaton, could do about it.

From the edge of the road, Rafe could look under the arch of the trees toward the ruin of the square and the little knoll where the courthouse had been once. Rafe thought he knew what it had looked like; he had fleshed out the building by talking to men who remembered it. He could imagine it now—the warm bricks, the tall windows thrown open, the classical portico gleaming white at the end of the tunnel of trees. Nothing remained but the columns, blackened by the fire that consumed the square ten months ago, and behind them a pile of bricks and ashes. Around the knoll lay a moat of deep black mud, churned by horses and the wheels of heavy wagons. Ringing the moat were more ashes, more piles of brick, isolated chimneys, charred timbers reaching skyward like the limbs of the dead. Here and there the dingy flanks of a wall tent, or a flimsy, windowless, clapboard hut, rose sullenly from a cleared space. One of these last, a quarter mile back down the southerly road, was painted peacock blue and sported a narrow gallery furnished with overturned kegs to accommodate the clientele. Hanging from the gallery roof was a sign:

THE CITADEL OF DJIBOUTI
L. W. Thomas, Prop.

Rafe knew that Frye's Tavern once stood on this site—an old inn from the post-road days, ancient, sagging, comfortable, of two stories with a pair of rock chimneys and a mossy shingle roof, where local companies had been raised for the Confederate army in that first glorious spring. Now old Frye was dead, and his tavern burned and gone, and the site would be empty still were it not for L. W. Thomas, a Union man.

Thomas arrived in Cumberland during the cold, empty days of January on a government train from Grand Junction. Among the articles in his valise were a roll of Federal banknotes; the deed to the old Frye place, duly signed and witnessed by the executor of the Frye estate—another Union man—who had fled to Memphis when the yankees secured it in '62; and a sutler's commission signed by General Washburn himself. Without delay, and in spite of the winter weather, Thomas hired a crew, cleared the rubble of the old tavern away, and built the Citadel of newly planed lumber from the sawmill beyond Leaf River. He contracted with Mister Audley Brummett to haul his wares from the steamboat landing at Wyatt's when the roads dried out. Finally he discovered, in the attic of an abandoned house, seventeen pots of the peacock-blue paint which would transform this shanty, with its canted stovepipe and smell of raw lumber, to a curio set down among the elms and cedars like a bright bird strayed from some unimaginable clime.

Rafe Deaton wished he was at the Citadel now, in this close afternoon with the rain coming. Queenolia Divine, who cooked for Mister Thomas, offered stew, turnip greens from her early garden, fresh perch caught out of Leaf River, ham sometimes, and gumbo, served with great flagons of beer on a raw trestleboard in the blue-painted, dimly lit interior: a cornucopia like no one—soldiers or civilians—had seen in years. But Rafe was not at the Citadel, nor was he likely to be this day.

Rafe Deaton watched up the road and felt the hours close around him. Long years ago, when he was a boy in Mulberry, Tennessee, he would journey to a certain high ridge on summer days and spend a solitary hour looking down on the broad earth below. In the rank, sweet grass at his feet, he could hear the drowsy voices of insects. But beyond, where the green fields and woods fell away to the haze of the world's end, there was only a great stillness, where hawks and buzzards floated on silent pinions, and the air was hushed in timeless, unassailable peace. He used to believe that a portent lay in that noon's quiet suspension—that if he could just look hard enough, or listen long enough, he might perceive his own fate in the voiceless reaches of the air. All that was a long time ago, and he believed in portents no longer, but as he looked down the road toward Cumberland, he felt that something lay huddled in the hour's stillness, some answer perhaps to a question he had not yet thought to ask. He smiled. There was too much mystery to peace, he thought, and too much complication. War was a good deal simpler. He knocked out his pipe and was about to turn back to the house when a soldier came into the yard, a corporal whom Rafe had known since the old days at Jefferson Barracks. The man was off-duty and wore his frock coat open save for the button at the collar. A stream of blood trickled from his nose, and as Rafe watched, he wiped at it and smeared it on his cheek. He approached shaking his head, as if he had seen something too absurd to be believed.

"Rafe," he said, "you ought to come quick. They's trouble at the Citadel."

✦   ✦   ✦

AS RAFE DEATON was trotting down to the Citadel of Djibouti to investigate the disturbance, Colonel Michael Burduck was sitting his horse in the southerly road, trying to remember how he had come to be there. His watch told him it was one o'clock; the hour was gray, and thunder was muttering to the west. When last he consulted the time, on the overturned pot at the Wagner place, it was nine o'clock and the sun shining. Four hours gone then, and no accounting for them. The Colonel checked himself. His uniform was buttoned, he wore his saber and sash, his hat was in place, the lap desk was properly stowed in a saddlebag, his pistol was unfired. He was intact.

"What happened, Sally?" he asked his black mare, but the horse only rolled her eyes at him and pulled at the bit. The thunder was close now, and she was nervous. "All right," said Burduck, and pushed the mare up the southerly road. Just beyond Leaf River bridge, it began to rain.

✦　✦　✦

THEY WERE ALMOST to town when Gawain stopped again. He drew up in the middle of the road and dropped his bag. "Dammit," he said.

"What's the matter now?" asked Stribling. He was mounted, his left leg cocked up, reins tied over the pommel of the saddle. His hat was off and balanced on the top of Zeke's head.

"Maybe I just won't go on atall," said Gawain. "Maybe I'll turn around, go back south. I liked it down around Mobile. You ever been there, Harry?"

"No, but I been to New Orleans," Stribling said. "If we are goin back south, we ought to go to New Orleans. But we are not goin south, we are goin to Cumberland." He looked at the sky. "And anyhow, it's fixin to rain—we got to go."

"Maybe I won't go," said Gawain.

"Well, good God," said Stribling. "It's not but a quarter mile." He removed his hat from between the horse's ears and jammed it back on his head.

They had come to the place where Mister John Walker's house once stood, just south of the Cumberland square. The road climbed a little rise just here, before dipping down to the square. Not many trees grew this close to town, the old timber having long been cut for sawmill or stove or hearth, or more recently for soldiers' fires. The trees that remained were lofty and grand, musing like old gentlemen along the road, left clustered here and there for shade over cabins and feed lots and in the yards of houses. Walker, a bachelor, had been of Gawain's regiment, been hurt bad and captured at Franklin, or perhaps Nashville, Gawain wasn't certain. He *was* certain that this was the place where the house had been, but no house was here now: only a grove of oaks, a pair of chimneys, and between these a jumble of ashes and timbers, and in the middle of it all the charred remains of an upright piano. "I knew that fellow," said Gawain, nodding toward the house. "I guess he ain't home."

"No," said Stribling, "he don't appear to be. Now, what is all this? Have you forgot that Miss . . . blame it, what's her name, anyhow?"

"You mean Morgan?" said Gawain.

"Have you forgot that Miss Morgan is pining away, not a quarter mile up this road?"

"Morgan Rhea," said Gawain.

"That's her," said Stribling. "Now, what's the matter with you?"

Gawain shook his head. "Back yonder on the road, before I run into you, I got the feelin—ah, Jesus, Harry, you were right. We are all strangers here. This ain't a place I remember. Look at it! Look at John Walker's house, at that piano there! And everything all hacked down and trampled, and over the rise yonder—what? Maybe I don't want to see that."

Stribling shifted in the saddle, the leather creaking. "I wish you wouldn't think so much," he said.

"It's all I *been* doin, Harry. I—" He stopped, his eyes narrowed, looking down the road. "Now, what the hell is *that*, pray tell?"

Stribling followed Gawain's pointing finger, and looked, and after a moment said, "Well, damned if I know, but ain't it gay?"

"That's where Mister Frye's old post-tavern used to be—see? The chinaberries and the big elm still stand."

"What do you suppose it is now?" asked Stribling.

"I don't know, but it certainly is blue, ain't it?"

The two men marveled at the ramshackle building by the roadside; windowless it was, with a slanted woodshed roof and a flimsy gallery and a canted stovepipe—but nothing in all that land partook of color in the way that shanty did. Against the leaves, gone gray now in the light of afternoon, it shimmered dreamlike, seemed carved from some great gem or raised from the iridescent feathers of birds. Gawain and Stribling blinked at it. Their eyes were accustomed to grays and browns and comfortable woodland greens; this unexpected burst of color astonished and delighted them, as if the sun itself had broken peacock blue through the clouds.

Then, as they watched, the blue began to spill out into the yard—a riot of light blue and dark blue, of faces and hands and the voices of men. For a moment, Gawain could not comprehend—then it struck him, hard. He felt the old cold turning in his stomach. The sweat came out on his forehead, and the blood drummed in his ears, and for an instant he could not breathe—weeks and months and all the long road fell away, and he was falling with them, back and back, and felt again the mad glee of chaos waiting just beyond the next step—a little run, the line bending into a V behind the slanted colors, smoke and fire and the old cry rising in their throats.

"Ah!" he cried, and shook his head, willing himself back to the road, the summer day, the prosaic carpet bag at his feet.

"Yes, goddamn," said Stribling. "See the yankee sons of bitches!" His voice was strained, he had straightened in the saddle, was leaned forward with the reins in his hands. Then, as Gawain watched, he relaxed. He looked down, grinning. "Good God," he said, and laughed.

Gawain laughed in return. "What's the matter, boy?" he said. "Yankees make you nervous?"

"Hah," said Stribling. He looked back up the road. "That's a right smart of em, and they're mad with somebody. Look—some of em are armed."

"No doubt somebody called out the guard," said Gawain. "Look, there's a brave sergeant."

"Coming at the trot," said Stribling. "Now—hey, see that big fellow in his shirtsleeves? And the lanky one—there, in the sack coat!"

"Why, they have taken on the whole lot," said Gawain. "Whoa! There the big one's laid a fellow out in the road!"

"Well struck!" cried Stribling, standing up in his stirrups. "See that one with the crutch? My, how he does lay about with it—see it? Damn, Harper, we must ride to the rescue!"

"Rescue, hell," said Gawain. "Let the bluebellies save they own selves!"

"Indeed, sir," said Stribling, "but nevertheless—" and jammed his spurs into Zeke's flanks. The horse squealed and shot forward, hooves throwing gobbets of mud. Gawain scrambled to his feet, watched Zeke slip and slide and find his footing and gallop away, Stribling lashing the horse's rump with his hat, hollering. Gawain waved his arms and cried out, all to no avail. Harry Stribling was making the last cavalry charge of the war, and all Gawain could do was take up his carpet bag and follow, running clumsily in the mud for the second time that day.

The mud caught and tugged and pulled at him, and now a wind came up, pushed ahead of the storm, and the leaves showed their undersides, and the trees began to thrash and sigh. The gray sky lit up with lightning, a quick white flash like the burst of a shell, and Gawain ducked in spite of himself, and when the sharp report of the thunder rolled over him, he gritted his teeth and ran on. *It is only lightnin,* he thought, and then remembered he was afraid of lightning too. Then the first fat drops of the summer rain fell, coming straight down like stones, then the rain in earnest, a solid sheet of it—the world was suddenly white with rain, and Gawain stopped in the road, the water pouring off the brim of his good straw hat.

He stood in the road, blind and soaking wet, and listened to the rain hammer around him. He could no longer hear the voices of the lads up ahead, nor the sound of Zeke and Harry Stribling passing up the road, nor anything at all but the cracking thunder and the good pounding of the rain. He turned his face to the sky, let the rain strike him, felt it run down his collar—and all at once he was overcome with the desire to make water himself. He stood in the middle of the southerly road and fumbled open the buttons of his trousers and began to relieve himself. In the thrashing of the storm, he did not hear the rider's approach.

"See here, sir—are you pissing in the road?"

The voice startled Gawain so badly that he almost dived into the roadside weeds, but he caught himself just in time and pressed on manfully, trying to finish—it seemed to take forever—until at last he could button up his breeches and turn. He looked up and made out the shape of a horse and rider shrouded in the white rain. He was about to comment when a bolt of lightning struck a tree in John Walker's yard; the report, sharp and concussive as a howitzer, made Gawain duck, and in the brilliant flash he saw the horse rear on its hind legs, saw the rider in his Federal officer's coat and sword and broad hat, heard him curse as he fought his mount.

"Dammit, sir, make way!" said the officer, and clapped his spurs hard into the horse's flanks and sent him leaping forward over Gawain's carpet bag and up the road.

"Good God," said Gawain Harper, and took up his bag and began to walk toward town. He was done with running; whatever was happening up ahead would have to wait until he got there. It occurred to him as he walked along that when he left Cumberland three years ago, he had gone north on the cars. Now he was coming from the south. A full circle, then, and enough walking to have circumnavigated the globe. Suddenly a light burst in him, like the fire from the lightning-struck tree: he was alive, and up yonder was Morgan and Aunt Vassar and his old mad Papa. And freedom, too, whatever that meant. He didn't know for sure, couldn't know— except that it had to do with being alive. He thought of the little fyce, sleeping on the banks of Leaf River, and of his cousin, and Sir Niles, and young Fitter—and he might have thought of all the rest who were gone in the smoke, might have seen their faces one by one and heard the echo of their voices down the long corridor of time if he'd wanted to. Perhaps he would want to someday, but not *this* day. He could put off grieving for a little while. Let the summer rain grieve for now, and the sighing trees, and the earth over which they'd all passed their little while. He was alive, and he would live to claim the long days left him. Whether he deserved them or not, he could not say. He only knew that they were his, and he would do his best by them.

Gawain Harper lifted his face to the rain again. "Oh, me," he said to his God, who dwelt up there beyond the thunder and the clouds. "You make sure I do all right, won't you?"

For answer, he had the rain. It was enough.

PART 2

Long Remember

· VII ·

In June 1865, the only jail in Cumberland County was a United States Military Railroad boxcar set out on the old house track behind the ashes of the depot. It had been there long enough for the wheels and the strap rails beneath them to rust, and for weeds to flourish around it, and for a gang of sparrows to build nests under the roof-walk. Over the winter and spring, the car had hosted a variety of inhabitants whose only amenities had been a smoky Sibley stove, a collection of vermin-ridden blankets, and a bucket for waste. The provost, Lieutenant Rolf von Arnim, was not much disposed to extravagance regarding the jail and its tenants.

Only one inmate could be said to be permanent, and then only because he refused to leave. This was a man known as Old Hundred-and-Eleven, so called because years of chewing tobacco had left three indelible streaks on his chin, one from each corner of his mouth and one down the middle, startling in their clarity because Old Hundred-and-Eleven was a beardless albino. His long hair was linen-white and tangled. He wore greasy leather breeches and a ragged frock coat. He had been barefoot since birth; his knobbed and horny feet were so tough that he could dance on the red-hot stove, or so it was told by some who claimed to have seen it. His only possessions were an umbrella and an enormous illustrated Bible that he had worn to tatters, that leaked pages covered with his penciled annotations.

Harry Stribling had not heard the story about dancing on the stove, nor did he know that Old Hundred-and-Eleven was originally jailed for assaulting a chaplain. He *did* know that the man, like some grotesque Bartleby, refused to leave the jail—though he went foraging now and then, and made himself useful to von Arnim as a swamper and a digger of graves. Stribling also knew that Old Hundred-and-Eleven was by far the most peculiar human being he had ever seen, and so a proper study for the philosopher.

Stribling had been brought to the boxcar jail after the affair at the tavern, in company with the other civilian participants who were even now sleeping in a pile at one end of the car: a big, bearded man named Nobles, a one-legged former artilleryman named Marcus Peck, and a wiry, nervous little fellow who introduced himself as S. Cragin Knox. They were all Confederate veterans, but the fight (Stribling learned to his disgust) had not been a matter of national loyalties. It was simply the old, tired contention of one branch of service with another. The trouble began when Peck declared that the artillery was the supreme arbiter of battle, that the infantry was superfluous on the modern field of war, that in fact the infantry had lost the war for the Confederacy just as it had for the British in the Revolution. These and other arguments inspired Knox and Nobles to comment that Saint Barbara, the patroness of gunners, was a rapid old whore whose privates could accommodate gun and limber and horses too, a thing they would not have said had they been sober. But they were not sober. In fact, none of the patrons of the Citadel of Djibouti in that early afternoon was sober—not the former rebels, nor the Federal infantrymen, nor the Federal gunners from the regular battery. All joined in the fray, but only the civilians had been clapped in jail. The troops were remanded to Lieutenant von Arnim, who set them to marching around and around the square with barrels over their heads as an act of contrition.

Had he known the true origins of the affair, Harry Stribling might not have ridden in so eagerly. As it was, he had a blackening eye, a broken knuckle on his right hand, and the memory of an unusual fight. The downpour had been a novel twist, but the thing that made the incident so memorable was the arrival of the irate Federal Colonel who finally brought things to a halt by firing his pistol in the air.

Gawain Harper had arrived last, his wet straw hat hanging down around his face like an umbrella. By that time, Stribling was sitting in the mud with the other lads, the sergeant of the guard watching over them.

"Why, Harry, what have you done?" asked Gawain.

"You know this fellow?" asked the sergeant. He was leaning on his musket and smoking a curious pipe—Gawain wished he could get a closer look at it.

"I should say so," said Gawain. "This is Harry Stribling, the well-known bushwhacker."

The sergeant removed his pipe and spit. "He just told *me* he was Gawain Harper, the well-known scholar."

"Well, good God," said Gawain.

Stribling shrugged.

"You best go away," the sergeant told Gawain, " 'fore I haul you off with the rest."

"All right," said Gawain. "Can I tell the prisoner somethin?"

The sergeant nodded, and Gawain knelt beside his comrade. "Now, Harry," said Gawain, "when they turn you loose, if they ever do, you hunt up my house. It's up on the Holly Springs road, just where the road bends. I am fixin to go there straightway."

"You ain't goin to see Miss Morgan?"

"I look like a drowned mushrat," said Gawain. "I am not fit to call on anybody. Besides—" He stopped, and looked away.

"Besides what?" asked Stribling.

"Nothin," said Gawain. He rose stiffly to his feet and turned to the sergeant. "He ain't really a bushwhacker," he told the sergeant. "He is just a little peculiar in the head, from a fall, you understand."

The sergeant nodded sympathetically. "A good night's rest will do him wonders," he said.

"I will come see about you, Harry," said Gawain.

Stribling lifted his arm and watched Gawain Harper slog away with his carpet bag, pulling hard against the mud.

Now Stribling sat swinging his legs from the open door of the boxcar. There were no bars, no grate, nothing at all to keep him from leaving, though he'd been told not to, and figured he better not. At least, not before dark. Stribling pulled his watch. A few hours to go before suppertime—might as well wait for some rations.

He raised his eyes to the fresh afternoon that still smelled of rain, to the mist that rose from the grass, to the sky empty of clouds now. His gaze roved over the green woods that lay beyond the railroad, and the deep shadows there. A bored sentry paced nearby, and there was old Zeke, tethered to a fence post, sleeping with his off hind foot cocked.

Then the boxcar creaked with movement, and Stribling smelled sweat and rancid ham fat, and Old Hundred-and-Eleven eased into the door beside him. The man grinned at Stribling, his eyes like a pair of pale rubies. "That was a good shower, warn't it?" he said.

Stribling nodded. The man waved his arm, his long finger (the nail yellow and hooked like a dog's) pointing to the afternoon. "Cleans it all up, y'see? Makes it all new again, same as the first mornin old Adam woke, when he still had all his ribs. Rah!" The man's voice was strangely musical. He edged closer to Stribling, laid a hand on his leg. "D'ye think they'll hang ye?" he asked. "Them yankees?"

Stribling's flesh crawled from the touch of the man. "No, sir," he said. "I do not believe they will."

The man seemed disappointed. He removed his hand from Stribling's leg. "Well, they ort to," he said. "No offense, I'm sure."

"Oh, no," said Stribling. "However, I think they intend to dangle *you*."

Old Hundred-and-Eleven pulled back in surprise, his mouth a perfect O, his eyes wide. "Ye *don't* say! Hang *me*?"

"Yep," said Stribling.

"Rah!" huffed the other. "Arrah! Bavardage!"

"You may think so, but even now they are buildin the gallows down on Leaf River. On inquiry, they told me it was for 'the pale man that spoke in tongues.' Them was their words, not mine. 'You mean Old Hundred-and-Eleven?' says I. 'The same,' they said. So there you have it."

"Ye must be mistaken, sir," said the old man. He waved his hands, his voice quivering now. "I am a fixture, well respected in these parts. I am the personal friend of Gin'ral von Arnim; he told me hisself I could stay long as I wanted, never mentioned any hangin."

Stribling smiled and shook his head. He leaned close to the man, lowered his voice. "I heard em talkin. They taken you for a prophet."

"Hell, I *am* a prophet!" shouted the old man. "God damn, I been slingin prophecies sixty-eight year! Why, hell, I prophesized *all* these war and tumults—t'warn't any news to *me*. And freein these niggers? Why, I knowed about that 'fore they ever *was* ary Year of Jubilo. Don't tell *me* about prophesizin!" The old man slapped his hands on his knees and began to rock back and forth. "The Lord God Jehovah!" he said. "The twelve tribes of Isr'el!"

"Calm yourself," said Stribling. "They's one person I know can help you."

The old man clamped his hand on Stribling's arm. "Who is it? But speak the name, and I'll plumb the levels of perdition to fetch him."

Stribling thought a moment, rubbing his brow. "If I tell you, then you must promise to fetch em here."

"If they's in Californy, I'll fetch em. I seen a feller hanged once—it ain't for me."

Stribling drew a deep breath, leaned over and whispered a name in the man's ear. Old Hundred-and-Eleven started in surprise again. "Say it ain't so!"

Stribling nodded.

Old Hundred-and-Eleven pulled Stribling close and kissed him noisily on the cheek. "I'm gone for town," he said, and dropped out of the box-car door and began to shamble off, his ragged coattails flapping behind him. The sentry glanced his way. "Go it, Ol' Hundred-and-'leven!" said the man, and laughed.

Stribling did not laugh. He took a handkerchief out of his coat pocket and scrubbed his cheek.

✦ ✦ ✦

GAWAIN HARPER STOOD on the front porch of the house he was born in. His eyes were fastened on the peeling paint of the front door, but it was not the door he saw. Rather, he saw the whole moment in which he stood, as if it were a bright globe and he turning in the center of it. He was surprised to discover that all his expectations, all the fanciful images he had dreamed of over the years, deserted him now, and in their place was the brief, ordinary passage of a summer afternoon.

The house was clapboard, two-story, with an ell that had been added just before the war. It had been painted white once, but was peeling so badly that the gray of the pine weatherboards was the dominant color now. The shutters were open, save for a few that had swung partly closed on their hinges. The broad gallery on which he stood was crowded on one end with rocking chairs, like old women huddled in gossip; the other end was empty, for there the porch had given way. Someone had propped a broomstick in the hole for warning.

A few of the trees that once had shaded the house were gone, but enough remained to dapple all with light and shadow, and to fill the air with the smell of their damp leaves. The tangle of sweet-shrub by the porch still thrived, and the crepe myrtle, and the rife lantana Aunt Vassar always planted in the spring, and the fleshy cannas that Gawain, when a child, had always been fearful of. He never knew why, even then. The old wood of the house was warm and gave of a warm smell; the afternoon was quiet, the air a little cooler after the storm. In the grass, in the gnarly privet along the western line, in the solemn trees, the old summer voices buzzed and whispered, and the birds sang, thankful for the rain. Gawain heard the drip-drip-drip of water in a gutter pipe, the creak of a limb, the flutter of a sparrow in the eaves. It was all so homely, so ordinary and so beautiful, and Gawain understood that these things would be the same whether he was standing here or not. The afternoon was passing, the sun falling and so changing the slant of light, the minutes disappearing one by one down the long corridor of time, and Gawain himself already disappearing with them.

No, he thought. *No, it has to change a little for my being here.* He held up his hands, saw them against the door, made himself believe that he had shifted the universe just by stepping up on the porch. The moment took its shape, its texture, from him now. Were he not here, it would all be different, might not exist at all.

He dropped his hands. For a moment longer he stood watching, suddenly aware that he was balanced on the thin edge of time between one moment and another, between one life and another. The thought hung in his mind and left him immobile. He wondered how long he could sustain these last seconds of the war; he found in his tired heart, just for an instant, the smallest glimmer of regret that it was over and something else about to begin. What it was he couldn't imagine, wasn't even supposed to imagine now; he only knew that every breath brought him closer. He swallowed hard, and took off his hat, and lifted his hand to knock.

The door opened before he touched it; he stopped with his fist poised in the air, and the globe of time rushed inward until it was a single brilliant point of light, and again he was in the center of it, though all he could hear now was the drum of blood in his ears. "Oh," he said, "well," and dropped his hand.

"It's about time you got here," Aunt Vassar said. "Mind that hole in the porch."

◆　　◆　　◆

NOTHING ELSE IN the world was so interesting to young Alex Rhea as the weather. Worms were good—the yard was full of them now, and he poked and prodded them and gathered them in clumps. Ants had their charm, and birds' nests, and the dark, mysterious things he believed dwelt in the upper rooms of old Mister Carter's house. But nothing held his attention like the weather, that garment that the world changed at will—violent and sweet and illogical, but always present, always inescapable.

He had loved the passage of the storm, though it scared him some, too. He'd watched from the safety of the enormous bed in which his sister slept, peering out from a part in the curtains at the tall windows of the upper bedroom. Framed in the window light was the glorious rain, dropping straight down and heavy at first, then slanting in the gusts and hammering at the windowpanes until he feared they would break, and the wind howling and thrashing among the oaks, and the thunder drumming, and how the lightning did crack and flicker against the rattling glass. Then a moment when it all turned, and the rain settled into a steady percussion, going gentler and gentler, and the thunder murmuring farther away, and the lightning seemed to be looking back over its shoulder as it passed eastward—and then the sun. Inexplicably, as if it had never left at all, the sun spread itself over the dripping trees and the silver-puddled yard, bringing steam from the grass and lighting the birds that shivered their feathers in the branches. He could go out then, and breathe the electric air, and ponder the worms that writhed in the sweet sunlight, and still, way off beyond the eastern hills, the thunder grumbled, reluctant to leave but leaving anyhow because God said it had to. Alex wondered if everybody had weather. If the yankees had it.

The boy was down by the road, studying the wiggletails in the ditch water, when Old Hundred-and-Eleven appeared. The man had his breeches rolled up and was lifting his feet high, like a crane. His feet made a squelching sound in the mud. Alex watched him nervously; he was never sure about this ghostly fellow with his pink eyes. "Hey, Mister Eleven," he said.

"Lord God Jehovah," said the old man. He was breathing hard, and the sweat was streaming down his face. "Ere Miss Morgan to home, pray? Please say she is."

"Yes, sir," said the boy. "She is yonder in the back yard, lookin for the cat. He run off yesterday. She won't find him, though. You can't hardly—"

"Rah!" said the old man. "Never mind the cat, no offense. Will ye go and fetch her? She must save me from a cruel fate undeserved. Say you will."

"Why, surely," said the boy, and turned and ran for the back yard.

✦　✦　✦

THEY DID NOT embrace. Not even in his most elaborate fancies had Gawain envisioned them doing that. But Aunt Vassar touched him. Her hand moved back and forth between them, touching first her bosom, then some part of Gawain Harper's body: his arms, his hair, his breast, and at last his face, her fingers brushing his cheek. Finally, Gawain captured her hand in its flight and held it. Her hand closed around his for an instant, then dropped away. "You look pretty bad," she said, her voice barely audible.

Gawain smiled. He knew she was willing herself not to cry, turning all her strength inward for this moment to spare herself the waste of tears. It was all right; he had imagined it thus, and she had not disappointed him.

For himself, Gawain struggled not to register his shock at her appearance. He had left her a great, buxom, shiplike woman, always in black and smelling of rose water and lavender powder. She was still in black, but she had shrunken and dried. The eyes behind her spectacles were hollow, curiously still and lightless, as if she had just awakened from a long, uneasy sleep. She smelled different, too—a dry, weary smell, like a milkweed husk, or something left in the attic for years. Gawain performed his own act of will then, driving away the memory of her until he could see clearly the woman who stood before him. "You, on the other hand, are beautiful," he said.

"Hah," she said. She looked him over again, from head to foot. "Have you been wrestlin hogs?" she asked.

"Somethin like it," he said. "But never fear—I shall go to the well-house and wash. Maybe young Vincent can bring me some of my clothes."

She laughed dryly and waved her hand. "Young Vincent went off with the yankees last summer. I'll send Uncle Priam, who is still here underfoot and forever a nuisance. Go on, now—I'll watch you go, then I'll tell your papa you are . . . home."

"Papa," said Gawain. "Is he—"

"Time for that," said his aunt. "Go on now."

So Gawain left the wide porch, went around the house and through the muddy yard to the cluster of outbuildings in back: the kitchen, the well-house, the crib, the chicken coop and, fifty paces downwind, the privy. The grass was tall around all of them; only the privy and the well had paths worn to the door. Gawain had never seen the kitchen, winter or summer, without a curl of smoke out its chimney, but there was no smoke now, and the brick walk that ran to the house was almost hidden in the grass. Gawain figured they must be cooking on the hearth, what little they had to cook. Certainly they had no chickens—the coops were a ruin.

Standing at the door to the well-house, Gawain sensed that something was missing, something removed from the familiar landscape he had carried in his head. He compared what he saw to the plan of his memory and realized it was the barn—yes, the cow barn and the fence that surrounded the lot. Gone for soldiers' shanties, Gawain decided, or for fires, or for breastworks. He wondered briefly if the Federal government would be interested in paying for all that wood, now that he was a loyal citizen once more. Doubtful, he thought.

It was cool inside the well-house. The sun slanted in ribbons through the boards, and by its light Gawain could see the spiderwebs that festooned the ceiling, nasty things where great surly spiders lurked. There was the usual wasps' nest too, tucked in a corner, busy with inhabitants. They didn't bother him, but the spiders made him nervous. If one were to drop on him—but he forced the thought away and began to peel off his clothes.

He was nearly done washing out of the well bucket when old Priam tapped on the door and entered, his arms full of clothing. Gawain had never known Priam when he wasn't old, so he looked no older now than he ever had. A little bent perhaps, but no grayer, and his eyes still glittered with flecks like gold in the irises. "Here's your clothes, young Marse," said Priam matter-of-factly, as if Gawain had not been gone at all.

"I ain't so young anymore," said Gawain.

"I ain't noticed," the old man said. He studied Gawain in the dim light for a moment. "Well, you never was much to look at nekkid," he said, "but you *have* fell off some. Been a long time—is you farin well gen'rally?"

"Gen'rally," said Gawain. "Aunt said young Vincent run off. How come you still here?"

The old man laughed softly. "I knowed you gone ask me that. Now I turn it around, ask you: what you come back for?"

Gawain understood that he had been a fool. "Same answer as you," he said. "Can't go no place but home."

"Mmm-hmm," said Uncle Priam.

Gawain indicated the muddy clothes on the floor of the well-house. "I bought these down south. Reckon you can clean em up? Ought not to be any graybacks in em, just mud mostly. Maybe a flea or two."

The old man nodded, bent slowly and gathered up the clothes Gawain had traveled the road in. "I shave a little lye soap in the water, kill most anything. Brush your coat out, dry it in the shade, it'll be all right. Marse Gawain?"

"Yes, old Priam?"

The old man narrowed his golden eyes. "You killed some, didn't you, back endurin the war?"

"I reckon," said Gawain. "It's what you do. There ain't much gettin around it."

"Well, then." Uncle Priam looked up at the gray rafters where the spiders lived. "You didn't bring none of em back with you, did you?"

"I hope not, old Priam," said Gawain. "I surely hope I didn't."

The old man nodded again. "I put your bag upstairs," he said, "in your old room. Opened the windows, see could I let a little air in there." Then he turned and passed through the door and closed it behind him.

Gawain dressed in the clothes Uncle Priam had brought: cotton drawers and socks, a muslin shirt, a pair of brown plaid breeches, and the old boots he used to hunt birds in. All but the socks and boots were a size too large now. Old Priam had brought a handkerchief, and, folded inside, a gold watch and chain. There was a comb, too, and a bone-handled clasp knife. When he had dressed and run the comb through his hair, Gawain felt better than he had in a long time. He looked up at the wasps' nest. "Why don't you boys do somethin about these spiders?" he said. As if in answer, a wasp sortied out from the nest and spun lazily around his head, then disappeared through a crack in the boards. For an instant, Gawain saw him burnished golden in the shaft of the sun.

✦ ✦ ✦

SOME OF THE men who had passed through the boxcar jail had carved their names on the wall of the car, and some had scrawled them there with a burnt stick. The four current residents, all awake now, had pondered this and built a discussion about the way some men yearn for immortality, and some move through life leaving no more trace than they would in water. To illustrate his own view, S. Cragin Knox was carving his name with his clasp knife, in letters bigger and deeper than any before. The others, meanwhile, sat in the open doorway and watched the afternoon.

"I hope you are satisfied, Peck," said Carl Nobles, "now that we are jailed." Nobles was a big man, bearded, in a checked gingham shirt and jeans pants. Marcus Peck, too, was stout; it had taken them all to hoist him into the boxcar when they'd first arrived. Peck had lost his left leg outside Atlanta when a limber chest he was serving exploded from counterbattery fire. When he was first home, Peck made up a tale about being blown up in the air while his severed leg spun aloft beside him. When he found that people believed him, he quit telling it.

"Well, it wasn't me started that affair," said Peck. "Look to yourselves—I was only makin an observation, and for that, I was set upon by ruffians. This used to be a free country, as I recall."

"And what would a bloody fat Irishman know about a free country?" snorted Nobles.

"Sirrah!" said Peck.

Nobles and Peck went on arguing—out of habit, Stribling supposed—while Knox went on carving.

Cragin Knox had been a cabinetmaker once, and a fixer of delicate things, and a crafter of mandolins and violins, and a fine gunsmith. He was an expert shot, and served much of his time in the war as a sharpshooter with General Cleburne, who gave him a Whitworth rifle and allowed him to travel at large along the division front. After Cleburne's death at Franklin and the terrible winter defeat at Nashville, Knox left the line of retreat and began walking home, hundreds of miles across the barren winter landscape. Almost within sight of his mother's house in Cumberland, he was captured by Federal cavalry and sent all the way up to the Rock Island Prison in Illinois. He had not been home long now, and he still had the prison thinness on him; the skin of his face stretched taut against the skull, and his clothes hung loose upon him. He had a wracking cough that, at times, seemed about to burst his narrow chest. Stribling was astonished that Knox had been able to join in the fight at the tavern; the act of carving his name seemed to exhaust him. Still he worked on, stopping now and then to rest, saying nothing until he was done. "I am finished, boys," he said at last.

They all turned at once to look at Knox's work. He had fashioned, in perfect Roman font, the legend

S. CRAGIN KNOX, GENT.
1830–1865

No one spoke, for each had learned, in his own way, at whatever expense, that a soldier's self-prophecies were never to be taken lightly, and never acknowledged until the invitation was made. Knox invited no response. He sat down against the wall under his carving, stretched out his legs, clasped his fingers, and began at once to snore.

"Well," said Peck after a moment, watching his comrade. "The kind maiden, Sleep. How soft she comes."

"And the thief, Time," said Stribling.

They were silent for a while then, watching the afternoon die around them. They had all traveled a long way and had gained a costly wisdom in the journeying. They did not need to be reminded that few such golden afternoons were left to S. Cragin Knox, Gent. This vanished rain, this twilight, the season grown old—then the dark sister of sleep would call. By then, no doubt, the boxcar would be far away, the carved name traveling on in darkness.

"Where do you come from, Mister Stribling?" asked Nobles suddenly.

Stribling shrugged. "No place in particular," he said. Then, to temper his rudeness, he added, "Alabama, mostly." He told about meeting Gawain on the road, and, in brief, their subsequent adventures.

"I don't know the fellow at the grave you mentioned, though it is a good story," said Nobles. "However, I do know Molochi Fish. He is fearful strange for certain. I wouldn't be surprised, now the niggers are free, they don't get him some dark night. So Gawain Harper is home at last?"

"Yes," said Stribling. He looked past the sentry, up the road that led to town. The shadows were growing longer. He slapped at a mosquito. *Pretty soon now,* he thought.

"That's a good horse," said Nobles, pointing at Zeke.

"Oh, Xenophon will do," said Stribling, "though he is a little spare right now."

Nobles shifted, rubbed his thighs. "I have to ask you a question, sir—a favor, I reckon."

"You can ask it, Mister Nobles," said Stribling.

The other shifted again, as if he had to be situated just so for the words to be right. "I am in a bind," he said at last. "My ox is in a ditch."

Stribling waited.

"You see," said Nobles, "I had not thought to include this fracas on my afternoon's itinerary."

"Nor I," said Stribling.

"Plainly put," said Nobles, "I need to be somewhere this evenin, and . . . "

"You need a horse?" said Stribling helpfully.

"More than anything in the world," said Nobles. "I'd gladly pay—"

"No, no," said Stribling. "I won't need the horse tonight, and he could stand the exercise. However—" He looked around at the boxcar. "We *are* in jail, you understand."

"Pah!" snorted Nobles. "That is only a formality." He put out his hand, and Stribling took it. "Thank you, sir," said Nobles. "You are a friend."

"Now, let me tell you about Zeke's peculiarities," said Stribling, and he did.

✦   ✦   ✦

THE HOUSE WAS cool and smelled as it always had in summer, of mildew and damp, of dust, of old books and tobacco and candles. Through the tall open windows came the light breeze, bringing with it a clean smell of oak leaves and the faint, buttery perfume of the lantana. Gawain stood in the dim front hall, the wide space made gloomier somehow by the light from the open front door. When he was a boy, this hall was a frightening region to him, and he rarely lingered here. But he lingered now, remembering how it was, breathing the old stale air among the old familiar shapes: the coat tree, the table, the stiff chairs where no one ever sat, the horsehair settee and the portraits covered with gauze against the summer. The house was utterly silent, save for the tinkle of a lamp pendant moved by the breeze, and the slight rasp of his aunt's inhalation. She stood beside him, her hands together at the front of her dress, watching him from the corner of her eye. After a moment, she looked away; when she spoke, her voice was hushed almost to a whisper. "I cannot imagine what it must be like," she said.

"What, darlin?"

She lay her palm on the marble top of the hall table, then brushed absently at the dust. "I have lived in this house since it was raised, nearly thirty years. I was already an old maid when I came here—your papa was kind to take me in, his old-maid sister-in-law." She studied her palm. "He was kind to me, Gawain, always. Whatever else he was, you cannot forget that. You have to give him that."

"I will remember it," said Gawain, knowing that he really would, if only for his own peace. He knew the story of Vassar Bishop's life, how she had been the sister elected to stay with the old folks in Alabama until they died. By then her prospects were gone; there was nothing for her to do but follow her sister west, to the new territory, where her sister's husband promised a place for her. She came to this house then, and saw it raised and finished out of the wilderness, and saw the Choctaw trading post of Frye's Tavern wax and grow into Cumberland: houses built, and churches, and the beautiful Georgian courthouse, and the mercantile anchor of the old square. And saw it fall again to ashes and dust. And, Gawain had no doubt, would live to see it rise once more.

"I have never left here," Aunt Vassar said, more to herself than to her nephew. "Maybe a night or two, I could count them on my fingers. So I don't know what it must be like to come back." She looked at Gawain then. "What does it look like to you? Has it changed much? That's a foolish question, maybe."

"No," said Gawain. "No, it ain't foolish." His eyes traveled to the row of portraits that hung on the west wall; they peered back from the plaster above the wainscoting, dim behind their curtains of gauze, watching another day wane in the long procession of days that had passed since Frank Harper, Gawain's father, had hung them there. Gawain's grandfather was there, in the high stiff collar and cravat of the 'twenties; Frank Harper himself, in the black frock coat he wore every day, winter and summer; his bride, Ellie, Gawain's mother, fragile and beautiful and remote, more real than she had been in life. Gawain as a callow young man of twenty was there, and his sisters. And Aunt Vassar.

The portrait of Aunt Vassar, painted when she was a girl in Alabama, was like none other Gawain had ever seen. Her young face—almost Byronic, with short-cropped hair and eyes that seemed to dart away when they were looked at—leapt out from a vague and stormy background. She wore a blouse open at the throat with the collar turned up, like a poet or a harlot, and in his time Gawain had looked on that portrait and felt every stirring the blood is capable of. The image was scandalous, immeasurably fine, and, by life's mad chemistry, the saddest of them all.

"No, darlin," Gawain said at last. "It is just as I remembered."

"Then what do you feel? Is time that heavy that it never moves at all? Where have you been, then?"

Gawain shook his head. "I don't know how to answer you. I have been a long way, and all of a sudden I'm in the front hall again. I am . . . I reckon I am too tired to think about it now."

His aunt laughed. "I know no more about it than I did a while ago, except that you have learned to lie in the army—not that you were any slouch at it before. Come then, and see your papa."

She led the way up the creaking stairs to the landing, then down the upper hall to the last bedroom door. It was open, and she stopped just short of it and turned and put her hand flat against Gawain's breast. "You know more about time than you let on," she said, "and you must have been seein this moment in your head for a long while."

"Yes, ma'am," he said.

"All right, then. I will tell you, and let you decide how close it comes to whatever it was you imagined. Gawain, your papa is senile, infantile, he can't remember what he had for breakfast—though all he'd have to do is look at his shirt front—and he is deaf as a lamp post, so speak up when you talk to him. Not that it matters—he won't know what you're sayin anyhow. There now. Go on in. When you are done, I will fix you somethin to eat."

She stood aside. Gawain stepped past her and into the room.

Frank Harper sat with his back to the door, gazing out the tall windows at the leaves of a hackberry tree. Gawain could see the bare dome of his head above the chair back; it was feathered with wisps of white hair that shone like spun silk in the light. From this angle, too, he could see the gnarled, spotted hands where they gripped the arms of the chair. "Papa?" he said. When there was no reply, he looked back at his aunt. She shook her head and motioned him further into the room. He took a step, then another, and at last stepped around the chair and looked at his father's face.

The eyes were sunk deep and glittered like chips of coal. The skin of the old man's face stretched taut around his cheekbones, and his nose was sharp and bladelike. His thin lips were moving, but no sound came. As Gawain watched, he raised his hand and dug at his nose, then his fingers moved downward to his watch chain and stopped there. He seemed to be watching something in the leaves; he did not look up.

"Papa," said Gawain.

"Speak up," said Aunt Vassar from the doorway.

"Papa!" said Gawain, louder now. "How you doin?"

Old Harper started, looked around him. "What?" he snapped.

"I said How you doin!" bellowed Gawain into the hairy cup of his father's ear.

"Yes, yes," croaked the old man irritably. "I done told em that already, the sons of bitches."

"Good God," said Gawain.

The room smelled of camphor. Gawain looked around at the familiar furniture, heavy and dark: the wardrobe, the chairs, the dresser, the bookshelves crowded with ancient tomes, the sagging bed, the rug worn threadbare. The hearth spilled cold ashes across the floor, and the clock on the mantel tick-tocked as it always had. But the clock lied, Gawain thought.

There was no time here, not by the clock, not by day or night or season. His eyes darted to the chair by the hearth; it was empty, or so it seemed.

"Good God," he said again, and backed away from his father's chair. Then Aunt Vassar was beside him. "Listen to me, Gawain—it is your life you have come back to, not mine nor his nor anybody else's. Yours. Can you understand that?"

He did not answer. The sun was dropping lower now, and the light in the room was strong and burnished, moving with the shadows of the hackberry leaves. A squirrel sat in the crook of a limb, turning an acorn in his paws. The old man blinked at the sun, muttered and sneezed and rubbed his eyes. He spoke a name Gawain could not understand. Gawain turned away then. He looked at his hands; they were shaking. "Oh," he said, "I got to eat somethin."

Aunt Vassar took Gawain by the arm. "I know, boy," she said.

"I really got to eat somethin," Gawain said again. "My hands get shaky when I don't eat. See?"

He held up his hands for her to see. "I know they do," she said. "I know."

✦   ✦   ✦

THERE IS A moment when the day's axis turns, when time begins to slide away toward night again. The exact moment is imperceptible, though if a watcher is careful, he might perceive the signs. He might see how light and air conspire to make a stillness, to soften the sharp edges of the world. He might note how sounds no longer ring so brightly, and how shadows creep into places still warm from the sun. Shadows, the first sure tendrils of night, reach into fence corners and woods and up the eastern face of houses, and with the shadows come the birds again, hurrying against the night, and timid feeders move quivering over the grass, who know the hawks have folded themselves away, and the owls not yet awakened.

In his early life, Harry Stribling made a conscious effort to mark himself in time. Among other experiments, he tried endlessly, in every season, to close his hand around the exact moment when day gave way to evening. But at length he decided it was impossible and gave it up, as he gave up trying to touch the moment when sleep arrived. Now he contented himself with knowing only that the turning had come. He was thinking about that when he saw her. She was moving down the shadows, under the trees that lined the townward road. "Ah," he said.

Nobles and Peck and Stribling still sat in the doorway. "Well," said Peck. "There comes Old Hundred-and-Eleven again, and he's got . . . my, who *is* that?"

The woman was slender and tall, in a pale blue dress that she held up out of the mud. From this distance, they could not see the details of her face, only that her skin was pale and her dark hair pulled back in a bun. They did not have to see her face to know that she was agitated; her whole body communicated that news. Old Hundred-and-Eleven was lumbering along behind her with his hat in his hand. They watched the two of them approach the sentry, who stood stiffly at attention for a moment or two while the woman talked at him. When the sentry pointed toward the box-car door, the woman turned her face that way and scowled.

"Why, that is Morgan Rhea," said Peck. "What is she doing here, do you suppose?"

"I always thought she was handsome," said Nobles.

"I, too," said Peck. He leaned back on his elbows and laughed. "I danced with her once, at a barbecue on the Fourth of July." He laughed again and thumped the stump of his leg against the boxcar floor. "The thief, Time," he said.

Stribling pushed himself away from the boxcar and landed on his feet in the mud. The knee of his bad leg buckled, and he almost fell.

"Where you goin?" said Nobles.

"I have an engagement with Miss Rhea," said Stribling.

"You?" said Peck. "She don't even *know* you."

"I reckon she's fixin to," said Stribling. He moved away from the box-car, at the same time raising his hand to the woman. "Hey!" said the sentry, but Stribling ignored him. He watched Morgan Rhea move across the muddy space between them.

"This is the feller!" said Old Hundred-and-Eleven when they were a dozen paces away. They came up to Stribling then, the old man breathing hard, Morgan gritting her teeth. Now that he could see her face, Stribling allowed she was handsome indeed, even with the smallpox scars that pitted her cheeks. He liked her hands, too; they were long and slender, and the finger she raised in his face was steady.

"Who are you?" she demanded.

"This here's the feller sent me to fetch you," said Old Hundred-and-Eleven. "He said you could save me from the rope—didn't you, Cap'n?"

"I suppose I did," said Stribling. He took off his hat and made a slight bow. "I am Harry Stribling, and I am—"

"A liar, I should say!" spat Morgan. "What is all this business about hangin? Why, I have known this man since I was a baby, and he has never done—"

Stribling held up his hand. "Please," he said, without prelude. "I bring you word of Gawain Harper."

Stribling regretted his haste at once. The woman recoiled as if he had slapped her. She tried to speak, but no sound came, and when she staggered, Stribling put out his hand and caught her. She shook him away. "Dead!" she said at last. "I knew it, all this time!"

"Now, hold on," Stribling began, but she shrank away from him.

"Oh, I have been waitin for you," she said. "I didn't know who you'd be or what you'd look like, but I knew you'd come. I watched for you, I—"

"Oh, Lord," said Old Hundred-and-Eleven. "Oh, Lord, what's the matter!"

She turned, put her hand against the old man's chest, pushed him gently, her voice forced into gentleness. "Go along. Nobody's goin to hang you, it was all a great joke and now it's over. Go along."

The old man scratched his head, put his hat back on, took it off again. "Well," he said.

"Go on, now," she said, and Old Hundred-and-Eleven nodded and turned back toward the boxcar. Stribling was about to speak when she whirled on him. "Don't tell me anything about it," she said. "Nothin, you hear? I don't want to know how or where, or how gallant it was, or what his last words were." She raised her hands, palms outward, and began to back away. "How dare you bring me here for this. If I were a man, I'd kill you. I might do it anyhow."

Jesus Christ, thought Stribling. He was aware that the boys were watching the scene; the sentry had joined them at the boxcar, and they were all waiting to see what would happen next. Stribling cleared his throat. "Now, see here," he said. "I did not *say* that he was dead, did not mean to *imply* that he was dead—fact is, he ain't dead atall, and you must quit this foolishness so I can talk to you."

The woman lowered her hands, looked at Stribling with eyes narrowed in anger. "Foolishness, is it?" she hissed. "First you scare that old man nearly to death, then bring me here on a lie, and now you speak a name I had already put away and didn't want to take out again. What do you mean he isn't dead? What do you want? Who *are* you?"

Stribling, who had envisioned a rational conversation once his deception was revealed, found himself irritated. "Good God," he said. "Will you settle down? I just want to talk to you about the boy. I have good tidings, if you will get off the ramparts for a minute. Good God."

She drew herself up and brushed at a loose strand of hair. "What happened to your eye?" she asked.

The irrelevancy of the question startled Stribling. He unconsciously touched his eye and winced. "I was in a fight, which landed me in the jail yonder, which is why I couldn't seek you out myself."

"What kind of fight was it?" asked the girl.

"Recreational," said Stribling. "Now, Miss Morgan—"

"How do you know my name, sir?"

Stribling was growing weary of her questions. "Since I met Gawain Harper this mornin, I have only heard it a hundred times." She blushed at this, and Stribling felt a twinge of satisfaction. Then he looked back at the boxcar again where the boys were watching. Nobles waved at him and smiled. "Can we walk up the road a bit?" asked Stribling. "I am harmless—Mister Marcus Peck and the rest of those fellows will vouch for me."

"That is hardly a recommendation," said Morgan Rhea. "However, I will walk with you. How is it you can stroll about when you are supposed to be in jail?"

"We like to think of ourselves as prisoners at large," said Stribling.

They went up the road, and as they walked Stribling told her of the morning's adventures—excepting the incident with Molochi Fish—and by the time they reached the edge of the square, she was smiling. *Mercurial,* thought Stribling, nodding sagely to himself. *Very mercurial.*

"You told poor Old Hundred-and-Eleven that yarn just so he would fetch me, so you could tell me this?"

"I figured you wouldn't come otherwise," Stribling pointed out again.

"Quite right," she said. "But now you may explain to me why Gawain himself isn't standing here tellin me all this?" Her voice caught in her throat then, and for an instant Stribling thought she might cry. But she didn't, and Stribling wondered why. Instead, she looked back down the road, squinting into the evening sun. "Did he send you to tell me this? Was it his doing?"

"No," said Stribling, and was glad he could say it, for it seemed a relief to her.

"I'm sorry," she said. "When you first said his name, I thought he was . . . dead—" She interrupted herself. "Why did I do that? Why did I assume—"

"There has been a great deal of bein dead," said Stribling. "Perhaps we have grown to expect it."

"Perhaps." She shaded her eyes with her hand. Stribling thought the light on her face was pretty. "When you told me that, it came to me all at once how the last time I saw him—the very last time—was yonder at the depot, the cars pullin away. I watched 'til they went around the curve and that was the last I saw of him, sir, three years almost to this very day. And now the depot is ashes and dust, and the world—" She stopped, turned to Stribling. "What do you have to tell me that I have not understood already? There must be something. I have always thought I must have missed something.

What is he like now? How far is he from the picture I carry in my head? If you can tell me that, then you have done me a service."

"I can't tell you that," said Stribling. "I do not know the picture you have, I only know the fellow I met on the road this mornin. He is the one who is home, not the other one."

She thought a moment. "The other one *is* dead, I suppose, isn't he."

"Yes," said Stribling, too quickly. "I mean, most of us are. You cannot—"

"How much do you get to keep?" she asked. "How much can you bring along when you die and come back as somebody else?"

"That is what he is wonderin himself," said Stribling.

"What?"

Stribling touched her shoulder, lightly. "The mosquitoes are bad here in the shade," he said. "Let us walk yonder where there is still a little sun."

They walked out into the square. They could hear bullbats squawking overhead now, and the chittering of chimney swifts. They stopped then, and Morgan sat down on a mounting block and looked at Stribling. "Tell me then," she said.

"He is afraid," said Stribling.

"Afraid?"

Stribling knelt beside her, looked out over the square. "We have all been to a strange country, all us boys. I do not say that to condescend nor to elicit sympathy, mind—I only state it as a fact that you must agree to if you are to begin to understand."

"All right," she said. She wrapped her arms around her knees and watched him.

"A strange country indeed," said Stribling. He shifted, aware for the first time how tired he was, how his bones ached. He rubbed his swollen knuckle, then laughed. "I used to think I would know when we left it, used to dream of the day when I could look behind me and there would be the bourne of that unhappy place—the ramparts or fence or stone wall or whatever it might be—and, having seen it, could turn my face from it and look up the road to home. But I was mistaken. You don't ever leave it, not altogether, not all of you—some part is always there, and that's the boy you knew, I reckon. What comes out is whatever is left, and something new as well, something you picked up on your travels—does that make any sense atall?"

"Go on," she said.

"All right. Have you ever known a person who nearly died and was come to life again—or maybe seen one of these old-time river baptizins where the person comes up out of the water?"

"I have seen them, yes."

"Then you know how that fellow looks around—and you know that he is lookin at the world in a way he never had before and might never again. Suddenly it is all a bright mystery and nothing is familiar, not even the ones he loved in the old life. I have seen that, and seen, just for an instant, how afraid they are. You can't be not afraid when you wake to life again."

"All right," she said.

"All right. So he is afraid, Gawain is. That is why he didn't come see you today. That is what I want to tell you. I don't know how much you get to bring out with you, I only know it has to be enough." He looked at her, smiled again. "You know exactly what I am talkin about, don't you?"

She nodded and rested her chin on her knees. "Yes. There is more than one strange country; that is why I am afraid, too."

"Then you know he will come in his own time," said Stribling. "He ain't so afraid that he won't do that."

She let out a long sigh and shook her head. "We are all gone mad, aren't we?"

"I don't see how it could be otherwise," said Stribling.

They sat awhile longer while the dusk gathered around them, talking of things beyond madness, beyond sorrow and fear: the color of the sky, the sweet rain, the ephemeral promise of tomorrow. Harry Stribling had not talked to a woman in a long while, and he was glad to discover that he had not forgotten how. But it could not last; Stribling knew that such a moment was not supposed to last, that it had its own axis, its own turning, one that was easy enough to detect. So he played it out as long as he could, waiting for her to bring up Gawain again. At last she did, but not in the way he expected.

"You are a strange man, Captain Stribling," she said. "I can see why Gawain Harper would take to you, for he is pretty strange himself. But why did you do this, go to all this trouble?"

Stribling shrugged. "I don't know. Because I am a busybody. Because we were soldiers, I guess." He laughed. "The great fraternity of fear."

Her face darkened then. "I *shamed* Gawain Harper into joining the army, you know." She looked at Stribling. "Why did I do that, do you suppose?"

Stribling shrugged. "Why do we do anything?"

She laughed then, real laughter, and lighter now. "A glib answer, sir, worthy of a philosopher."

"That's my trade now," said Stribling, grinning.

"I thought so," she said. She rose, walked a little way up and down, her hands clasped before her. "Do you suppose that's why he hasn't come around? Because he blames—"

"He blames nobody, least of all you," said Stribling.

She looked at him. "And you, sir? Who do you blame?"

"Nobody," said Stribling. "Not yet, anyhow. If I find out who was responsible, I'll let you know. In the meantime, you might give us old soldiers a little rope."

"I suppose I must," she said, and smiled. "Well, I am awfully tired," she said. "And there is a curfew."

"Will you let me walk you home?" said Stribling, rising stiffly to his feet.

"No, thank you," she said. "And you are supposed to be a prisoner anyhow." She half-turned as if to go, then stopped. "I am obliged to you," she said. Then she laughed again. "When he first went away, in the springtime, I used to imagine him returning on horseback—can you imagine?—among gay banners and pennoned lances and music—*Gawain*, for pity's sake. Oh, I cringe to think on it now."

"Well, he was *kind* of on horseback," said Stribling. "There was a horse in the party, anyway."

She put out her hand, and Stribling took it, and they stood thus for a moment as the twilight grew around them. Then she turned and was gone. Stribling watched her walk away, lifting her skirts out of the mud, until he could see her no more. He stood a moment longer, looking out over the burnt square, listening to the crickets, the katydids, listening to the sound of an axe chopping somewhere. The light was soft now, dissolving; the treetops glowed as if the light was leaving them upward. "Morgan Rhea," he said. Then he turned at last, and as he moved back through the deepening shadows of the trees, he thought of Zeke. The boy had been too many nights in the open; it would be nice to find a place for him.

He was still thinking about Zeke when he came into the clearing, so was surprised to find the horse gone from the fence and nowhere in sight. Then he remembered Nobles and his errand.

"Brother Carl has left us," said Peck when Stribling came up to the boxcar. "I would escape myself, but I think they might feed us after a while. And, oh—Carl said he would try to find some corn for your horse."

Stribling nodded and looked away toward the south. Yes, he thought, some corn would be nice for the boy—maybe Nobles could find some. And a little good water, too: clear and shining, warm from the sun, so smooth it would mirror the stars.

· VIII ·

The twilight was long in passing, as it often is in summertime, and the dark slow to come. At the old Wagner place, the ruined brick cookhouse gave of the sun's light for a long time, as if reluctant to surrender any token of life. Somewhere in the brush-choked fields, a whippoorwill began to call.

A man sat on the overturned cookpot, his saddled horse grazing nearby. It was not Colonel Burduck, though the man was examining the Colonel's whittled stick and the drawings—a sun, a moon, a star—that the Colonel had made in the dirt. Across the man's lap lay a Henry rifle. "Curious," he said to himself, and laid the stick on the ground exactly where he'd found it.

This was the second time in as many nights that Captain King Solomon Gault had visited the old Wagner place. Last night he had come to survey the ground as any good commander might be expected to do. Tonight was business.

In the twilight, Captain Gault seemed calm and thoughtful. If he was aware of the ghosts collecting in the ruins, he gave no sign. He himself believed that he was calm, in a contemplative mood, unhurried and in control of his unfolding destiny. Had he been able to view the inner landscape of his soul, he would have been surprised to find the red shapes that rose and fell there, that spiraled upward in tortuous columns and fell back into the darkness. Others—those who knew him well—would not have been surprised.

Captain Gault was called "Captain" because he once held a commission in the Confederate service—a roving commission, he liked to say, for he never served an hour in the regular army. His troops—sometimes a hundred and fifty or more—had been partisan rangers raised from Cumberland and Yalobusha Counties: piney woods farmers, hard men contemptuous of uniforms and discipline and drill, who could be sum-

moned by mysterious signals and handshakes and messengers in the night
to foray against the yankees. Armed with pistols, shotguns, knives, muskets lifted from the hands of the dead, they would mount their famished
horses—or mules lately harnessed to the plow—and rendezvous at some
lonely place where their Captain waited with his sleek thoroughbred, his
English saddle, his gray officer's frock and Henry rifle. From there, they
would go and tear up the railroad, or steal livestock, or terrorize the
Unionists of the county, or dangle by his heels some elderly farmer thought
to have money buried in his garden. But they could fight, too. They liked
to fight, preferred to fight, and they showed no quarter.

In July of 1864, Gault and his men fought their last battle. In the piney
summer twilight, with the rain just passed and a mist rising from the river,
they set up an ambush on the north bank of the Tallahatchie, and sprung
it on a column of Indiana cavalry escorting a pair of smoothbore
Napoleons to Cumberland. Perhaps the attackers were too eager, made too
bold by past successes. Certainly some of them were drunk. Whatever the
reason, by the Federal artillery lieutenant's pocket watch, the fight lasted
twenty-five minutes. Many of Gault's men spent the first five minutes
learning that their paper cartridges were wet, while the yankees, armed
with Spencer repeating carbines, were under no such encumbrance. Worse,
the smoothbores belonged to a veteran battery that could unlimber and
open fire in a matter of minutes, which they did, with canister. The battle
dissolved at last in a wild chase through the second-growth timber, during
which five rebels were dispatched and three captured. Although they had
suffered no casualties themselves, the Indiana men viewed the incident as
a criminal act; before another half hour had passed, their captives were
swinging from picket ropes in the limbs of a red oak tree beside the road.

The defeat put an end to Gault's command. Some of the rangers joined
Forrest when he began operating in the area in August. A few decided to
move west into the territories. Most simply went home, where they spent
the rest of the war hiding out from both sides. None of them forgot the
humiliation suffered in the Tallahatchie fight, for which they blamed the
yankees, the rain, the gods, even Solomon Gault; in short, everybody and
everything but themselves.

For his part, Gault wisely chose to give up soldiering for a while.
Casting about for other ways to serve, he discovered the lucrative smuggling trade that ran out of Memphis. In this adventure he was so success-
ful that, when the war ended, Solomon Gault found that his fortune was
not only intact but increased severalfold. The war had cost him his wife
and child, the country was a wasteland, his house was burned, and the
fields over which he once rode were tall in broomsage and black oak

saplings—but Solomon Gault had things to do, a plan to accomplish that only a calm, clear-sighted man could bring to fruition. He was, by anybody's calculation, the richest man in the country. By rights, then, he should have been the most powerful. However, that distinction belonged to one who was not rich at all: Colonel Michael Burduck, U.S.A. Gault planned to alter that galling circumstance, and much more besides. So he waited in the gathering dusk at the old Wagner place, his good Henry rifle across his knees, listening to the whippoorwill.

Presently, at near dark, he heard another sound, the one for which he'd been waiting. The horse lifted his head and whickered softly, his ears pricked forward. Gault rose, pulling his watch; he glanced at it, then snapped it shut and turned toward the road. The sound of walking horses, and the muted voices of men, grew nearer; they were coming from the south, two of them. Gault waited. In a moment, the riders turned off the road and materialized in the dusk, walking their mounts carefully through the cedars toward the open space where the old cookhouse stood. In the tricky light, they seemed larger than they really were. One of them stopped just inside the clearing, but the other rode close enough that the Captain could grasp the horse's bit.

"Well, Lieutenant Stutts," said the Captain, looking up into the sharp, bearded face shadowed by the brim of a slouch hat.

The other made no move to dismount. "Evenin, Cap'n," he said, and grinned. "I been promoted, I see."

Wall Stutts was the only ranger to stand by the Captain in the months following their defeat on the Tallahatchie. Stutts' adventures in the smuggling trade refined his sense of avarice and earned for him the conditional trust, if not the affection, of King Solomon Gault. Again, the Captain might have been surprised had he been able to see into the deep chambers of a soul, but probably not in this case. He knew Wall Stutts better than he knew himself, and understood that the man was useful only so far as his meanness was useful. Stutts enjoyed looking down on his Captain from the back of a horse, but that was all right for now. Let the man have his small moment.

"Yes, a promotion," the Captain said. He peered into the dusk at the other man waiting in silence. "Who's that," he said.

The rider urged his mule forward. He was a short man, his face hidden by his hat brim and the upturned collar of a rain slicker. "Ah, the high sheriff," said the Captain.

The man pushed his hat back to reveal a round, grinning face. He had dropped his stirrups and was twisting the mule's bridle in his hands. "Hidy, Cap'n Gault," he said, and giggled, and climbed down from his mule.

Ben Luker was a stunning illustration of the possibilities Captain Gault envisioned. He had once been the turnkey at the old jail under Sheriff Julian Bomar. With Bomar gone to the army, Luker and Constable John Talbot carried on as the law in Cumberland. John Talbot was shot down in the street by the wild Kansas troops who occupied the town briefly in '62, leaving only old Ben Luker. When Colonel Burduck arrived and established martial law, one of his first acts was to seek out for civil liaison, for sheriff, a man so invisible, so inept, and preferably such a coward that he would give Burduck no argument whatever. Ben Luker seemed the perfect choice, and he was already in place, so the sheriff he became.

Unfortunately for the Colonel, old Ben Luker was now in a situation to serve in ways Burduck did not suspect. Ben Luker had kinsmen with the rangers, had always been sympathetic, and had even ridden with them now and then when the sortie was not too strenuous. So, in the end, he was Gault's man, not Burduck's at all. The Captain enjoyed this joke on Colonel Burduck.

For now, however, he ignored Ben Luker and turned to Stutts. "The other one's late—any trouble?"

Wall Stutts threw his leg over his horse and dismounted. "Yonder he is, you can ask him yourself," he said.

The third rider had come quietly and now sat his horse just outside the clearing, hands folded on the pommel of his saddle, watching. Just enough light remained for the Captain to see that the man was hatless, bearded. The Captain did not need the light to detect the uneasiness he pushed ahead of him into the clearing. He was a little too solid, too inscrutable for the Captain's taste. But that was all right too, for the moment.

"Don't be shy," said the Captain. "We're all friends here."

The rider dismounted, tied the reins to the spiky branch of a dead cedar tree. He walked with a slow, deliberate, rolling gait into the clearing. "I'm late, all right," he said. "There's a sentry on the bridge, nights. I had to hunt the ford."

"I heard you was jailed," said Stutts, and spat.

Carl Nobles looked at Stutts for a long moment. The other grinned in return. At last Nobles turned to the Captain. "I'm here now," he said.

Captain Gault was keenly aware of the distance that lay between this new arrival and the other two men in the clearing. Unlike Stutts and the sheriff, Carl Nobles was a bona fide veteran of a regiment that had served in the East; he had been in great battles, had marched and fought under leaders whose names already rang like mighty bells in the folklore of the region. The Captain did not go so far as to admit that any such contrast existed between Nobles and himself; still, he could not rid himself of a certain *awareness* of the man and, worse, a covert envy. For the moment, he told himself. Only for the moment. For what he envied in Carl Nobles was, at last, only the means to an end.

"Tell me the news," he said.

Nobles shrugged. "I got some boys interested. It ain't easy. I ain't good at this."

"How many?" asked the Captain. "A dozen? Twenty?"

"One," said Nobles. "Two, countin myself."

"Jesus," said the Captain. He looked away in disgust, knowing he had to control himself.

"And the other son bitch ain't got but one leg," Stutts said.

"Watch your mouth," said Nobles.

Stutts grinned. "Any time you want to shut it, you jes let me know."

"Goddammit, man," said the Captain, turning to Nobles again. "I called on you because I thought you had some influence. What the hell have you been doing?"

Nobles closed the space between them; without thinking, Gault stepped back, then checked himself and stood his ground. "You listen to me," said Nobles. "These boys are comin back wore out. They ain't like your damned peckerwood rangers that never left the country. They are tired of fightin."

"What about you?" asked the Captain. "You tired, too? But you are in it now, sir, and there is no backing away. This is serious business—I could hang for it, and so could you. Don't forget that." The Captain stopped then, and made himself relax. When he spoke again, his voice was easy, amiable. "Look here," he said. "You don't have to like me, nor Stutts here, nor the men who served with me, but we're the only chance you have. What you have to do is believe. That's all I'm asking."

Nobles looked at the ground for a moment, then raised his face to the Captain. "Fact is, I *don't* much like you," he said. "But, like you say, that don't matter. I'm game, and I will keep tryin."

"Good man," said the Captain, and lay his hand on Nobles' shoulder. Nobles looked at the hand, and the Captain took it away.

"Just one thing," Nobles said.

"And what is that, sir?"

Nobles looked at Wall Stutts. "It better be for the right reasons," he said.

"Freedom," said Gault. "That is the *only* reason."

Nobles gave a slow nod, then turned, walked back to where he had tethered Zeke. He mounted slowly, crossed his hands on the pommel again. When he spoke this time, he wasn't looking at any of them. "I am long past bein afraid of dyin," he said. "Just remember that." Then he turned the horse and disappeared into the black shadows of the cedar trees. In a moment, they could hear the horse's hooves in the mud of the road.

"You gon' trust him?" said Stutts.

"Not anymore," said the Captain. He looked at the sheriff. "Good night, Ben. You keep an eye on things, let us know how the wind changes."

"Sure thing, Cap'n," said Luker. After a moment, he spoke again, diffidently. "You want to know what I think, I—"

"Good night, Ben," said the Captain.

When the sheriff had gone, Wall Stutts cut a fresh chew of tobacco. "What you bring me here for anyhow?" he asked.

The Captain clasped his hands behind his back, looked thoughtfully at the stars. "We won't get any help from town—I should have known it all along. But no matter. With or without them, the time is nigh," he said.

"I been hearin that for months," said Stutts, but Gault ignored him.

"It's time to make a statement, Wall," the Captain said. "I have a job for you." As the other watched, Solomon Gault went to his mount and took a pencil and a leaf of good linen paper from his saddlebag.

"I ain't no goddamn mail rider," said Stutts.

"You'll like this delivery," said the Captain. "It's right in your line." Then he sat down on the overturned cookpot and, by the light of the stars, began to write.

◆　◆　◆

THE MOON, LIKE a guest arriving after the party, rose diffidently, a little shyly, as if it expected to be turned away. It was a three-quarters moon, pale against the spray of stars, but in the lampless dark it gave of a good light, made shadows, sculpted romantic shapes out of ordinary things. By the moon's light, cedar trees grew ominous, charred timbers and tumbled walls became the ruins of a mysterious civilization, empty windows the eyes of watchful giants. The soldiers' tents gleamed in the moonlight, and the smoke from their dying fires curled straight up in the windless air. The strident voices of the day and of the twilight were stilled to a thin drone of a cricket here, a katydid there. Great owls hooted in the oaks, and now and then sortied with a rustle of wings to glide across back yards, pastures, the empty black square of Cumberland. Dogs, stirred by the moon's rising, spoke to one another across the night.

Colonel Burduck had imposed a curfew on the towns within his reach, so, in the hour the moon rose, the only living men apparent in Cumberland were the sentries. These moved in a studied walk, eyes forward, their bayonets gleaming in the moonlight, guarding the Shipwright house, the box-car jail, the company streets, Audley Brummett's old livery where the stores and munitions were kept—guarding all these from the sinister possibilities of the night. But neither curfew nor sentries could deter the wakeful ones who traveled outward over the moonlit roads and into places where the shadows lay dark.

Molochi Fish did not know about the curfew, and would not have obeyed it if he had. Several times a week, he would leave the dogs shut away in the old pens where his pack used to live, and cross Leaf River at the gravelly ford. Then he would move through the woods and fields to town. He liked to go to town at night. He liked to watch the soldiers from the shadows. He would peek in windows and see what went on there by candlelight, observe the secret lives of people who crossed the street to avoid him by day. He would listen to their talk, their arguments, their love-making, hear the voices of children, the sounds of cooking, the rustle of a shuck mattress as a sleeper turned. He heard them mutter in their dreams, cry out. He watched them stumble groggily to the privy.

Dogs never barked at him; they would tremble, bare their teeth, back away to the length of their tethers or crawl under the house, but they never barked. Now and then Molochi would choose one, court it night after night until he could lure it out—it would come sooner or later, slinking, fawning, grinning at him—and he would put his hand on it, quiet it, give it a piece of bacon or bread.

On this night, Molochi was in town before moonrise. He was moving up the shadowed road when a great owl sailed out of the darkness, intent on some rat or possum. The bird was in Molochi's face before it saw him, pulled up, startled, and flapped away. Molochi never saw the bird, only the shape of it against the stars, and the soft rustle of it. He felt something about the silence of the owls, the great hunters. He was afraid of them, but he wished men could hunt at night like they could, or like the foxes, mov-ing quiet through the shadows where there was no sun to scald and burn.

The rising moon found Molochi hidden in the deep shadows of a clump of cedars near the place where old Frye's Tavern used to be. There was a new tavern now, and every night it was full of soldiers; he could hear them talking, laughing. Now and then he came here to watch them. He saw them come out and fight in the yard, or steal away into the bushes to vomit or relieve themselves. Always he would study them as they moved, singly or in groups, from the tavern to their camp—follow them even, gliding through the shadows at a little distance while they stumbled home, singing sometimes.

Tonight, Molochi felt something new hovering around the yard. He had come from the creek side, so whatever it was lay across the road where the cedars also grew thick and black with shadow. As he watched, he heard a soft rustle in the sky; he looked and saw the dark birds circling, then alighting one by one in the moon-fringed tops of the cedar trees. They made no murmur among themselves, though Molochi could hear them moving in the branches. From this, he knew that another watcher lay among the shadows across the road.

Molochi never carried a gun on these excursions, but he always had his knife. It was an old knife—he had forgotten where it came from—crudely made on the Bowie pattern, the hickory handle riveted together, the blade still bearing the marks of the original file but sharpened so often it had all but lost its original shape. Now it appeared in his hand; he could turn it and make it gleam in the moonlight.

The night smelled late when the tavern door opened and threw its rectangle of light into the yard. A soldier stood silhouetted in the open door, turned to say something, then closed the door behind him. He lingered unsteadily on the narrow gallery a moment, then carefully negotiated the steps, muttering to himself. Once in the yard, he stopped and raised his face to the moon. "Annie!" he cried, waving his arm across the sky. He stood a moment more, as if listening for a reply, then crossed to the road and staggered off toward the square. He had gone only a little way when a man glided out of the cedars across the road and followed him.

Molochi left his own watching-place then. Under the three-quarters moon, he followed the drunken soldier and the stalking man. The soldier went unsteadily up the road, stopping now and then to talk to himself; the other moved boldly in the moonlight a little way behind. Molochi stayed in the shadows, the knife still in his hand. Overhead, the dark birds circled against the stars.

The hour was late, and of a silence and emptiness that was almost tangible. When they neared the Shipwright house, the stalking man moved off the road and into the shadows, while Molochi passed down the creekbed behind.

A fog lay in the creek bottom, pale in the moon and thin as pulled cotton. Molochi felt it on his face, watched it swirl around his feet as he moved. He had to be careful on the slick bank lest his feet betray him; pale branches reached for him, and in places the brush was thick, and he had to move slowly. Passing behind the Shipwright house, he could see the sentry by the back porch standing motionless in a pool of moonlight. He was almost past when his foot slipped and broke away a chunk of the muddy clay bank. The splash was loud in the stillness.

"Who comes there?" said the sentry.

The moment that followed was like a glass dome lowered over Molochi Fish and the foggy creek bank and the soldier in the yard. Molochi saw the man lower his rifle, peer into the dark. "Who comes there?" the man said again, his voice taut with fear and with the loneliness that visits in the deep ruin of night. Molochi stood absolutely still, wrapped in the shadow of a sycamore tree. A dark bird lit in the branches and watched him in silence. Time passed, and there was no sound but the creak of frogs and insects and the whisper of the moving water. Molochi did not believe the sentry would move out into the dark, not by himself anyway. Sure enough, after a little while, the man relaxed. He searched the darkness for a moment more, then moved up onto the porch out of the moonlight. Molochi saw him lower his musket and put his hand against the boards, as if to reassure himself that he was not alone.

When it was safe then, Molochi moved on through the cool breath of the fog. He had no hope of catching the soldier and the stalking man, but he went on just the same, following the night birds now. They flew from branch to branch before him, still voiceless, making only a little flutter with their wings. He followed them into the ruins of the south side of the square, through the hollow shells of buidings, over rubble and ashes. Molochi had never entered these buildings when they were whole, and he moved through them now without any brush of memory.

Then he was in the fog again, once more moving slowly along the bank of the creek. He could see the bridge where the Oxford road crossed. The bridge was an indefinite shape against the stars, and under it was a deep pool of shadow in which something moved. Molochi passed into a stand of willows and stopped, kneeling, the knife blade lying across his thigh. He heard a sound, a sighing rush of air that came from the shadows under the bridge, and no sooner had it passed than he heard one of the night birds shriek: a high, piercing sound that drove across the darkness like a spear of light, then gone. The insects and frogs fell silent, and through the silence came another sound, a man breathing hard, in quick gasps, as if there were not enough air for him to breathe. In an instant, the man himself emerged from the shadows under the bridge, slipping in the mud, moving fast, bent over like a man running under fire. His moon shadow ran beside him, the legs scissoring. Molochi saw the gleam of the knife in his hand, saw him stop and look back once, then kneel and thrust the blade of the knife into the mud, and again, and again. Then the man rose and came running, breathing hard, and Molochi saw his face in the moonlight as he passed.

In a little while, it was quiet again. Molochi moved out of the willows and approached the bridge, watching the shadows beneath it. As he drew closer, he saw that it was not all shadow; the moonlight fell in dim ribbons through the planking and touched something there, a point of light, a reflection that winked with movement. Then he heard a low and sighing sound, like air moving through a bellows. Molochi knew then what he would find, and he crossed the threshold of shadow with the image already in his mind.

The soldier lay on his back, his eyes wide open, the air rushing through the glistening slash at his throat. Molochi squatted beside him and saw that he was very young, just a boy. The soldier turned his eyes on him, and Molochi saw the wetness of them, and as quick saw the light pass out of them. With his free hand, Molochi touched the boy's throat and felt the warm blood coursing. He could smell it, too, heavy and rank and mingling with the smell of raw whiskey and mud and dead fish in the shadows under the bridge.

· IX ·

Aunt Vassar Bishop made her nephew a good supper of biscuits and greens and the tiny breasts of robins old Priam had snared that morning. Afterward they went into the parlor where, in a little while, Priam appeared with a silver tray and a pot of English tea Aunt Vassar had saved for this moment, which she had never doubted would come.

The room was dressed for summer, with rush mats on the floor and linen covers on all the uncomfortable parlor chairs, and cheesecloth over the pictures on the walls (still lifes, mostly, and one of a lady playing a harpsichord, and a framed wreath fashioned from Gawain's mother's hair) and wispy linen curtains where, in winter, the heavy drapes hung. Gawain was surprised to see this old seasonal arrangement, and even more surprised to find that he had expected it.

"My lands, Aunt," he said, laughing. "The whole town burnt, and the war lost, and yankees everywhere, and you have put the parlor in summer dress."

"Well, it's summer, ain't it?" she said.

She did not press him on the war. In fact, she hardly spoke at all, sitting in her chair by the cold hearth with the teacup balanced on its saucer, and on the table beside her the glass of clear corn whiskey that she took every night since she weaned herself of laudanum. She let Gawain talk, and listened as he spoke a little of his travels—not much, and not of battles or marches, but of towns he had seen, and rivers, and high mountains, and of lads he had known who were gone. He asked after his sisters, whose faces and voices he could hardly remember, and Aunt Vassar told him what she knew of their lives and fortunes: of childbirths and of deaths, of scenes played out among people Gawain would never know. When he questioned her about his father, she answered plainly: he was incontinent, mad, and not likely to live long, and he had nothing left but the house and the ground it sat on. Before his sickness, Frank Harper had been vice president of the Mississippi Central Railroad and so was entitled to a pension. In the war years, the pension had been issued in Confederate notes, worthless now, and since the yankees came, the money had stopped altogether. The yankees had managed with great difficulty to keep the railroad intact, but they were not in the pension business. Gawain Harper heard these things, acknowledged them, and put them away.

Aunt Vassar reminded him that his own prospects, as a professor with no one to profess to, were not much better. Did he have any ideas?

"Sure, darlin," said Gawain. "I will turn to crime."

"Excellent," said Aunt Vassar. "Only, who are you goin to steal from? And to whom would you sell it if you did?"

"Mere details," said Gawain. He rose from his chair and paced before the mantel, the smoke curling from his pipe. He had finished the tea and now he, too, was sipping at a glass of corn liquor. It was imported stuff, brought across the hills from Tippah County by King Solomon Gault, who had also run the tea through the lines from God knew where. A little of the whiskey made Gawain dizzy. He hoped it would take the edge off his restlessness, but it didn't.

"Well," said Aunt Vassar at length, "I suppose we will make out."

"I do not intend to be idle," said Gawain. "I will do for you and Papa and"—he stopped, his hand poised in the air—"and any other orphans we might pick up."

"Hmmm," said Aunt Vassar. She rocked awhile, studying the whiskey in her glass. Gawain paced around the room—it was dimly lit by a pair of candles on the mantel—looking at the books and plaster fruit and statuettes of unlikely shepherds and maidens, picking up this one and that one as if seeing them for the first time. He came back to the mantel then and regarded the face of the curlicued porcelain clock that sat there, which Aunt Vassar brought from her trip to France long ago.

"Have you seen Morgan?" asked Aunt Vassar then.

"I have not," said Gawain, tapping his pipe stem on the clock's face. "Have I ever mentioned how much I hate this thing?" he said.

"So you have not made any attempt to—"

"Aunt Vassar Bishop," said Gawain, "this day was long before it even got started. I have not the energy to face the Judge, and I am too tired to go slippin about in the rose bushes right now."

"I see," said Aunt Vassar. She stirred a little sugar in her whiskey, the spoon tinkling in the glass. When she was done, she licked the spoon and set it carefully on the table and looked at Gawain. "I suppose you are right to be circumspect," she said, "given Nathaniel's temper, though most of that is put-on."

Gawain laughed. "I never heard that said of him."

"Never you mind," said Aunt Vassar. "I know him better than you, by twenty years. Truth to tell, his honor the Judge is scared to death right now that the yankees will haul him off to jail. Not this bunch, maybe—they are about as wore out as we are. But the vultures and the politicians will follow soon, now the fighting's over and the danger's gone. Having read the papers, they'll be jealous, and therefore less tolerant of the Judge's reputation. He was quite outspoken about all that secession foolishness, you remember."

"My God," said Gawain. "They already burned his house. How much does he have to pay before they let him alone."

Aunt Vassar shook her head and laughed. "You have a good deal to learn about the passions of them who have never been shot at. The Judge himself used to be a prime illustration, for the one year out of four it looked like we might win the thing. In victory, his kind ain't so quick to let bygones be bygones. You will see."

"Well, let it be amongst em," said Gawain. "You won't find me linin up to register for the vote."

"That's all right to say, when it don't touch you."

"Well, it don't."

"Yes, it does," said Aunt Vassar.

Gawain looked at his aunt then. The candlelight lay soft on her face, and he could see, in the light's illusion, the ghost of the girl in the portrait. Gawain turned away and spoke to the clock on the mantel. "No," he said. "I insist that it doesn't."

"You may insist all you want, and I with you, but that don't change what is."

"Then tell me what *is*," Gawain said testily.

"The Judge is going to Brazil and taking his folks with him," said his aunt. From her seat, Aunt Vassar could see the muscles tighten in her nephew's jaws. She went on. "The king down there has promised full citizenship, land—niggers too, for all I know—to anybody who wants to come. Nathaniel has said he will get up a party to go. He is trying to talk other malcontents into the thing before it gets too warm around here. All their families, too. It is madness, but I suppose we ought to be used to that by now."

Again Gawain made no reply, but stared hard into the clock's face, as if he might will it to stop, or vanish, or merely cease being what it was.

Aunt Vassar watched him a moment, then slammed her glass down on the table by her chair. He jumped at the sound, turned to find her glaring at him, the candle flame flickering in her spectacles. "I just thought you might be interested to know," she said.

"What would you have me do about it?" he asked.

"Do? Oh, I would have you do nothin atall. I am sure Morgan will flourish in the valley of the Nile."

"Aunt, the Nile is in—"

"I *know* where it is, sir," said Aunt Vassar. "Never mind. I won't mention it again."

Gawain knocked out his pipe in the hearth. "Aunt, I am told it was Solomon Gault who killed Lily. Has the Judge taken any action in the matter?"

"You mean, has he shot him down in the street?"

"*Yes!* That is just what I mean!" said Gawain. His voice was loud in the silent house. He reached up, snatched the clock in both hands.

"Don't you break that clock," said Aunt Vassar.

He put the clock down gently, but kept his back to her. In the mirror over the mantel, he could see his face.

"That burns you up, doesn't it?" she said. "Even worse than that other thing I said I wouldn't mention."

"It is none of my business," said Gawain.

"Just what exactly *is* your business, sir?"

"Aunt—"

"Don't 'Aunt' me. Point of honor: Nathaniel should avenge his daughter. Do you think it would change anything if he did? Would it make you less afraid of him—or more?"

"I am not afraid of him," said Gawain. "And anyhow, that is not the question."

"Oh, I thought it was," she said. "But you must not feel yourself ashamed. Morgan or the Judge—it is a point of honor either way, and you will do the right thing by both."

He turned from the mantel, hesitated an instant, then bent down and kissed her on the forehead. He had never done that before, not even at the depot on the day he left for the war. Aunt Vassar flinched away. "Quit that," she said.

"Point of honor," said Gawain. "I will see to it."

"Go to bed," she said.

So he bade her good night and took a candle and made his way up the shadowed stairs to his room. He stopped by his father's door, listened, heard nothing, passed on. In a moment he was standing at the window of his old room, looking out at the murmurous dark. The bed he had slept all his life in, covered by the same counterpane, lay waiting, but he had no interest in it. Tired as he was, he suddenly had no desire to sleep. He could smell the sweet-shrub and the damp oak leaves. " 'The curfew tolls the knell of parting day,' " he said aloud, wishing he had thought to say it at sundown when it would have made more sense.

A mirror hung over this mantel as well, and once more he considered the reflected image of his face, ghostly in the candlelight. He thought of the other face hidden behind the glass and wished he could draw it out somehow, bring it into the light again just so he could assure himself that he'd been here once. Again he was surrounded by the shapes and the artifacts of his old life, left just as they were on the day he turned from this room and closed the door behind him—forever, he had thought then. Maybe forever. Now he had returned, and all of it should have been familiar to him: the curtains, the bed, the fowling piece propped in a corner, the books slanted on their shelves—but in the wavering light of the candle he could find no corner of memory to accommodate these things. Then, moving restlessly about the room, he spied the carpet bag and hat and canteen, and the brushed frock coat that Priam had hung from the coat tree. These were his, he knew. Of all that had lain waiting for him in this room, these things alone could he touch and know they were still his own.

He sat on the bed and drew the carpet bag up beside him, and from it he took the ambrotype of Morgan Rhea. He opened the case and ran his finger across the crack in the glass. Her face was barely visible in the candlelight, but there she was, staring out at him with that same thoughtful expression, as solemn and remote as any of the portraits in the hall below. *Brazil,* he thought, and another line of old Tom Gray's ponderous "Elegy" came to him. " 'Full many a flower is born to blush unseen, and waste its sweetness on the desert air,' " quoth Gawain Harper, embarrassing himself.

He closed the case and laid it beside him on the bed, then rooted in the carpet bag and found his rosary. Father Denby Garrison, that old high-churchman, had sent the beads to Gawain while the regiment was still at Corinth, and he had carried them in his haversack throughout the war. Not once had Gawain Harper gone into a fight without the beads around his neck. When he searched for Sir Niles at Franklin, he had them in his hand. He held them now in his palm and studied the yellowed ivory beads, the medallion of Our Lady, the crucifix with its head-bent figure. All at once, he closed his hand around them, feeling the shape of the beads in his palm. "Point of honor," he said. He rose, quickly, and slipped on his frock coat. He put the beads in one inside pocket, the portrait of Morgan in the other, and left the room, closing the door softly behind him.

In the hall, Gawain stopped to consider. Since arriving in Cumberland, his only contact with the Federal authorities had been at the tavern when he had spoken with the pipe-smoking sergeant. He supposed there was some protocol for returning orphans of the defeated Confederacy; he also supposed that someone would tell him if there was. Certainly no one had officially informed him of the curfew. Aunt Vassar had mentioned it in passing, but Gawain did not consider her remarks on the subject official. And anyhow, for three years Gawain had been testing the limits of his luck; he saw no reason to end the experiment now. "All right, then," he said aloud.

He found he remembered which stair treads creaked, and he avoided them on his way down. The parlor was dark, his aunt gone to her room in the back of the house. The pictures in the hall were dark rectangles shrouded in cheesecloth. He stopped under the portrait of himself, peered at it, believed he could see in the ambient light the outline of the composed, solemn face looking down at him. Then he went on down the hall. The front door clicked softly behind him and he stood for a moment in the soft night, listening. Then he set out across the yard.

✦   ✦   ✦

MORGAN RHEA SAW the pale light of moonrise creep in her window. It fell across her brother Alex where he lay on a pallet on the floor; he stirred as if the light had brushed him, muttered some incoherent plea, then flung his arm out. His open hand lay like a night-blooming flower on the dark rug. Morgan watched him, wondering, as she always did, what pictures moved in his dreams. He had not slept well since their house was burned.

Morgan remembered the burning. The yankee General Hatch's men had forbidden them to take anything from the house but the clothes they wore that afternoon. They had stood in a cluster on the lawn—Mama and Alex and Morgan and the old negro Robert, who had not run away but who would die before the leaves turned—and they watched the house burn. Morgan forced herself to watch it, from the moment the flames licked through the windows until the last wall had crumbled, fallen back into the glowing ashes of everything they had owned, every material thing that had defined them. Her father's reputation had brought the yankees swarming into the yard, had sent the smoke rising in a great black pillar toward the sky. His intractable will had torched the house as surely as if he'd laid the fire himself, and now he stood apart from them as he had when the news of Lily came, offering no comfort, his back turned to the burning house, his eyes fixed on whatever it was he imagined lay beyond tomorrow. On that afternoon, she had hated her father with a bitterness hotter than the fire itself, and she believed, hoped, desired—demanded, almost—that it consume her as the fire consumed the house, wishing it would use up everything inside her and leave nothing but a shell, graceless and unfeeling and cold.

Not long afterward, she thought that what she had wished for among the smoke had been accomplished. At first, waking and sleeping, her mind prowled through the rooms of the vanished house, noticing things in memory that she had forgotten, hardly looked at, in life—things she needed, wanted to put her hand to and couldn't because they were gone forever. Then the emptiness she had wished for seemed to come upon her, and she put all that away at last. If she had made herself watch the house die, she could make herself quit watching it in memory, and so she did. Her waking hours became a long, vacant corridor through which she moved. When she walked about the town, her skirts dragging in the ashes, she had to remind herself that she was alive, that the faces she looked into were alive, that the faces and voices and the footprints in the mud were real and would not vanish with the cock's crowing. Then, when her father declared his intention of leaving this place forever, even the fact that she was alive ceased to matter. She had taken the news without interest. South America, Mexico, California, any one of the planets that whirled among the stars— no matter. A widow without prospects, she would go. She would take care of the old folks, and of Alex until he grew away, and one day she would be old, and another day she, like Lily, would cease to be at all.

Now she sat on the bed while the moonlight filled the window. She was still clothed, though her feet were bare; in the last hour, she had told herself a dozen times she would put her nightgown on and climb under the covers where it was dark and no one could get at her, but she hadn't. For the first time in many months—seasons, years it seemed—Morgan wished she could cry.

Crying was good, once. She had never been ashamed to cry, never thought of it as a weakness, never hesitated to employ it to her advantage. All her life she had cried easily, when she was angry or happy, sad or tired or sick, when the mystery of life moved her, when she wanted something she could get by no other means. All these, she felt, were legitimate reasons to cry, and the tears themselves but outward signs of her fervent heart—or (she was not afraid to admit) the handiest weapons in her arsenal. But crying was another thing she had lost the means for; it had come to seem so paltry a thing, and she had scorned it so long, and though she wished for it now, she knew it was denied her.

So she sat and listened to the night sounds, and to her brother's soft breathing, and to the tick of the clock on the mantel. That clock had been the Carter boy's. This was his room they occupied in Mister T. J. Carter's house, his bed she slept in, his things that lay on the dresser and hung in the wardrobe. Mister Carter had left them just as they were, and she had touched them all, remembering the boy's face, trying to see the room as he had seen it before he went away with the Cumberland Rifles and never came home again. Once in the early spring, she thought she had seen him. She came in the room at dusk and caught something that had just gone away—a shape, more a shadow than anything. She had not been afraid; in fact, she spoke his name, half-believing, half-hoping he might appear. But there was only the quiet end of day, golden and soft, and the silence of the empty room. She had not seen him again, nor had any sense of his being there. He was gone; she did not believe he would return.

So many were gone, and Morgan wondered sometimes where they were now—even her husband, whose face she could barely remember, who had died in California long before there was any war he might have gone to. She believed ghosts dwelt in the places they had known in life, but somehow these lost ones were different. They seemed not ghosts but empty intervals in the air, the light, as if the spaces were there waiting with nothing to fill them. As she moved about the town, past the galleries of houses and the blank doorways of burned-out stores, she had felt, in spite of herself, a strange sympathy with those who had gone. Here was a certain clump of chinaberry trees, there the pond by the old cowpens, there the hollow shell where Terrible Miss Chastain kept her school once. In all these places, Morgan felt—could almost see, she thought—an emptiness more complete, more final, than her own. The lost ones were dead, of course; she knew that, could understand that. But it was as if they had all returned once, like the Carter boy, and then gone again, leaving behind these vacancies in the air. She thought it might be the violence of their passing, the infinite waste and madness into which their lives had disappeared. Or the sorrow of it, perhaps—of coming once more to the places they had known, only to find that life was trudging on without them. Morgan could not say; she only knew that they were gone, and none of them lingered. She was glad, in a way, for she did not believe their souls could be at peace here. Let them go; it was enough that they had come to say goodbye.

Eventually she had allowed herself to believe that Gawain Harper was one of these lost ones. She had not grieved—*that* she could not allow—but she had taken to watching for him as she walked past Vassar Bishop's old house at odd times of the day, or strolled among the grim, eyeless walls of the burned Academy. She believed that she would see him if he returned, and that it would be in one of those places. She pictured him in a short gray jacket like the one the Carter boy had worn, with the same sad look in his eyes. He would be standing by the porch or perhaps in the place where his classroom used to be, where he had leaned on the mantel and listened to her read in a distant springtime. She knew that, if he came, she would have only time enough to lift her hand to him and speak. She could see it all in her mind, could see her hand and see her lips move. But she could not hear what it was she said to him, nor what he might say in reply. Then he would be gone, and she could see in her mind the empty place where he had been.

But he had never come, and now she understood why. Because he was alive too. That was the news the stranger had brought. Gawain had lived after all, was in the world, was even home now, probably at his Aunt Vassar's house this very moment. The thought brushed over her with a chill, and she realized she could not picture him now. She could see him dead, but not alive—what did that say about her? What did it say about them all? Only this afternoon, listening to the words Captain Stribling spoke, did she know how strongly she had believed in Gawain Harper's death, and how completely it had shaped the empty corridors of her days. Now the rules had changed, or at least the players had, and the pieces. Now the knight was back on the board.

She heard a whippoorwill. She had heard him every night since the early spring, but tonight he seemed closer, almost under her window. The query of the bird made her shiver again, as if he had spoken her name. She rose, found her shawl and, with one more glance at Alex, passed out of the room and closed the door behind her.

The house was still. It smelled of mildew, of neglect, of old people with their powders and physics and rusty clothes. Mister T. J. Carter had long since ceased to care about the house, and nothing Morgan or her mother said could stir the old man from his dream; no amount of bustling or cleaning could rid the house of its emptiness. Worse, Mister Carter still talked of his boy as if he were only gone down to the post office and might return at any moment, and there was nothing anyone could say to that.

She passed the front parlor, saw the dim flicker of a candle there, and by it the white crown of old Carter's head where he sat by the cold hearth. He was waiting even now, she thought, listening for a footstep on the porch, a tap at the window, the creak of a stair. One day soon, her family would be gone, and old Carter would be left here all alone, listening still. But not for long, she thought. He would not be here long.

Morgan, silent in her bare feet, glided by the parlor door, and in a moment stood on the broad gallery, looking up at the square columns that had taken the light of the moon. The whippoorwill had hushed his calling, but there were other voices, solitary and indifferent: the crickets, an owl, the reedy piping of toads down by the garden pond. She gathered her shawl around her and sat down on the front steps. "Gawain Harper," she said aloud, testing the sound of it. Then, louder: "Gawain?" She spoke into the dark, got only the sound of crickets in return. They fiddled blithely, and gave no answer she could use. "Gawain Harper, damn you anyhow!" she said, and her voice caught in her throat, and without any warning she began to cry.

✦　✦　✦

GAWAIN HARPER HAD never felt so alone. Never. He almost regretted leaving the house, almost wished he would stumble on a provost guard or a sentry just so he could hear a voice. But he kept to the shadows away from the main road, moving through the silent streets and yards toward something he could not name, was not sure he wanted to find. He knew only that he had to seek it, whatever it was, and that this was the time. And he knew this was better than the house, better than the dead air and the silence.

He marveled at how far he'd come in twenty-four hours. Last night at this time, he was lying on his cousin's gallery, watching the starlight on the road, wondering what he would find in the day ahead. Now he was here with the day behind him, and old Dial Ethridge, and the little fyce, and Molochi Fish, and Harry Stribling, and the fight at the tavern, and Aunt Vassar and his father. He wondered how old Harry was doing. In the morning, he would find out where he was and go see him and try to get him off. For now, though, he had to—

Had to what? He knew the answer to that, though he was careful with the thought. Honor was more fragile than he had ever imagined—that was one lesson he had learned amid the smoke.

He was behind the ruins of what had been the north side of the square when he heard them. Heart pounding, he slipped into the deep shadow of a wall and watched as a pair of cavalrymen—a provost guard, no doubt— passed by on the road, their horses' hooves squelching in the mud. They passed so close he could have counted the coils around their picket pins: Federal cavalry, for God's sake, taking their ease in the moonlight on the square in Cumberland, while Gawain Harper, citizen, cowered unarmed in the lee of the old Jenkins Hardware.

He waited in the shadow until his heart settled down and his breath had returned. What was the worst that could happen if they found him? Run him home. Clap him in the guardhouse. *They will not shoot you, boy,* he told himself.

The Carter house was east of the square, almost to the Episcopal cemetery where his mother lay beneath her weeping maiden of stone. In a little while, he turned that way, crossing the broad Holly Springs road, crouched and running like a fugitive. Had he looked up the road, he might have seen the shape of his own house where it sat in the bend, windows dark under the looming of the oaks. Instead he glanced south, and what he saw made him stop in the shadows and look again. On the far side of the square, a soldier was passing. Aunt Vassar had said the soldiers could go down to the tavern at night, and sometimes they got into devilment along the way. But Gawain saw in this lad the unmistakable carriage of one who wanted only to get to his blankets; forward-leaning, weaving at the quick march, the soldier reminded Gawain of himself on many a night in camp. The notion made him grin, and in spite of himself he felt a sympathy toward this unknown drunk who, but for the fortunes of war, might have been his comrade. He was about to turn away when another movement caught his eye. There, in the indistinct shadows across the square, might have been a second man; Gawain couldn't say for sure, and he peered hard across the moonlight, strangely uneasy all at once, as if his mind had registered something that his eyes had not seen. But the soldier had disappeared, and there was no more movement, and after a moment Gawain turned and passed between the chimneys of the old Bank of Cumberland, rattling boards and making a mess of his boots in the sodden ash.

❖   ❖   ❖

OH, CRYING HAD always been a good thing, yes, but tonight it was different. When she used to cry, first her emotions gave notice: an overture of sniffling, a burning in the eyes, a peculiar sensation under the bridge of her nose. Tonight, as she sat on the porch under the rising moon, Morgan Rhea was caught by surprise. The tears burst out of her, pushed out by a great sob that she had no time to stifle. The sound of it shocked her, as if she had shouted some obscenity into the dark, and she doubled over as if from a physical blow. Rebounding, she flung away her shawl and struggled to her feet, her face already wet; she wiped at the tears, wiped again and again until her hands, too, were wet, and now she heard the sounds she made. They seemed torn from her, a groaning and wailing dragged from somewhere deep in her throat. She had not summoned them and could not will them to cease, any more than she could have willed herself from retching. They seemed louder than any sound in the world, and they terrified her. She crammed her fists in her mouth and moved away from the house, out into the tall grass of the yard where her bare feet and the hem of her dress were instantly soaked from the dew. She saw herself alone then, spinning in the moonlit yard, and now her aloneness frightened her—but she

LONG REMEMBER ♦ 125

couldn't go back, not to the house, not even to her mother who slept in a
room heavy with darkness and defeat, and close with the dry smell of old
people.

She made her way to one of the oaks that stretched their muscular
trunks out of the grass. The trunk of this one glistened with roaches, but
she didn't care. She leaned against it, her chest hurting now, tears rolling
in great drops and a thick fluid running from her nose. She wiped at this
and brought away a ropy strand of it, but she didn't care.

She heard a sound overhead as if a flock of birds were passing, and out
of the shiny leaves, like rain, dark memories fell. Through the tall grass
coiled long serpents, bright of scale, each one reciting its own peculiar
litany of death, loss, smoke and flame, soldiers running, trains leaving—
one murmuring the names of those who had gone, another hissing *Who
are you to think we would not come?* and *Nobody is strong enough—
nobody, nobody*—until she pulled at her hair and cried for them to cease,
but they would not. Their time had come at last; they had found her in the
dark alone, and she had found the grief she wished for. She sank to her
knees, her body pressed tight against the oak, and covered her face and
wept.

♦   ♦   ♦

GAWAIN FINALLY GOT through the rubble of the bank (he had tripped,
barked his shins, nearly fallen into the cellar) and emerged behind the
buildings on the northeast corner of the square. Just beyond them, two
houses still stood facing the cemetery road; he passed warily through the
back yards, watching for dogs or for citizens who might take exception to
his wandering at this late hour. But the houses were dark and silent, and
all Gawain encountered was a cat, who allowed him to pet her before gliding off into the moonlight.

Presently, he came to the Church of the Holy Cross. He put his hand on
the arched red doors and for a moment thought of entering—of going no
further than the quiet, candle-smelling darkness of the old sanctuary where
even time trod gently, where the silence held you for as long as you would
be held, for as long as you needed to be held in the suspension of grace. It
was an illusion, of course, but Gawain suspected that God worked by illusion sometimes, that the deepest chamber of a man's heart was not so different from a child's: he craved a benign mystery and the assurance that
forces beyond his comprehension were working in his favor. So the temp-
tation was strong for Gawain to enter in, to surrender himself to the silence
and thus be absolved of his own foolish aims, his own will. Except he knew
that would not be an illusion, it would be a lie. He had journeyed long

with Death, and Death had refused him, and now he was left with freedom and life. To these he owed the responsibility of his will, and to cower in the church would satisfy nothing of the debt.

Yet, if he didn't enter, he could at least linger in the shadow of the church for a while. He found a dark place in an angle of buttress and wall, and there he knelt. He reached into his pocket, took out the rosary, and held it. Father Denby Garrison was no more; he had shot himself in the sacristy—by accident, so Aunt Vassar had said, repeating the common wisdom. But Gawain did not believe this any more than Aunt Vassar did. The notion was as absurd as keeping horses in the Presbyterian church; it was the groping of people trying to explain by simple means a truth so complex they could not grasp it, and feared it because they could not. Gawain made the sign of the cross with the beads and offered a prayer for the priest, that good man whose thoughts, in his last moment, no one would ever know.

Gawain hardly knew what his own thoughts were, as he knelt in the shadow of Holy Cross. He had never cared much for the night; his imagination always peopled the dark with mysterious prowlers, with watchers and whisperers who knew all about his sins and showed an interest in them. And though he might tell himself that the dead were only dead, in the dark he could never be sure *they* believed it. If there was ever a time when the dead might visit, this ought to be it, so he clutched the rosary tightly and prayed for all the dead, trying, as he prayed, to recall the faces of those he knew, and prayed even for those he did not know, that vast assemblage who lay sprawled across the wreckage of the past three years. When he was done, he leaned against the warm bricks of the church and prayed for himself, for Morgan, for all his people, and for grace to abide.

At last he arose and moved out into the moonlit emptiness of the old glebe where Father Garrison's milk cow used to graze. The far gate stood open, and Gawain went that way. At the gate, he stopped and listened. Just across the lane, beyond a grove of sentinel oaks, rose the pale flank of the Carter house, silent and dreaming. In one of the dark corner windows, a gauzy curtain trembled in the night breeze like a spirit beckoning. Gawain wondered if Morgan was sleeping in the darkness beyond it, and what she might be dreaming about up there.

Gawain moved across the lane and into the yard, trampling a bed of irises along the way, until he reached the corner of the house, and there he stopped, listening. Something out front, a sound above the night sounds. A mosquito stabbed him in the cheek, and he crushed it. He waited, pressed to the side of the house, one hand gripping the wire that ran down from the lightning rod.

He knew what he was hearing, and it scared him: a woman crying in the dark, alone in the deep midnight. For some reason, he thought of the stone maiden over his mother's grave, weeping like this when no one was about. *No, you don't,* he thought. He shook the image away and moved out of the shadows and into the moonlit yard.

He found her sitting on the ground, her knees drawn up, face cradled in her arms. She had reached the place in her crying where she could not catch her breath; the sobs were torn from her, strangling and hoarse. As he approached, he whispered her name, but she did not respond, and now the intensity of her grief almost panicked him. She seemed to be at the unraveled end of some immediate terror, some violation that still shuddered in the cool evening, so close it still threatened. Gawain felt a tingle at the base of his skull and remembered the figure he had sensed, but never seen, in the ruins of the square. He looked back, half-expecting the man to be crouched in the shadows behind him. But there was no one, nor any other sound but the monotonous drone of the crickets. Then he thought *No, I have seen this before* and remembered how it was: how a man might be sitting by the fire, or cleaning his musket, or bending to tie his shoe, and all at once he would crack open, lift his face in terror as some dormant image burst unexpected out of his fragile heart. Gawain had seen men cry like this, had heard the sounds they made as they tried to push closed the door of memory. Most times they succeeded and would slink away abashed while their comrades pretended to be busy with the fire. But sometimes a man could not close the door again. Then he might cry out and wave his arms and run madly away, the demons pursuing like a cloud of hornets— or he might sit upon the ground, moaning, rocking slowly back and forth, gone to a place where no one could reach him. This was the worst, for when his comrades knelt before him, they could see their own fate in the dull mirror of his eyes.

Gawain knew he had stumbled into a moment like that. He had no idea what demons had come, but he could feel them all around in the dark, and he held up the rosary so that the crucifix dangled from his fist, and he spoke her name again, not whispering now: "Morgan!"

This time she lifted her face, eyes wide, and struggled to her feet, her hand outstretched as if to push him away. She backed up toward an oak, and Gawain saw that the tree was covered in cockroaches, a glistening encrustation curved about the trunk like a sheet of smoky glass. "Don't!" he said. He spread his arms wide. "See? It's me, Gawain Harper, plain as day."

She stopped then, pulled her fists up under her chin and looked at him, struggling for breath. He could see her face clearly now: it was the face in the ambrotype, with a shadow blading across it where the crack was. He took a step toward her. "What's the matter?" he asked.

Suddenly she came alive with an energy he would not have expected. "Hah!" she said, mocking him in a harsh whisper. "What's the *matter*! The time to ask me that was—oh, I don't know, about last winter"—she stopped to cough; Gawain took another step toward her, but she halted him with her lifted hand—"about last winter, with all those battles in Tennessee, and nothin from you, not a word—"

"But I wrote you, Morgan! From Nashville and Tupelo and from 'way down in Alabama!" Gawain was a little pricked by the way things were developing, this clumsy arguing in the dark by a tree full of roaches, after he'd come all this way. But she wasn't through with him yet.

"Well, where have you been all the day?" she asked. "I had to find out from somebody else that you been in town since before dinner. Why didn't you let me know? Why didn't you!"

"Why Morgan, I—" Then he stopped, for he had no answer.

"Damn you, Gawain Harper," she said.

Gawain had a thought. He reached in his pocket, held up the gutta-percha case. "Look, Morgan," he said lamely. "I still have your picture." He opened the case, held it out to her. "It's broke, but I still have it."

She took a tentative step toward him. "I thought you were dead," she said.

"I am sorry," he said. "I wrote you. Good God, Morgan, why would I *not* write you?"

She took another step, then another, her arms clasped over her breasts, until she was close enough for him to smell the sweat of her. She lifted one bare foot and scratched it. Then she reached out and took the ambrotype from his hand, and in that moment, Gawain understood that, whatever else happened, he had closed one circle at least.

She looked at the picture, turned it into the moonlight so she could see it better, ran her finger down the crack. "It's broken," she said.

"I told you it was," he said.

She closed the case but didn't return it. "You know, I had nothing of yours," she said. She laughed softly. "I never saw you in a uniform. I thought you'd come back in one."

"But you said you believed I was dead," he reminded her.

"Yes," she said. "That's what I mean."

He understood then, and a chill touched him.

"What's that in your hand?" she asked, pointing.

Gawain opened his hand; the beads slipped through his fingers and dangled in the moonlight.

"Ah, Gawain Harper," she said. "Of course you would have that, out here in the dark." She put her hand out, touched the lapel of his coat. "Are you whole? I mean—"

He captured her hand and held it. "Oh, yes. I been hungry, mostly. I suppose the Judge has had a hard time. What about your mother? Young Alex? Yourself?"

"All well," said Morgan, "though I suppose that don't mean what it used to." After a moment, she said, "Papa is changed a good deal, after all these troubles."

That's real good, thought Gawain.

"How did you know to find me here?" she asked.

"My Cousin Rena," said Gawain. "I stopped at their place last night. She told me about your house. About Lily."

"Ah," said Morgan. "We have a lot to talk about, I reckon."

They were silent then, for a little while. Gawain heard the whippoorwill, and had the odd thought that perhaps it was the same one he'd heard in the fields last night, keeping watch. "It is grievous late," he said finally. "I will come tomorrow, if I may."

She did not reply, but lifted her face, her lips parted a little, and he kissed her then, lightly. From the roof of the old Carter house, a mocking-bird began to sing, as if Gawain had planned it himself.

✦　✦　✦

MOLOCHI FISH BELIEVED (though the notion had never taken any definite shape in his mind) that all men were guided by some elemental Mover, as a blown leaf, a night bird, a floating log are moved by air and water. Thus he was driven away from the bridge and through the town, through the bricks and ashes of the square. He moved silently behind tents where no lanterns glowed in this late hour, where people sometimes moaned in their sleep or their rutting, or talked in whispers about things he could not imagine. He shied away from these hushed voices, for whispers had a way of following him in the dark. He stopped once to wash the boy's blood from his hands in a puddle in the road. Kneeling there, he smelled the rank mud of the creek on his boots, so he washed them too, scrubbing the mud away with his hands.

Later, he rested within the hollow shell of a building. The air was dead there, and it reeked of ashes and old pigeon droppings. An iron safe, its door yawning open, crouched in a corner. Molochi could see stars through the empty windows, and he saw the restless night birds perched around the roofless walls. They dipped their beaks at him. They swiveled their heads and nudged one another, and their eyes caught the moonlight like little jewels. Then, all at once, a stirring moved them, as if they'd caught some signal from among the stars, and, as Molochi watched, they all took flight, their wings beating the dead air without sound as they lifted from the wall. He followed them, and in a little while found himself in the burying ground that lay beyond the town on a hill all its own. He squatted in the deep shadow of a wall, breathing hard. Nothing stirred in this place, not even the wind, and the voices of the summer night were stilled. All around, the stones and monuments gleamed in the moonlight and threw black shadows over the rank grass. One of these was a tall shaft, and atop it stood a woman, arrested for eternity in an attitude of grief, her cold hand outstretched toward the sleeper below. A dark bird perched on her shoulder. In a little while, Molochi crept toward her and knelt at the base of the shaft. Even in the moonlight, he could discern the strange marks cut deep in the stone:

HARPER

JANE ELLEN
b. Herefordshire July 18, 1805
d. Cumberland, Miss. July 18, 1855

Seek him that maketh the seven stars
and Orion, and turneth the shadow
of death into the morning . . .

As he had done on other occasions, Molochi ran his fingers over the marks. He did not wonder what they meant, for he was not aware that they meant anything at all. Presently he looked up. The bird had flown away, and Molochi found himself looking at the woman's face, at her eyes mysterious with shadow, her outstretched hand graceful and white against the stars. Her gown seemed to flow in liquid movement where the moon lay upon it. Molochi wanted more than anything else in the world to touch her face, to feel the smoothness of it under his hand and trace the eyes, the cheekbones, the lips, the curve of the throat. But she was too high, out of his reach, and all he could do was look up at her.

He could not say how long he knelt there, but at last he curled himself against the cold marble and slept until the constellations dimmed and the sun began to rise. Then he rose himself, cold and stiff and bitten by mosquitoes, and looked at the woman again. The sun was just touching her face, and now he could see it with startling clarity against the pink sky. The life wreathed about the woman by the moon was gone, the face empty, the eyes become blank orbs and the hand mottled with mold. Molochi, standing now, found her within his reach after all; he touched her feet where they rested in stone sandals, and he found them cold, like his mother's feet as she lay on the cooling board in the cabin by the mill. Molochi looked at the woman now without any feeling at all; he saw in her transformation evidence of the only truth he knew: that life was illusory, and when it passed, nothing was left but stone.

· X ·

At the first break of day, the dog opened his eyes to discover a yellow tomcat sitting on the woodpile, not a dozen paces distant. A mockingbird perched overhead in the branches of a hackberry tree, flicking its tail and chipping irritably; now and then the bird would sortie, diving on the cat, actually brushing it with a wing. Then the bird would settle on the end of a log in the woodpile, hop nervously for a moment, and retreat to the tree again. The cat, meanwhile, stared straight ahead, only flinching a little at the touch of the bird, his eyes narrowed into slits. *Just a little closer, you son of a bitch,* the cat seemed to say.

It was a morning ritual, and the dog, whose name was Beowulf, took no interest in it. He lapped out his tongue in a yawn, raised his hindquarters and stretched. He had his own ritual: yawning, stretching, scratching, licking. He champed with his teeth at the wakening fleas that swarmed on his belly; he inspected his privates and gnawed his tail. Then he was ready.

Beowulf belonged to Mister L. W. Thomas, and his usual sleeping place was under the Citadel of Djibouti. It was dry under there, and comfortable, though there were a good many fleas and it tended to get noisy sometimes, what with all the stamping on the floor above. Last night the racket had driven him out, and he had slept in the muddy yard with mosquitoes whining about his ears. As a result, he was stiff, and damp from the heavy dew, and he seemed hungrier than ordinary, as if his fractious dreams had used him up. He knew his boss would not be astir so early in the day, but no matter: Beowulf had his morning rounds, and these would take him through the soldiers' camp where he could always get a handout if he looked pitiful enough. That was easy for Beowulf, who was naturally pitiful with his ribbed flanks and rheumy eyes.

He set out across the yard, ignoring the cat who bowed its back to him. The morning was fresh and full of smells, the light pink and soft, and all the shapes of things soft, too, as if the night had worn away the world's hard edges and angles. Spiderwebs, silvered with dew, hung in the grass, and a delicate mist floated in the air. Beowulf flung his nose up and took it all in—too much, and he had to stop and sneeze. Then, as he was about to set out again, he smelled the dark thing.

He had come to the cedars that squatted in a clump by the road. Daylight had not yet penetrated among them, and the smell was coming from the shadows there, so strong that his hackles raised. He knew the scent. It was there sometimes in the morning—in the grass or among the cedars—and always it seemed to make a black hole into which he might fall if he got too close. Beowulf circled the little cedar grove, his nose down among the leaves and needles and mud, and on his first circuit, he found the place where the dark thing had come out. He raised his head and looked up the road. He did not want to follow the smell; he wanted to go on up through the yards to the soldiers' camp where they would be frying bacon and making corn cakes and coffee like they did. But this morning the scent seemed to draw him; it was a message he had to unravel. Beowulf could recognize Purpose, as when Mr. L. W. Thomas set him to find squirrels or rabbits in the wood. This time there was no man with a gun, no commands, but Purpose was there just the same. So he lowered his nose again and began to trot, tacking from side to side, his long hound's ears dragging the ground.

So many smells, but the one scent stood out among them all. Beowulf tracked through the weeds beside the road, ignoring the town coming to life around him. He was led behind things: behind a greasy wall tent where a man stood half naked, splashing himself with water while a woman built up her fire; behind the Shipwright house where some of the soldiers lived (here the smell took him on a wide circuit, down along the bank of Town Creek which flowed behind the house); then at last behind the rubble of the old buildings on the south side of the square. Here he had trouble, for the dark thing had moved in and out among the ruins, and the wet ashes were bad for the nose. But Beowulf straightened it out and found the trail again, and suddenly he was on the Oxford road, on the bridge over Town Creek, then down in the tall slippery grass of the bank, down to the water, under the bridge.

He stopped, and his lips curled up over his yellow teeth. He moved back, legs stiff, feet sliding in the gray, slimy mud that smelled of dead fish and of the crusty droppings of swallows. He stopped again, quivering, then eased forward, his nose thrust out. Closer he came, and closer, the scent of the dark thing mingled now with the smell of the shape that lay before him. Flies rose from it, swarming angrily. Beowulf jerked back when a rat popped up; the creature watched him over its folded hands, then dropped to all fours and scuttled away. Beowulf sat down carefully in the mud. He began to howl, low at first, then rising to such a mournful note that men came querying. They peered down at him from the road. After a moment, one of them made the slippery descent and peered into the shadows under the Town Creek bridge.

✦   ✦   ✦

THE CARTER BOY'S room was on the southwest corner of the house, so it got no sun by its windows in the morning. However, at a certain moment each day around the summer solstice, when the sun broke above the trees around the cemetery, a single bright ray pierced an eastern window. It slanted across the hall and through the open door and struck the mirror on the west wall, where it would flash against the eyes of a sleeper in the bed. So every morning this June, Morgan Rhea awoke to the notice of the sun.

This morning she was laughing, and the sound made young Alex stir on his pallet. She heard herself laughing, then woke to it: a bright sound like a bubble bursting, like a bell or a fall of water. She loved the sound of her laughing and raised her arms out of the damp sheets and flexed her fingers, feeling the grin on her face. She felt light and airy, felt bright inside, and clean.

She leapt out of bed and crossed to the open front window, leaned out into the cool air smelling of rain and oak leaves and smoke. There was the yard, the oaks, and beyond them the cemetery road. The sun streamed in golden banners down through the trees and through the mist that lay along the ground. "My God," she said. Her hands flew to her hair, then down her face, over her breasts and down to her hips. "My God," she said again, and her face burned with shame and unbelieving and delight.

Alex stirred on his pallet beneath her; she realized she was straddling him, her nightgown over his head. "Lordy!" cried the boy. "Where am I!"

"Hey, boy!" she said, hopping away, laughing. "Get up! Turn out!" The boy curled himself, pulled the quilt over his head. She prodded him with her foot. "Hey!"

The boy snatched the quilt down and glared at her. "What's the matter with you, can't you let a feller—it ain't a school day—it ain't—"

But she was gone, out the door and into the hall and at last out onto the upper gallery where the morning wrapped itself around her like soft cotton. A carpenter bee was drilling under the balustrade, wasps were building overhead, a sparrow flitted past with a straw in its mouth. She gripped the railing with her hands and felt her face grow hot again. Shame indeed!

"Morgan, what are you *doing*, child?"

She whirled at the sound of her name. Judge Nathan Rhea stood in the hall, the sun from the east window cutting across the white of his shirt. "Papa?" she said, and crossed her arms over her breasts, realizing all at once how naked she was.

"You seem to be standing on Mister Carter's gallery in your night-clothes," said the Judge, coming into the doorway. "Unaccountable behavior." He looked at her bare feet, as if he had never seen them before. "My lands," he said.

"All right, Papa," she said. "I'll come in."

But the Judge didn't move. He stood in the doorway a moment, looking past her, fumbling with the key that dangled from his watch chain. Then he came out on the gallery and stood beside her at the balustrade. Morgan felt the strangeness of it; since the burning of the house, she had spoken to her father hardly at all, nor stood this close to him with no one about. Now he was so near she could touch him, and she found herself wanting to, if only to test whether he were really alive. He seemed suddenly frail, as if something had gone out of him since the last time she had really looked at him, that afternoon on the lawn with the smoke rolling by. She wondered what he saw out there in the bright morning, if it was the same world she saw. She touched his sleeve, felt the living flesh beneath it. "What do you see, Papa?" she asked.

"I was only thinking," said the Judge. He turned then, and again Morgan understood how long it had been since she'd looked at him. "Then what were you thinkin about?" she asked.

"Freedom," said the Judge. Then, without looking at her again, he passed through the door. She could hear his footsteps in the hall, then descending the stairs, then the closing of a door somewhere in the house.

Morgan turned back to the morning. She felt the breeze move through the thin cotton of her gown, felt the grit of the gallery floor under her feet. She leaned out and turned her face eastward toward the sun; there, through the trees, she could see the musing stones and monuments of Holy Cross cemetery. She caught a glimpse of movement: a woman, all in black, passing up the rise toward the circle of cedars on the crest. Someone calling on the dead, moving slowly, remembering. Squinting her eyes, Morgan could see that the woman carried a basket over her arm, and in the basket a white blur—daisies, Morgan thought, such as grow by the roadside in the early summertime. Now came the old, familiar tingle under the bridge of her nose, and in a moment Morgan Rhea was crying, but easily, without pain. "Long remember," she said to the woman yonder on the hill. "Long remember." Then she turned away, and passed into the cool hall where the sunlight slanted.

✦   ✦   ✦

WHEN THE SUN had warmed him, but before it got too high, Molochi
Fish left the burying ground. The night birds were gone now, and he was
glad of it. At the iron gate, he met a woman entering. She was all in black,
and carried a basket of white flowers. When she saw Molochi, she made a
wide path around him, never looking at him. Molochi passed through the
gate and made his way down the road.

He had gone just a little way when he saw the house among the oaks.
Molochi knew the place—he had sold firewood here in past winters—and
he stopped for a moment to observe it. The white houses of the town had
been a mystery to Molochi all his life. Though he had never entered, he
would often visit one or more of them on his nocturnal scouts and peer
through the windows. Save for chairs and tables, he had no name for anything he saw, nor could he imagine what use any of it would be. He watched
the people move among the rooms, and sometimes he could hear them talk.
What they said was as meaningless to him as the chatter of birds.

Now he looked toward the house—it seemed not so white now, he
thought—and saw a woman on the gallery. For an instant he thought it
was the woman from the cemetery, the stone maiden by whom he had
slept, only alive again, the breeze moving in her gown. He knelt in the
roadside weeds and watched carefully. He hoped it was not her. He could
not have her following him, did not want to see her among the others who
moved about his cabin in the dark. Then another person came out: a man,
white-haired, in a black frock coat that reminded Molochi of some of the
night birds. They stood together, looking out over the yard. Molochi knew
the man, and now he knew who the woman was. He had seen her in the
town, the daughter of old Judge Rhea, the man who'd sat on the high seat
in the courtroom and looked down on Molochi after the killing of old
Harper's nigger boy. Molochi remembered that. He remembered how the
words he could not understand flowed over him as he stood beneath the
Judge's seat, and the people looking at him, murmuring. He remembered
the month in a cell in the county's jail where he'd nearly gone mad with
pacing, pacing, and the barred window too high for him to see anything
but the sky—light and dark, light and dark, to mark the slow passage of
time—and the voices of other men, and the howling of dogs in the night,
and the night birds perched on the sill of the high window, watching him
as he slept curled on the stone floor. He watched now until the old Judge
went away. He saw the woman look off toward the cemetery and speak
words he could not hear, then she, too, was gone.

Molochi carried the vision of her in his head as the Mover drove him through the morning, down to the soldiers' burying ground to see if they were digging the grave.

✦ ✦ ✦

GAWAIN HARPER HAD been awake a long time when daylight came. He watched it from the back gallery, watched the light diffusing out of darkness, the shapes of trees and the well-house and the old kitchen taking their places in the world again. The morning smelled of cedars and oaks and wood smoke, and of the mist that hung above the grass. Squirrels were busy. Out of the wood beyond the yard a buck emerged, and after him a pair of does, and they grazed calmly in the grass, the mist moving around their feet. The hollow place in his stomach spun a thought: he would find a rifle, borrow one if he had to, and tomorrow— but he shook it away. He would not kill that deer. The squirrels maybe; though, as Stribling had said, you shouldn't take squirrels in the summertime. He watched the buck lift his head. "Hey!" Gawain said, and marveled at the swiftness of them, how they disappeared into the brush without even the quiver of a leaf.

He had slept in his clothes a little while, but rose while it was still dark, and crept once more down the stairs, this time with the tin cup and boiler and sack of coffee from his carpet bag. He had built a little fire in the back yard and boiled his coffee, and now he had it with him on the back gallery, watching the morning come. He had his pipe, too, though it always made him cough when he smoked it so early. He had a thought and smiled at it: for years he had dreamed of being home in his old bed, of sleeping the clock around with no sergeant to come and roust him, no drums beating reveille, none of the farting and belching and loud talk men indulged in when they woke in camp. Now here he was, sleepless, his bed not even turned down, awake at daylight even though he was free. *Ah,* he thought. *Freedom, freedom, freedom.* It was all right. He was awake because he wanted to be.

He remembered the night, and how he found Morgan in the yard of the Carter house. Now it was morning. Gawain sipped the last of his coffee and lay the blackened, dented cup beside him on the paintless boards of the gallery. He filled his pipe, struck a lucifer and touched it to the bowl and sent up a plume of smoke. He thought of the way Morgan had felt against him, and the remembrance caused a stirring in him, a movement that pleased and embarrassed him all at once. He shook his head and was blushing pink as the day's beginning when Harry Stribling came around the corner of the house.

"Good God," said Gawain, rising to his feet.

Stribling was startled as well. He turned a little dance in the wet grass, his hand against his breast. "Dammit, boy," he said. "What you doin out here, ambushin me again?"

"Dammit yourself," said Gawain. "Sneakin around here, and the day just breaking. I thought you was hauled off to the guardhouse."

"I was," said Stribling. He took off his hat and fanned himself with it. "When they changed the watch this morning, that provost—von Arnim?"

"I don't know him," said Gawain.

"Well, of course you wouldn't. Anyhow, he told us to skedaddle, told us we would get no more free meals off the national government. I think it was his way of being kind."

"Well, did you eat last night?"

Stribling laughed. "I should say. 'Bout dark, that man from the tavern came down—Thomas? but you don't know him either—with a boy pullin a handcart with a pot of stew in it and some bread and coffee. The stew had chunks of—"

"Hush," said Gawain. "My stomach is rubbin my backbone this mornin."

"Well, mine too, but at least I am a free man. Did you spend a good night?"

"Hah," said Gawain. "Let me poke up this fire—I got some coffee left. Then I will tell you of my adventures, and you can tell of yours." He looked at Stribling. "You got a noble black eye," he said.

Stribling nodded. He knelt by the fire, began to rearrange the unburnt sticks and twigs that lay around the white scattering of ashes. "A soldierly fire," he mused, almost to himself. Then he said, "The bluebellies are restless as ants this mornin—somethin happened in the night to stir em up, I think."

Gawain looked up sharply. Again he saw the soldier on the square, saw the vague suggestion of movement among the hollow walls. The image, he realized, had been fluttering in his mind like a bird trying to light. Now it had found its place.

"What?" said Stribling. "What's the matter?"

Gawain shook his head. "I'll tell you," he said, "but for God's *sake* let's boil the coffee first."

✦　✦　✦

AS GAWAIN AND Harry Stribling boiled their coffee, Colonel Michael Burduck was balancing himself in the greasy mud under the Town Creek bridge. He ignored the flies that hummed around his head, ignored the citizens clustered on the bank behind him, ignored the voice of the creek and the fresh morning that had come after the rain, ignored the officers who stood beside him with their hands on their swords. His attention admitted nothing but the thing that lay before him in the barred sunlight under the bridge.

Private Tom Kelly lay on his back, forearms lifted, hands knotted into fists. His mouth was open, and beneath it another, darker, mouth gaped where his throat lay open to the backbone. The mud around him was murky with his blood.

Burduck stood in a pale cone of fury, completely isolate and out of time, as if the earth and all in it were the business of a remote and alien star. He felt the air against his skin, felt the blood bulging in the veins of his temples, heard the mechanical pumping of his heart as it maintained the illusion of life. But he was gone deep into the core of himself, where nothing lived but the white-hot furnace of his anger. He was in a place where there was no room for logic or humanity, no capacity for regret or sorrow or desire or anything but vengeance, where even the voice of his own reason was muted and distant, like a lost child calling in a fog. Still, the voice was there, and he knew he must heed it, else he would be lost in time again, and useless. He closed his eyes and followed the voice, and as he listened, it became that of Rafe Deaton shouting, "Give way! Give way, goddammit!"

Burduck opened his eyes, turned and saw Deaton—hatless, in his shirt-sleeves, suspenders dangling—shoving through the crowd of civilians by the creek bank. He got clear of them, slipped and sank to one knee in the mud, made to rise and slipped again. He raised his face; his eyes focused on the officers who were all watching him now. "Colonel?" he said.

Captain Bloom began to speak: "Deaton, where's your—" but Burduck gave an almost imperceptible shake of his head, and the officer stopped.

"Colonel?" Deaton said again, as he rose carefully to his feet. His hair, shot with gray, was ruffled with sleep; his eyes moved quickly, darting from Burduck's face to the shadows behind him. Rafe Deaton had been first sergeant of Burduck's first company, way back when the regiment was at Jefferson Barracks before the war.

"What is it, Deaton?" asked Burduck.

The sergeant, suddenly embarrassed, drew himself up and nodded at the officers. "Beg pardon, sirs," he said. Then, to Burduck: "Colonel, is it really Tom Kelly?"

"I am told it is," said Burduck. "Tom Kelly was the boy's name."

"Ah," said Deaton. "Of course it would be him, of course it would."

"He was one of yours?" said the Colonel.

"He was," said Deaton. "He ain't ever hurt anybody."

Burduck looked at his shoes; the others stood quietly, waiting. A king-fisher planed down the creek, chattering, and disappeared into the willows. After a moment, Burduck looked up again and spoke quietly. "Sergeant Deaton, you know better than to walk out like that. Go back and fetch your blouse and your kit. Assemble a detail, five men. Bring a litter." Then, as an afterthought: "Roust out some musicians. They can play this boy back to camp."

"I will, sir," said the sergeant. Out of uniform, he did not salute, but bowed slightly from the waist and turned.

"Deaton!"

The sergeant stopped. Burduck moved closer, almost touching the man. "Steady, Rafe," he said, so low that only the sergeant could hear. "We will have the son of a bitch. We will put him against a wall."

"I will hold you to it, Colonel," said Deaton, and moved away. Burduck watched until he was gone, then stood a moment longer, staring at the crowd. They began to shift uncomfortably under his gaze, and Burduck had to struggle against the urge to speak to them. Finally, he turned back to his officers. "Mister von Arnim," he said.

"Sir."

"Cover this boy. Clear away these citizens, post a strong guard on the bridge until Deaton returns. Then fetch me that fellow from the tavern. Mister Bloom?"

"Sir."

"Parade your company, sir. Inform them that until further notice, no one is to leave camp unless his duty requires it, and any man leaving camp after retreat will be bucked and gagged. Have a negro dig a grave in the cemetery. Mister Osgood?"

"Sir," said a fresh Second Lieutenant of infantry, West Point class of '65.

"Stay with the body. When Sergeant Deaton comes with his party, you must bear it to the color line. Inform me when this is done, I'll be in my quarters. Keep these goddamned citizens away, too."

"Sir," said the Lieutenant, throwing a nervous glance at the body of Tom Kelly.

"Be about it then," said Burduck.

When the two officers had gone, Burduck lingered a moment. He knelt by the body for the first time and examined it, waving the flies away. The boy's legs, in their sky-blue trousers, were stretched full length, the shoes caked with drying mud. He wore his fatigue blouse open, and a striped shirt buttoned to the throat. The skirt of the blouse was twisted under him, the shirt pulled out of the waistband. Such was the way of dying men; they seemed to always tear at their clothes, as though they might shuck off the dark thing that was enveloping them. Burduck looked at the boy's face. The eyes were half open, the irises dry and fixed on the bridge timbers overhead. Burduck tried to close them, but they were stiff with rigor. He was about to turn away when he noticed a sliver of white under the flap of the boy's blouse. He moved the garment aside and, with two fingers, removed a square of folded paper. It was good paper, not the pulpy stuff soldiers usually wrote on, and it was free of blood. Even before he opened it, Burduck knew that the paper was not Tom Kelly's, that he would find in it a message from out there in the night country where he had been himself and where he did not wish to go again. He looked at the paper in his hand and knew that, when he opened it, the easy times would be over and nothing would be the same again. He had thought it would be the women, that somehow their intractable hatred, which transcended all suffering and even defeat itself, would set the sky aflame once more and bring the horsemen galloping in the dark. But the women's hatred, he saw now, was more tragic than that, and had nothing to do with this boy under the bridge, nor himself, nor the uniforms they wore, nor even the victory of which they were avatar and reminder. The women, he thought, hated the night country itself, and would always hate it and never forgive it, and might even vanquish it as the soldiers had not, could not, by the mere exercise of force. But that was something for another day, Burduck thought, as he unfolded the paper and read.

Deo vindice, it said.

Burduck lifted his eyes. Beyond the bridge, he saw the light falling through the leaves, glazing the creek with silver. Near the bend, a heron stood motionless in the shallows; as Burduck watched, the bird speared the water with its beak and brought up a wriggling fish that shook droplets clear and bright as ice into the sunlight. Burduck rose to his feet, his knees popping, and the heron flapped away with its prize. "Mister Osgood!" Burduck said.

The Lieutenant had been watching from the creek bank. "Yessir," he said, springing to attention.

"Come over here, Osgood," said Burduck. "This boy won't hurt you."

The young officer approached, his mouth a thin line, his eyes straight ahead.

"You were never in battle, Mister Osgood," Burduck said.

"No, sir."

"This is worse," Burduck said. "You are not going to be sick, are you." It was not a question.

The Lieutenant swallowed. "No, sir," he said. "I won't be sick, sir."

"Carry on, then. And Osgood?"

"Sir?"

"It will be all right if you stand down by the water."

"Thank you, sir," the Lieutenant said.

✦   ✦   ✦

"IT WAS A white soldier, jes a boy," old Priam was saying. "They found him under the Town Creek bridge with his th'oat cut year to year."

"God above," said Aunt Vassar. She was in her chair by the hearth again, a plate of hoecakes on her lap. Gawain leaned on the mantel, and Harry Stribling, also with a plate of hoecakes and a three-tined fork and a tin cup of coffee, sat on the parlor organ stool. Priam stood with his back to the fireless hearth, his hands tucked under the tail of his frock coat as if he were warming himself. He had just come from town where Aunt Vassar had sent him to learn the news.

Gawain had talked with Stribling before his aunt came down. He had told of his meeting with Morgan, and of the odd thing he had seen on the square. Now both men thought of this in the light of Priam's report. They swapped a look, but said nothing.

"It might have been one of their own that did it," said Aunt Vassar. The men were silent. Stribling swabbed at the molasses in his plate. "Those yankees are not like ordinary people," Aunt Vassar went on, as if no one in the room had ever seen a yankee. "They have peculiar ways."

"Surely," said Gawain.

"Still, it is a vicious thing," said his aunt. "You say he was just a boy?"

"Yes'm," said Priam.

"God above. Who would do such a thing?" Aunt Vassar said.

Later, Gawain and Stribling were smoking on the gallery, where Zeke was tied to the balustrade. "You will stay around here for a little while, won't you?" Gawain asked.

Stribling shrugged. "I have no immediate prospects. Might hang about, marry a rich widow, run for the legislature."

"I thought you had principles now."

"Ah, yes," said Stribling. "I forgot."

"Well, you can stay in my sisters' room, if you can stand the frills and the wallpaper. I expect their diaries are still there; they make interesting readin, as I recall."

"I am obliged," said Stribling. He went down the steps and gathered Zeke's reins. "This boy ain't had the saddle off him in two days. Is there a place I can put him up?"

"We got a crib in back. Might be an old currycomb in there. We'll shin around, get him some feed. Mister Audley Brummett will have some, I bet."

"Obliged," said Stribling. "That would be good."

Gawain felt suddenly animated, as if he had drawn into himself the life of the new summer day. "Why, we can go to lodge," he said. "Go fishin down on Leaf River. Maybe start us a business—a school maybe. I been thinkin—"

"Gawain," said Stribling.

"What?"

"Who you think cut that boy's throat?"

Gawain looked off into the yard. "What do you care?"

"You don't mean that," said Stribling.

"No, I do not," said Gawain. "It grieves me. It is not like killin one in a fight."

"Do you think it was the fellow you saw on the square last night?"

"I never really saw him," said Gawain. "It was more like I saw where he'd *been,* if you know what I mean. Hell, it was spooky out there—might not've been anybody at all, just shadows, or imagination. I have a wondrous imagination. Besides, there was yankee cavalry all over the place."

"A lot of good they did," said Stribling.

Gawain tapped his pipe on the balustrade. "La, la, la," he said, gazing out at the yard.

"What?"

Gawain looked around in surprise. "Why, Harry, I forgot you was here. I was just thinkin about the mounted arm and all the times they was so very useful in the war. You know, I once saw a cavalry man cut down a live Plymouth Rock with his saber, and that at full gallop—the hen, I mean. The cavalryman was standing still, or his horse was anyhow, and—"

Stribling snorted. "You may kiss my leathery buttocks, sir, not having any of your own to speak of."

On the road, just visible through the trees, an army wagon creaked ponderously townward, a crowd of black children following in its wake. Their voices rose in a high, sweet gabble, like the calling of young birds. Stribling threw the near stirrup over Zeke's saddle and loosened the cinch; the horse looked around curiously, as if such a thing had never happened to him before, then heaved a great sigh, like a woman coming out of her corset.

"Harry," said Gawain.

"Now what?"

"Harry, I have to go see the Judge today, there is no way around it. If I don't go today, I might not go at all."

"All right, let us go then," said Stribling.

"You don't have to."

"Oh, I wouldn't miss it," said Stribling. He dropped the reins and moved to the bottom of the steps, his eyes on a level with Gawain's. "You ever feel like things are runnin off and leavin you?" he asked.

"Yes sir, I have felt that way in my time," said Gawain. He looked off into the yard again. "I feel that way now, if you must know."

"Me too," said Stribling, "and I don't know why. At least you have a reason. Maybe I am just wore out. Maybe—" He stopped, and cocked his head as if he were listening to something. "Gawain?" he said.

Uh-oh, thought Gawain. "What?"

"He crossed at the ford, by the gravel bar," said Stribling.

"Who did?"

Stribling didn't answer. Zeke stamped his foot and whisked his tail silkily at a fly. The morning was still, no breeze, nothing moving in the leaves above. Then a blackbird sailed through the yard like a fugitive thought, or a word someone had forgotten to speak.

◆   ◆   ◆

A STAND OF willows, delicate and lightly green, grew along the railroad. They were fed by a ditch that held water in the rainy times, and the ground beneath them was marshy and soft with leaves, and smelled of decay. Anyone passing among them was well-nigh invisible, so he might observe unseen the soldiers' burying ground that lay just to the west. That was Molochi Fish's intent as he eased across the weed-grown cut of the Mississippi Central and into the green shadows of the willow trees. He crossed the ditch on a fallen log, pausing long enough to let a water moccasin slide out of the way. In a moment he was squatting at the edge of the willow brake, peering through the morning haze at the melancholy wooden grave markers faded by the weather, and the paling fence that surrounded them.

Molochi was glad to see that men were already working on the grave. He could see the heads and shoulders of the diggers above the hole, their shovels flinging up clumps of dark earth. On the edge of the grave stood a white man with an umbrella. No soldiers were anywhere around, except dead ones. Molochi remembered the dead man under the bridge and wondered where they were keeping him. He thought of the man he'd seen running: Wall Stutts, who lived on the Gault place a few miles from Molochi's cabin. He remembered Wall Stutts very well.

It was two summers ago, by Molochi's calculation, before the yankees came who burned the town, and before the ones who whipped him. The weather had been dry for a month, and the woods were crackling, the leaves curling on the trees, the dust thick. The dry wind rattled in the leaves and brought the smell of a big woods fire somewhere to the west; the air was hazy with smoke, and when the sun set every day, it was round and coppery.

Molochi had a woman that summer. He had bought her from a party of Choctaws passing through on their way to the south, had given a jug of liquor for her, and some clothes he had stolen from a yard in town. She was young, they said, and strong. They did not mention that she was insane; Molochi found that out for himself that very afternoon when he caught her squatting behind the cabin, eating a blacksnake alive. He watched her peel the skin back with her teeth, the snake writhing in her hands. He noticed then that her head was too big, swollen like a goatskin filled with water. But that was all right; Molochi did not give a goddamn about that.

She was strong, sure enough. She could haul firewood and run down rabbits in the field and carry water from Leaf River as long as Molochi wanted her to. She had a round moon face and brittle hair, and her feet were splayed and leathery, and her eyes were black and flat as river rocks and seemed never to move. Her one garment—a faded trade dress—had holes cut away for her breasts, and sometimes they hung out, and sometimes they didn't. Molochi did not know that Indian women were modest by nature; he supposed they were all as careless as this one. Thinking back, he realized that her companions had been afraid of her, and it wasn't long before he noticed that the dogs were, too. That was a good thing, for he could turn them loose at night, and they wouldn't try to catch her when she went out to make water.

One smoky afternoon in that summer, Molochi was sitting on the cedar bolt he used as a step to the cabin door, probing with a little shard of broken glass at a toenail that was bothering him. He had smashed the toe with a chunk of wood and was drilling the nail to let the blood out. He had the dogs tied under a blackjack oak; they sprawled in the shade with their tongues lolling out, the dirt around them boiling with fleas. Molochi had just broken through the nail and was squeezing out a little bead of black blood when he heard the dogs move. They were standing now, the two of them looking off to the east. Molochi looked that way too, just in time to see the horsemen emerge from the woods. He watched them pick their way among the stumps that littered the clearing: four of them, bearded, broad hats shading their eyes, dressed in the poor, shapeless garments of dirt farmers but carrying shotguns and wearing pistols. The two dogs made no sound, but strained at their tethers, their teeth bare. Molochi stood up, thinking to turn the dogs loose, but the leader jumped his horse ahead and pointed his shotgun. "You leave them goddamn dogs where they at," said

Wall Stutts. In a moment, the riders were arranged in a half circle before the cabin door.

"What you want, Wall?" said Molochi.

Stutts, his shotgun resting on his thigh, grinned down at Molochi. He was wearing a blue yankee blouse; beneath it, his shirt was yellow with sweat. "We heard about your squaw," he said. "Injun told us all about it, thinkin maybe we wouldn't hang him. He was misguided in that, poor feller. Where she at?"

"Ain't here," said Molochi.

Stutts grinned again, his teeth white behind his whiskers. "Tom," he said without turning his head, "why'nt you look in the cabin yonder."

A tall man, his shotgun slung behind his back with a length of plow line, dismounted and dropped his reins and crossed the little way to the cedar bolt. He stepped up on it and disappeared into the black square of the cabin door. Then he was back again, and with a single quick movement flung the woman out the door into the yard. She landed in the gray, powdery dirt on her hands and knees, her breasts swaying heavily beneath her. The tall man jumped down and pulled the woman to her feet. She stood in the midst of them, her face empty.

"Aye God, she ain't much to look at," said Wall Stutts. "Tom, see if they's anything under there."

The tall man pulled up the woman's dress and thrust his hand between her legs. She blinked once and turned her head and looked at Molochi. The tall man removed his hand and sniffed his fingers. "Well, it's ripe," he said, "but Gah damn if it ain't dry as a corn shuck."

Wall Stutts laughed. "Look around, see can you find some lard," he said, and dismounted.

The tall man found a tin of lard in the cabin. Stutts went first, then the others took their turns while Stutts held a pistol under Molochi's chin and whispered in his ear. It took two of them to pin the woman in the dirt. She fought them at first, and it was all they could do to hold her, but at last she gave it up and lay staring at the leaves rattling over her head. All the while, even in her fighting, she made no sound. Then Stutts gave the pistol to the tall man and went again. When he was finished, he rose, buttoning his trousers. "Well, Molochi," he said, "that just might be the worst I ever had." He turned to his men. "Boys, I'm like that monkey that was fuckin a skunk—you hear about that?"

Naw, they said. Naw, tell it, Wall.

"Was a monkey fuckin a skunk," said Stutts as he swung into the saddle. "Monkey went back home, his pards says 'What happened?' Monkey says, 'Boys, I ain't had all I want, but I had all I could stand.'"

They laughed at the joke. The man with Molochi slapped him on the back. " 'At's a good 'ern, ain't it, Molochi?" he said.

"Come along, Junior," said Stutts. "Molochi don't think that's funny."

They rode away then, crossing the clearing at a walk, not looking back. In a moment, they were into the woods and gone. Molochi Fish stood looking at the place where the trees had closed behind them; he could hear their horses moving in the dry leaves, heard the snap of a branch, a man laughing. When he was sure they were gone, he looked down at the woman.

She lay on her back, her thighs streaked with blood and shiny with lard, the dress balled up at her waist. The black buttons of her eyes were almost hidden in her swollen face, and, though her cheeks were wet, she made no sound of crying. She was more silent even than the dogs, who were sitting on their haunches now, panting. Molochi watched her for a moment, then turned and searched in the dirt until he found the sliver of broken glass. He knelt by the woman and held out the sliver. She sat up and looked curiously at the shining thing, then took it gently between her pudgy fingers. She turned it in the sun, making it glint, and tested the sharpness of it. Then, as Molochi watched, she drew it down her forearm from the heel of her hand almost to the elbow. The flesh sprang open, pink and white, then the severed veins erupted in blood that fountained over Molochi's bare feet and in an instant soaked the woman's legs and dress and breasts. When the dogs smelled the blood, they could be silent no longer; they leapt against their tethers, the tarred ropes jerking them off their feet again and again as they lunged and snapped and growled. The woman cradled her ruined arm in her lap and looked at Molochi and made the only sound he ever heard her make: a whimper, like a child. Molochi turned away and took up his cudgel from the feed bucket where he kept it and waded into the dogs, beating them until they lay senseless among their own droppings and foam. Then he walked to the edge of the clearing and sat down on a stump, his back to the cabin, his breath coming ragged and harsh and dry through his mouth.

That was two summers gone, and now Molochi heard his own breathing in the bright morning, among the green of the willows. In the burying ground, the darkies were singing as they dug the grave where the dead boy would lie. Molochi did not know what singing was; he cocked his head and listened and felt the sound run deep inside him like strange blood coursing in his veins. He looked up through the delicate tracing of the willows and saw the blue sky. The sun would be high pretty soon, and Molochi did not want to be out in it, but he knew he would go and look at the grave. It did not occur to him to wonder why.

· XI ·

The guards stood at support arms, their bayonets pointed toward the cloudless sky. Two of them were on the bridge itself, and four more down below: regular infantrymen in their dark frock coats and blue trousers and forage caps, their leather blacked, their belt- and box-plates polished. Six months ago, they would not have been so well turned out.

Sergeant Rafe Deaton left his musicians and escort on the bridge and brought the litter bearers down through the grass, which by now was trodden and more slippery than ever. The soldiers, carrying the rolled litter, moved carefully, their leather-soled shoes slick and treacherous.

"Stand here," said Deaton when they had reached the bank. The men nodded and began to unroll the litter. They were silent, as the guards were silent. They did not look under the bridge.

Lieutenant Osgood returned Deaton's salute and inclined his head toward the body, covered now in an issue blanket of gray wool. "We are to take him to the color line. Colonel's orders," said the officer.

"The color line, sir," said Deaton. He thought a moment, then leaned his musket against one of the muddy bridge pilings. He did not look at the Lieutenant again, but brushed past him and knelt by the body and gathered the hem of the blanket in his fingers. Then Rafe Deaton, who had seen many dead men in his years of soldiering, hesitated. He knelt a long while, still holding the blanket, the muscles in his jaw working. At last he dropped the blanket without pulling it back. Osgood spoke his name. Deaton stood and walked past the Lieutenant again, out into the sunlight. He looked at the men with the litter. "Take him up," he said.

They tried to lower Tom Kelly's arms under the blanket, but he was stiff by now. Then they discovered that the boy was glued to the ground by his own congealed blood. They worked to free him; he came loose with a wet, tearing sound that sent Lieutenant Osgood to the creek at last.

As the soldiers struggled to bring Tom Kelly up to the road, Rafe stood a little distance behind the Lieutenant and waited for him to finish. The officer wiped his mouth on his sleeve, turned to find Rafe watching him. "Goddammit, Sergeant," he said.

Rafe came to attention, saluted. "We are ready, sir," he said. The Lieutenant straightened, searched Rafe Deaton's face for some sign of irony or derision, found nothing there at all, not even pity, which would have been worse than either. "Very well," said the Lieutenant.

Thus they brought Tom Kelly back to camp. "Guide around the courthouse," said Rafe to the musicians. "Let the goddamned citizens get a good look." So they set out: first the drummer and fifer, the drum snare muffled with a rag, and the fifer playing "The Banks of Allan Water" and "MacPherson's Lament" to the beat of the slow march. Even in these melancholy tunes, the notes of the fife leapt up into the morning air like birds, and it was fitting for a young life that they should. The musicians were followed by Sergeant Rafe Deaton, his musket at the shoulder, and Lieutenant Osgood, sword at the shoulder, bayonet and blade polished and glinting in the sun. Then the escort, arms reversed, and the body on its litter, stiff beneath the humble pall of the wool blanket. The detail passed once around the square where a good many townspeople had gathered. They watched in silence, most of them, their faces grave, telling nothing. One man spat into the road as the body passed; if the soldiers saw it, they gave no notice. Then they were gone, back across the bridge and up the road toward camp, the drum's reverberation like the beating of an old heart.

◆   ◆   ◆

FROM THE BACK parlor of the Shipwright house, through the open window that looked out on the muddy back yard and the trees along Town Creek, Colonel Burduck could hear the drum and fife. He stood at the window, his hand pushing back the heavy winter drape that still hung there. He could see the ivy-shrouded cookhouse, the paling fence that leaned around the weedy ruins of the old truck garden, a wheelless carriage set up on cedar bolts, its top and seats stolen away by the soldiers for their camp. Among these remnants of an old, vanished life, the tents and fire pits and stacked arms of the headquarters guard ought to have seemed alien, intrusive; as it was, Burduck had long since grown used to the juxtaposition, and the only odd note registered on his mind was that the ramshackle garden fence was still unburnt. No one thought any longer of the civilian world as a safe and separate realm, but as a landscape that existed solely to accommodate the soldiers—one of the fruits of a war fought in towns and cornfields and pastures, along country lanes and railroads and through back yards where laundry was hanging. At times, Burduck had looked out this window and felt sorrow nudge him like a finger at his breast. Not for the rebels, not even for the Shipwrights who were all dead of war or grief—save the old man, who lived in the attic but prowled the lower rooms, peering into them with his face shriveled like an old pecan, his hands curled into impotent claws. Burduck felt the loss of beauty as a diminishment of all men, no less the beauty that must have hovered over this plot of ground, contained here in shadows and silence and the peaceful curl of kitchen smoke—beauty that now was vanished, made irrelevant by the slow beating of the drum. At last, he turned from the window to the others waiting in the room.

Lieutenant Rolf von Arnim leaned on the mantel, his spurred, muddy boots crossed, his fingers tapping lightly on the mantel. Mister Henry Clyde Wooster, special correspondent for the Cincinnati papers, spread his bulk across a horsehair settee, his mechanical pencil poised over a notebook. He was an elegant man, though given to sweating in the unaccustomed heat of Mississippi. Beside him, in the little space remaining on the settee, Sheriff Ben Luker sat stiffly, hands in his lap, his pistol holster pulled awkwardly across his belly. He had taken a fresh chaw before entering, and now he wished he hadn't, for there was no place to spit. Finally, in a parlor chair across the table from the Colonel, sat Mister L. W. Thomas.

Thomas was dressed in tan breeches, a waistcoat of the same material (with a gold watch chain looped across it), a dark butternut sack coat, and a wide cravat of yellow silk. He had fetched as well his broad hat of brown felt, which he now held in his lap. Thomas uncrossed his legs and looked from one officer to the other.

Colonel Burduck sat down at his table, picked up a pencil, waved it vaguely. "Mister Thomas," he said, "you occupy a unique place in the community. You have always enjoyed the protection of the government—without seeming to need it. Remarkable accomplishment."

Thomas fidgeted in the chair. "Yes, well—I am—I am loyal, of course, but I have few prejudices—if you understand me."

"I understand, sir," said the Colonel. "And be at ease, I won't hang you today."

Thomas nodded. "That's real good to know," he said.

Burduck went on. "You can hear the fife and drum, sir. I don't have to tell you what it means."

"No," said Thomas, "it is for the boy that was killed at the bridge last night. Tom Kelly. I knew him. He was . . . a good boy."

"Did you see who left with him? Or soon after? Was he in any kind of argument, do you recall?"

Thomas looked at the faces around him, then back at the Colonel. "No, there was a fight out there yesterday, a little skirmish, but Kelly wasn't in it."

"No," said von Arnim, addressing the Colonel. "He was on guard detail in the afternoon. Fact is, he was not at liberty to go off last night. He paid a man to take his place on the guard."

"How was I to know that?" asked Thomas.

"Never mind, it is immaterial," said the Colonel. "Go on."

"He came in, drank too much, got tighter'n Dick's hatband—not like him atall. He was agitated about his wife, seems like. Anyhow, I made him leave—I always do when they get too full. Now I wish I hadn't. That's all I know about it, Colonel."

On the Colonel's table lay the sheet of paper he had found. He slid it across to Thomas. "What do you make of this?" he asked. "It was discovered on the body."

Thomas picked up the paper and read aloud. " '*Deo vindice.*' God has vindicated. God will vindicate us." He looked up at the Colonel. "I never got good marks in Latin."

"God vindicates," said von Arnim.

Thomas looked at the provost. "Thanks so much," he said, and tossed the paper on the table.

"Well," said the Colonel, "can you attach any particular meaning to it in the circumstance?"

"I suppose it means what it always means," said Thomas.

"And what is *that,* sir?" asked the Colonel.

Thomas shrugged. "Everybody thinks God is on his side and not the other fellow's."

Burduck closed his eyes, felt the ache beginning in the base of his skull. For an instant he saw the bright morning again, the mist rising from the creek, the mud bank and the willows—and in the shadow under the bridge, among the trash and leaves and branches left by the high water, the boy with his arms uplifted, his eyes that would not close. *Requiem aeternam dona eis Domine, et lux perpetua luceat eis.* The boys' faces lifted in the candlelight among the bells, and the incense smoke drifting, rising toward the dark ceiling, and the words rising *Libera me, Domine, de morte aeterna* into the darkness where carved faces no living man had seen leered from the vaulted arches. The darkness drew him, so he would not look but kept his eyes on the frayed hem of the priest's chasuble, letting the words and the smoke go up without him among the hovering souls that waited. Then another bell rings, four clear strokes, each one dying away in solemn reverberation, then gone into time. He is in the eyes of the ship; he can hear the hiss of the water under the bow, the creak of lines, the wind plucking at the shrouds; he can feel the rail, the deck moving beneath him. No stars, no moon tonight; he lifts his hand, it is invisible against the great dark that lies all around, the infinite blackness through which the ship moves, seeking her way *Requiescat in pace*—

"—insight into this matter," Burduck heard himself say, and the room took shape again, folding out of the darkness.

Thomas was stroking his beard. "I might have, but you won't like it."

When Burduck did not reply, von Arnim tapped the mantel with his knuckles. "You may try us," he said.

Again Thomas shifted in the chair, wincing now, as if in pain. "What is it, sir?" asked the Colonel.

Thomas grimaced again. He looked down at his hat, ran a blunt finger around the brim, his head cocked as if in contemplation. "You know I am a Southerner, sir," he said.

Burduck was surprised. "No," he said. "Your speech does not betray you."

Thomas stood then, slowly, and lay his hat on the chair behind him, and straightened, and looked at the Colonel.

"Now, sit down," said von Arnim, moving away from the mantel. "Be at ease."

Thomas ignored the provost. He gathered his shirt in his fingers and pulled it back over the white flesh of his belly. There, in his flank, was the puckered spray of a bullet wound, still angry looking and oozing a little from the half-healed tear of the ball's entrance. The pus had left a yellow stain on the shirttail. Thomas looked down, daubed at the wound with his fingers. "That is from a rebel ball in the Wilson's Creek fight." He raised his eyes, turned his body so the provost could see. "I was with the loyal Missourians—I have my release, signed by General Halleck in St. Louis, if you want to see it. The hole still pains me, don't want to heal. It makes a mess of the bedclothes every night."

"An impressive wound," the correspondent said.

"You miss my point, sir," said Thomas. "If I wanted to impress you, I'd show you where it came *out*."

Burduck waved them silent. "I am sorry for you," he said, "but your loyalty is not in question here. What *is* your point?"

Thomas gingerly tucked his shirttail in. "My point is illustrative," he said. "You ask for insight, and I'd as soon you know my qualifications. I know these people very well, and I would ask a question of you, sir. Have you any idea how much some of them hate you?"

Again Burduck was surprised, though he tried not to show it. "We are not here to win their affections," he said.

"Of course not, though many will say they've been fairly treated—so far. But you won't be here forever, and them who come next will not be so fair, and the people know it, and some of them make no distinctions." Thomas waved his hand toward the window. "The woods out there are full of men who would slit that boy's throat for recreation—but you know that. What you may not understand is that a great many would do it out of hate—pure Old Testament hate, red with vengeance. Did you hate the rebels, Colonel?"

The correspondent scribbled furiously. Von Arnim waved his hand. "Now, see here—," he began, but Burduck motioned him silent. He leaned back in his chair. The ache in his head was moving forward, lurking behind his eyes. He pinched the bridge of his nose. "Yes," he said at last. "Sometimes I did."

Thomas pressed on. "It's a grand feeling, ain't it? Clears the air, makes everything so much simpler. When did you hate em most, out there in the field?"

"When we lost," he said. "No—I take it back. I hated them the most when they *believed* we had lost."

Thomas thought about that a moment. "Yes," he said. He picked up his hat. "Yes," he said again, nodded, and went out, closing the door behind him.

"Well," said von Arnim, folding his arms over his chest.

Sheriff Ben Luker had grown more and more uncomfortable during the interview. He wondered what kind of man would have no spittoon about. But he had to speak now, and when he did, the juice ran from the corners of his mouth, and his voice was garbled, as if he were speaking under water. "Aw, hell, Colonel, Thomas is all right. He don't know nothin."

Burduck looked at the man as if he'd materialized out of the air. Luker wiped his mouth with his hand, his eyes moving from the Colonel to von Arnim and back again. "I'll keep a eye on him, though," he said.

"I am glad to hear it," said the Colonel.

"Well," said von Arnim again.

"Well *what,* sir?" said Burduck.

Von Arnim shook his head. "I hate to agree with the constable, but I think he's right—Thomas don't know anything."

Burduck laughed. "You believe he was shot up in Missouri?"

The provost stroked his moustache. "I believe he was shot somewhere, Colonel," he said.

Henry Clyde Wooster consulted his notes. "An unusual character, this Thomas," he said. "I would trust him about as far as I could throw an anvil."

The two officers ignored the correspondent. Deep in the house, a clock chimed nine. Through the open window, voices drifted, and the crowing of a cock. Burduck rose from his chair and leaned over the table, steepling his fingers on the scarred top. Then he raised his open hand and brought it down hard, making pens and inkwell jump and papers flutter to the floor. "God *damn* it," he said.

The provost moved circumspectly to the window, pulled the drape aside and looked out into the morning. "I will say this, Colonel. Some bad men live out yonder in the county, just as Thomas said. I would not like to see us get tangled up in a bushwhacking war."

"Nor I," said Burduck. "But that's what's about to happen, isn't it?"

The provost turned and leaned against the sill and folded his arms. He looked at the Colonel. "Maybe," he said. "But why would they telegraph their intentions? Why not just come out of the woods one night and murder us all in our sleep?"

"They are cowards," said Wooster.

"No, sir," said Burduck. "On the contrary. I think whoever wrote that message wants us to be ready, is so sure of himself that he prepares us for a fight to make the victory sweeter."

"Or maybe ashamed," said the provost. "These local yahoos took a noble thrashing up on the Tallahatchie just before we got here."

Ben Luker was made even more uncomfortable by the turn this conversation had taken. In fact, he was about to gag on his own spit. Clearly something had to be done. He looked at his companions. Burduck was deep in thought, the provost had turned to the window again, Wooster was writing. Luker took the opportunity to open his coat and pull open the inside pocket with his finger. Into this he emptied the sodden chaw and all the accumulated ambure. When he looked up, a thin brown string suspended from his lower lip. Wooster was watching him in disgust.

"Good God, man," said the correspondent, and rose from the settee. Luker smiled and wiped the string away with his fingers.

Burduck was thinking about the incident on the Tallahatchie. "Now here is something," he said at last. He looked at the provost. "Who led the partisans around here? He still around?"

"Don't know, sir," said von Arnim. He looked at Luker. "How about it, Ben? Were you in that fight?"

"Oh, no, indeed," said Luker. He was aware that the ambure was seeping through the front of his coat. Von Arnim pointed to the spreading stain. "Damnation, you got one of those leaking wounds, too?"

"Who led the partisans, Ben?" said the Colonel.

Luker hunched forward on his seat, tapping a pudgy hand on each knee.

"Oh—," he began. He looked at the ceiling, at the walls, at the floor. "Oh, seems like that feller was from down in Yalobusha County, somebody I never heard of. I never did mess with them rangers, Colonel. They was a bad lot. I mean—but they was hanged, most of em, and them that wasn't—no, they won't give you no trouble, depend on it. Why, after the Tallahatchie, they wouldn't come back for pie, nosiree. Why, they would no more—"

"All right," said the Colonel. He turned to the provost. "You find the man that led the rangers."

"I can do it, Colonel," said von Arnim.

"I'm tellin ye," said Luker, "ain't nobody around here—"

"That'll do," said Burduck. "Ben, why don't you go out in the yard and spit. You are about to make me ill."

The sheriff lost no time in making his exit. When he was gone, Wooster returned to the settee. "Will you close down the Citadel?" he asked.

Burduck thought a moment. "No. The tavern is not the problem. Besides, it is all the men have in this damn place."

Von Arnim nodded thoughtfully.

"I will send to LaGrange for another cavalry company," said Burduck. "Double up the patrols. The men may leave the camp for the tavern, but only in pairs—we'll read the order at evening post. And Mister von Arnim?"

The provost turned from the window. "Sir?"

"You tighten up that civilian curfew. I do not want to see a goddamned *house* cat on the streets after seven o'clock."

✦   ✦   ✦

GAWAIN AND STRIBLING discovered that the crib behind the house would not be usable without a good deal of cleaning up; it was full of the tendrils of trumpet vines, pale yellow in the gloom, and rats' nests and swallows' nests and wasps' nests, and the crinkly webs of furtive black spiders. These last were not the brutes of the well-house, but the glassy orbs called cherry spiders by the old people—though the only red about them was in the hourglass each sported on her belly. So Zeke was tethered in the yard for the moment, and curried with a scraggled brush, and left to crop the new grass as best he could. That done, Gawain and Stribling curried themselves, and brushed the caked mud from their cuffs, and set out for the Carter house.

They went down through the trees that lined the Holly Springs road; here, on the north end of town, the trees seemed to have fared better at the hands of the soldiers, though there were some stumps here and there, baring their stark white faces to the light. In a moment they passed a grove of oaks among which stood the hollow shells of buildings, and Gawain detoured through the gate. He led Stribling across an overgrown lawn to a fire-crumbled wall of red brick. Curiously, the door remained intact, though the windows were sightless, their wooden sashes charred into black velvet, tongues of soot lapping from their upper edges. Gawain brushed the broken glass off the steps and sat down, his elbows on his knees. Stribling watched him. After a moment, Gawain said, "Why do you reckon they burned such a thing as this, that never did them any harm?"

"Well," said Stribling, "what was it, anyhow?"

"The Academy," Gawain said. He looked over his shoulder at the wall, then back at Stribling, then beyond him. He shook his head. "The sons of bitches. The perfidious sons of bitches. Harry, did you ever burn anything?"

Stribling shrugged. "Some bridges. A barn once—I don't recall why."

"It was fun, wasn't it?"

"Yes," said Stribling. "Yes, it was."

They were quiet then, remembering. After a moment, Gawain spoke again. "This was the Cumberland Female Academy—the name used to be over the gate yonder, but it's gone now, I notice. I used to teach here. Literature, if you can imagine. To girls. Good God."

Stribling looked up at the wall, then bent and picked up a loose brick. He tossed it through a paneless window; they heard it clump in the rubble on the other side. "Nothin there, pard," said Stribling. "Just air is all. Now come on."

Gawain dusted off the back of his breeches. "I had a good time here," he said. "Why you reckon they burned it?"

"Meanness, I guess," said Stribling.

Gawain looked at the wall again (through the upper windows, he could see the blue sky and the feathering clouds), and beyond it to the hulls of other buildings already going green with vines and creepers. A silence lay upon them, deeper than the songs of birds and the morning voices in the grass—a silence like that in a room where strangers sat, each one waiting for another to speak. Once more he thought he ought to see them: the shapes of them who were gone, himself among them, walking the sward in clawhammer coats, heads bent to an opened text, smoke curling from their pipes—or blithe and gay, the young ones, the girls like young lambs dancing in the spring, their dresses white, their voices light as music. But once more there was nothing, only the empty air, as Stribling had said.

They went on, out the gate again and down the road to the square, where they arrived in time to view the last journey of young Tom Kelly. The procession entered from the Oxford road and moved around the rubble of the courthouse; in a moment, it passed along the north side where Gawain and Stribling stood among the citizens.

"Ah, Jesus," said Gawain. The drums disturbed him, and the sight of armed Federals so close. "More dead people."

"Odd that you should use the plural," said Stribling.

"Beg pardon?"

"Never mind," said Stribling. Then, almost to himself, "Mind the citizens; he is here somewhere, I'd guarantee it. Or at the grave."

"Who? Dad blame it, Harry—"

But Stribling said no more. They watched until the procession rounded the square and disappeared up the Oxford road, over the same bridge where it had begun.

"Well," said Gawain, "it is a relief not to hear the drums anymore. I hope to never hear another one in my lifetime."

There were no clouds yet, but a little breeze sprung up and creaked a sign over their heads. Gawain turned to look at it.

DR. STEPHAN E. TEICHMILLER

Absolutely Painless Dentistry

Practice Limited to Extractions Only

"I wonder how the doc is faring," mused Gawain. "I spent a couple of weeks up there one day."

"I do not believe any enterprise is absolutely painless," said Stribling. "Especially the present one. Tell me about the Judge. You said he is bound to go to Brazil?"

"Yes, yes," said Gawain. "And if he goes, Morgan will go too."

"She ain't exactly a child," Stribling pointed out. "Maybe she can follow her own mind."

Gawain sat down in a splintered chair by the wall of the dentist's office. "I will tell you about Morgan Rhea," he said. "When she was sixteen, she got married off to a lawyer named Turban, Turpin, somethin or other—damn if I can remember. That was in 'forty-eight; I remember because the University opened that year, and I went up there. Next year, they had a child, a little girl, but it died after a week or so. In 'fifty, the lawyer got the gold fever and took off for California—he was half crazy by then anyway, so they said, because of the girl that was lost. Then one day Morgan got a package by the post. Inside was the lawyer's pocket watch and wedding ring and a lock of his hair. The note said it was all the hair he had left after the injuns got their portion. After that day, she never called herself by his name again. She moved back in with the old folks in time to help raise Alex—he was a surprise to everybody, Miz Ida having gone beyond the usual years for such things—and she is froze to him now, as if he were her own, and in a way, he is. Yes, she will go to Brazil when the Judge goes."

"Well," said Stribling, "when you talked to her last night—"

"She never mentioned it, and I never let on that I knew."

"Well, good God," said Stribling. "Then you don't know *how* she feels about it."

"I just told you," said Gawain.

Stribling paced up and down, shaking his head, his arms crossed. At last he stopped, looked at Gawain. "You just gon' sit there and let her go?" he asked.

Gawain shifted uncomfortably. "Well, then there's the Judge—"

"I am tired of hearin about the Judge," said Stribling. "Come on, boy. Let us go and see what develops over to Miss Morgan's. The Judge might even have us for dinner."

Gawain pulled himself up from the chair. "You believe that?" he said.

"No," said Stribling.

They went on then, through the bright morning, up the cemetery road toward the Carter house.

✦   ✦   ✦

WHEN L. W. Thomas left the Shipwright house, he nodded to the guard on the porch. He knew the man, of course. He knew them all, even Tom Kelly, who had drunk too much the night before and cried for his young wife and made an ass of himself, and now was dead. The guard, a squat, red-faced, bat-eared fellow from Illinois, looked like a troll in his oversized frock coat. He said something in the harsh twang of his tribe; Thomas missed the remark but acknowledged it with a wave of his hand and moved quickly across the porch. He almost stumbled going down the steps, and he winced when the dull pain thumped in his side. He pressed his hand to the wound, felt the gummy fluid penetrating his shirt. *It will never quit,* he thought.

But the hurt was familiar at least, like an old regret, and it went almost unnoticed among the more immediate symptoms that followed L. W. Thomas across the yard of the Shipwright house. His hands were trembling, sweat beaded on his forehead, his heart was hammering like the clapper of a fire bell. Though he walked as fast as he was able, he seemed to be moving dreamlike through air thick as muscadine jelly, over ground that refused to pass beneath his feet, toward some indefinable point he would never gain. He listened for voices behind him, shouts, orders, the cocked lock of a musket leveled at his back.

Then he was in the road. An army wagon was lumbering up from the south behind its four-mule team, and Thomas found himself standing square in the way of it, glued in the deep gumbo mud, the object of the driver's curses. The jingling team came to a halt close enough for Thomas to count the nose hairs on the leader.

"Outen the way, ye dod-derned idjit," snarled the driver. "Bless God if I ever get em started agin!" He slapped the lines over the mules' backs, and the animals leaned into motion. Thomas hauled himself aside, almost stumbling again, and looked up at the driver and tried to speak, but too late. The mud-rimmed wheels of the wagon creaked past inches from his face. He could feel the compression of the great weight they bore, and smell the grease of the axles. He found the roadside and set off for the Citadel.

He felt transparent, could imagine his nerves like glistening blue wires and the blood coursing red through the glass pipes of his veins, and in his breast the dark loaf of his heart beating, beating like the drum he'd heard through the open window. There it was: the dead boy, borne to the soldiers' graveyard above the camp, who only last night was crying like a child. Thomas had told him to be gone, to get him hence, to quit his blubbering before he marked himself a fool—Go, boy, get your rest. And now he was resting sure in a far country, and the wife was shelling early peas perhaps, or strewing corn to the chickens in the yard, singing "Go Ye Lightly to the Well," and soon—not today, but next week or the next—she would turn her eyes up the road to where the Post came riding with the Colonel's letter in his bag.

Well, he was an actor still. God! what a bluff to pull on von Arnim and the Colonel, not to mention an actual yankee newspaperman. But he had done all right, he told himself. Not too much help, not too little—just right. And what a splendid exit! But there was the boy—

He looked fearfully at the few people he passed—a man with a bundle of sticks, a negro driving a cow, a woman and her child picking their way townward through the mud—and marveled that they did not turn from him in disgust, or point accusing fingers at his transparent soul where all his memory lived. *It will never quit,* he thought again, and pressed his hand, not over the wound this time, but against his heart.

Another wagon came from behind; he heard the horses' hooves sucking in the mud and the creak of the wheels. He turned to watch it pass, and the heart beneath his hand nearly stopped when he saw that it was no wagon at all but a hearse, ancient and ungreased, wanting paint, the oval glass window cracked, and on the box a man bent like a vulture in his black coat and tall hat, a plug of tobacco swelling his blue jowls. And worse: no mourners or mutes, and no nodding plumes on the horses' heads, only a negro with a shovel following behind. Through the cracked window, Thomas saw the cheap painted coffin like a slab of black stone. The whole collection seemed to repel the sunlight, as if it moved in its own shadow.

Thomas found his voice. "Who . . . who is that?" he asked of the bird-like driver, the undertaker's man. The fellow swiveled his head and looked down over the rims of his spectacles. "Sewer-cide," he drawled, dragging the syllables out. He grinned, showing his big teeth. "Any more questions, brother?"

"But who?" persisted Thomas, without knowing why. "*Who* is it?"

The driver halted the team. Then he laughed, a low, phlegmy sound. "Oh, *God* knows, brother—him and the black demon that's waitin to take delivery. Them's all that matters, don't you agree? Gon' bury him tonight when the moon is dark, down at the Mount Zion church. Gon' dig a good grave three-by-six and six foot perpendic'lar just outside the fence, put him down in it where he can't contaminate the sanctified. Such is the way in a Christian country. Tomorrow daylight there'll be naught but a mound of fresh dirt—ain't that somethin? Le's ponder that a while, think about the demon perched on the fence with his leathern wings folded, rubbin his little hands, while Jacob here opens up the ground, prowlin down through the roots and the worms—"

"No," said Thomas. "No—you get on away from me. You get on."

The man laughed again. "Some folks don't like to think about it," he said, and clucked to the team.

Thomas stood and watched until the hearse went out of sight over the rise to the south. Then he went on. It was not far, and in a moment he was climbing the steps of the tavern. In the cookshed behind, a plume of white smoke curled from the chimney where Queenolia Divine was making her fire for dinner. Beowulf was lying on the porch; he lifted his head and thumped his tail on the planks. Thomas knelt and stroked the hard pan of the dog's head and spoke through his teeth: "What'd you have to do that for? Why'd you have to be the one?" Then he was through the door, and when the door closed behind him, L. W. Thomas was safe for the nonce in the cool, rank darkness of the Citadel of Djibouti.

The interior of the place smelled variously of stale beer, mildew, cold cigars, wood smoke, and men—this last commodity a rich medley of odors in itself, as if there emerged from the anonymity of these men a single personality that could stand for them all. As his eyes grew accustomed to the gloom, Thomas could discern fantastic shapes: a deer head, its glass eyes wide in perpetual astonishment; a stuffed alligator gar the size of a small canoe suspended from the rafters; a cuckoo clock that clung to the wall like some complicated beast, whose yellowed ivory hands kept good time, though no cuckoo ever appeared to announce what time it was. The bar was a tall door laid across two barrels; the door, like the rest of the collection, was pilfered from the same abandoned house that yielded the blue paint. Above the bar, dimly illuminated in the light that shown through the gaps in the weatherboards, hung a garishly framed portrait of a reclining nude. The portrait was lurid and cheap and improbable, but it had always moved Thomas in an unexpected way. At first, the more he looked at it, the more he found it vaguely familiar, and he had often searched back through his adventures for some corresponding shape. He had found several, but their names and faces, voices and desires, even the cities and hotels where they'd crossed his life—all these eluded him, shut away in rooms to which he had long ago lost the key. He wished he could remember just a single name, so that one of them at least might have the dignity of remembering. Ah, well, he had decided at length—maybe they didn't have names. Maybe they never were at all.

Thomas felt his way across the room to the curtained doorway of the lean-to. The stump of a candle still burned there, revealing his bunk among the boxes and barrels. One empty crate contained his worldly goods: a scattering of books, a tin plate and cup, a mandolin, a great sheaf of dog-eared papers covered with his scrawl, a Remington pocket pistol with a tin of caps and a powder flask and a bag of conical balls. Above these hung the cloudy shard of a mirror, and by the candlelight Thomas examined his face. "Why did you do that?" he asked his image. Then his eyes moved to the tattered bill nailed to the wall by the mirror:

MR. LAWRENCE THOMAS
will appear on **SATURDAY AFTERNOON** in his
Great Character of
METACOMET!
being most positively his last appearance
in that character in Boston.

• • • • •

THE BEAUTIFUL CUBAS
will appear.

• • • • •

THIS SATURDAY AFTERNOON, NOV. 16,
will be performed the celebrated
Indian Tragedy entitled
METACOMET!!!
or, King Philip at Bay!

Thomas looked from the bill to the mirror and back again. He reached out his hand, touched the letters of his name. Then he undressed, climbed into his bunk, and blew out the candle. In the dark, riven only by a slant of sunlight through a crack in the wall, he pulled the covers over his head.

✦   ✦   ✦

BEN LUKER FOUND Captain Gault sitting on the portico of his burned house. He was in his shirtsleeves, his breeches tucked into his boots, skinning a rabbit he had shot in the yard. His fine, long-fingered hands were bloody. Beside him was a pail of water and, leaning against a smoke-blackened column, the Henry rifle. Luker, standing at the foot of the steps, told of the interview at Colonel Burduck's headquarters. Gault listened without comment.

"They wanted to know who it was led the rangers," said Luker. "They asked me who it was, I told em it was somebody down in Yalobusha, but von Arnim said he would find out. What you gon' do?"

Gault had finished his skinning. He slit open the rabbit's belly and scooped out the innards. They lay in a glistening red-and-blue pile at his feet. He picked them up and flung them past Luker into the yard, then dropped the carcass into the pail and rubbed water over his hands to wash off the blood. He dried his hands on a rag. "Tell me about Thomas again," he said at last.

Luker scratched the back of his neck. "Well, I guess he done all right—but it was him got em to thinkin about the rangers. He ought not to've said what he did when he didn't have to. I don't know, Cap'n. Looks to me like he could've kept his mouth shut."

"Well," said Gault, "you keep an eye on him. He is not one of us, after all."

"What you gon' do with them lookin for you?" said Luker.

Gault folded the rag and rose from the cane-bottom chair he was sitting in. He looked out across the yard and the overgrown fields beyond, as though they contained a shape that only he could discern. "What do you think, Ben?" he said at last. "You think I had that boy killed?"

The sheriff looked at the ground. "Well . . . well, *naw,* Cap'n, I never said—"

"Don't worry about it, Ben," said Solomon Gault. Then he smiled. "I'd ask you to stay for dinner, but, as you can see, there is only the one rabbit."

· XII ·

The soldiers' graveyard was just north of the camp, close enough to the railroad so that the ground trembled at the rare passage of trains. Around the cluster of wooden markers (thirty-six in all) the men had erected a soldierly fence of stolen palings, neat and plumb and white-washed. Outside the fence stood three additional markers; under these rested a black teamster killed by a mule, and two black soldiers who had died in a skirmish with rebel cavalry in the early spring. Also beyond the fence was the grave of a Confederate deserter, marked only by a depression in the soggy ground.

Of the thirty-six buried within the fence, most had been taken by measles or dysentery. One was a suicide, one had broken his neck in a fall from a horse. A few had been killed in the same skirmish as the black rifle-men over the fence. Their markers, save one, were identical wooden shingles, rounded on top, painted with the name, the regiment, and the date of departure of the sleeper beneath. The one odd marker was the Tuscan capital of a courthouse column; on the remnant of the shaft was written the name of a major of infantry whose life had ebbed away in a fever. His people were expected to come fetch him when the roads were dry.

As the morning grew, the sky was still clear, though soon the white clouds would begin to pile toward the afternoon's rain. The sun shone hot on the soldiers' graveyard, and the two men digging the new grave were sheened with sweat. They were young men, and their black skin glistened with the sweat, and heavy drops beaded on their faces and dripped into the sour turned earth of the grave. With every thrust of the shovel, their muscles stood out like skeins of tarred rope. They sang to each other as they worked.

On the lip of the grave stood a third man, Old Hundred-and-Eleven. He wore a broad straw hat and carried a spavined umbrella to protect him from the sun, and in his jaw he worked a great wad of tobacco. Under his right arm, he held his great ragged Bible, which he would unlimber now and then to shake at the gravediggers in silent benediction. The two men, brothers called Dauncy and Jack, ignored him and went on singing to the rhythmic plunge and toss of their shovels. Their voices were high and sweet, like boys' voices, and they sang in a language they knew only through the song. The words meant nothing to them, so far had they traveled in their generations from the old tongue, but the sounds spoke of something peaceful and green and sad, of old lost ways and the end of life. It was a burying song, fit to carry down into the earth.

Old Hundred-and-Eleven liked to hear the negroes singing. He liked the sound of the digging, and the smell of the ground and of the sunlight, though the sun hurt his eyes and would scald him if it touched his skin. Just a little while before, von Arnim the provost had sent him here with these contraband to dig in the earth, to prepare a place for one of the newly dead. He liked that, too: the idea that here was a life neatly rounded out, and he chosen above all others to preside over the temple of its end.

There had been no more talk of hanging; apparently Judge Rhea's girl had fixed it just as the stranger said she would. In the sunlight, in the sweet music, Old Hundred-and-Eleven thought of Morgan and felt a warm glow in his heart. Awkwardly, for he had to keep the umbrella aloft, he palmed his great Bible and turned to a place he remembered: a picture of some children sleeping in what appeared to be a hayrick, and over them, keeping watch, a winged angel in flowing robes, its hand raised in a graceful way. Old Hundred-and-Eleven believed the angel looked a good deal like Morgan Rhea, though it was blond-headed and Morgan was not, and it was bigger and hadn't any pox scars. But no matter; the more he looked, the more he became convinced that here was a portrait of the girl who had saved him. "She's right here," he said to Dauncy and Jack. "Stamp *my* vitals if she ain't!"

"Who right where?" said Dauncy, reaching for the canteen that lay by the graveside. But the old man had already turned away, absorbed in the study of the picture.

"That ol' genneman give me the willies," said Jack. "He smell like a goat, too."

"I knowed him for years," said Dauncy. "Ain't no harm in him when he ain't conjurin. You ain't no rosebud yourself, by the by."

Jack was about to reply when a shadow fell across them. They stopped and looked up toward the sun. A man in a broad hat was standing there. At first they thought the old white man had come around behind them somehow. The brothers shaded their eyes and looked, and the blood slowed in their veins. They moved their bare feet nervously in the earth, feeling the clammy coolness of it.

It was a man all right, but not Old Hundred-and-Eleven. Later, Dauncy would tell how he believed for a moment it was a man risen from some other grave, for his skin seemed to be falling off him, and his eyes under the broad hat brim had no shine to them, and his mouth moved with his breathing as if he couldn't breathe the air of this world. He had appeared without herald, without sound, out of the hot light of morning, and thrown his shadow over the new grave, and Dauncy thought maybe he wanted it for himself, and if that was the case then he—Dauncy, who wanted to live at least long enough to find himself a last name—would be glad to oblige. Then he thought *He made a shadow,* and knew by that it was a man, flesh and bone that once had sucked his mama's paps, and in some ways this was worse.

"What you lookin at?" said the man. His voice was flat and quiet, as if he had no lungs but only his mouth to make the sound with. Dauncy looked away. "Nothin, sah, just diggin. Gon' dig right now, ain't we, Jack?"

Jack was frozen in place, his eyes wide, his hands wrapped tight about the mud-crusted shovel handle. A swirl of old stories rose like swamp gas in his memory, tales of a white man and his tracking dogs, how his skin peeled like sycamore bark. He saw his grandmother's face in the firelight, shriveled and toothless, a snuff stick jutting from her gums: *Ol' Molochi gon' get you, you don't straighten up.* "Ol' Molochi," breathed Jack. "Sweet Jesus."

The white man spat into the grave. "You best get to diggin, nigger," he said.

Dauncy nudged his brother, and they set to work again, watching each other from the corners of their eyes, understanding they were nearly done with the hole and once done—what? They dug. The man watched them. In a moment, Old Hundred-and-Eleven shambled up and peered over the rim of the grave.

"Gah damn, you boys is fools for excavatin," said the old man. He looked up at the stranger. "Here now, who are you to be tellin these boys anything? Don't you reckon they know how to make a grave? Anybody they put under will want a pick and shovel if he's to rise on time at jedgment day—who are you, anyhow, and good God but you are truly ugly, amen!"

The stranger moved then, without sound. He rounded the grave. Dauncy, bent nearly double from the waist, shook the dirt loose from his shovel blade and gripped the shaft. A word appeared in his mind: *Freedom.* He tried to get hold of it, look at it in its separate parts. "Freedom," he said softly to himself, as he had for months now. Did it mean he could whack a white man on the head with a shovel if he had to? He doubted it. Still, Old Hundred-and-Eleven, crazy as he was, had always been good to him, and if the stranger so much as lifted a hand against the old man, Dauncy would test the limits of his new condition. "Free-dom," he crooned softly, and began to make a song of it, watching the stranger with the peeling skin. "Freedom brung the children out of Pharaoh's land."

And Jack, picking up the line: "Sho' brought Jonah from the belly of the fish."

"Ol' Jonah," said Dauncy.

"Ol' Pharaoh," said Jack.

Up above, the stranger was close to Old Hundred-and-Eleven now. He stopped, and cocked his foot up on the mound of dirt. "Who you buryin here?"

Old Hundred-and-Eleven shifted his umbrella, bringing the shade across his face. "Gah damn," he said, "if you ain't the ugliest white man I ever see—uglier'n a fart in church, by God. I know you, don't I? You Molochi Fish. Thought the ha'nts and demons had got you down in the Leaf River bottom long ago."

"*Free*-dom," grunted Jack, thrusting his blade into the earth. "Freedom in the bosom of *A*-braham." He flung the dirt out of the grave, careful not to hit the stranger.

"Just never you mind," said Molochi Fish. "Who you buryin here? Is it that soldier what was cut last night?" He took a step closer, wrapped his hand in the lapel of the other's frock coat. "Tell me who it is."

"Can't say," said Old Hundred-and-Eleven agreeably. "Might be the Prince of Wales, all I know."

The stranger let go, peered down into the hole. Jack and Dauncy froze. "They gon' put him in a box, set him down in there," the stranger said, as if to himself. "They gon' cover his th'oat with a handkerchief." Then his eyes fixed on Old Hundred-and-Eleven again. "You make sure this hole's dug deep. Don't want that boy to get out. They's enough of em around as it is."

Old Hundred-and-Eleven snorted. "Done told you, these here boys is near 'bout to Chiny now. As for you"—he shook the Bible in the man's face—"the dog returns to his vomit, the fool to his folly. Go on with ye!"

"Lord Jesus," whispered Dauncy.

But the stranger was paying no attention to Old Hundred-and-Eleven. He seemed to have forgotten them all. He was looking past the grave toward the railroad, his mouth opening and closing with his breath. His gaze seemed fixed on something only he could see, as if some familiar shape were moving among the willows by Town Creek, or through the clumps of sumac along the right-of-way. "This ain't the end," he said. "This ain't all of it." Then, without another word, he began to move away, eyes still fixed on what he had seen. The three men at the grave watched until the man had crossed the railroad and was out of sight beyond the willows.

"Whoosh," said Jack. "That genneman warn't right, what I say."

Old Hundred-and-Eleven sat down in the dirt and crossed his legs, holding the umbrella upright, the Bible in his lap. "I ever tell you boys 'bout the vision I had one time? They was a dark beast, it was wintertime—"

As Old Hundred-and-Eleven began to tell his vision, making shapes in the air with his free hand, Jack and Dauncy resumed their digging. Just a little way now, and they would be done. Dauncy flicked the sweat from his eyes and thrust the shovel into the yielding earth.

"Dauncy?" said Jack.

"What?"

"It's good to be free, ain't it?"

"Shut up and dig," said Dauncy. "Be dinnertime soon."

✦   ✦   ✦

IN THE LEAN-TO room behind the Citadel of Djibouti, L. W. Thomas was thrashing in his sleep. He had kicked the sheets off; the bare mattress was soaked in sweat and suppuration. A fly was investigating his nostrils, and he brushed at it fitfully. Young Tom Kelly, barely visible in the dark, sat on a barrel in the corner of the room, one leg crossed over the other. The wound in his throat, barred by a slant of daylight, gleamed wetly. He had a tankard of beer, and when he drank, the beer leaked out of the wound and onto his shirt front. He didn't seem to mind.

"Whoa!" said Thomas, jerking upright in the sodden bunk.

"Sleepin in the daytime always give me bad dreams," said Kelly. "You oughtn't to do it."

Thomas shook his head. "Here lately, I been sleepin all the time," he said. "What you mean, comin up in here botherin me?"

"Oh, I'm a ghost," said Kelly. "I come to ha'nt you. I won't be no trouble, however." Then he let out a cry that shook Thomas to his bones.

"Well, you will damn sure have to quit *that*," said Thomas. "Now, look here—if you think I had anything to do with your—"

Kelly held up his hand. "Oh, not at all. No, you was always kind to me. If anybody'd asked me 'Where's a fellow you can trust, a fellow who won't do you any harm,' why, I would've sent him straight to you."

"No!" cried Thomas. "Don't be sayin that!" He threw the covers off and made to sit up, but the wound in his side sent a lance of pain through him, and he fell back groaning. "Ah, Jesus. Don't be sayin that to me."

Daylight flooded the room, except it wasn't the room at all but a narrow, empty street in a great city—St. Louis, Thomas thought. The buildings cast long shadows; they were of red brick and sooted with coal dust, their windows like pools of dead water. Though Thomas had always liked St. Louis, he was not comfortable here—it felt too much like Sunday morning, early, before the church bells. A lonely time.

Thomas stood in the street while dead leaves, golden and brittle, rattled across the sidewalks. Up ahead, the street curved away, and Thomas found himself watching there.

Presently a hearse, drawn by a single black horse with a nodding plume, emerged from the shadows beyond the curve. No one was on the driver's box, nor any mourners walking behind—just the hearse, its wheels silent, and the horse's hooves silent. Overhead, a flock of blackbirds passed across the sky between the buildings, throwing swift shadows on the bricks. As the hearse grew near, Thomas peered into the glass oval in its side, saw nothing there but his own reflection, pale and disembodied. The sight chilled him so that he recoiled, backed away, feeling for the stone curb behind him. He couldn't find it, and at last he turned, found himself still in the street. Before him was a store window festooned with spiderwebs. When he moved closer, the window disappeared, and he was looking into the hollow shell of a building all in shadow. He could hear birds in the rafters; they ruffled their feathers and murmured, but Thomas couldn't see them. Then he was inside, and he could smell the damp and the ashes, and Solomon Gault sat regarding him across a wide table. "Hear the fife and drum?" said Solomon Gault. "You know the meaning of it, sir?"

"I am not in this," said Thomas.

"Sure you are," said Gault, only he was Colonel Burduck now, and he slid a knife across the smooth surface of the table. It fell over the edge, glinting in the light from somewhere, and rang like a bell when it landed at Thomas' feet.

When he woke, he was sitting on the edge of his cot, soaked in sweat, staring at the barrel in the dark corner. In the gloom, he heard a mouse scuffling among his papers, and he wondered vaguely where the cat was. Then he lay back for just a while longer, listening for Queenolia to come and set up for dinner.

· PART 3 ·

The Citadel

· XIII ·

When a summer morning came, it drew the night out of houses where people lived. If a house were empty—or if it were drawn and shuttered against the coming day, as the houses of the sick often were, or the dying, or the frightened—then night would hold on, lurking in the corners of rooms, crouching at the end of dim halls and under furniture and in the folds of curtains. In such a house, the air went on smelling of the dead hours when the blood slowed in the veins, when the mind crept up dark avenues of memory and all the senses grew sharp to the creaking of a board, the flutter of a moth, the subtle movement of shadows. But stand in the yard of a house flung open, at the moment when day was established at last, and you could feel the night leave through the windows like an exhalation of breath. You could smell the night as it passed you, see it almost, as you might see a blackbird rising from the grass.

Old man Tom Carter paused and listened as the night left his house. He was in the yard, in his nightshirt, barefoot, his long white hair still tangled from sleep. He was looking for the place he had buried a dog once. It was important that he find it. The thought had come to him deep in the night, how his boy would naturally want to know where the dog lay. The creature had been old, toothless, feeble, but she had followed the boy when he left, had stumbled blindly down the lane after him until the boy stopped and knelt, petted her, said "Go home, France—you can't follow where I'm goin." Then the boy had gone, quickly, not looking back, and the dog had sat in the road and nodded her head, swayed her gray muzzle back and forth trying to find him again, until Tom had lifted the old dog up and carried her home.

Now he was searching for the place where France lay, and just as he thought he might be close, he smelled the night leaving his house. He stopped, looked up: there was the house, all the windows open and the curtains moving in the little breeze of morning, and he realized he was in the front. He had buried France in back, seemed like.

He went around the east side where the sun was already warming the boards, where the volunteer morning glories had opened their blue bells among a tangle of vines. Old Tom Carter blinked in the sunlight; for a moment the house seemed strange to him, alien and unexpected, as if he had just stumbled upon it in the grove of oaks. He tugged on the lead rope of his horse, felt no resistance, looked around in puzzlement. His hand was empty.

"Well, I'll say," he murmured, looking at his hand.

In the rear of the house, a gallery ran around the ell. Old Tom sat on the steps and looked across the yard. His feet were cold from the dew, and he rubbed them together. The open door of the barn was a great black square. *Maybe it is still night in there,* he thought. "France!" he called out. "Here you, Scotland! Here now!" He could see the pen where the dogs lived, the old setters, brother and sister out of a dog—what was her name?—he got in Grand Junction once. France had a litter out of one of Sam Hook's dogs—*No, that ain't right,* he thought. *France was dead when Sam Hook was breedin—* The thought struck him: France was dead by then, and Scotland, too. *Then who was it followed him down the lane?* He looked around expectantly, as if he had spoken the question aloud and someone might be there to answer it. But there was no one. In the dog pen, the grass was high, and morning glories grew through the board fence.

A spring morning, and the boy had gone to join his company on the square, and the dog went after him. Or was that the one who went to sea and was lost? Old Tom had not thought of that one for a long time, and he had to search the back rooms of his memory for the name. Owen, it was. So it was. No, Owen was up plenty early, gone before daylight, and it was wintertime when he left. He hadn't said he was leaving. Old Tom remembered looking down the empty lane where the boy had gone, at the trees lacy with ice. He stood by the gate, telling himself he could catch the lad if he tried, but he hadn't tried. A year later he got a letter from a man he'd never heard of, telling how the ship lost her masts and foundered in a typhoon and Owen Carter was swept over the side. That one was gone, then, no question about it. But not the other one, the young one. *He* would want to know where France was buried.

Behind the place where old Tom sat, a door led onto the gallery from the dining room. Now he heard the door open, scraping as it always did in damp weather. Alex Rhea came out on the gallery, carrying a cat draped in his arms like an inverted U. No sooner had the door closed behind them than the cat twisted free and thumped on the boards of the gallery. "Well, go on, then," said Alex, and the cat slipped past the old man and across the yard to the barn where he paused by the open door, looked back once, and disappeared.

"Here, now," said Tom Carter. "What you doin?"

"Nothin, sir," said the boy. He looked at the place where the cat had gone, then slouched across the gallery and sat down on the steps. He wore a muslin shirt, muslin braces, and a pair of jeans pants. He, too, was barefoot; he arranged his small feet beside the larger ones of old Tom Carter. The boy's were tan, calloused, pimpled with mosquito bites. The old man's were like slabs of blue-veined marble. The boy sighed and looked up into the bright leaves of the oaks. "It's mighty clear this morning," he said. "You can look all you want, you won't find no clouds."

"Be some after while," the old man said.

"Sister got me up," said the boy. "She is actin peculiar, like it was her birthday or somethin. I wisht I had a dog. That cat ain't much for company. Papa says we'll get a dog in Brazil, says you got to have em down there. I'd just as soon stay here and have one, though."

The old man nodded, looking out across the yard. There was the barn, the privy, the silent cookhouse with moss growing on the chimney and over the shingles of the roof. In the wall of the cookhouse was a perfect hole where a stray round of solid shot had come calling during the fighting around the square last year. The cook had run away after that, never to return. As the old man watched, a spear of sunlight penetrated the oak canopy; it grew until it resembled a gossamer curtain falling among the trees. It illuminated a spot of ground just beyond the cookhouse, toward the pasture grown rank with grass and honeysuckle and bull thistles.

"Don't see why I can't stay here *and* have one," said the boy. "Other boys have dogs. How come I can't stay with you, Cousin? We could have us some dogs, couldn't we?"

The old man didn't answer; he was watching the place where the curtain of sunlight fanned through the trees. He watched a fat robin land there and kick around in the leaves. In a moment, he put out his hand, fumbled, found the boy's and held fast to it.

"What, Cousin?" said Alex, but again the old man didn't answer. He struggled to his feet, breathing hard with the effort, and pulled the boy up with him. For an instant he swayed on the step, gaining his balance. The boy's hand felt hot and impossibly small, delicate, fragile as a leaf. His own encompassed it completely. Still grasping the boy's hand, he moved down the steps and out into the yard, across it, past the cookhouse and into the oaks, the boy following behind. The curtain of light was gone now—it couldn't last long, for the sun was climbing—but his eyes were fixed on the place where it had been. When they reached it, the old man fell to his knees, the boy standing beside him. The robin did not fly, but cocked his head and watched them from an arm's length away. Old Tom Carter reached out with his free hand and cleared away the leaves. "Here," he said.

The boy looked a question at his old kinsman, then knelt, waiting.

The old man was silent for a long while. At last he released the boy's hand and leaned forward and spread his fingers out over the earth. His breathing was deep and steady; the only other sound was the robin flock talking to one another in the grove, and from the pasture the carol of a meadowlark. The boy settled himself, his hands on his knees.

"It was right here, you see," said old Tom. "This is where I put her. I should've made a mark, a rock or somethin, so you'd know."

"Who?" said Alex. "Put who?"

The old man captured the boy's hand again, guided it to the cleared patch of earth, cool and damp. The wet undersides of the turned leaves glistened, and the smell of them was strong in the boy's nose. He had a vision of bird dogs moving in a field at morning, saw their feathery tails switching over the broomsage. And he smelled the dry, papery smell of the old man, and the sweat of his sleeping. Heard his breathing and knew, somehow, that he was searching for words—that he saw a picture too, and wanted the words to tell it. "What, Cousin?" the boy asked in a whisper. "What is it?"

The old man shook his head, as if a fly were buzzing him. Then he looked at the boy. "I'll get you another one," he said. "We'll go up to Tennessee, I promise—I know a fellow up there. Or maybe Sam Hook has one—I've not seen him in a while—" He turned his head, looking past the boy. "I wonder where he got to?"

The boy knew the name—Sam Hook, lawyer, preacher, breeder of fast dogs and horses, a legendary wing shot, who went with the army as a chaplain—from stories the old men told, and a half-remembered image from early childhood, before the yankees came, of a man riding a sleek mare up the steps of the courthouse and into the main hall where Judge Rhea's court was at recess, laughing at something his father said—no, laughing *at* his father, he remembered. And his father's anger, tangible as a cold stone, and a pistol drawn, and the man on the horse laughing at the pistol in his father's hand, but not his eyes laughing. "Sam Hook," said the boy. "Why, I heard them say he was lost—"

"No!" said the old man. He turned to the boy now, dragging around on his knees, grasping tightly the boy's hand. "Never mind—you listen to what *I* say. They ain't gone, none of em. It's all right, it's all the same as it was, just the same. I'll get you another good dog, I promise. You don't have to go, you are only a boy. Bushrod? You hear me?"

"You mean I can stay?" said the boy. "Did you ask Papa?" Behind them, at the house, the door scraped open again. The boy heard it, looked and saw his sister on the gallery, her hand shading her eyes. "Can Morgan stay, too?" he asked.

"It's all right," said old Tom Carter. "It's all right now. We'll get a new dog and raise him up, don't worry." He let go of the boy's hand then, and struggled to his feet. He turned an awkward half circle. The robin flew at last and joined his mates in the trees overhead. "Bushrod?" said the old man. "I found her for you!"

Morgan was there then. She wore a checked gingham dress, yellow and brown, and her hair was pulled back, and at her throat a silver locket on a chain. She came gliding over the yard and lifted her hands and fitted her long fingers to old Tom Carter's face. "Oh, Cousin," she said, and pulled him close to her. She stroked his long white hair. "Oh, Cousin," she said again. "Hush, hush." The old man tried to pull away but she held him fast.

Alex rose and brushed the leaves from his breeches. "He said we might stay, Sister. He said—"

"You, too," said Morgan. "Hush." She put out her hand and the boy came to her, puzzling. She pressed him against her, holding them both against their will, as if she would keep them from flying away like the robins.

+ + +

HARRY STRIBLING HAD not told Gawain of his meeting with Morgan the afternoon before, and apparently the woman had kept the secret too. Stribling thought that commendable. "I suppose you have got your speech lined out," he said to Gawain now, as they stood in the road by the Episcopal church.

"Not atall," said Gawain. He was looking across the way at the Carter house in its grove of oaks. The house looked quiet, serene, not so lonesome as it had in the moonlight. Yet, even by day, it gave of something indefinable: a sense, pehaps, that it was only waiting now.

"That's all right," said Stribling. "I remember my time at the bar—I leaned a good deal on Providence when it was time to sum up."

"The Holy Ghost descending," said Gawain.

"Speaking of that," said Stribling, "I just had a thought. You know what day this is?"

Gawain pondered a moment, counting up from the last time he had known what day it was. "Ah!" he said. "I calculate it is June the twenty-fourth, year of grace eighteen hundred and sixty-five. Saint John the Baptist Day."

"I thought so," said Stribling. He smiled. "Old days, the lodge would've had a feast."

Gawain nodded. "Yes, well, there ain't any lodge now, not here. Maybe next year." Then he smiled as well, remembering. "We had a travelin lodge in the regiment, Harry. Thirty-eight members, I was senior warden. We hadn't of surrendered, I'd of been master next year. This day *last* year we caught a chicken. It didn't go far, but we had a good time."

"We will have a good time again," said Stribling.

"You reckon?"

"Well, sooner or later anyhow."

They went up the road then and turned into the Carters' lane. In a moment they were through the trees and standing by the bottom step of the portico. Gawain saw the irises he'd trampled last night and felt a pang of guilt; his mother would have skinned him for that.

The paint was peeling from the house, and in places the gray cypress wood showed through. Woodbine covered nearly all the front, climbing to the rusted gutters, invading the upper windows. All the windows were open; in one of them, a spider had spun her web. Looking up, Gawain saw that the gallery door was open too, and he wondered if anyone had been watching them from there.

"This house is dyin," said Stribling. He had his pipe out, and was filling it from a silk pouch.

"What?" said Gawain, startled.

Stribling knelt and scratched a lucifer on the boot scraper by the steps. He lit his pipe deliberately, as a man will do when he is thinking. At last he shook the match out and stood up. "It is dyin," he said.

Gawain saw that it was. He looked up at the gray, paintless, bird-streaked facade, at the gutters sprouting with seedling oaks, at the shingles covered with moss, and he thought of the faces of some old people he had known, or of soldiers sometimes, waiting.

Stribling gestured toward the front door with his pipe stem. "Go on," he said. "Let's get it over."

Gawain mounted the steps, crossed the porch to the front door. He looked back, saw that Stribling had moved a little into the yard, was smoking, his arms crossed. He was looking toward the corner of the house.

"Ain't you comin?"

Stribling waved him away, went on smoking. Gawain shrugged and rapped on the door. He waited, rapped again. Up above, some sparrows were fussing in the eaves. He knocked again, hard this time. When no one answered, he turned. "Harry—," he began. But Stribling was gone.

Gawain stood on the porch, thinking maybe he would run, maybe he would do this tomorrow, when the door opened behind him. He turned again, quickly, and in the turning expected all at once to see old Robert the Butler there, as if this were Judge Rhea's house again and all the three years had been a dream and it was still that April evening when there was no Perryville, Stones River, Chickamauga, Chattanooga; no Atlanta, no Franklin nor Nashville, no long retreat in the ice, no defeat—still that April, still Lent, and the moon fixing to rise—all that in the turning, the years folding in on themselves and Gawain Harper, in that instant, for the last time, a ghost of himself, already fading in the sunlight.

But it was no house servant, no Robert with his fine old imperious face and woolly hair and gold half-spectacles. It was a white woman, handsome, her hair shot with gray, smelling faintly of lavender. She stood timidly in the open door, clutching her breast, seeming smaller than she really was, and as Gawain faced her, he felt time opening out again. Women opened doors for themselves now—he had seen it over and over in cabins and great houses along the journey, but he would never get used to it. This woman wouldn't either, he knew. She had no idea how to answer a knock nor confront a stranger without someone in between.

Gawain made his voice gentle and bowed slightly from the waist and was glad he had a hat to sweep off. "Miz Ida Rhea," he said. "What a long time it's been."

The sound of her name seemed to surprise her. "I don't know you," she said, looking curiously at him.

"Gawain Harper," he said. "You may remember me; I came to call on Morgan, a long time ago. May I say that you have changed not at all?"

"Gawain—," she began. Then her eyes grew wide. "My Lord, yes. That professor. Why, wherever did you go? I know—you went in the army, didn't you?"

"Yes, ma'am."

"You lived!" she said. "Through all that trouble! Well, bless God!"

"Yes, ma'am. I prevailed, through much hardship and danger," said Gawain. "And now I have come to ask—"

"Ida, who is that?" came a voice from the dark hall.

The woman started as if she'd been caught lifting hens. "Oh!" she said. "Why, Judge, it's that boy who used to call on Morgan—"

"I believe I know who it is," said the voice, and Judge Nathan Rhea appeared in the door as his wife backed out of it.

Judge Rhea was sixty years old now, by Gawain's calculation. When last he'd seen the Judge, the man's hair and chin whiskers had still been Indian-black, and the bones of his face were chiseled and the skin drawn tight. He'd had no wrinkles save at the corners of his eyes and deep-etched in the space between his bushy brows. The eyes themselves were black and sharp and glittering, and when he spoke, his voice seemed to resonate from somewhere deep inside him, filling a courtroom or parlor as if there could be no other voice in the world.

Now Gawain hardly recognized the man, would not have known him if he'd passed him on the street by light of day. His hair was white and thin, and where the chin whiskers once flourished was only a gray stubble. The eyes were still black, but the lids drooped, the brows had thinned, the skin of his face seemed translucent and had no color at all. The Judge stood in the doorway, his shoulders sagging, the black frock coat hanging loosely, the front of it stained with food. He fidgeted with the key on his watch chain. His hands were thin and hairless; when they began to tremble, the old man thrust them into the pockets of his waistcoat.

"Gawain Harper," said the Judge.

Gawain stood speechless. Here was the moment he had imagined over and over in his head, trying to think of what he would say, and what the Judge would say—and now he couldn't say anything at all. He swallowed, cleared his throat, but still his voice failed him. Finally, he managed a single word: "Judge."

The old man shuffled out onto the porch and stood a hand's-breadth away. He took out his spectacles, fumbled them on, and peered hard into Gawain's face. Gawain could smell him, a smell like dust, like the leaves of old books. "You have changed some," said the Judge.

"Oh, well," said Gawain, finding some remnant of his voice. "I have been a long way, sir."

"Yes," said the Judge. "So you have. A long way. And now you are back again." His voice trailed off, and he moved past Gawain to the edge of the porch. Gawain turned, still holding his hat like a schoolboy.

"The last time you called at my house, I sent you off with a note as I recall. Is that right?"

"You did, sir. I read it sitting on a bench on the square. Then I set a match to it."

The Judge chuckled, a strange sound. "Well, you couldn't call at my house now—oh, you *could* I suppose, but you would find only ashes there, and a curious silence. I go there almost every day, and I am always puzzled by the silence."

"I know the kind you mean, sir," said Gawain. "I have heard it myself."

The Judge looked at his hands for a moment, then tucked them back in his pockets. "I wonder if you really have," he said.

Gawain looked down at his hat. His sweat had stained it, and the rain yesterday had ruined the roll in the brim. "Judge Rhea," he said, "I am sorry for your troubles, and I am not here to add to them. I have come—"

"I never supposed you would make a soldier," said the Judge, as if Gawain had not spoken at all. "Frankly, I thought you were a coward."

Gawain laughed. "Well, you had that part right," he said.

"On the contrary," the Judge went on. "I was wrong in that. You acted well, against all my expectations, and now here you are again—your honor intact, I suppose?"

"I don't know what you mean, sir," said Gawain.

"But you agree it ought to mean something, eh?"

"Maybe it's easier to understand when you win," said Gawain.

The Judge turned and looked at Gawain over the tops of his spectacles. "No, sir," he said. "I have discovered, in the eleventh hour, that victory and honor are best understood by them who lose. My grandfather was in Washington's army. He always said that he despised the British for proud and arrogant soldiers, that he never saw anything noble in them until they marched out to surrender at Yorktown. Their fifers played a tune that day called 'The World Turned Upside Down.' It certainly had for them, eh? And for us, too, now. I wonder—how do you see the world, Mister Harper, after all your adventures?"

Gawain shrugged. "I find it much the same, sir," he said. "A little damaged perhaps, but in the essence, all the same. I want to think so, anyhow. It is what I've been counting on."

The Judge smiled, nodded. "You belonged to that English church, as I recall. And I know you are a Freemason, and therefore a freethinker. Still believe in God, do you? After all this?"

"You are Presbyterian, as I recall," said Gawain. "Do you mean God, or God's will?"

"Is there a difference?"

"I have seen nothing to lead me to doubt," replied Gawain. He waved his hat toward the yard, and beyond it the memory of fire and smoke and ruin. "All that out yonder—we sowed it, and we reaped in turn. I do not believe any of it was His will, and I can't imagine He approved of most of it. Anyway, it wasn't Him burnt your house, it was the yankees. He didn't kill—" He stopped then, just in time, biting the words off hard. If the Judge noticed, he didn't show it.

"I see," said the Judge. "Still a freethinker, then. Well, forgive my catechism, but I am curious to discover how you perceive, as you put it, the *essence.*" The Judge rested his hand on one of the great square columns. "When my daughter told me you'd gone with the army, I laughed in her face. When I discovered it was true, I considered apologizing but didn't, for it is not—was not—in my nature, and I supposed you'd come crawling back by winter anyhow. But you didn't, and again I was checked. I was forced to admit at last that you had done the honorable thing. But then, you see, circumstances took their turn. All was lost, the end was obvious even to me, and I began to believe we'd been betrayed—by you and your kind, the ones we had depended on to save us from shame. Oh, Mister Harper, betrayal is not too strong a word, though even it has a loftier connotation than what I had in mind."

Betrayal, Gawain thought, the anger rising in him. "And what do you believe now, sir?" he asked.

The Judge held up his hand. It was steady now. With a deliberate movement, he hooked the first two fingers in Gawain's waistcoat and drew him near, their faces almost touching. When the Judge spoke, his voice was almost a whisper. "You see? Honor means something to you after all, doesn't it? You have come away with yours intact, you and the rest, and immortal myths will be fashioned about you, and great epics will be wrought. In the end, all that will remain is the honor, the sacrifice. It is the way of primitive peoples, sir, and we Southerners—but never mind. I have learned to accept that. I understand what you did now—*made* myself understand it, look it in the face, because I had to. I would even ask forgiveness, if it were yours to give—but it isn't. Only the dead can offer that gift."

"Then why don't you ask her for it," said Gawain.

The Judge's face colored for an instant, then his hand tightened in the fabric of Gawain's waistcoat. "You know about Lily?"

"Yes, sir," said Gawain.

The Judge's hand relaxed, but still he held on to Gawain. He looked away, and for an instant Gawain thought the old man might collapse. "Sir," said Gawain. He grasped the Judge's arm. "Sir, it was never my intention to—"

The old man snapped his head around, eyes glittering. "I am sensible of your intentions, but we were talking about honor. Are they the same?"

"I hoped—I believe they are," said Gawain.

"My daughter thought you were dead. She grieved for you in her own way. I could tell, though she never spoke to me about it, has hardly spoken to me at all since the house burned—she blamed me for it, and rightly so perhaps, and for Lily—"

Gawain started to protest, but the old man shook him silent. "Listen!"

he said. "I never believed you were dead, not for a moment. God has taken so much from me, but I knew He wouldn't take that. In return, I had to come to terms with what I perceived as your betrayal. *Quid pro quo*, sir— it is often thus when dealing with God. I allowed you—all of you—the honor I thought you'd lost with defeat. I had to, you see, to preserve my own."

"Judge—," began Gawain.

"No," the Judge went on. "I have been waiting for you, knowing you would come. You may deny God's hand in it, but here you stand never-theless—with your honor and your intentions. Do you really want to con-nect the two?"

Gawain understood then. *Quid pro quo.* He almost laughed, so far had he come from his own expectations. He removed the Judge's hand from his waistcoat, but held on to it, was surprised by the strength in it. "Yes," he said.

"Good," said the Judge. "Then you will stand with me when I go to kill Solomon Gault."

✦   ✦   ✦

STRIBLING FOUND THEM, as he supposed he would, on a bench in the old kitchen garden: Morgan and the old man side by side, and the boy sit-ting on the ground with his knees drawn up. The old man was talking, telling a story, his hands clasping and unclasping in the lap of his night-shirt. The woman was listening, the boy was studying something in the grass. Stribling, standing in the garden gate, smoking quietly, listened him-self for a moment to the old man's disconnected tale about people Stribling had never known, getting into some mischief on a day long vanished from the earth. At one point the old man laughed, and Stribling found himself laughing too. When he did, the woman looked up, startled, and the boy jumped to his feet. Stribling snatched off his hat. "God bless all here," he said.

Morgan rose. "Why, Captain Stribling," she said. Meanwhile, the old man had quieted.

"Forgive me," said Stribling. "I was only out for a stroll this mornin."

The woman laughed. "Do you often stroll through people's gardens? Not that there's any harm in it, I suppose. And don't you ever stay in the guardhouse, or whatever they call it?"

"I was set free before breakfast," said Stribling. He waved his hand. "Thought I'd walk about the town, heard you all back here, knew your voice right away—"

"You are a poor liar, Captain."

Stribling laughed then. "No, actually I'm real good at it, but only under pressure."

"I am glad you do not feel pressured now," said Morgan. "Will you take some breakfast?"

"Oh, I have eaten," said Stribling. "However, there *is* something you could do for me—only a little kindness, won't take a moment."

She eyed him suspiciously. "What is that, sir?"

"Take a turn with me around front, where your father has Gawain Harper cornered on the porch."

Her eyes widened, and she clutched at the locket around her neck. "Good Lord, sir, do you mean it?" She turned quickly to the boy. "Alex, will you look after Cousin? See him to the house—through the back, mind. Will you do that? And go find Mama?"

The boy nodded his head, looked at Stribling. "Are you a stranger?" he asked.

"Pretty strange," said Stribling, bowing. "And you are . . . ?"

"I am Alex Rhea, ten years old on the third of Feb-wary," said the boy. "That is my sister you are talkin to. She is a widow. Are you come courtin?"

"Alex!" said the boy's sister.

Stribling shook his head gravely. "Would that I were," he said, "but I am only the humble instrument of Providence."

Morgan smoothed her hair, her dress, looked toward the house, then back at Stribling. "My father," she said. "And Gawain."

"He told me he came to see you," said Stribling. "I am glad of it."

"Oh, yes," she said. "In the middle of the night. I suppose he would've climbed a trellis or somethin, had I not been in the yard."

"Well, he has come again," said Stribling. He held out his arm. "If we leave now, we can catch the closin arguments."

She took his arm then, and together they walked toward the house. "No hurry," said Stribling. "Plenty of time—they're just gettin wound up. What're these little blue flowers here?"

✦   ✦   ✦

ONCE MORE GAWAIN Harper saw, in all its parts, the moment he was standing in. A pair of flickers were moving in a courtship dance in the yard. A wagon was passing on the cemetery road. Through the open door of the Carter house, he could hear voices—a child's, a woman's—the words lost to him. Judge Rhea was still watching, his eyes sharp and intent behind the spectacles, waiting. Gawain wished he could wait himself, rearrange all this to fit the shape he had carried so long in his head. But he understood that this moment, not some other, was the one prepared for him since the day Lily died. "If I stand with you, then," he said at last, "you will allow me to call on Morgan?"

"Plainly put," said the Judge.

Gawain shook his head. "You would make a pawn of her? Is that your notion of honor?"

"Dammit, sir," said the Judge.

"You'll give up this foolishness about Brazil?"

"I didn't say that. She will have to choose."

Gawain still held the old man's hand. He let go of it now, stepped to the edge of the porch and looked out at the yard. The flickers darted upward, circled, lit again. "I could call on her anyway, Judge, with your permission or without. I could keep her from going—you know I could."

The old man laughed dryly. "Again, that would depend on Morgan, wouldn't it?" he said.

Now Gawain laughed. "I suppose it would," he said. "Strange, though—" He turned, looked at the Judge. "You never gave her any such choices before. You sent a note, you recall."

"Yes," said the old man. "That was so you would make a choice, and you did. Now you must make another because of it."

"What if it's God's will that I not choose?" said Gawain.

"If that were so, sir, He would not have brought you here," said the Judge. "But you *are* here, and I have asked it of you, and you will choose because you have to now. Your choice don't come back to God or to Morgan, sir—never did. It comes back to honor."

Gawain threw up his hands. "Why me, Judge? Why anybody? If Gault killed . . . if he did that thing, then why—" Gawain stopped, knowing he was going toward a place he did not want to go. But the Judge finished the thought for him.

"Why haven't I confronted him before now? Is that what you want to know?"

"Yes, sir," said Gawain, looking away.

The Judge removed his spectacles, folded them, pointed with them toward the square. "A good many out yonder would like to ask the same question," he said. "The answer is quite simple, really. I am too old to face Solomon Gault alone, and I am afraid."

"You? Afraid?"

"Does that surprise you?" asked the Judge. "Or does it merely offend your sense of chivalry?"

"Maybe a little of both," said Gawain. "She was your daughter."

"Yes," said the Judge. "Yes, she was."

"But why me?" asked Gawain. "Why did you wait for me?"

"Because of her," said the Judge, and pointed again, this time toward the corner of the house. Gawain looked, saw Morgan and Stribling walking up along the box hedges. There was no time left now for thinking.

"I will go with you, Judge," said Gawain quickly, "but I won't trade."

"Of course not," said the Judge. "That's what I meant about honor."

· XIV ·

*H*onor!" said Morgan. "Is that what brought you here with your hat in your hand?"

"I came here to see your daddy," said Gawain. "He brought up the question, I didn't."

They were alone in the garden, Morgan on the bench, Gawain pacing up and down before her. She sat erect, her feet together, hands knotted in her lap. "Quit that walkin up and down," she said. "You are makin me nervous."

Gawain stopped his pacing, jammed his hands in his pockets and rocked on his heels. "She was your sister," he said. "I should think you'd be glad."

"Glad?" said Morgan. "Let me tell you something, sir. I have lain awake every night for a year now, wondering why Papa didn't kill that arrogant, self-righteous ass. Then I would lie awake a little longer, thinkin of ways I could kill him myself. But this . . . this *covenant,* and I the surety, as if I were a hecatomb or a piece of good bottomland. My God."

"It ain't like that," said Gawain. "I can't explain it. It is impossible to explain."

"Perhaps you should try," said Morgan.

Gawain came and sat beside her on the bench. "Look here," he said, "I told your daddy I would not trade—"

"Oh, *that's* flattering," said Morgan.

"Hah!" said Gawain. He stood up and began to pace again. "You can't have it every which way, Morgan. Your father demands some proof of me—I expected that, and you *ought* to be flattered. I just didn't expect the thing to turn the way it did."

She was silent, watching him from the bench.

"I have no job, no fortune, no prospects," Gawain went on. "I went soldierin and look what happened. What else *could* I offer him, pray? At least he owns up to it—that he waited—that he—" Gawain stopped, waving his hands in frustration. "Do you have any idea how hard it was for him to wait, to raise not a hand, and everybody, includin his own daughter, wonderin why he didn't—why he didn't—"

"Do the honorable thing?" said Morgan.

"Yes."

"Well," she said, "I am sure he suffered."

Gawain looked at her, sitting on the iron bench in the ruined, over-grown garden. When she spoke again, her voice was quiet and contained: "When my husband left for the gold fields, I was eighteen years old with a child buried in the graveyard yonder. I waited a year without a word from him, until one day a parcel came. When I opened it, a curl of hair fell out. It was white, and still had flakes of scalp in it, and it was pasted together with dried blood. Only when I read the letter did I understand whose hair it was. His was black when he left, you see. No doubt people will have told you that my husband's wedding ring was among his effects."

She looked at Gawain, expecting a reply. "Yes," said Gawain, suddenly ashamed by the knowledge, remembering how he'd told the story to Stribling. "Yes, I have heard that."

"Come," she said then, and patted the bench beside her. Gawain sat, and she half-turned to face him, laying her hand on his sleeve. "There was a ring," she said, "but it wasn't the one *I'd* given him." He started to speak, but she touched his lips with her fingers. "I said I would never wait for anybody again, but I did. I waited for you. When I believed at last that you were dead, I knew there wouldn't even be a parcel this time. Please do not lecture me about waiting; I know all I ever want to know about it."

She dropped her hand, and Gawain took it with his own. The garden, with its overgrown wisteria, its fences covered in honeysuckle, its weedy patches where once flowers and herbs grew, lay warm in the morning sun. The wisteria was heavy with pendulous blooms; their odor was sweet, so strong it was almost visible, and bees swarmed among them. A pool, encum-bered with vines, reflected the brightness of the sky like a sheet of old glass; from its shadows, now and then, ancient goldfish rose to gasp at the air, then sink again, their bronze backs glinting for an instant in the sunlight.

♦   ♦   ♦

ON THE WAY back to Aunt Vassar's, Gawain and Stribling avoided the road and passed behind the old Academy through the woods. As they went along, Gawain told about the conversation with the Judge and the trouble with King Solomon Gault.

"This man Gault," said Stribling. "What's he like?"

"In the old times, I only knew him by reputation," said Gawain.

"During the war, he had one of these irregular cavalry outfits, like we had so much trouble with in Tennessee. He killed a friend of mine, a woman." Gawain paused, not wanting to shape the words. "Morgan's sister," he said at last.

"My God," said Stribling. "Tell me."

So Gawain told about how Gault and his men had killed Lily Landers and hanged her no-account husband, and how the boy Willy had wandered off or been taken off, nobody knew which, only that he was gone. When Gawain was finished, Stribling shook his head in disgust. "He needs killin all right. Wonder the Judge ain't done it by now."

"I don't know, Harry," said Gawain. "I guess he needs a second, and I am it. If he don't do it at all, I am still it. I can't let that go."

"Well," said Stribling, "it's a thing needs doin, all right. But the Judge is right—some things a man ought not to have to do alone."

They had paused in a place where the ground was covered in moss. Stribling knelt and brushed his fingers across the soft green carpet. "Seems to me you have got yourself in a fix," he said.

Gawain nodded. "Yes, I have. I thought I was finished killin people, but there ain't a damn thing I can do about it. Anyway, there is Morgan."

"Yes," said Stribling. "She is worth it."

"So was Lily, I reckon," said Gawain.

"Yes, of course she was."

They went on. In a little while, Stribling spotted a young possum in the fork of a tree, tail curling down, blinking in the light.

"You ever eat one of those?" asked Stribling.

"A time or two in the field, when pressed," replied Gawain.

"What do they taste like?"

Gawain thought a moment. "Grease," he said.

So Stribling shot the possum with his pistol, and Gawain carried it home by its tail and gave it to Uncle Priam.

"Now that's a tender shoat," old Priam said. "We'll bake him in the ashes, be just right for Sunday dinner."

Later, they ate in the dining room, on the good dishes: new potatoes, watercress, some dandelion greens seasoned with fatback, a little broth from a boiled ham bone, and, in a stone pitcher, some good spring water. Old Frank Harper slumped in his chair at the head of the table, a napkin tucked in his shirt front; Stribling, as the guest, sat to his right. Aunt Vassar was at the other end, Gawain to her left. The doors and windows were open, and a good breeze, scented with grass and lantana, blew in and stirred the light curtains.

Gawain told his aunt about the meeting with the Judge, leaving out the part about Solomon Gault and emphasizing the possibility that Morgan, at least, might be saved from Brazil.

"Saved how?" asked his aunt, regarding him over her spectacles. "And what about that boy? What would he do without his sister?"

"I do not have all that figured out yet," said Gawain testily. "All I know is, I won't have her goin off down there to eat coconuts and live in a hole in the ground. Anyway, the Judge said I might call on her."

"You're turnin red, boy," said Aunt Vassar. "Will you have some more potatoes?"

They ate in silence for a while, then Aunt Vassar nodded at the old man. "Mister Harper don't come down for dinner much," she said. "I am glad he felt up to it today, you boys being home and all."

Old Harper picked up his fork and prodded among the greens on his plate. "There's goats up in the house, Ellie," he said. "One of em has shat on this plate."

No one spoke for a moment. Then Aunt Vassar lay down her fork. She put her hand on Gawain's arm, but looked at Stribling. "Captain Stribling, we are grateful for that good possum," she said.

"I was only the instrument of Providence, Miss Vassar," said Stribling. He was about to go on when old Harper jabbed him in the elbow with his fork. Stribling winced.

"Who're you!" shouted the old man. "What're you about!"

"*Mister* Harper—," began Aunt Vassar, but Stribling held up his hand.

"It's all right," he said. "I am glad to be in his company, and especially in yours. I look forward to the possum on Sunday—truth to tell, I never ate one. What do they taste like?"

"Oh," said the aunt, coloring slightly. "They are noble fare, sir. Noble."

Stribling nodded, went on with his meal.

"Let me tell you a story, Aunt," said Gawain. "One time Jack Bishop— you remember him?"

"Oh, yes, poor boy," said Aunt Vassar.

"Goddamn goats all up in here," said old Harper.

Gawain took a drink of water. "One time Jack Bishop and I were foraging in the woods up in Tennessee? Came upon one of these country people camped out in a railroad cut, had a fire and a bird turnin on a green willow stick. Jack says to him—we were hungry, as usual—Jack says, 'What you got on that stick?' Fellow was cuttin up a onion, tears all down his face, he says, 'Well, it's a hawk.'"

"Good heavens," said Aunt Vassar.

"Yep," said Gawain. "Still had the beak on it, talons too." He clawed his hands like talons. "Jack looked at him, said, 'Well, good God.' Fellow said, 'You want some? It's real good.' Jack says, 'Well, what's it taste like?'" Gawain stopped, forked a mouthful of cress.

"Well," said Aunt Vassar after a moment, "what did the man say to that?"

Gawain laughed. "Looked at Jack like he was a fool, said, 'Oh, 'bout like a owl.'"

Aunt Vassar looked blank for an instant, then her eyes widened and she began to laugh—carefully at first, as if laughing were an art she had neglected and now was taking up again. "An owl!" she said, and with the words her laughter grew until it was full accomplished. It was a good sound, the old woman laughing in the cool dining room, the breeze tinkling in the lamp pendants again, the smell of grass and summer. Gawain, watching his aunt, suddenly ached with recognition, as if time had reeled backward and touched on some vanished nooning they had known. He remembered the geese looking down on converging roads in the starlight, and all at once he could see them traveling in time: all them he knew and loved, and them he didn't like much, and the myriad whose lives he would never know, each one with his carpet bag following time. He felt the quick tears come to his eyes, blinked them away before they could fall. "That's a good story, ain't it?" he tried to say, but his voice caught and betrayed him, and suddenly he *was* crying, silently, not much caring now, having come too far to be ashamed. He rose, pushed his chair back, and without saying more, fled out the door to the side gallery and was gone.

✦　✦　✦

ONCE THE COURTHOUSE bell would have tolled the hour, the slow, measured strokes of noon, and the hotel dinner bell would ring. No bells now, but still the pause, the moment when the day seemed to turn, and the morning ceased, and afternoon began. The clouds, impossibly white against the blue sky, gathered pile upon pile, shifting, moving across the sun then away again so that the earth was by turns shadowed and bright. Now and then a strong breeze, moving ahead of the coming rain, shuddered in the trees, and the leaves of maples turned their pale undersides to the light. Chimney swifts swirled above the houses, riding higher and higher on the rising heat. Hawks circled, and buzzards over the country fields. A southbound locomotive, with four empty flats and a cabin car, crept uneasily over the ramshackle Tallahatchie River bridge; when it blew for an isolated crossing, the sound of its whistle could be heard for miles. Everywhere, through the color and the brightness and the shadow of afternoon, all things followed time, and all persons followed time.

In the Carter boy's room, Morgan was reading *Les Misérables,* now and then watching out the window toward the lane. Alex practiced sword fighting in the yard and kept an eye on the weather, and the Judge paced in the library, and old Mister Carter searched for France's grave in the woods behind the house.

After dinner, Gawain's father nodded in his chair by the window, muttering and moving his hands, while below Uncle Priam poked at the fire on the kitchen hearth. Stribling went to work on the crib to make a place for Zeke, and in a little while, Aunt Vassar brought out a pitcher of water and spoke to him:

"I am sorry about all that in yonder," she said, waving her hand toward the house.

"I can think of ten thousand reasons why you ought not to be," said Stribling, and they talked a long time while the wasps buzzed about their heads.

At the Citadel of Djibouti, L. W. Thomas leaned his elbows on the bar and talked quietly with Marcus Peck and Carl Nobles. Sheriff Luker propped his chair against the wall in the shadows and listened. Behind the tavern, Queenolia Divine sat on a keg by Town Creek, fishing. Old Hundred-and-Eleven, worn out from his morning's exertions at the graveyard, snored in a corner of the deserted boxcar jail while the sentry walked to and fro. In the shade beneath the car, Dauncy was showing Jack the best way to sharpen a pocket knife. In the camp, Captain Bloom's company stood at parade rest on the color line and listened as their Colonel spoke to them. Their eyes were drawn to the blanket-shrouded litter at the Colonel's feet, but Rafe Deaton would not look at it; he twisted the socket ring of his bayonet and looked off toward the railroad. In the woods below Leaf River, Molochi Fish set a pot of greens on the fire; a few miles away, Wall Stutts was still asleep after the rigors of the night, lying in the dogtrot of his cabin on the old Gault place. King Solomon Gault himself sat at his desk in the farm office where he lived now that his house was burned. Soon he would ride out to Yellow Leaf Church to visit his wife in the graveyard, but for now, he was taking an hour to work on his memoirs:

> For what is defeat or shame, what the delusion of freedom under oppression? Only self-imposed shackles of the mind; debilitating in some; in others, subject to the will, readily broken, cast away, then forgotten in the tasks of renewed struggle or in the oblivion of the grave. That last morning, as I bid farewell to my gallant troop . . .

So all these followed time as they must, all traveling together through the noon and afternoon, while the rain moved in from the west where the

Great River lay. Gawain Harper journeyed that way, too, with this difference: only he, among them all, was aware of it, could sense their passage, could hear it almost like the long flocks of blackbirds that whispered overhead in a winter twilight.

When he left his aunt's house, Gawain retraced the path he and Stribling had taken earlier, through the side yard, through the woods and around the back of the old Academy. The path he was taking now was not a conscious choice, any more than the geese had chosen what arc they would take in the night, or what star to navigate by—but it *was* a choice, he told himself. He merely went, trusting in the way.

Presently, he found himself on the grounds of the Academy again. In the shifting diffusion of light among the trees, the buildings rose like old ruined abbeys. Speckled with leaf shadow, vines already taken hold, they seemed the ancient remnants of a struggle long healed and forgotten, too old even for ghosts to remember. But Gawain Harper remembered. He put his hand against the bricks and knew that they were real, knew he had been here once and now had returned and too much had happened in between. In that moment in the dining room, he had glimpsed, perhaps for the last time, the world that had shaped him. Now he was following time again, he and all the rest, toward something—the stones in the burying ground, confrontations, freedom perhaps, or peace, he couldn't say. It should not have bothered him, he knew—he would make his choices, they all would, and the seasons would go on, and the moon and sun, and the planets in their wandering. But right now he could see beyond the light a darkness he did not want to enter, but that drew near him, near them all, as surely as the coming night.

After a time, Gawain came to the shell of the building he and Stribling had visited that morning. This time, he climbed the steps, his feet crunching in the glass, and tried the door. The latch gave to his hand and he hesitated, knowing full well what he would see, and knowing he could never be ready for it. He pushed the door. It opened on nothing. Gawain blinked and almost fell, pulled into the emptiness. He caught the door frame and hung there, leaning out into space. In a little while he steadied himself, pushed away and sat on the step again. He took the rosary from his pocket and began to tell the beads.

Saturday's rain terrified and delighted Alex Rhea beyond all his imaginings. A little after two o'clock, the clouds thickened and turned black, and the day darkened so that birds sought their roosting. Presently, the sky turned a sickly green behind the clouds, and the lightning flickered. There were distant rumblings, and the wind thrashed in the trees. Alex, his face stung by dust and leaves driven by the wind, stood on the widow's walk atop old Carter's house and watched in awe as the slanted veils of rain swept in from the west. Suddenly a blinding flash drew all the world in stark outline, and an instant later the thunder seemed to explode just above his head, and Alex ran for the trapdoor and the narrow stairs. When the rain struck, it did not announce itself with patterings but came all at once and full blown like old Noah's deluge must have done.

All evening and night the rain hammered the earth, the lightning sparked, thunder rattled windows in their sashes. Trees groaned and sighed, and some in their writhing uprooted themselves and fell, and shingles flew like leaves, and tents pulled up their stakes and fluttered away like frantic ghosts. A man was killed by a falling limb, an infant drowned in the high waters of Town Creek.

Sunday morning, as if in apology, the sky was clear and benign, and the air washed clean. People emerged from whatever shelter they had found and looked meekly about, as after a great battle. They had been humbled, reminded of how little power they possessed and how helpless they really were. They seemed astonished, disappointed almost, that the world had not changed to any great degree. Then the axes began, and the saws, and the sound of voices calling to one another across the morning, and the people forgot until next time.

In the Federal camp, the soldiers repaired their tents and rebuilt their fires and ate breakfast squatting on their heels on the sodden ground. Then the drums beat assembly, and Captain Bloom's company was paraded on the color line for church call. Tom Kelly was about to be committed to the earth, his vessel a plain box nailed together from the weatherboards of an abandoned house. The box waited on the color line. On the lid, a cavalry farrier had burned the soldier's name, his regiment, his dates—a futile gesture, for such a coffin would not last long down below.

These troops had a chaplain once, a Unitarian and vocal abolitionist from the East. He had not been in Cumberland long before Old Hundred-and-Eleven called him out on the doctrine of the Trinity. The discussion heated up, Old Hundred-and-Eleven smote the chaplain with a stick of firewood, and the man left the next morning for Massachusetts again, shaking the dust of the wild frontier from his feet. So it was that, when the troops had been paraded and inspected and read the orders of the day, Colonel Burduck came out on the field accompanied by a wizened little man in an old-fashioned black frock coat and wing collar and steel spectacles: the Reverend Roy Spaulding of the Cumberland Methodist Church who, because Kelly had been a Methodist himself, had been asked to preside. The old man accepted at once. He did not mention that his own church had been reduced to cinders by the army to which Tom Kelly belonged.

The minister stood beside the Colonel for a moment, clutching his Testament, his head bowed. Then he lifted his face and spoke. His voice was strong and clear; the soldiers would say later that it was more of a voice than such a dried-up little fellow ought to have. Moreover, they would tell how the man never once mentioned sin or hell or the futility of earthly deeds, never once invited them to look into their own souls to see if salvation dwelt there. Instead, he began by asking their forgiveness that he should presume to speak of a boy he never knew. Then he spoke of humility, of mercy, of grief—even God's grief that such a boy should be finished so soon. When he was done, he turned to the Colonel and asked if the men might kneel. The Colonel spoke to the Captain, the Captain gave the commands, and the men grounded arms and knelt in place in the mud. Above them the regimental and national colors whisked in the warm breeze. Old Spaulding turned his voice to God then, and asked that young Tom Kelly be forgiven for whatever sins he had managed to commit in his twenty years, and that God welcome him and be kind to him, for he would surely be afraid. When he was finished, the troops were brought to attention again, the musicians called to the front, and Tom Kelly was borne to the graveyard to the beat of the slow march.

The soldiers' burying ground was deep in mud and standing water. Captain Bloom's company formed a hollow square around the grave, the first time this ground had seen such a display for a private of the line.

Reverend Spaulding offered a final prayer, then the box was lowered with ropes by four soldiers, Rafe Deaton among them; it made a squelching sound at the bottom, for the grave was deep in water. Colonel Burduck, at the head of the grave, nodded once to Dauncy and Jack who were standing by with their shovels. The brothers bent to their work, with Old Hundred-and-Eleven looking on from beneath his umbrella. As the first heavy clods of mud struck the coffin lid, the troops were brought to shoulder arms. In a moment they marched away, the drums beating a quick march now.

A scattering of civilian spectators watched a little distance from the grave. Henry Clyde Wooster had already filled three pages in his notebook. At the edge of the gathering were L. W. Thomas and Carl Nobles, and Marcus Peck leaning on his crutches. Their eyes were red and swollen from drink, for they had spent the night in the Citadel listening to the wind pushing at the boards. Now they stood without speaking, their faces showing nothing. Nearby stood Captain King Solomon Gault. His eyes were lively and quick, darting here and there under the brim of his broad straw hat. This morning he wore a tan sack coat and fawn-colored breeches and a brocade waistcoat and good boots, for he was on his way to morning prayer. He nodded approvingly as the Federal troops executed the maneuvers necessary to come from a hollow square into line. When they marched away, the drums stirred him as they always had, and it was all he could do to keep from applauding. If only he could have commanded such troops as these—but never mind. He would do the best with what he had. He turned to the man lounging next to him in the sparse gathering of townsmen. "Well done," he said.

Wall Stutts nodded and spat a stream of ambure after the departing soldiers. "Sho', Cap'n," he said. "Whatever you say."

✦   ✦   ✦

HARRY STRIBLING HAD left the house at daybreak. He saddled Zeke in the cool dawning and rode north up the Holly Springs road for a few miles to take the air, then doubled back to Cumberland. Just past the house again, he cut cross-country, guiding Zeke through the fields and woodlots, feeling like he was on the scout again. It was hard going in some places; the storm had done great damage (though he had slept through it all in Gawain's sisters' room, in a girl's narrow sleigh bed that still smelled faintly of talc) and they had to hunt for a passage now and then. The swollen creek was a problem, too, but they found a ford just south of the railroad bridge. Once across, the going was easier; they sauntered past the burned depot and the boxcar jail and approached the Federal camp;

the wind was from the south, and they could smell the fires and the breakfast cooking, and Stribling's stomach growled in response. When he heard
the drums beating church call, Stribling found a place among some willows
near the railroad, dug out his spyglass from a saddlebag, and waited.
Presently he lifted the glass and through it watched the column enter the
burying ground, the drums beating a slow march and the infantry coming
along at right shoulder shift. Again he felt like he was back in the old times,
scouting for Chalmers, counting bayonets, but he shook it off and concen-
trated on the civilians tagging along at the end of the procession. He was
surprised to see Nobles and Thomas; they were shambling along, helping
the one-legged Irishman Peck through the mud. The others he did not
know, though one of them caught his eye: a well-appointed gentleman in
a tan sack coat whom he somehow recognized, though he had never seen
the man before. "Solomon Gault," he said, lowering the glass. "It's got to
be him, Zeke."

"That's him all right."

For an instant, the mad notion cut across Stribling's mind that the horse
had answered him, but Zeke was already sidestepping nervously and about
to tangle himself in a blowdown, and Stribling had to fight to get him settled. By then he had seen the man—he had appeared out of the trees without a sound. Stribling cursed himself for a greenhorn, a fool who could be
bushwhacked three times now in the broad light of day. "Goddammit," he
said. "I am tired of these surprises. What you doin here?"

"It's a free country," said Molochi Fish. "Or ain't you heard?"

✦   ✦   ✦

GAWAIN HARPER WOKE to a grievous headache; he had been afflicted
by them ever since the fight in Georgia when he was knocked in the head
by a rock-hard lump of clay. That is how he thought of it, for being
knocked in the head had always been his aunt's idea of the worst thing that
could happen to anybody. When he was a child, she would say, "You keep
goin in those woods by yourself, somebody gon' knock you in the head."
Later, it was "You go up to Memphis by yourself, somebody gon' knock
you in the head" or "I wouldn't put my foot in that place, be afraid I'd get
knocked in the head," and so on. Gawain always made light of her fear,
but when he finally *was* knocked in the head, he understood the gravity of
it. He was reminded of it this morning, as he groped in his bag for the
physic powder a druggist in Meridian had sold him.

He felt better after breakfast and declared his intention of taking his aunt
to morning prayer. He looked for Stribling to invite him as well, but that
gentleman, old Priam said, had saddled up before daylight and ridden off

somewhere. Aunt Vassar took a while to get ready, so the bells were already ringing when they set off through the morning for Holy Cross church.

The troubling thoughts of the previous day did not follow Gawain Harper into the sunlight. Although his head still pained him some, his mind was clear, and no weight rested on his heart. He thought he looked pretty dashing in his brushed clothes and watch chain and walking stick, with his hat slanted over one eye and the prayer book under his arm. Nothing bad was happening to him right now, and he walked in the moment as he had learned to do when he could. Aunt Vassar was in her usual black, but she, too, seemed at ease, and talked lightly as they went along. Gawain's only immediate regret was that Morgan was not Episcopalian, so would not be there to admire him. Well, maybe after dinner he would slip over to the Carter house in his finery.

They sat in their old pew, and Gawain looked about him determined not to be hurt by what he might see. Many of the old faces were gone, and those remaining had a gaunt look. They had aged some, his friends of the old time. But they spoke to him kindly, and in their voices Gawain heard the echoes of all they had been to him, and by their touch he knew them to be real. The church itself was shabbier than he remembered, the pews and the floors creakier, the windows grimy. But the smell was the same—candles, old women, books—and the same wasps still buzzed lazily over their heads. The women's fans still fluttered, and the men ran their fingers around the inside of their collars as they always had.

Father Garrison's successor was a younger man, tall, nervous in his movements. His speaking voice had all the marks of the Virginia seminary from which he'd graduated. As the priest began the litany, Gawain had a thought. He leaned over to his aunt and whispered against her ear: "Say, Aunt."

"Hush," she replied.

"But I want to ask you somethin," Gawain persisted.

"*What?*" she hissed.

"I want to ask you—back last summer, did the yankees keep their horses up in here?"

"What in the nation are you talkin about?" said his aunt.

"Thank you," Gawain said.

"The Lord be with you," intoned the priest.

"And with thy spirit," said Gawain and Aunt Vassar and all the others.

Gawain was a little disappointed that the priest failed to mention Saint John the Baptist in his homily. Still, the man was a good high-churchman like Father Garrison, and when the service was over, Gawain felt satisfied.

There was the usual bustle and talk at leaving, and the usual delay in the aisle as each person stopped to speak to the priest at the door.

As Gawain stood facing the rear of the church, calculating how long it would take to get out, he noticed a man sitting alone in the back pew, waiting. Suddenly the light went out of the day, and Gawain felt the clutch of anger and of fear, old familiar partners, and with them the thought *Not here. Not here.* Then the red light breaking behind his eyes, and the trembling, and at last the calm, all passing in a moment as he stood behind Aunt Vassar in the nave of Holy Cross.

King Solomon Gault sat with his legs crossed, his arm across the back of the pew, his eyes fixed on the altar. He seemed to be lost in thought, his face reverent and at ease.

Gawain did not look at Gault when he passed. He managed to slip around the priest, an easy task, for Aunt Vassar was ahead of him, and she would hold the man's hand and ask about his family and comment at length on the homily while people bunched up in the nave behind. Gawain moved out into the churchyard and dropped his prayer book in the grass. He was breathing deeply of the clear air, thinking *The son of a bitch the goddamned son of a bitch* while absolution and grace and joy slipped away. His thoughts drove him away from all who were gathered there, and he thought *I could do it now, get it over* except he had no pistol, no knife, nothing but the walking stick, and he had never been any good at knocking a man in the head. He fought himself then, hearing the priest's voice not twenty minutes gone: *Let us confess our sins unto Almighty God—* He felt the weight of his sins and wished that Stribling were here so that one man, at least, might understand what had descended upon him so quick in the holy light of Sunday. Except Stribling would try to talk him out of it, and what good would that be? And no sooner had he thought of Stribling than he raised his eyes and saw, at the end of the overgrown brick walk, Harry Stribling himself sitting on old Zeke, leaning forward in the saddle, his hands crossed on the pommel. Gawain, at first sight, thought man and horse an apparition, so silent had they come. But the horse nickered at him, and Stribling grinned and lifted his hat, and Gawain knew they were as real as anything else he might put his hand to in that moment. He went on down the walk in the leaf-dappled sunlight, a long way it seemed, and the voices in the churchyard seemed distant and without meaning. At last he had come far enough; he took hold of Zeke's army bit and looked up and said, "Gault is here, Harry. What am I to do?" And Stribling, shaking his head, thumbing his hat back and looking toward the church: "He's here, too? Good God." Then he said the very thing Gawain Harper knew he would say: "This ain't the time, pard, believe me," and it wasn't any good at all, no help at all.

Now the bell was tolling again. Gawain let go of the bit, backed away, watching Stribling's face. At last he turned; Aunt Vassar was huddled with a pair of old gossips, all in black, and in the yard stood Solomon Gault, an unlit cigar in his fingers, watching him.

"Gawain," said Stribling behind him, but too late now. Gawain was already moving, slapping the brass head of the walking stick in his palm, his eyes on Solomon Gault's face.

All right. He could knock a man in the head all right. He had done it once before anyhow, on the works at Franklin, took his musket by the first band—hard to swing a musket with a fixed bayonet, but he had done it all right. The point of the bayonet had jabbed him in the stomach, but he had done it and the boy's head cracked—he could hear it crack, even over the terrible detonation, the solid wall of sound that surrounded them, impenetrable, and Gawain Harper moved on through it and into the smoke beyond—he who had once read Keats to the young girls in a room full of sunlight—

Then the horse was in front of him, turned by the flank, and Gawain said, "Get out of the way, Harry," and Stribling reached down from the saddle and gathered Gawain's shirtfront in his fist and said, "Goddamn you, stop." But Gawain was still walking, pushing at the horse. The people were looking, and the priest had stopped, still shaking someone's hand, and was looking too, and Solomon Gault was walking. Then Aunt Vassar was there, and Stribling released his hold.

"Gawain," she said. "He has a pistol in the tail pocket of his coat. There is no honor in dying like a dog, boy."

Gawain stopped. He couldn't seem to get enough air. "All right," he said. "All right. All right." Then, looking at Stribling: "You got a pistol. Let me borrow it."

"Nope," said Stribling.

"Harry—"

"Leave it alone, Gawain," said Aunt Vassar. "This is not your affair."

"All right," he said. "All right, all right." But it was too late then, for Solomon Gault was there, touching the horse's nose. Stribling backed Zeke a few steps and sat watching, his hand inside his frock coat. Aunt Vassar stood her ground.

"You have business with me, sir?" said Gault. He was relaxed, holding the cigar in two fingers.

"Yes," said Gawain. "Yes, I do."

"Get on with it, then," said Gault.

Gawain looked around him. He was not afraid, though he knew he would be later. And later he would wish he had never seen Solomon Gault in the pew, though he would know that he'd have to wish a lot further back than that to fix things, to reshape the universe so that he did not have to stand here now in the sunlight saying, "Gault, you are a goddamned coward. You killed Lily Landers and must answer for it."

Gawain's boldness was rewarded with a momentary look of surprise in the man's face and, more than that, a brief glint of knowing. But he recovered quickly and bought a little time by lifting the cigar and studying it. Then his eyes moved to Gawain's again. "You mistake me, sir. I never met the lady."

"Then you are a liar as well as a coward," said Gawain.

"Jesus God," said Aunt Vassar.

Gault pondered his cigar a moment, shaking his head, then he looked at Gawain and smiled. "You have the advantage of me," he said. "I do not know you, but no matter. I'll let your remarks pass for now, saying only that, when I have a free moment, we'll discuss the matter in more detail. In the meantime, sir—" He glanced at Stribling, then back at Gawain. "In the meantime, you might do well to go armed like your comrade here. You never know when I might find the time to learn your name."

"It's Gawain Harper. I am a friend of Judge Rhea's—perhaps you've heard of him, at least."

Once more a look of surprise passed over Gault's face before he could stop it. "Ah, yes," said Gault. "I do know that gentleman, by reputation anyhow." Then he smiled again. "I would have thought he'd send a *man,* but I reckon they are in short supply these days—the war and all. Good day, now." He pushed past Gawain and went on down the brick walk into the lane and was gone.

"Well," said Stribling after a moment.

Aunt Vassar handed Gawain his prayer book, wet from the grass. She looked at him hard. "Why don't we all go have some of Captain Stribling's possum," she said.

◆　　◆　　◆

THEY WERE ON the gallery again, smoking and drinking coffee, though the afternoon was hot. Sunday dinner had been tense; Aunt Vassar was in a brown study, more or less ignoring them all, even old Harper, who rhythmically tapped his fork against his plate through the whole meal until Gawain thought he might go mad from the sound. The possum had not gone far among five people, though Priam got a double portion: his own and most of Stribling's. By tacit agreement, the confrontation at the church had not been mentioned, but Stribling brought it up now. "You played hell with Gault," he said. He was sitting on the balustrade; Zeke, still wearing his tack, was grazing in the yard.

"I know," said Gawain, "but there it was. I thought maybe I could get it over with."

"You are a brash and hasty man for a scholar," said Stribling, sipping his coffee.

Gawain had no answer. In fact, he was deeply embarrassed by the episode and wished Stribling would change the subject. He said: "Where'd you get off to this mornin? I looked for you to go with us."

"I went to a funeral," said Stribling. Then he told about those he had seen at the burying ground. Gawain listened in astonishment. "So Gault was there," he said. "And those other boys—Nobles and them. Are they that starved for amusement?"

"I can't say it was all that amusing to em," said Stribling. "Or to Molochi Fish either."

"*Molochi* was there?"

"He wasn't just there," said Stribling. "He was standin right next to me. He came out of nowhere—upwind, so Zeke never smelled him. Old Molochi is quite a talker when his dogs ain't around to distract him."

"Well, everybody was there but me," said Gawain. "What did you all talk about?"

Stribling told how at first Molochi Fish had ignored him completely. "Then all at once he pointed to my glass and wanted to know if you could see afar off with it. Then he wanted to borrow it. I don't mind sayin I was reluctant, him with those rheumy eyes, but I give it to him, and he looked a long time, then he said some peculiar things. I tell you, Gawain, he is as crazy as a Chinee with the Holy Ghost. He hears things out in the woods at night, people talkin to him, dead ones mostly."

"Dead people," said Gawain. "Well, what do they tell him?"

Stribling set his cup on the balustrade. His hat was off, and a breeze ruffled in his long hair. Zeke lifted his head and pricked his ears, as if the same breeze had brought some message to him. But the yard was peaceful, the road empty. "He looked a long time," Stribling went on, "movin the glass back and forth, then he give it back without so much as a word. I said, 'What you know about this Gault?' He chewed his gums awhile, then he told me a story. He said a dead boy came in his yard one night. The dogs had him, of course—apparently, he wasn't so dead that he couldn't be mauled by those devils before Molochi beat em off. He said the boy's eyes were like glass marbles, a detail I could have done without. Boy never said but one word, and that a name: Gault. What does that tell you?"

Gawain felt a dark wing brush his heart, as he had three days before when his cousin's wife told him about Lily. "Oh, blessed Jesus," he said. "Willy Landers, tryin to get home."

"Yes, Molochi found the long-lost boy," said Stribling. "Buried him, too. I trust a merciful Providence that he really was dead by then."

"Gault," said Gawain Harper, while the little wind moved among the oaks.

"Yes, but that ain't all," said Stribling. "Old Molochi come to town Friday night. He followed that boy, the one under the bridge."

Gawain blanched. "Molochi! I should've known—the thing had all the marks of—"

"No," said Stribling. "It wasn't him. Somebody else was ahead of him. Molochi saw him with my glass, standin by the grave."

"Molochi knows the man that done it? I don't believe it."

Stribling lit his pipe, taking his time, and Gawain waited. In a moment, Stribling told the story that Molochi Fish had related among the willows: of how he had followed the boy under the moon, and of what he had seen as the dark birds swirled above him. "He called the man's name, too," said Stribling at last.

Gawain waited again. Stribling, like most storytellers, was getting the most he could out of the suspense, and Gawain waited until just the right moment to ask, "Well, who was it, dammit?"

"The name he gave was Wall Stutts. Do you know him?"

"Ah, shit," said Gawain in disgust. "He is a damn peckerwood, worked for my daddy once, drivin mules for the track gang. Papa, of all people, run him off because he was too mean to the niggers. He worked out on Gault's place, too—lived out there, I think. Damn, Harry, you think Gault was behind it?"

"Molochi left me with that impression," said Stribling. "It was no idle killin."

"What should we do? Go to the yankees? Let's tell em, Harry—even if it wasn't Stutts, he deserves hangin anyhow."

"Let's hold off," said Stribling. "There is more to all this than we care to know, but we better find out anyhow. I mean to talk to those boys at the tavern."

"My God," said Gawain, shaking his head. "If I'd of known all this, I'd of stayed in Mobile."

✦　　✦　　✦

AUNT VASSAR BISHOP stood in the perpetual twilight of the hall, arms folded, watching her nephew and his friend through the side lights of the door. Like most women, Aunt Vassar had no qualms about eavesdropping; in fact, she considered it the only genteel way to gather information for later use against the parties involved. This time, however, she had not come to spy, would not have expected to learn anything new even if she had, for intuition had already informed her of the game afoot. This time, she stood hidden in the cool shadows of the hall for no other reason than to contemplate the two peregrine spirits lounging on her porch.

She thought of Gawain that way now: a strange spirit dwelling in the shape of someone she thought she had known once, had pretended to recognize only two days ago as if, by simple refusal, she could vanquish the alteration of time. Then this morning, in the churchyard, she saw what those three lost years had wrought in her nephew, and she could fool herself no longer. Time had won out anyway, as he always seemed to do, and he would carry them all down paths of his own choosing, and it was folly to deny it. She supposed she ought to have learned that long ago, and perhaps she had. It was the sort of thing one had to learn over and over anyway.

Forty years ago, Vassar Bishop had watched as the boy, not even named yet, emerged from the agony of her sister's labor. Vassar heard him draw his first breath and make his first complaint against the light of the world as if he'd been awakened from some deep and comforting dream. She had seen other new-born creatures—cats and dogs, horses and cattle and men—do the same, and she always watched with wonder and not a little envy at the pain and privilege of engendering life. She had thought that creation held no puzzles for her, but on that distant morning she looked at her nephew lying on the blooded sheets—hairless, squirming, still wet, flushed and wrinkled like a boiled squirrel—and thought to herself *My God—he is too raw by half, he is not finished yet,* and now on this twenty-fifth day in June 1865, she was still thinking it: *He is not finished yet, not by a long way, and he is as much a stranger to me now as the day he arrived.*

So she lingered in the hall and watched the two old soldiers talking on the porch in the illusory peace of a Sunday afternoon—old soldiers indeed, who were not really old, who had been but children once, and that not long ago. At last she turned away, fumbling in her sleeve for the lace handkerchief, wishing for the instant that she had a vial, just a vial, of laudanum to ease the passing of the day. But the blockade had put a stop to that—not even Solomon Gault could procure that blessing—and she supposed she was glad, though in trying times she missed the sweet elevation of the poppy. In any case, she had no choice now but to push against the hard edges of reality. So she daubed her eyes with the handkerchief, and turned away, and set her shoulder to one of the big pocket doors that opened into the library where old Frank Harper had his desk. The door rumbled sullenly in its track, and the various smells of the closed room greeted her: dust, mildew, the odor of old books bound in crumbling leather, of trapped sunlight and time. Into this she moved, her skirts rustling like the wings of frightened birds.

+   +   +

COLONEL MICHAEL BURDUCK was not immediately aware that it was Sunday—only that he was in his office at the Shipwright house. Even that knowledge came to him gradually, line by line, like a sketch emerging from a blank sheet of paper. First the light, then the familiar shapes of furniture, then smaller details: his pen and inkwell, his revolver on the table before him, his watch with the case shut but the key lying there as if it had just been wound. He did not recall taking the watch from his pocket, but there it was. He looked up, disturbed by the sense that someone had been in the room with him, but the room was empty, the door closed.

Burduck turned his chair to the window and looked out on the yard. It was full of broken limbs from Saturday's storm, and trash from where the creek had overflowed. He looked upon it as if seeing it for the first time. The skeleton of the abandoned carriage had been blown off its cedar props and looked more forlorn than ever, listing in the mud like a beached derelict. The sight of it woke in Burduck's heart a profound sadness he could not put a name to, as if the night's wild passage had imbued the carriage with a fresh portent. Burduck rubbed his eyes. He had lost time again; that much was plain from the afternoon light that dappled the yard. He remembered standing on the color line with Captain Bloom's company on parade, young Kelly's plain coffin at his feet. He recalled the drums beating the slow march, the column passing through the camp, past the tents and smoldering fires and stacked arms where the men watched in silence. The last thing he remembered was the sound of the clods striking the box and splashing in the water. Now here he was, in his office again, the mud of the burying ground on his boots, the stink of the grave in his nose.

Clearly he needed a rest. More than that, he needed a month or so out on Long Island with nothing but the sea and the lonely beacon of the Montauk light. Maybe he would ask for a furlough. He had not had one since the war began, not once in all those years, and now that the war was over—

Over? he thought, catching himself. He laughed out loud at the notion. Wars were never over, not this one anyway. Too much had happened, was still happening, and enough remained for generations to wallow in bitterness, making charge and countercharge, revising and accusing and apologizing long after the smoke had drifted away on the wind, and those who had walked through the smoke were dust. Then he remembered the anger he had felt the day before when he stood under the Town Creek bridge and looked at the remains of Tom Kelly. How quick to hand his anger had been, how easy to embrace and how infinitely difficult to control—and it was in him now, he knew, like a shadow moving under the calm waters of . . . was it Sunday? Yes, God's own day, morning and evening. Yesterday the man Thomas had spoken of hate. *Did you hate the rebels, Colonel? It's a grand feelin, ain't it?* Thomas had said.

The slaver's crew was sent below to loose the shackles and draw out the chains, and the captives came tottering and blinking to the main deck where they bunched like cattle, save one man who flung himself overboard and swam with such unaccountable strength that the Nimble's *boat could not reach him before the sharks. The rest watched this melancholy drama in silence until an old woman with withered dugs began to hum, then to wail, and presently they all took it up, and the nervous sailors looked at one another in the keening, the groaning, of the voices. Then Captain Burduck fired his pistol in the air and in an instant there was only the creaking of the shrouds and the slapping of water against the motionless hull.*

A score of dead remained in the hold. To these Captain John Burduck chained the slaver's crew, and secured the hatchway. Then, under steam, they towed the dead ship two days back to the coast and ran her aground at the foot of a nameless town. As the people came down to view the spectacle, and the slavers sat in irons (some of them gone mad, raving of old journeys or burning their eyes out watching the sun) and the blacks huddled bewildered on the beach, Captain Burduck himself set fire to the slave ship and its cargo of dead. A long time she burned, the smoke reeling skyward black and greasy as mortal sin.

All so quick to hand it was, and so easy to make use of. But you had to be careful. His brother burned four ships in all, and drove a score of men insane, and killed that many more. A fever was on him, it seemed to Michael, and would have consumed him had he not been recalled. At Dakar, Captain John Burduck was relieved of command; the two brothers stood at the rail of the Commodore's flagship and watched *Nimble* sail away until her masts sank below the horizon and she was gone. You had to be careful. You had to keep control of it, especially now, when there was sufficient madness for all.

He turned back to the table, and all at once he remembered who'd been in the room just now: Captain Bloom's first sergeant with the dead boy's papers. They lay at hand on the table, the history of Tom Kelly's life as a soldier. On top was a sealed envelope addressed in the boy's scrawl to Annie Kelly of Louisville, Kentucky. To this person, Burduck must now address a letter of his own. He did not try to imagine her; he would not even acknowledge that Annie Kelly existed, was moving in the world this very moment unaware of what was about to descend upon her. She must remain a name only, abstract and bloodless, incapable of grief. It was a trick Burduck had learned only after writing many letters to the wives and mothers of men who had gone their violent ways: *Dear Madam, I regret to inform you—*

But not right now. He would write no letters today. He even thought that he might have Captain Bloom write this one, knowing all the while that he would do it himself. But not right now. He took up the papers and shuffled through them, his glance touching the mundane details of the boy's career. On the fifteenth of October 1864, Tom Kelly had been absent in hospital with a bad tooth. Three days later, he was issued a new canteen. Burduck riffled the pages. *Absent, detached duty. Paid. Present for duty. A fatigue blouse issued. Request for furlough denied. Paid. Brass insignia, Infantry. Absent, sick. Request for furlough denied. Paid. Absent. Present. Paid—*

"You have to be careful with it," said Burduck aloud, the papers trembling in his hand. At last he laid them down again and evened their edges, picked them up again and tapped them on the desk. "Careful, careful," he said. Finally, he laid the papers gently on the tabletop and set the inkwell on top of them. For a while he sat with his elbows on the table, fingers pressed against his eyes, studying the little motes swimming in the dark. He could hear the watch ticking. Then, like a man waking from a troubled sleep, he sat up straight and looked about him. The walls of the room seemed to have moved closer in the interval, and he could hear his own breathing. The ticking of the watch was louder now, persistent and demanding, as if no other sound in the universe were so essential. Burduck imagined he could hear the gears and wheels making their infinitesimal movements, jerking in tiny increments toward tomorrow, and he knew the hands were moving under the closed case. He brought his fist down hard on the watch and heard the glass of the crystal break, and the watch stopped, and the only sound then was his breathing. He stared at the watch as if waiting for it to begin again. When it didn't, he shifted his gaze to the pistol, and a thought brushed across his mind: *Go ahead, it's easy, take a good long furlough, one you won't ever have to come back from—*

He stood up then, so quickly that the chair fell backward with a crash.

"Orderly!" he shouted, and had to call again before the man put his head in the door.

"Bring my horse around. Be quick now."

"Yes, Colonel," said the man, and disappeared.

A rest was all he needed. Just a little while by himself. He buttoned his coat and found his sword belt and buckled it on. He detached the sword but holstered the pistol. He knew the place he was going to.

✦　✦　✦

STRIBLING HAD JUST swung into the saddle when Aunt Vassar came out the front door. "Surely you are not leaving us?" she said.

Gawain rose to his feet, and Stribling took off his hat. "No, ma'am," he said.

"Good," she said. "Somebody needs to fix that porch."

She stood just outside the door, cradling in her arms a flat, rectangular box of polished mahogany that Gawain recognized at once. "Now, Aunt—," he began.

"Hush, Nephew," she said. She crossed the porch and held the box out to Gawain. "Take it," she said. "You will need it sooner or later."

"My God, Aunt," said Gawain. "Papa will have a fit."

Aunt Vassar snorted. "Your papa, in case you haven't noticed, has checked out of his hotel. Anyway, he left it to you in his will. Now, take it."

Gawain took the box then, cradling it in his arms just as his aunt had done. He stood awkwardly for a moment, balanced on the step, then moved his right hand across the smooth mahogany lid. "I'll be," he said.

"Open it," said Aunt Vassar. "Let Captain Stribling see."

Gawain moved the brass latch and opened the box. It was felt-lined and divided into compartments by narrow strips of felt-covered wood. In the largest of these lay a Colt's Model 1851 Navy revolver, barrel and frame of blued steel, grips of oiled walnut. Like all Navy Colts, the cylinder was engraved with the scene of a naval battle and a date in 1843. Gawain had known dozens of men who carried Navy Colts in the war, and not one of them had been able to say what battle was represented. Other compartments held a bullet mold, a box of percussion caps, a powder flask, and a quantity of .36-caliber round balls clustered like gray spider's eggs. The pistol gleamed in the sunlight, a perfect shape that begged to be handled and admired. Its beauty denied the purpose for which it had been created.

Gawain stepped out into the yard and held the box up for Stribling's inspection. Stribling leaned down and took the box and balanced it on the pommel of his saddle. "May I?" he asked.

"By all means," said Gawain.

Stribling lifted the pistol from the box and held it with the muzzle pointing skyward. The thing seemed to fit itself naturally to his grip. "It is beautiful indeed," said Stribling. "I used to have a Confederate copy—piece of trash, it was. When I got a Navy Colt, I thought I was in business. I wish I still had it." Then his brows furrowed, and he looked down at Gawain. "I always wondered why Mister Colt made it for such a little ball."

Gawain shrugged. "Maybe sailors don't take as much killin as we did."

"No," said Stribling, "it always worked for me." Then he remembered Aunt Vassar. "Beg pardon, ma'am," he said. "I have a loose tongue."

"Nonsense," said the old woman. Then, to Gawain: "It is yours now. So far as I know, it has never been discharged. Your father always preferred a weapon he could hide."

"Yes," said Gawain. "Well, I will try to protect its maidenhood."

His aunt looked at him. Gawain could not decipher what was in her face and looked away. "It is yours now," she said again. Then she turned and passed back through the door and into the house. Gawain could hear her footsteps in the hall.

Stribling latched the box and handed it down. Gawain took it, once again holding it awkwardly, as if he were afraid he might break it.

"When I get back," said Stribling, grinning, "I'll show you how to load it."

"I know how to load it," said Gawain. "Wish I could get some cartridges for it."

"We could steal some from the yankees, like in the old times."

"Or I could put it back in Papa's desk and forget about it," said Gawain.

Stribling flexed his injured hand, watching his fingers as if he were inspecting a piece of machinery. Zeke stamped impatiently, tired of standing. Gawain spoke again. "I said I could put it back—"

"I heard you," said Stribling. "You was wantin to borrow mine this mornin. Now you got one of your own. Before you load it, make sure all the oil is out of the chambers. In fact, I'd boil that cylinder, I was you."

"Yes, Father," said Gawain, grinning himself now. But the grin lasted only an instant. "I won't put it back," he said. He looked up at Stribling. "I will have to use it now."

"Maybe not," said Stribling.

Gawain shook his head. "No, Harry, you know yourself that ain't so. Ever since we run into old Molochi at the river, it's been all shit and no sugar. I was you, I'd pack my bags and light out for Alabama."

"I'll pretend you never said that," said Stribling. "I am fixin to go to the Citadel, see who's around. Trouble is comin upon us, and if I can find out

about it, maybe we can arrange to be fishin that day." He grinned again
and turned Zeke's head and rode out of the yard at the canter.

Gawain watched his friend until he was out of sight down the
Cumberland road, then he sat on the steps again, the pistol case beside
him. He opened it and withdrew the Navy Colt; it fit to his hand as it had
to Stribling's, and when he cocked it, the action was smooth. For a while
he sat there, holding the Colt in the casual way of a man long familiar with
firearms, looking out at the yard. The ground was littered with branches
and with windrows of leaves where the water had stood in pools after the
storm. Last night he had lain awake in his old bed listening to the hammering rain, the thunder that pealed and crashed and shook the windows,
and he thought how it was in the old times. Back then, on nights when
storms came prowling and threatening out of the west, his mother would
call Gawain and his sisters to her bed. There she would surround them
with all the down and feather pillows in the house, for, as everyone knew,
geese and chickens were never struck by lightning. Secure behind that
redoubt, they would tell stories and laugh and, in time, fall asleep, safe
from all hurtful things, even in their dreams. They had believed in safety
then; Gawain watched the light lie blue on the pistol barrel and wished he
could believe in it now. In a little while he rose, took up the case, and
moved into the shadows of the house.

♦   ♦   ♦

SOLOMON GAULT HAD always hated slavery, not because he found it
morally repugnant, but because he could not bear to be around black people. When his father died, Solomon Gault inherited the farm and fifty
slaves, and the word around the Quarters was that he might free the whole
lot, and there was much jubilation. Instead, Gault sold them all as quickly
as they could be brought to the block in Memphis. Even before the last one
was gone, Gault dismantled the cabins in the Quarters and with the hewn
logs and shingles erected four dogtrot houses, one in each corner of his
thousand acres. In these he installed white families—only a notch above
the blacks on the social scale, but free and white nevertheless—and provided them with cotton seed and harness and a pair of mules to work the
ground. His neighbors viewed the change with outrage and scorn, but
Gault had never cared much for his neighbors anyhow. He anticipated the
sharecropping system in Cumberland County a generation before it would
have a name, and he made it work, and if his neighbors could not quite
forgive him for it, they could at least be envious.

Now, on this Sunday afternoon, Gault sat on the overturned cookpot at
the Wagner place and marveled, as he often did, that others had not seen

things as clearly in the old days. The ruins around him were a perfect object lesson, there for all to see. They illustrated the evils of a system that enslaved the enslavers, that bound them to a primitive and unpredictable people whose capacity for violence was limitless. The damn fools, Gault thought. Without the niggers there would have been no war, no ruins, no Colonel Burduck swaggering among his well-drilled troops. And Solomon Gault would not have had to swing Simon Landers from a white oak tree nor split his woman's head with a saber, and he would not be sitting in the ashes now, waiting for a man he despised. Well, it was all right. The details could be worked out, and anyhow, daring ventures were always messy.

Damn the Harper boy, thought Solomon Gault. The old Judge was all talk—Gault had never feared him and wouldn't now. But here was Gawain Harper bruiting threats in the churchyard, opening a line of discussion that Gault had no time for. If the man went to Burduck—but, no, Harper wouldn't run to the yankees. He might be a schoolteacher (Gault had learned that much in the course of the afternoon), but he had been in the war, and he was of the same race as Gault himself, weaned on the old code of personal responsibility in matters of blood. So he was commissioned by the Judge, for whatever reason, and sooner or later he would come around with a pistol in his hand. That wouldn't do. Gault could beat him, of course—there was no doubt of that in his mind—but he couldn't afford that kind of attention right now. He was too close, too many things were falling into place. The time was fast approaching when Solomon Gault would make his bid for greatness.

The rain had washed away the curious drawings that had been in the dirt, but Gault remembered them now: a moon and stars, heavenly signs that men sometimes looked to for guidance, for planting times, for success in love, for procreation. Gault did not believe in signs, any more than he believed in the God whom the new priest had evoked so eloquently this morning. Men lived and died by their own will, and what they made or broke around them was their only testimony.

He heard the horse then, and rose, his eyes toward the road. He heard the creak of leather as the rider dismounted, and the crackle of brush as the man led the horse through the tangle left by the storm. In a moment, man and horse were in the clearing.

"You sent for me," said Wall Stutts. It was a statement, not a question. "I could have just as easy come to your place."

"This is the meeting place," said Gault.

Stutts nodded. He dropped the reins of the horse and squatted on his heels. From his pocket he took a plug of tobacco, bit off a chew, and offered the plug to the Captain. Gault only looked at him. Grinning, Stutts returned the plug and spat a preliminary stream of clear spit into the leaves. Wall Stutts had been the first white tenant on the Gault place and the only one remaining after the war. In all those years, he seemed to have never changed his clothes nor taken off his hat. "What about it, Cap'n?" he asked. "Time to make another statement?"

"Yes," the Captain said.

Stutts snorted. "We kill em one at a time, hell, they'll die of old age before we get shut of em. Why'nt we just take the whole lot?"

"This is a . . . *personal* favor," said the Captain.

Stutts looked at the Captain for a long moment. Finally he grinned. "That kind of work comes high," he said.

"Twenty dollars," said the Captain.

Stutts spat into the mud. "Shit," he said. "Who is it, anyhow?"

When the Captain spoke the name, Stutts laughed out loud. "Aye God, Cap'n, what you scared of him for?"

The Captain's face burned. He looked off for a moment, studying the light where it lay on the leaves. When he could trust his voice, he said, "You know the man, then."

"Used to work for his daddy. Son bitch fired me off the line. It'll cost you a hunnerd."

"Fifty," said Gault.

"You come up a little, I'll come down a little," said Stutts.

They settled on seventy-five dollars and the loan of the Henry rifle. "At that price," said Stutts when the bargain was made, "I'll even spook the yankees again, no extra charge."

Gault thought about that for a moment. At last he said, "Since you are feeling generous, allow me to make a suggestion. Select your target at the tavern again."

"Any particular reason?"

Gault drew his boot across the place where the moon and stars had been. "Thomas has become a burden. He is . . . superfluous now, and can best serve as a diversion. Do you understand?"

Stutts winked and grinned. "Sure, Cap'n," he said. "But, aye God, you a hard man." He spat again, crossed to the Captain's horse, and drew the Henry out of the saddle scabbard that Gault had had special-made in Memphis. He checked it for loads, then he gathered up his own horse's reins and, without another word, disappeared into the brush. The Captain listened until he heard the creak of leather again and the horse's hooves trotting north toward Cumberland. Then he went to his mount and opened the near saddlebag and removed from it a sheaf of papers, the manuscript of his memoirs. Seated on the cookpot again, he drew his reading glasses from his pocket, and a stub of pencil, and began to write.

Wall Stutts, with the Henry rifle lying across his pommel, crossed Leaf River at the gravelly ford, then stayed in the woods out of sight of the road. Had he kept to the road, he would have found Colonel Burduck riding south.

✦   ✦   ✦

ON HIS WAY to the Wagner place, Burduck passed the Citadel of Djibouti. He gave it a glance, and for a moment he considered stopping. L. W. Thomas bothered him for reasons he could not name, and he wondered what would happen if he faced the man in his own territory. But at the last moment he rode on, deterred by the image of a Federal field-grade officer in such a place. Besides, Burduck thought, there was nothing to be gained by another interview. Not yet, anyway.

In a few moments, Burduck came to the bridge across Leaf River, and halfway across he paused. He could smell the trees, lush and green and heavy with moisture, and the hot planks drying in the sun. The birds were quiet at this hour, but in the grass the crickets sang, their incessant voices punctuated by the click of grasshoppers. A flight of gnats swirled in the sunlight. Sally did not like standing on the bridge, but Burduck held her there; she bobbed her head in protest and swished her tail at the gnats.

Burduck shifted in the saddle and looked around him. He remembered a place like this in Brooklyn: a stream that in summer ran cool and slow, where the trees arched over the water and dappled it in shadow, where cattle came to drink and the boy driving them could sit in the grass among the secret voices and dream of the sea. Sally stamped a forefoot, and Burduck let her go; they walked off the bridge, the horse tossing her head. On the other side, Burduck turned her and looked back.

The tattered mob of slaves moved behind the army like a vast, ragged quilt—old men and crones; women, some of them suckling; and frightened children, some naked; and young bucks with the sweat glistening on corded muscles—singing and praying, raising a dust cloud that could be seen for miles, and Forrest's cavalry out there somewhere. They crowded up on the rear guard, and the soldiers could not be stopped from going among them with government rations and water and chickens stolen along the way, so Burduck went to the rear of the battalion and, with a picked detachment of men, kept them at bay, the men sometimes walking backward with fixed bayonets. So they swarmed out into the fields and marshes, lapping around the rear guard, singing and praying. Some, older

*ones mostly, collapsed in the heat, and around these sprang up little knots
of wailing women.*

Burduck shook his head to clear it. The bridge and the road beyond lay
empty, peaceful in the light and shadow. Overhead, a kettle of buzzards
came drifting from the west, circling, their great wings motionless.

*Now and then, rebel horsemen appeared, emerging suddenly from some
empty space among the trees, their carbines propped on their thighs. They
would call to Burduck's men, "What you gon' do with all them niggers,
Billy?" and Burduck's Regulars would holler back "Gon' bile em down for
gum blankets!" or "Maybe gon' run em for Congress down here—say,
won't you like that?" and the rebels: "Man, yes! And if that don't work,
you can make em gen'rals!"*

Burduck felt the sweat running down his body under the frock coat. He
shook his head again, took off his cap and ran his hand through his thinning hair that was soaked with sweat. Through the trees, the sky was blue
and endless, without clouds. The buzzards had gone, driven east by the
winds aloft. The bridge shimmered in the heat, seemed to sway as if suspended by wires.

*The engineers laid pontoons across the nameless river, and the army
took all day to cross while Burduck and his men kept the negroes back
with their bayonets. It was nearly sunset when the orderly came on his
lathered horse and saluted and gave Burduck the message, hastily penned
on the back of an advertisement for Wheaton's Bitters: "Hold the contraband on the east bank. You must not let them cross." And Burduck, covered with dust and the sweat running in his eyes: "What the hell does this
mean?" And the orderly: "Sir, I reckon it means don't let the niggers
cross." And saluted again and put spurs to his horse.*

"That can't be right," said Burduck on the Leaf River Bridge. He
seemed to hear them in the woods again, the shuffling of their bare feet,
their singing, their voices lifted to God. Going down out of Egypt, they
sang. Crossing into Canaan.

*So the soldiers drove them back with bayonets, Burduck riding among
them, striking with the flat of his saber while they clutched his legs and
begged and prayed because they knew. When they saw the river, they knew.
The engineers stood ready to pull in the pontoons, and Burduck himself
was the last one onto the bridge, and the engineers cut loose the pontoon
behind him. On the bank, the women knelt and threw up their hands and
wailed, and the old ones stood looking at the water, silent and resigned, letting their bundles drop at their feet in the churned mud. But some took to
the water, and the current snatched them and spun them down under the
arching trees. Others set across on logs, and Burduck's men were running*

downstream on the far bank, throwing branches and driftwood in the water. Burduck backed his horse across the pontoons, the engineers pulling up the bridge behind him, and once a sergeant said he would send a pontoon back across and Burduck told him "No, damn you!" and had to threaten the man with a pistol. And he saw them drown, saw the brown water take them, their hands always the last thing to go under.

"Freedom!" said Burduck, his voice loud in the quiet Sunday afternoon. Time was gone. He had lost it again, the old, comfortable progression of minutes and hours carried away on the brown water, swirling downstream, clutching at the sky. He dropped his cap and pressed the heels of his hands against his temples, feeling the blood pounding there, hearing the rush of it, but not loud enough to drown their voices, their singing and praying.

"Close up! Close up!" Burduck cried, urging his horse up the muddy slope of the far bank. "Rally on the colors! Close up!" And the officers shouting and cursing, pulling the men together, forcing them away from the river and up the road after the army, and Burduck turning his horse to look for one last time: the ragged host was spread out along the far bank, all of them kneeling now, singing again, their high, keening voices echoing off the sandy bluffs. And out of the treeline a company of rebel cavalry appeared, their red flag bright against the trees, and one of them raised his carbine and fired, and Burduck heard the ball rattle in the leaves above him.

He was crying now, his face wet with the unfamiliar tears that flowed with rivulets of sweat down his cheeks. Ashamed, he wiped his coat sleeve fiercely across his face, the broadcloth stinking of sweat and wood smoke. Then he sat absolutely still in the saddle, his arm outstretched, hand open like that of a man reaching for the next rung of a ladder. He listened, still hearing the single report of the rifle that had come to him across the afternoon. It seemed uncannily real, not something out of time but in the here and now, still echoing in the stillness. He dismounted and retrieved his cap from the mud, and for a moment he stared at the embroidered infantry bugle sewn to the front of it. The gold thread was tarnished, the enameled visor cracked and brittle. In a little while, he mounted again and turned Sally's head to the south. As he rode, he fixed his mind on the bridge over the stream in Brooklyn, and tried to remember the last time he crossed it, and how the planks were warm under his bare feet.

Meanwhile, at the old Wagner place, Solomon Gault lifted his eyes from the manuscript page before him. He found himself smiling, though he couldn't say why.

· XVI ·

Mister L. W. Thomas was carried on the army rolls as a sutler, one of those civilian entrepreneurs licensed to sell food, dry goods, and spirits to the soldiers. According to the Articles of War, sutlers were not to conduct business after nine at night, or "before the beating of reveille," nor upon Sundays during church call "on the penalty of being dismissed from all future suttling." However, in Mississippi in June of 1865, the finer points of the Articles were often obscured by realities of circumstance, especially when they applied to the Citadel of Djibouti. Thus, on this Sunday, the Citadel was still open, unreeling the spool of Saturday night into the bright hours of morning.

The air in the room was close and stale; moreover, the place was full of smoke—everyone present seemed to have a lit cigar—and the light, as always, was dim even though the door was standing open. The patrons, few at this hour, were not saying much; they seemed content to slump in their chairs, sweat glistening on their faces, moving only to lift their glasses, and when they did speak, it was in a low, desultory way that suggested they would rather not speak at all. Sheriff Ben Luker sat in his usual place in the shadows, resting a mug of beer on the swell of his belly, a cigar stuck in the center of his mouth. His coat was pulled back to reveal a pistol in a flap holster, butt forward. He watched the room carefully, flicking his eyes toward every movement. Rafe Deaton sat alone, still in the dress coat, complete with shoulder scales and service stripes, that he had worn to the burying. In less than an hour, he had drunk his way through a bottle of Thomas' cheapest whiskey, and now he had begun talking softly to himself. At another table, Nobles and Peck sat drinking quietly and smoking, a bottle between them. They had been at it for nearly twenty-four hours now, and the strain was beginning to tell in their faces. With them sat Stuart Bloodworth and Patrick Craddock, lately returned from the Army of Tennessee. At a third table sat Professor Malcolm Brown, the daguerreotypist, and Mister Henry Clyde Wooster, more animated than the rest, working in his notebook with a mechanical pencil, recording impressions for his subscribers.

L. W. Thomas, leaning on the bar, regarded the scene and wondered idly if this was what purgatory would look like. He expected to visit that place sooner or later, and was grateful to have this time to practice for it. The damp weather made the wound in his side ache, and the nagging of it put him in mind of his mortality. Then, of course, there was the excursion to the burying ground this morning.

He thought about that, about the boy who was put down into the cold, sodden ground, who should have been lying in his tent with a hangover. Even now, Thomas was not sure why they had gone to the burying, especially Nobles and Peck. It was none of their affair, nor any of his either, Thomas thought, as he daubed at a puddle of beer on the bar. He, L. W. Thomas, was a spy—a scout, they had called it during the war. He was good at the trade, had worked it for nearly four years in Memphis, Nashville, Chattanooga, Atlanta, all behind the Federal lines, with nothing between him and the noose but the discharge paper with General Henry Halleck's signature cleverly forged by Thomas himself. Now he was working at it again, not for the Confederacy but for King Solomon Gault.

Thomas had seen Gault at the burying ground, and now he thought about the man and how, in another smoky bar on a vanished afternoon, Gault had drawn him into his design. That was at the Gayoso house, away last fall, when the war was dying on the vine and everybody in Memphis was scrabbling for a place in the new order of things that lay just beyond the horizon. At the time, Thomas had marveled at the serendipity of the incident. He was "at large," as he liked to phrase it then, and open to possibilities, and behold, Gault had insinuated himself into the crowd at the bar and in a little while—circumspectly at first, then made bold by the whiskey—began to speak of the vacuum of power, and of opportunity, and of gain down in Mississippi. That moment had led to this, and now Thomas was leaning on a makeshift bar thinking of a dead boy and purgatory with the rats gnawing at his side.

But that was all right. Gault had set him up here and paid a good wage for Thomas' sketches of the camp and the powder magazine, the barn where the stores and munitions were kept, and the blockhouses along the railroad. He received with great solemnity Thomas' detailed weekly submissions of troop strengths, ration issues, and railway schedules. Gault enjoyed the notion, encouraged by Thomas, that the Citadel of Djibouti was a froth of conspirators, secret messages, midnight cabals, where every Southern ear was tuned to the loose talk of drunken bluebellies. In fact,

Thomas encouraged all of his patron's broad fantasies, so long as they were made incarnate in genuine Federal notes, of which Thomas now had a goodly store tucked away in a leather valise under his cot in the back room. So it was all right, this lingering in a smoky, foul-smelling tavern in a burned-out backwater village. Soon enough, Mister L. W. Thomas would take his fat valise and board the cars for the north—St. Louis, he thought, where there were good doctors—and Gault and Nobles and Peck and the rest of these damned fools would be left to fry in their own grease. For Mister L. W. Thomas had no faith whatever in Captain Gault's design, and when the play opened, Thomas intended to be sitting at the bar in the Planter's Hotel, reading about it in the St. Louis papers.

And the sooner the better, Thomas reflected, as he poured a beer for himself. He blew the foam off, then lifted the glass and held it at eye level and watched it tremble in his hand. He was thirty-eight years old and had long ago learned to dispense with all illusions about himself, and he understood that he had finally lost his nerve. He had seen it happen to others, and he had seen them make fatal mistakes because of it. That was not the way of Thomas. He was an actor above all, and he knew very well when it was time to make his exit.

Yet he had gone to the burying this morning, contrary to everything he had learned in his years on the scout. He had fallen asleep about daylight, sitting upright in his chair, while the storm wore itself out in distant mutterings to the east. Then Nobles woke him and announced that they were going to see the boy put under, and Thomas had gone without question, violating his own rule of invisibility. He had, in fact, felt *compelled* to go, not by his companions but by an inner voice he had labored for years to silence. It was the voice of remorse, and its nagging persistence was the final proof that his nerve was gone at last.

Remorse had no place in the trade. You did your job, and usually men died because of it, and sometimes they were innocent. That was the nature of war, and there was no getting around it. When you started feeling, it was time to quit.

Only this was not war. The boy under the bridge had lived through that, suffered that, and was supposed to be safe from it now. Thomas looked out at the room. The bright, sunlit rectangle of the open door beckoned to him. He could do it right now; he could go behind the curtain and pack his few books and his pistol and mandolin—hell, he would leave the mandolin and get him a better one—and walk right past Luker, the Captain's watchdog, and out the door and down to the railroad and away from this wretched hole forever. He could go to a place where the war really was over, where he would never again have to hear the clods splashing in the bottom of a water-filled grave. He could do it. Right now. There was nothing to keep him from it. *Nothing nothing nothing,* said the voice in his head. *Go on now, while you got the chance, before you do something you'll wish you hadn't—*

Then the light from the door was broken by the silhouette of a man, and Thomas squinted his eyes, thinking with a sudden pang that his scheming might have evoked the presence of Gault himself. But no, it wasn't the Captain, thank God. Thomas went on sipping his beer, watching the stranger while the voices in his head spoke urgently of freedom.

✦ ✦ ✦

WHEN HARRY STRIBLING stepped out of the bright afternoon and through the door of the Citadel, he was nearly overcome by cigars and sweat and stale beer. The stink was palpable and wrapped around him like a damp garment. He stood blinking in the dim light, waiting for his senses to adjust, conscious of the faces turned his way. Finally, when he could see to navigate, he moved across the room to the bar where I. W. Thomas was watching him.

"Hey there," said Stribling amiably.

Thomas nodded. "Hey," he said.

"Hot, ain't it?"

"Yeah," said Thomas. "It is."

"Looks like the rain's quit for a while."

"Uh-huh," said Thomas.

Stribling turned and leaned his back against the bar and looked out at the room. He nodded at Nobles and Peck. From the corner of his eye, he could see a fat man watching him from the shadows. Stribling grinned. "God bless all here," he said.

"What you want?" asked Thomas.

"Who is the little fat man over yonder?" asked Stribling, still smiling out at the room and its sulky occupants.

Thomas snorted. "That is the high sheriff his own self," he said. "Why?"

"Just curious," said Stribling. "Did you vote for him?"

"I don't think anybody did," said Thomas.

"I wonder if Solomon Gault did."

Caught by surprise, Thomas almost let his face betray him. "I wouldn't know," he said.

Stribling nodded, as if everything was clear to him now. He looked at Ben Luker and smiled and tipped his hat. "Hey there," he said.

Luker leaned his chair away from the wall, stood up, moved to the bar and set his mug down. He had to look up at Stribling, who was nearly a head taller. "I ain't seen you before."

"No," said Stribling. "No, you ain't."

Luker moved closer, sliding his mug down the bar so that it left a wet trail. "You just travelin?" he asked.

"I was until I got here," said Stribling.

Ben Luker grinned, showing a single upper front tooth with a crescent of decay. "Is that right?" he said.

"Actually," Stribling went on, "I thought I might linger awhile. I make enough friends, I might run for sheriff next election day."

"Job's already taken," said Ben Luker.

"That's too bad," said Stribling. "I'd like to meet the man."

"You already did," said Luker. He pulled back the skirt of his sack coat so that Stribling could see the pistol and the dull gleam of a badge that reminded Stribling of the star-and-crescent pins he had seen infantrymen wear on occasion. Luker said, "You know what? I think I have seen you before. You the feller they th'owed in jail last Friday, damn if you ain't."

"Well, I suppose I am," said Stribling. "Yes, I am he—Harry Stribling, the famous outlaw."

"They didn't ask my help," said Luker. "If they had, you might not be so goddamn smart."

"Aw, Ben," said Thomas, "let the man alone. Have another beer." He moved to take Luker's mug, but the sheriff covered it with the palm of his hand.

"Let me ask you a question," said Stribling in a confidential whisper.

"Sure," said the sheriff, leaning toward him, grinning.

"Why you reckon Solomon Gault killed that boy under the bridge?" Stribling said.

What little sound had been in the room ceased, and the men turned to look. Thomas covered his face in his hands. The sheriff's eyes grew wide. "Well, goddamn—," he began, but was interrupted by the clatter of an overturned chair as Rafe Deaton rose unsteadily, his eyes fixed on Stribling's face.

Stribling held up his hands. "Now, I don't mean to say Gault did it himself, you understand—he would've sent a man to do the actual deed. I just don't understand—"

"Well, goddamn—," began the sheriff again.

"Gault who?" said Rafe Deaton. "Who is Gault, and where is he?" The sergeant moved around the table, steadying himself with one hand on the tabletop. He crossed the room and approached the two men at the bar;

when he stopped, his face was an inch from Stribling's. "And who are you anyway?" he said.

"Now, you get out of it," said Luker.

"Fuck you, you little sawed-off son bitch, you," replied the sergeant.

"Watch your mouth," said Luker. "I'll—"

Rafe whirled, cocked his fist, but he was too far gone for such a move. He stumbled backward as Luker put his hand to the butt of his pistol and began to draw. Thomas was quick—he already had his hand on the truncheon under the bar—but Stribling was quicker with his pocket gun. Before the sheriff's pistol was halfway out, the muzzle of Stribling's Colt was pressed under his chin, pushing his head back.

"Don't worry," said Stribling. "It's only a little .31, it won't hurt much prob'ly."

"Well, God damn," said the sheriff.

Stribling laughed. With his free hand, he removed the sheriff's Navy Colt from its holster and thrust it into his own waistband. Then, still pressing the pocket gun's muzzle under Luker's chin, Stribling turned the man and backed him across the room and out the door. When Luker reached the edge of the gallery, he teetered a moment, windmilling his arms, then fell backward down the steps and into the mud. He rose quickly to his hands and knees and looked up at Stribling.

"You know Solomon Gault?" Stribling asked.

Luker rose to his feet. The sun was bright after the gloom of the tavern. Zeke, tethered by the woodpile, raised his head and studied the two men, his ears pricked with curiosity. At his feet, Beowulf slept on. The cat sat on the woodpile, studying the mockingbird in the limbs of the hackberry tree. Ben Luker wiped his mouth on his sleeve. "I know him," he said. "You have played hell. Now, you gimme my pistol back."

"No," said Stribling. "You tell Mister Gault that the hand of Providence is about to close on his nappy head. Now get on away from here before I forget I am a Christian."

Luker backed away a few paces. "You gon' be sorry you talked to me like that," he said. Then he turned and lumbered away toward the square. Stribling watched him go, and for a moment he felt painfully small and petty and dirty. He looked over at Zeke, who was watching him suspiciously.

"Don't look at me that way," Stribling said to the horse. "I attach no virtue to humiliating a man." Then he turned and went back through the tavern door and this time closed it behind him. In the candlelight, he sought out Nobles and Peck. They were on their feet now (Peck with his crutch thrust under his arm), and as Stribling watched, they began to clap politely, like gentlemen at the opera. Stribling blushed and crossed the room to the bar.

"Have a beer on the house," said Thomas. "Then you can tell me—"

"Who are you, anyway?" asked Rafe Deaton, who was sitting on the floor now, his back against the bar.

Stribling nodded gratefully at Thomas and took a long draught from the beer. When he put the mug down, he looked at the sergeant. "A philosopher," he said.

Mister Wooster approached then, his gray derby hat perched on the back of his head. "Just a minute of your time, sir," he said.

"Surely," said Stribling.

"Let me introduce myself," said Wooster, and did.

"I am pleased to meet you, sir," said Stribling. "I have never known a yankee journalist, though I have always wanted to."

Wooster flourished his mechanical pencil. "That was an extraordinary display," he said. "Tell me how you felt when the sheriff drew his pistol."

"He didn't draw it," said Stribling.

"You felt the white heat of anger," said Wooster, writing in his notebook. "Once more, unbidden, the lust of battle rose like a flame in your heart."

"Yes, that's it," said Stribling. "I felt . . . I felt the sting of outrage, to have come so far, over so many bloodied fields, only to be challenged by one of my own at the threshold of . . . of . . . "

"Of the home that for so long had been your beacon, your guide, now ravished by the iron heel of the oppressor," said Wooster, writing.

"Now, wait a goddamn minute," said Rafe Deaton. He struggled to his feet, aided by Stribling and the journalist, one under each arm. "These goddamned rebels—," the sergeant began.

"Infidels," said Wooster, writing.

"Infidels?" said Stribling.

"Perhaps that is a bit strong," said Wooster. "Did I hear you say you were a famous outlaw?"

"He is no outlaw," said Rafe. "He is a goddamned rebel comin in here."

Professor Malcolm Brown approached the bar. He, too, wore a derby, and a white linen duster stained with chemicals and ink. "Stop by the studio," he said to Stribling. "I'll make your image. No charge."

Wooster laughed. "Studio? Hell, you ain't got a studio, Mac."

"I got a tent," protested Brown.

"Gentlemen, gentlemen," said Stribling, holding up his hands. Still holding them up, palms outward as if he were delivering a benediction, Stribling moved out into the room. He turned, looking into the faces of the men sitting in the shadows. Nobles and Peck slouched in their chairs, watching him through eyes that seemed to have lost their focus. Bloodworth and Craddock, whom Stribling did not know, watched him, too. They still wore their short gray jackets, though all the buttons had been removed. Bloodworth seemed calm enough and regarded Stribling as if he were about to deliver an interesting lecture. Craddock's eyes sparkled with amusement. He crossed one leg over the other, and Stribling noted the paper-thin sole of his Jefferson shoe. Finally, Stribling looked at the journalist, who stood at the bar with his pencil ready.

"Mister Wooster, you can put down this," said Stribling. "You can say that a citizen named Wall Stutts murdered the boy under the bridge, and Solomon Gault put him up to it."

"Whoa, whoa, whoa, God damn," said Thomas, turning in a full circle behind the bar, his hands in the air.

"Stutts!" said Nobles. "How do you know—"

"There it is, boys," said Stribling. "But I am only a stranger here, and I am not used to your ways."

"You might be a little out of line," said Nobles.

Craddock's eyes were glittering now, his face frozen in a half smile. "I'm in," he said, rising to his feet, the chair scraping behind him. He looked at Deaton. "I ain't seen one of you sons of bitches yet that was dead enough to suit me."

Deaton pushed away from the bar, his hands opening and closing so that the knuckles cracked. He lurched forward, stumbling, and Stribling moved to catch him, pressed hard against him and gathered the collar of his frock coat in his hand. "Wait," he said, his mouth at the sergeant's ear. "Wait a minute, keep your wits." Deaton tried to push by, but Stribling easily forced him back against the bar. Then Stribling turned on Nobles. "Out of line? Well, I beg your pardon. Where I come from, murder and cowardice are not among the cardinal virtues, but I suppose the custom's different here. Carl, where'd you go Friday night, anyhow?"

"Goddamn you, sir," said Nobles. He rose unsteadily to his feet, and at the same time, Marcus Peck hauled himself upright on his crutch. Henry Clyde Wooster moved behind the bar with Thomas, writing furiously. Malcolm Brown held out his hands. "Now, gentlemen—," he began, but whatever he might have said was cut short by the crash of the bottles and glasses Craddock cleared from the table with one sweep of his arm. Bloodworth leapt up, cursing his friend for a fool, but Craddock ignored him and moved out to the center of the floor where he stood with his fists cocked at his side. Suddenly the whole room was filled with movement, with voices making words that were sound only, the odor of cigars and sweat and stale beer overcome by the raw stink of anger, the smell (Stribling thought) of the end of the line, the last moment before something was done that could never be undone, and he, Stribling, the cause of it, because he had forgotten how deep hatred could run, because he had never hated any thing nor any man in his long life. And he might have said *Stop, now—I take it back—I am only a stranger here*—except he didn't have to, for at that moment L. W. Thomas lifted a sawed-off, double-barreled fowling piece from under the bar and cocked both barrels and fired the left one into the ceiling of the Citadel of Djibouti. A jet of flame eighteen inches long illuminated the postures of the men like a tableau and opened a hole in the roof through which sunlight poured suddenly and unexpectedly like a message from God Himself. Then the right hammer, jarred by the detonation, snapped on its cap and set that barrel off; this time, however, the charge was damp: there was a great belch of white smoke, a pattering of shot like sleet, then a spew of sparks and flame like a Chinese firework. When it fizzled out at last, dense smoke swirled in the column of sunlight from the roof. The men stood gaping in attitudes of unbelief, their ears ringing, the thing they were about to create hanging in the air before them. The silence that fell upon them then was tangible and weighted like an anvil. It created a globelike vacuum that drew all their belligerence down to a black ball like solid shot, and into that empty place Stuart Bloodworth stepped, the front of his pants soaked in beer, his face calm, his voice without any inflection at all.

"I was never a very good soldier," he said. "Never could drill, and I always hated uniforms, even when we didn't have any. I stayed to the end"—he looked at Nobles—"but I don't intend to waste another hour of my life on this horseshit. You better talk to the man while you still can."

"Jesus Christ," said Craddock. He righted his chair and sat down, his elbows on the table. Nobles remained standing, his right hand touching the tabletop, his eyes cast down like a man peering over a precipice. The smoke had settled to the floor now, and Bloodworth, still in the center of the room, seemed to be standing in a ground fog. When he moved to his chair, the smoke swirled around his ankles.

"Rafe," said Thomas. He stretched his hand across the bar and touched the sergeant's shoulder. Deaton tried to turn his head, but it merely wobbled on his shoulders. "You need to go on home," said Thomas. "You come back later, I'll fetch you a bottle of the nastiest Irish whiskey you can drink, on the house, if they's any house left." He turned to the journalist. "Mister Wooster, will you—"

The journalist closed his notebook. His face was shiny with sweat, a wet strand of hair curling from beneath the brim of his derby. "Of course," he said. He came around the bar, glanced at Stribling. "That's S-t-r-i—"

"Come on, Henry, dammit," said Thomas.

"Of course, of course," said the journalist, and took the sergeant's arm. Deaton's eyes were unfocused now, his jaw slack. He tried to speak, but could make no words.

"Likely he's gon' be sick," said Thomas.

"Goddamned rebels," said the sergeant at last.

Wooster led the man across the room, their shoes crunching in the glass that littered the floor. Craddock turned in his chair to watch them, the glittering light in his eyes dulled with sudden self-awareness.

"Leave the door open on your way," said Thomas.

The sunlight and air that the open door admitted seemed unfamiliar to Stribling, as though he had been long underground. He blinked and turned away from the brightness, and found himself looking into the eyes of L. W. Thomas. The man gestured toward the smoky room. "It's your party," he said. "What'd you say your name was again?"

Stribling was about to answer when a single shot clapped sharply across the afternoon. Stribling and Thomas looked at each other, their faces mirroring the same question. Then there was a clumping from the porch, and the doorway darkened, and the patrons of the Citadel turned to see Henry Clyde Wooster standing in the rectangle of sunlight, holding out a hand that was smeared with blood. "Gentlemen," said Wooster. Then he spun dramatically and collapsed on his back among the sawdust and spilled beer and broken glass at Patrick Craddock's feet. Craddock bent down and prodded the journalist, then lifted the man's eyelids one by one. "Aw, he ain't hurt," Craddock said. "Just swooned."

Stribling was the first one out the door, with Thomas behind him. Zeke pulled nervously at his tether; Beowulf was on his feet, watching toward the cedars beyond the road. Rafe Deaton lay on his face in the mud like a toppled statue, his arms by his sides, the palms of his hands turned upward. The back of his frock coat was ragged where the ball had passed out, and already a trio of greenbottle flies circled the wound.

"Aw, mankind," said Thomas. He and Stribling clattered down the steps and knelt by the dying man. "Aw, no," said Thomas. "Not after all that way."

Stribling turned the sergeant over. He smelled of whiskey and bile; the wound in his chest sucked air as he tried to breathe. He lifted his hand, closed it on Stribling's sleeve, tried to speak but coughed blood in Stribling's face instead.

"What, Rafe?" said Thomas, bending close, his hand on the man's chest. "Tell me."

Deaton whispered, shaped a single word, and died. His eyes remained open, his face musing, as though he had at last discerned the mystery that lay beyond the ridge so long ago, in the emptiness where hawks floated, and time held no meaning, and dreams fashioned themselves out of light and air.

Stribling had to pry the man's hand loose from his sleeve. He rose and turned away, wiping his face with the handkerchief he kept in his sleeve. "My God," he said. "I never saw this. I wouldn't of come here."

"It wasn't you," said Thomas. He fixed the body, crossing the hands on the breast, closing the eyes. Then he looked off toward the cedars beyond the road. Beowulf was over there now, walking stiff-legged along the edge of the road. "He was over yonder, just inside the trees."

"Yes," said Stribling. He looked down at the body. "What did he say?"

Thomas didn't answer. He shifted to his other knee and went on looking at the cedars, the muscles in his jaw working. Beowulf returned from the road and crept around the body and thrust his muzzle under Thomas' hand. Thomas absently stroked the bony head.

By now, the patrons of the Citadel had gathered in the yard, all but Wooster, who was sitting on the top step in his shirtsleeves, mopping his face with the wet rag Mac Brown had used to revive him. Patrick Craddock knelt by the body and examined the wound.

"That one dead enough to suit you?" asked Stribling.

Craddock looked up. He was curly headed, his face smooth and unblemished as a boy's. "Let it go," he said.

Stribling looked at the blood on his handkerchief, then tucked it back in his sleeve. "Sure," he said.

"I figure we got about two minutes before von Arnim shows up," said Nobles. "What did he say to you, L.?"

Thomas rose to his feet, wincing, his hand pressed to his side. "Henry," he said.

"What?" asked Stribling.

"That's what he said. 'Henry.' "

"Henry who? Do you know?"

"Yeah, I know," Thomas said.

"Well, who is it? Not Wooster, surely?"

"No," said Thomas. "It ain't a *who* atall, it's a *what*." He turned to Nobles and balled his fist in the other's face. "*You* know what I mean," he said.

Nobles pushed the fist away. "Don't be raisin your hand to me," he said.

Marcus Peck balanced on his one leg and pointed with his crutch up the road. "Boys," he said, "I recommend we move this discussion to another venue, for yonder comes the cavalry."

They looked toward the square. A dozen Federal cavalrymen were coming at the trot, crowding the road in column-of-fours, their harness and sabers jingling. At their head rode Lieutenant von Arnim, his pistol in his hand.

"Time for the big skedaddle," said Craddock.

"*No!*" said Thomas. "Wooster saw it all. He can—"

"Are you daft?" said Nobles. "After the other night, they'll have us decoratin the trees by suppertime. Besides, we got to parley. I mean right now."

Thomas turned and looked at the Citadel of Djibouti. Wooster had retrieved his hat and coat and was bent over his notebook, writing. Mac Brown was reading over his shoulder. Thomas saw, as clearly as if he were standing there, the dim back room with its barrels and crates, the tattered playbill, the box with his possessions, and, under the cot, the leather valise full of U.S. greenbacks. Nobles was right, of course: the Federals would be stirred up like hornets now. He started for the door.

"Where you goin?" said Nobles.

"I got to get somethin," said Thomas. Then, as if they were planning an outing on Leaf River: "Where you all goin to be?"

Nobles raised his hands. "I don't—"

"Come *on*, boys," said Stuart Bloodworth. "My wife don't look good in black."

"Well, Jesus," said Stribling. He thought quickly. "You boys know the Carter house, up by the graveyard?"

"We're on our way," said Nobles. He put out his hand. "Come along, Marcus."

Stribling took Peck by the arm. "You can ride," he said, and led the man to the woodpile where Zeke was tied. "Quick now, put your stump in here," said Stribling, cupping his hands, but Peck shook him off and clambered up the woodpile and flung himself across the saddle as Stribling watched in astonishment. "Oh, never mind me," said Peck. "I am hell on retreat."

Stribling loosened the reins and looked back at the yard. It was empty, save for Wooster and Brown. "You all comin?" said Stribling.

"Lead the way, sir," said Wooster, his coat draped across his arm.

In the Citadel of Djibouti, L. W. Thomas stumbled blindly through the gloom. The column of light from the ceiling helped him find the tin box where he kept his ready cash; when he had emptied it, he looked for the last time upon the nude reclining behind the bar. She gazed back at him, unperturbed as ever. He wished he could remember who she reminded him of, but he knew he never would. "Goodbye," he said, and passed through the curtains to the lightless back room. He found his pistol and powder flask and a box of round balls and slipped them in his breeches pocket, then knelt and flung the blanket from the edge of the cot and fumbled in the cobwebbed darkness underneath until his hand was on the valise. The leather was cool to his touch; he gathered the handles in his fist and pulled. Then he stopped. He knelt there, the sweat pouring down his face. "Come on," he said to himself. Horses were in the yard now, and the voices of men. Something shifted behind him, and a board creaked. He turned his head; nothing was there but shadow. He looked at the valise. His heart was thumping now, driving the blood through his temples. "Ah, shit," he said, and took his hand away. He rose, kicked the valise under the cot, and was about to flee when he saw the playbill on the wall. He ripped it down, folded it, and stuffed it in a pocket of his sack coat. He looked around the room one last time, then he was through the back door. In a moment more, he had caught up with Stribling and his party in the trees along Town Creek. Behind him, he could hear von Arnim shouting his name.

✦   ✦   ✦

YOUNG ALEX RHEA had loathed Sundays for as long as he could remember, which wasn't all that long, though it seemed immeasurable to him. There was church, of course, as inevitable as the seasons, hollowed out of Sunday mornings rain or shine. Church was a great conundrum to him; he could never understand why time moved so slowly there, when it moved so quickly everywhere else. Moreover, his father required that Alex wear his shoes and good clothes all day Sunday, no matter what the weather.

This Sunday Alex was once again dressed in the blousy shirt and cravat and black jeans pants and hard black shoes that had once belonged to Mister Carter's boy Bushrod. All the clothes he owned now had once been the Carter boy's, for his own had gone up in the fire. He knew that Bushrod had been lost in the war, though Mister Carter didn't seem to believe it, and wearing the clothes gave Alex an odd feeling. Sometimes, when he was alone in some corner of the yard, and the light was just right—and especially in those strange moments when silence brushed the afternoon and the air grew still and watchful—Alex could feel his vanished cousin passing near or lingering in the hedges. It was not a scary feeling so much as a sad one, and at such times the boy would stop and listen hard to the silence, and sometimes he would speak the other's name out loud.

On this Sunday afternoon, Alex did not feel his cousin anywhere near. Indeed, the world seemed empty, deserted, as if everyone had gone off without telling him. He was bored almost beyond endurance, sitting in the rocking chair on the porch, trying to think good thoughts as his sister had instructed him to do. The boy was not sure which thoughts were good, but he was fairly certain that, being good, they would be dull and so would arise naturally on a Sunday, and therefore anything he came up with ought to qualify. He was thinking about frogs when the men came into the yard.

Alex recognized Harry Stribling at once. He was leading a horse upon which sat a one-legged man. Alex counted six other men whom he did not know following along behind, all of them looking over their shoulders. Alex leapt up from the rocking chair. "Hidy!" he said.

The men stood or knelt in the yard. Some of them made Alex think of the wild dogs that ranged in the woods around Cumberland, that he had seen crossing the cemetery one moonlit night. Stribling doffed his hat. "Young Alex, ain't it?"

"Yessir."

"You know where the Harper house is?"

The boy nodded.

"You run over there and fetch Mister Gawain Harper," Stribling said. "In return, I will let you ride this horse as long as you can stand it."

"Honor bright?" said the boy. "You'll let me ride him?"

"You can depend on it," said Stribling. "Now, be quick."

In another moment, young Alex Rhea was trying out his cousin's Sunday shoes on the road. As he ran, the shadows of leaves flickered across his face like magic lantern slides.

◆　◆　◆

WALL STUTTS MOVED quickly, was gone from his hiding place before the smoke of the shot drifted away. He knew he had hit the yankee sergeant and scared the living shit out of the fat civilian who was holding him up, and it was a good day's work already. Stutts knew that sharp-shooting the yankees this way was utter folly, but, the fact was, he enjoyed it. Nevertheless, he was pushing his luck. He figured, if he could just col-lect the bounty on Gawain Harper, he might ease off toward the Indian Territory and see what was what out there. Certainly he did not intend to be in the neighborhood when the Captain launched his rebellion. Moreover, he intended to take the Henry rifle with him.

The Henry lay across his pommel now as he guided the horse through the woods. He heard riders on the road and assumed them to be yankee cavalry, come to see what the commotion was; he grinned at the thought of old Thomas left holding the bag. Stutts had never liked the man, nor trusted him, not that it mattered much anyhow. What mattered now was getting a clear shot at the Harper boy, and in broad daylight, too, and right under the noses of the bluebellies. Quick. It needed to be quick. And it would serve old man Harper right, who had run Wall Stutts off the railroad for having a little fun with the niggers. Stutts grinned as he came out of the woods onto a back street off the square. He was enjoying himself, and he knew just the place where he could lie in wait behind the old Harper place.

✦   ✦   ✦

GAWAIN HARPER WAS not at the old Harper place, but way off down by the Mississippi Central Railroad, in a shallow cut dug by contract slaves in the 'forties with picks and shovels and wheelbarrows, while Frank Harper looked on from the back of a horse. Earlier, after Stribling left for the Citadel, Gawain had thought he might call on Morgan, and no doubt would have, had his aunt not presented him with the Navy Colt. But the pistol drew all his concentration, as if it were the thing he had been traveling toward for forty years, and it would not be put aside. He sat in his room, the smell of grass and lantana and oak leaves riding on the breeze through his open window, with the pistol and its implements laid out on the desk before him. He held the flask in the palm of his hand; it was smooth copper, shaped like an oversized fig, heavy with powder, with a tarnished brass measuring spout. Like the pistol itself, the flask was satisfying to hold, as though it were ripe with some secret purpose beyond mere utility.

Gawain Harper knew a good deal about guns, had seen what they could do to animals and to men. For most of his service (after he had rid himself at last of the worthless flintlock conversion), he had carried the same Enfield rifle, had polished its brass with ashes and water, had carved his initials into its greasy walnut stock, had cleaned it a thousand times (a job he loathed, but it was like bathing a bedridden old relative: you had to do it, so you did), had wiped blood and fragments of flesh from its bayonet, had looked down its barrel at living human beings and squeezed the trigger—sometimes he heard the report and sometimes he didn't, and sometimes felt the bruising shock against his shoulder and sometimes not—and seen them fling up their hands or clutch at themselves or run away. And, if the line was advancing, he might walk over them, and always he tried not to look, and always he looked anyway, as though that were a part of the bargain he had sealed with them in the instant he pulled the trigger. For a while, he could remember each of their faces, but in time they all became one face, vaguely familiar, like one he'd seen before on the street or in someone's parlor, eyes not accusing but startled and a little sad. He saw the face often. Waking in a dog tent on a moonlit night, Sir Niles snoring beside him, Gawain might see it in the random designs painted by the moonlight on the thin canvas. Or in the leaves or naked branches overhead when they had no tents. Or in dreams, or reflected in the smooth surface of a pond. He supposed he would always see it, only in wallpaper patterns now, or water stains on the ceiling, or on the other side of a hearth fire in a place where he ought to be safe. So Gawain Harper knew about guns and their ability to transform, not merely a single human life, but generations stretching away into the mist of long tomorrows.

Now here was the Navy Colt, blued and burnished and lying expectantly on the desk where he used to try to write poetry. Gawain did not like pistols; they always seemed to misfire on him, or fire off all their chambers at once, or let loose on their own later in the day when he least expected it, and they appeared to be useful mainly for driving tent stakes. As an infantryman, Gawain had never carried one, though for a time he did keep a single-shot Derringer in his haversack. It had a bore the diameter of a pencil and a trigger that appeared magically when you cocked it, and it took a microscopic percussion cap. One idle afternoon, Gawain found the little pistol in the bottom of his haversack among tobacco crumbs and grains of rice, and it occurred to him that he had never fired it, did not know if it *would* fire, nor what effect it would have on the candidate if it did. So he traded it to a comrade for a pair of wool socks. But this Navy Colt was different from all the other pistols he had seen and scoffed at. It had been his father's and now it was his, and he had a use for it that he would not have imagined in his most extravagant dreams.

So, in the end, he did not call on Morgan Rhea this Sunday afternoon. Instead, he put on his frock coat and slipped the pistol in the back of his waistband where it could not be seen, and put the flask and a dozen balls and a scrap of paper for wadding in his pocket, and took up his Panama hat and slipped out the door and, of course, met his father in the hall.

The old man was barefoot and in his shirtsleeves, a bristly growth of white whiskers on his face, his thin hair disordered. He was staring at the bright square of the window at the end of the hall where the gauzy curtains undulated in the breeze.

Gawain did not want to stir up his aunt, so he spoke softly to the old man. "Hey, Papa," he said. "What you doin?"

"Who is that?" shouted old Harper, lifting a crooked forefinger (a mule had bitten it nearly in two, years before) at the curtains moving in the sunlight.

"Who is what, Papa?" said Gawain, following the old man's point. "There ain't anybody there, just curtains, is all."

Old Harper squinted at his son. "She was gone before I knew it," he said, his voice loud in the silent house. Gawain winced. "Hush, Papa," he said.

"Gone like that," said Harper, and snapped his fingers, though they made no sound. "That boy of mine could tell you if he was here, but he ain't here—no, he's off whorin in Memphis." He gestured toward the curtains again. "You talk to her, see what she wants."

"Papa, I—"

The old man cocked his fist; the knuckles were hairy, and the knotted fist still seemed big as a ham to Gawain. "You do what I say! Go on!"

Gawain turned then, walked to the end of the hall, paused, and walked back again. When he came to the old man, Gawain put his lips against the hairy ear and said, "She wants you to lay down for a while, Papa."

In an instant, old Harper's face went empty, soft, the eyes puzzled now. "She does?" he said.

Gawain Harper led his father to the hot, foul-smelling room where he lived—the windows were closed and the curtains drawn—and sat the old man down in his chair. Then he pulled back the curtains and tied them in knots so they wouldn't move, and threw open the windows, and pulled down the bedclothes. At last he took the old man's elbow and guided him to the bed with its broken mattress. Old Harper lay down and arranged himself on the dingy sheet with his hands clasped on his breast, and Gawain adjusted the pillows under his head. For a moment Gawain stood by the bed, looking down at his father's face. The eyes were wet now, and held neither malice nor any memory of violence, only puzzlement, as if they looked upon something too quiet, too gentle, for Frank Harper ever to understand. When Gawain turned away, he found his aunt standing in the doorway. He walked past her without a word, down the stairs and into the sunlight.

He walked fast through the fields and stumps and young timber to the railroad. He did not expect to encounter any yankees back here, and he knew from old usage that the walls of the cut would mute the sound of his shooting, and if it didn't, that was just too bad. He remembered that a city ordinance used to be in effect against discharging firearms on Sunday, and the thought of it made him laugh.

He came through a stand of young pines, and there was the cut. He slid

down the muddy clay bank to the railroad, and for a moment he stood
transfixed in the solitude that embraced him, breathing in the hot smell of
the crossties and the heavy summer smell of Queen Anne's lace and blackberry vines. He noted that some of the ties were new-cut, no doubt laid by
the yankees, and the rails were spiked and lined and of a heavier weight
than he remembered. Taken all around, the Mississippi Central was in better shape than he'd ever seen it, and as he looked up the cut toward the
place where the rails curved gracefully into the trees, he realized that here,
at last, was one thing that had not only survived the war but been
improved by it. The thought took him by surprise, and he knelt between
the rails, the pistol dangling forgotten in his hand.

"Say!"

The voice startled Gawain. He looked up and saw an apparition standing on the lip of the railroad cut. "Say!" Old Hundred-and-Eleven said.
"You seen any ginsang down thar?"

✦　　✦　　✦

A QUARTER MILE away, Wall Stutts tied his horse in a grove of trees just
west of the Harper house. A low stone wall, one of the few in the county,
ran along the edge of these woods. It was overgrown with privet, honeysuckle, wild roses and morning glories, skirted with a white fan of daisies
and drowsy with the murmur of insects. From here Stutts could see the
front yard and the columned portico of the house. He sat down in the
leaves behind the wall and bit off a chew of tobacco, the Henry rifle lying
across his knees.

· XVII ·

When he heard the rider turn off the road, Solomon Gault's first thought was that Stutts was returning. Irritated, he set his manuscript aside and rose to his feet, wondering what fool thing the man would have to tell him. He was tired of these peckerwoods. At moments like this, Gault wished he had never stayed in Cumberland County. He should have crossed the river and gone to find Sterling Price in Texas. Should have gone down to Mexico. Should have, should have, should have—

He ripped off his spectacles and dropped them on the manuscript. The flame of his anger leapt inside him, burning away the thin veneer of reason that ordered his mind. He was choking on it, as his wife had choked and gagged when the diphtheria closed her throat, and the child's— *He had them placed in the same coffin and dug the grave himself and watched while Mister Garrison said the words over them. Then he filled it himself, ignoring the priest until at last the man went away, and they all went away, and it was only him then, and the slide of the shovel in the cool earth.* Then he saw the shape of a man through the trees, leading his horse. When Gault's horse nickered, the man stopped. Gault knew it wasn't Wall Stutts then—this man was too big, and cautious, as if he had not expected anyone to be here. "Who is that?" said the man.

Gault fought to control himself, to find a voice he could use. "A friend," he said, drawing the pistol from the pocket of his coat and slipping it into his waistband. Then, when the stranger walked into the clearing, Solomon Gault felt his anger evaporate, to be replaced by the scent of opportunity he had followed all his life. In that moment, he was willing to concede that perhaps there was a God after all.

◆　　◆　　◆

LIEUTENANT VON ARNIM had seen the men cross the road. He put his horse into a canter and, when he reached the spot, pushed her a little way into the cedars and listened. Then he backed out, turned the horse around, and saw the body lying in the yard of the Citadel of Djibouti. He pushed the horse into the yard. "Thomas!" he shouted. "You! Thomas!" When he got no answer, he turned to his escort. They were cavalry just come from the depot at LaGrange, most of them brand-new at the trade, the rest grown fat in garrison. They were sitting their horses, the youngest ones staring at the dead man, their eyes round as double eagles, and the sight of them pushed Lieutenant von Arnim into a room he had not visited in a long while. "Goddamn you!" he bellowed. "Don't sit there with your fingers up your ass! Get into the woods and find these goddamned rebels!" He did not wait to see his order obeyed, but holstered his pistol and slapped the spurs to his mount and forced her up the steps toward the black hole of the open door. He had to fight her, cursing through his clenched teeth; at last she went through, terrorized in the gloom, blundering into tables and chairs and benches, and von Arnim had to fling himself out of the saddle before she reared and crushed him against the ceiling. "Goddammit, get out then!" he cried, and broke a chair over her rump and sent her flying back into the sunlight. Von Arnim drew his pistol, looked around, saw the curtain and found the back door standing open. He kicked the cot over, pulled down a stack of boxes and sent mice scurrying. He picked up the mandolin by its neck and smashed it, then spied in the open box a stash of candles. He holstered his pistol again and dug through the box and found some loose matches. "All right, then, damn you," he said. He dragged the bedclothes into the front room, jerked bottle after bottle of raw whiskey from the shelves and poured the reeking stuff over the blankets, soaking them. His hands were trembling so that he could hardly strike the match, but he lit it and cupped the flame, then lit a candle, then another, and dropped the candles onto the blankets and saw the flame catch, leap greedily for more. He piled chairs onto it, old newspapers, books, a leather valise, the straw stuffing from the whiskey crates, while the smoke swirled into the shaft of sunlight pouring through the roof. Then the flames leapt at him and he backed away, turned and staggered out into the blinding sunlight, his face streaked with sweat and soot, and saw, with the same amazed and unbelieving jolt that Lazarus must have felt when he woke from the dead, the escort still milling in the yard, some of them dismounted even and gawking at the body as if it were a prize fish, or a slaughtered calf, or a goddamned pot of geraniums.

◆　◆　◆

BEN LUKER LIVED in a shebang he had built among the ruins of the courthouse. He was sitting on an overturned nail keg in the doorway, his mule tethered nearby, going over in his mind the incident at the Citadel. How much to tell the Captain? Maybe nothing. Maybe if he kept out of it, the thing would settle itself. As for the man Stribling, he, Ben Luker, could take care of that. He wouldn't be caught out like that again, and shoved around, and made a fool of. He was thinking about ways to do it when he became aware that men were running, shouting, and over the rise to the south, a column of smoke was beginning to boil skyward. He stood up, peering down South Street; he could see the Shipwright house, and the next thing beyond that was the Citadel. "Well, by God," he said, and was moving to his mule when Lieutenant von Arnim rode up. The man's horse was lathered, her eyes rolling; von Arnim pulled her up and slid out of the saddle, and Luker watched in astonishment as the Lieutenant pulled his pistol and stalked through the rubble of the courthouse toward him.

"Hey, Cap—," Luker began, but von Arnim was already there, and the pistol's muzzle was already thrust deep into Luker's belly so that he grunted in pain. "What—"

But von Arnim put out his hand and clamped it on Luker's jaws, twisting his head around. Von Arnim thrust his face an inch from Luker's ear and snarled into it, "You goddamned sorry son of a bitch, you have one minute—*one,* mind you—to tell me who—"

"It was Gault!" cried the sheriff, pulling away. "Gault done it! Him and Wall Stutts! I never knowed a thing about it!"

✦　✦　✦

THE REFUGEES FROM the Citadel of Djibouti, gathered in the yard of the Carter house, could not see the smoke rising to the south. Mostly, they wanted to get out of the yard, and to that end, Stribling was approaching Judge Rhea. The judge stood on the gallery, a walking stick in his hand. Behind him, Morgan Rhea stood in the doorway.

"What is all this about, Captain Stribling?" asked the Judge.

"We are a delegation, sir," said Stribling.

The Judge regarded the men in the yard. "A delegation?" he said.

"Yes, sir," said Stribling. "Can we come inside?"

"Inside?" the Judge said. "Captain Stribling, this is not my house. I do not know these men. I—"

"Great God, Papa," said Morgan, sweeping onto the gallery. "You know Captain Stribling, and I know some of these others. I know *him.*" She pointed at Peck, who grinned and lifted his cap, a greasy Mexican War relic with a blue-jay feather stuck in the band.

"Miss Rhea," said Stribling, "it is a joy to see you again, though I must say that the occasion is—"

"Come on, Harry," said Carl Nobles, "quit foolin around."

"Quite right," said Stribling. "Judge, we got to come inside right away. The yankees are after us."

"Well, why didn't you say so," said the Judge.

◆ ◆ ◆

"I LIKE TO come out here and hunt 'sang," Old Hundred-and-Eleven was saying. "Ain't had much luck, though. I ain't found enough to physic a snipe. What you doin, settin in the middle of the railroad anyhow? You gon' get runned over."

Gawain was loading the pistol. He had rammed the powder and ball, and now was ramming the wads, in the hopes that he might avoid the simultaneous ignition he expected. Old Hundred-and-Eleven had descended the bank and was watching from beneath his umbrella. "Well, I was gon' try this pistol," said Gawain. "What you want with ginseng, anyway? I heard it was good for the brain, and as long as I've known you, you ain't had one."

Old Hundred-and-Eleven grinned. "Naw," he said. "I'm to use it for a love potion."

"Go on!" said Gawain in surprise. "Who is the candidate?"

The other hunched his shoulders and looked around, up and down the rails and over the lip of the cut. Then he came close and sat down facing Gawain and crossed his legs. He put his finger to his lips. "Shhh," he said.

"I won't tell nobody," said Gawain.

"You promise?" said the other.

Gawain nodded.

Old Hundred-and-Eleven leaned close and tapped a yellow nail on Gawain's knee. "It's for Judge Rhea's gal," he said. "I think she likes me."

◆ ◆ ◆

ALEX RHEA STOOD on the porch of the Harper house, drinking a glass of water. Aunt Vassar sat in her rocker. "I am sure Mister Gawain will be back directly," she said. She leaned toward the boy. "You didn't say what you wanted him for."

"Captain Stribling sent me to fetch him," said Alex.

"Ah," said Aunt Vassar, rocking.

"Yes'm. He told me Mister Gawain must come right away. Captain Stribling was in our yard with a band of pirates; I believe they are formin a gang to rob and pillage, and I am to be a member, and he said I might ride the horse as long as I could stand it." The boy wiped his mouth on the sleeve of his cousin's shirt.

"Well, of course," said Aunt Vassar. "I can envision that."

Uncle Priam came around the end of the porch carrying a banjo. When he saw Aunt Vassar, he held the instrument up by its neck. The head was broken, and it had only one string. "I been lookin for this," he said by way of explanation.

"And I been prayin you wouldn't find it," said Aunt Vassar. "Do you know where Mister Gawain went off to? This boy is huntin him."

"I asked Mist' Gawain that same question when he left the house," said Priam. He tipped his battered hat to Alex. "How you doin, young master? I ain't seen you lately."

"What is that you got?" said Alex.

"A banjer," said Priam. He plucked at the single string, evoking a melancholy note. "I got to fix it, though."

"Well, where did he go?" asked Aunt Vassar.

"You mean Mister Gawain?" said Priam. "Lord Jesus, they always gone off someplace, these young peoples. Seem like they be wore out."

Aunt Vassar slapped her palms on the arms of the rocker. "*Where* did he go, dad blame it," she said.

Priam looked at her. "Said he was goin to the cut. Said to tell you that, if you asked."

"Well, why didn't you?"

"Well, you ain't asked 'til now," said Priam.

In a moment, Alex Rhea was on his way to the railroad cut. He walked along, enjoying the warm sun and the smell of the broomsage. He kept his eyes on the ground, hoping he might find a snake. He did not see the man watching from the clump of trees. Uncle Priam, however, who had been sent to watch after the boy, saw him plain as day.

✦   ✦   ✦

"WELL, MY GOD," said Gawain to Old Hundred-and-Eleven. "You can't court Morgan Rhea—she is spoken for."

"Rah!" spat the old man. "That don't matter to me. Hit's foredoomed. I seen it in the Testyment, in the pitchers. Say—" He cocked a red eye at Gawain. "It ain't that Stribling feller, is it?"

A little flame of devilment winked on in Gawain's head. "Well," he began, "it might very well be—" And stopped.

The old man was watching him, the umbrella shading his pale face where he sat between the rails. His ragged, buttonless frock coat was patched with mattress ticking; from the cuffs of his greasy leather breeches thrust the old man's bitten ankles, and his slablike feet twitched nervously. Once, years before, Gawain had seen Old Hundred-and-Eleven (he was old then, too; he had always been old, it seemed) from the cab of a moving train passing over the Leaf River trestle. Down below, Old Hundred-and-Eleven was preaching to a collection of negro children on the bank. Even over the steam and the clank and rattle of the cars, Gawain could hear the old man talking. The children, in their tattered burlap and flour-sack dresses, were wrapped in the cadences of the old man's voice, so that not a one of them raised his eyes to the marvel of the train passing overhead. Then, just before the locomotive cleared the trestle, Old Hundred-and-Eleven himself looked up—not at the train, but at Gawain—and when he did, all the little black faces turned that way. Gawain had never forgotten the sight of them, nor the penetration of their gaze, nor the way he had ducked back in the cab, clear to the other side, with the sense that he had been found out in some indeterminate sin.

"No," he said at last. "No, it ain't Stribling." He rose stiffly to his feet. "Come on," he said, "let's see if this pistol will shoot. You can try it, too."

"Rapidan!" said the other, grinning.

They found some rocks and set them up on the bank for marks. Gawain backed away a dozen paces. "That ain't very far," said Old Hundred-and-Eleven.

"My friend," said Gawain, "if I got any farther away, you could pose an elephant over there in perfect safety. Now, stand back." Gawain raised the pistol and cocked it.

"An elephant!" said the old man as Gawain was about to squeeze the trigger. "You ever see one of them?"

Gawain raised the muzzle. "Yes." He aimed again.

"Around here?" said the old man in astonishment.

Gawain raised the muzzle again. "No, they don't grow around here. This one was in a menagerie." Gawain set the front sight on the largest of the rocks and aligned it with the notch in the hammer. He drew a breath, let it out, tightened on the trigger—

"Well, what'd it look like?"

Gawain pointed the pistol skyward and turned to the old man. "Like an elephant, dammit," he said. "Now, how am I supposed to shoot if you keep botherin me?"

"Well, I just wanted to know."

"All right," said Gawain.

"You ort not to bring it up if you don't want to talk about it," said Old Hundred-and-Eleven.

"All right," said Gawain. "I will tell you all about it later. Now, you stand over yonder; this thing's liable to go off in all directions."

Old Hundred-and-Eleven took a step back. Gawain aimed the pistol again. His hand was not steady, and the brass bead of the front sight wandered over the target. Gawain took a breath.

"Mister Gawain!" said Alex from the lip of the cut.

Gawain sighed. He let the hammer down and turned and saw the boy. "Young Alex. What you want, lad?"

"Mister Gawain!" said the boy breathlessly. "Captain Stribling said you got to come to our house right away there is brigands in the yard and a one-legged man on a horse he said come quick so I could ride it is that a pistol?"

"Brigands?" said Gawain.

"Arrah!" said Old Hundred-and-Eleven. "That Stribling feller again!"

Gawain was about to question the boy when Uncle Priam appeared against the sky. "Mist' Gawain," he said, "you better come up here right away."

"I done told him!" said Alex.

"Well, good God," said Gawain. He gathered up his loading materials and, with the pistol in his left hand, grabbed the bony wrist of Old Hundred-and-Eleven with his right. "Come on," he said, "I'll help you up."

"Ain't we gon' shoot?" said the old man, but Gawain was already pulling him up the bank. At the top, Alex started to speak again, but Uncle Priam put his hands on the boy's shoulders and hushed him. "Mist' Gawain," he said, "you better step over here with me. I got to tell you somethin."

✦　✦　✦

THE AFTERNOON WAS growing long in shadow. Already the sun had left the clearing at the old Wagner place, though it still lingered in the tops of the trees, and the clouds overhead were bright with it. The two horses cropped the grass, shaking their heads now and then, and whisking their tails at the flies. Among the cedars, mosquitoes were swarming, and already the two men in the clearing were slapping at their ears and the backs of their hands.

"Have you ever thought to write your own memoir?" asked Solomon Gault. He was sitting on the cookpot; in his hand was a handkerchief that he used to wave at the mosquitoes. "I should think you would have a great deal to say."

Burduck was pacing. At first, he had been irritated to find the stranger in this secret place, but as they talked, the Colonel found his new acquaintance engaging. Gault had introduced himself as a planter lately returned

from the war in the East, who came to this place from time to time for solitude. They had spoken of the weather, of course, and the storm, and
horses, and the prospects for a late corn crop. Burduck thought he was suc-
cessful in steering the talk away from the war; then Gault had brought up
the subject of his manuscript, though he had not let Burduck examine it,
explaining that it was only a rough sketch and not yet fit for reading. For
his part, Burduck was glad the man had not offered.

"No," said Burduck. "I am more disposed to forgetting all that. Maybe
when I am old, and nothing is left but a tranquil recollection. Maybe
then—and only for my grandchildren, if I have any, so they can know how
unspeakably brave and noble I was."

Gault laughed. "You have a sense of irony, commendable in a soldier,
and rare in—if I may say so—one of your exalted rank. As for me, I was
only a humble private of the line, where irony was more regular than
rations ever were."

If you were a private, thought Burduck, *that horse there was a Major
General.*

"Speaking of matters military," Gault went on, "please allow me to
compliment you on the splendid performance of your troops this morning."

Burduck looked up in surprise. "My troops?"

"At the graveside. Oh, I was among the civilian spectators—happened
to be in town for church. You go to church, Colonel?"

"Not often," said Burduck.

"Let me see," said Gault, cradling his chin in his hand. "Your accent is
Eastern, but not New England—not Unitarian country. Your surname is—
Baltic? Russian perhaps? That means Orthodox, but you don't have the
whiskers for that. Let me guess—Roman Catholic?"

"Very good," said Burduck.

"*Pax Domine vobiscum,*" said Gault, smiling, but Burduck did not wish
to play. "And with thy spirit," he said.

Gault nodded. "I attend strictly for diversion, having long ago learned
to trust only myself in regard to destiny. But anyway, your troops are first-
rate at drill. Disciplined. Well-equipped. Would that I had served with such
a command."

"You could have," said Burduck.

Gault laughed outright, then grew serious. "A pity about that boy—the
one who was murdered. A drunken brawl, perhaps? Any ideas?"

"None," said Burduck. "How do you know he was murdered?"

Gault shrugged. "You can't hide such things," he said.

"Well," said Burduck, wanting to change the subject. "How fares it with your people? You say your place is nearby?"

"Yes, a mile or two. As for my people, they are . . . comfortable, I should say. In fact, when I saw them last, they were sleeping, and had not a care in this world."

"Well, I envy that," said Burduck.

"Do you?" said Gault. "Do you really?"

Burduck looked at his companion, aware that some unheard note had been struck, and wished he had not mentioned the matter of family. Gault smiled at him, but Burduck sensed a watchfulness, as if the man were waiting for the chance to turn them both down a darker path. It seemed inevitable, in fact, and all at once, Burduck was uncomfortable. "Yes," he said. "I envy anyone who has found peace. It seems in short supply these days."

Gault lowered his head. "On the contrary," he said. "A great many have found it."

Now Burduck laughed. "In the grave, maybe," he said.

The other rose and began to pace, his hands clasped behind him. In a moment, he turned and looked at the Colonel. "Have you considered how strange it is we should meet like this? Only yesterday, we were enemies, and now . . . ? I wonder if we could ever talk on the same plane, you and I? The victor, the vanquished, eh?"

"You don't look vanquished to me," said Burduck, irritated. "And, frankly, I do not feel victorious. But in one thing you are correct. It'll be many a day before we can talk about it. Now, if you'll excuse me, sir, I must be on my way back to town."

"Oh, don't go," said Gault. "Maybe we can find a way to bridge the gap. Maybe I can even help you understand the peculiar nature of our hatred."

Burduck turned on him then. "Hatred?"

"Beg pardon," said Gault quickly. "I do not mean of you personally."

Burduck snorted. "No offense," he said. "As long as you remember who started it."

"Oh, of course," said Gault. "But an educated man like yourself must surely recognize that knowledge, understanding, is power. You might use me to your advantage."

Burduck smiled. "Mister Gault," he said, "I am very tired. Come see me when I am in a better humor; I should be glad to hear what you have to say. For now, good evening, sir."

Burduck turned toward his horse. He paused to tighten the cinch strap, his back to Solomon Gault so that he did not see the man reach inside his frock coat, nor the curious light that had come into his eyes.

◆　◆　◆

LIEUTENANT VON ARNIM slammed open the door of the Shipwright house so hard that the oval ruby-glass pane shattered and fell around him like fragments of frozen blood. Old Mister Shipwright, just coming down the stairs, howled and put his hands to his head.

"Sorry, sorry," said von Arnim. He brushed glass from his uniform and strode past the man and into the parlor where the sergeant of the guard and officer of the day were staring at him open-mouthed. The officer was the same young Lieutenant who had kept watch under the bridge.

"Where is the Colonel?" said von Arnim without preamble.

Lieutenant Osgood paled. "I—he—I don't know," he stammered.

"You don't *know*?" said von Arnim. He turned to the sergeant. "Turn out your guard," he said. "*All* of them. Kick the musicians out of their blankets and have them sound the long roll. Take five men to the tavern and bring back Sergeant Deaton—"

"Sergeant Deaton?" said the young officer. "What has he—"

"He's dead," said the provost. "Get on, now. And sergeant—the tavern is on fire, and the cavalry has orders to shoot anybody who tries to put it out. Understand?"

The sergeant did not understand, but he was not about to bring that fact before Lieutenant von Arnim. He saluted, took up his musket, and was gone across the broken glass, bawling for his corporal. Von Arnim glared at the young Lieutenant.

"Osgood, damn you, *where* is the Colonel? Don't tell me you don't know."

The officer raised his hands helplessly. "He went off for a ride, said he would be back in a few hours. What is it? What's happened?"

"Bushwhackers," said von Arnim. "Captain Bloom is in command until we find the Colonel. Run fetch him. Be quick."

"Sir!" said Osgood, glad for the errand. He ran out, adjusting his sword belt over the diagonal red sash that marked him as officer of the day.

Von Arnim opened the door to the Colonel's office and walked in. The breeze from the open window had strewn the records of Tom Kelly across the floor. Von Arnim went to the window and banged his hand against the frame. He looked out at the yard and saw that the trees along the creek were wreathed in smoke from the Citadel of Djibouti.

Old Mister Shipwright appeared beside the provost; von Arnim was occupied with his own thoughts and did not realize the other was there until he spoke. "I remember when that was new," the old man said, pointing a crooked finger at the capsized carriage in the yard. "Don't seem that long ago, does it?"

"I don't know," said von Arnim. "I wasn't here."

"Not long atall," said Mister Shipwright. He squinted at the sky. "Be night before you know it," he said, then turned and shuffled away. Von Arnim heard the old man's slippers crunch in the glass and, a moment later, the slow tread of them up the creaking stairs.

Through the open window, the breeze brought the smell of burning and the shouts of men. Von Arnim took off his cap and wiped his forehead with his sleeve. *"Deo vindice,"* he said, hoping that it was so.

◆ ◆ ◆

WALL STUTTS WAS growing restless. He should have known that Harper would stick to the house on a Sunday afternoon, though it was reasonable to expect that he'd at least take a turn around the goddamned yard. Hell, maybe he wasn't even *at* the house. But Stutts had always had a reliable instinct about such things: where game would lie in the canebrakes, or what field held a good covey of birds. He knew he was in the right place; he just had to be patient, as if he were waiting by a salt lick. It was all the same.

He had seen the boy amble through the broomsage to his front, and a little while later the old nigger. Wall Stutts knew the boy—he was Judge Rhea's—and he wondered what the brat was doing out here. Was he looking for Harper? The thought crossed Stutts' mind that here might be a novel target indeed. If the boy came back this way—

Stutts grinned at the thought of the Captain's face if he should tell him he'd bushwhacked the Judge's boy. Or maybe he wouldn't tell him, just let him find out on his own when the Judge came to call. But, no—that was a complication Wall Stutts didn't need right now. One quarry was enough. And besides, there was the matter of the seventy-five dollars. Still, it was mighty tempting, and he might get lucky and fetch them both. He was trying to remember the boy's name when he heard the voices coming from the direction of the railroad cut.

Stutts' horse, who had never had a name, was restless too. He did not like being tied in the woods. In fact, he did not like anything much; the years with Wall Stutts had brought him little joy, and taught him to hate anything that walked on two legs. His reputation as a biter was well known among the men who associated with Stutts, and to walk behind him was to invite a crippling, as several had discovered too late. He had even bitten Stutts himself once. In return, Stutts had wired his jaws shut, hobbled him, and beat him to his knees with an axe handle. So he tolerated Wall Stutts, but watched him, waiting.

The voices, the smell of strangers from the place where the sun was going down, the sense that something was about to happen—these things bothered the old horse now, but not nearly so much as the other thing. He turned his head, watching the trees where it was coming. He stamped, and blew through his nose.

Stutts was hunkered down in the brush, eyeing the pair coming from the railroad. The boy wasn't there, but the nigger was, and the old fool they called Hundred-and-Eleven. Where did *he* come from? They were talking loud, laughing, the old man cutting capers with his umbrella. Stutts wanted to spit out his chaw, but he was afraid the smell of it would carry. Behind him, the horse moved again.

◆   ◆   ◆

WHEN THE COLONEL had gone, Solomon Gault reflected that the only god on the old Wagner place was Solomon Gault himself. The thought swelled within him, seemed to lift his feet off the ground and propel him into lightness and air. He had known the sensation before, when he watched men beg for their lives as Landers had done, crying out, not to God, but to Solomon Gault to deliver them. Yet, until today, he had never granted deliverance and so had not known the true nature of the power he embraced. At the last moment, and without knowing why, he had granted the Colonel life, had stayed his hand. Now he understood that, at the instant of decision, he had taken a lien on the Colonel's soul. And the man had never known, had mounted and bid good evening and ridden away never knowing how close he had come.

The clearing was all in shadow now, and a few early cicadas were tuning up in the trees. Solomon Gault gathered up his spectacles and the leaves of his manuscript and returned them to his saddlebag. He was momentarily puzzled at the sight of his empty rifle scabbard, then remembered where the Henry had gone. Gault wondered if it had been used yet. Somehow he knew it had, and at this very moment something was happening that would shape his own destiny. Again he felt the rush of heat in his veins, the power of holding a life—how many lives?—in the balance of his will. It was Sunday now, he thought; how appropriate if he could strike on the Sabbath. But it was too long, seven days and nights. The enemy was strong now, alert, watching for something to happen, wondering where the next blow would fall. Gault smiled at the irony, at the thing he had created. In their strength, the enemy was at their weakest. In the pride of their strength, they would not believe, *could* not believe, that the very thing they were watching for would actually come at them out of the smoke. Gault looked toward the sky, still blue above the trees, though soon it would soften to pink and violet. Night would come, as it always did, and then tomorrow. Gault looked around at the clearing, the meeting place. This time tomorrow, then. He mounted and pushed the horse through the trees. Once on the road, he set off southward at a gallop.

Meanwhile, Colonel Burduck, unaware that he no longer possessed his soul, rode north toward the square. He let the horse walk at her own pace through the cool shadows, through the voices of the woods and ditches, through the drowsy calm of a summer evening. Burduck was deeply sensible of the peace around him, the more so because it seemed so distant, as though he and Sally moved in a bubble of time and space all their own. For a moment, the Colonel wondered if he'd been out of time again—but no, the memory was too clear, too immediate: the stranger in the clearing, the talk that led nowhere, the irritation that was still with him. He had come looking for something and had not been allowed to find it, and the knowledge rankled him.

The man Gault stuck in his mind like a splinter. How many like him were in the country around—how many in the South? Cool men who looked on their defeat as they might some obscure event in classical history, something to be regarded with the intellect alone and thus unreal, abstract, offering lessons that no longer applied. Such men were more dangerous than all the ragged multitude with real wounds in their hearts, who had bled and suffered and wished to bleed no more.

Sally didn't want to cross the Leaf River bridge. Burduck spoke to her, nudged her with his blunt cavalry spurs, until at last she set her hooves on the planking. Once across, he took her in hand again and set her at a canter, and the breeze was cool in his face and brought the smell of greening trees and dampness—and smoke. Burduck frowned at that. It wasn't wood smoke, but the smell of a burning building, a foul, invasive smell that Burduck knew all too well. "Come up, Sally," he said, and slapped the spurs to her. She leapt forward, tossing her head, then stretched out her neck and let go, the mud flying in chunks from her hooves, her breath huffing in time with her stride.

So much for peace. So much for eluding the bitter anger that set ships afire, that left men drowning in their own blood in the dark. Ride then, and ride quick, into the black tunnel of the next minute, with its news of folly and madness and its record of despair. *It didn't have to be this way,* thought Burduck—*I could have told them, if they'd listen, but they wouldn't, and neither would we—*

He passed the gloomy ruins of a house to the left—the Walker place, old Boswell had said—and topped the little rise, and there was the smoke rolling in a black plume toward the sky, and men with their carbines drawn, sitting horseback in the road. One of them trotted out to meet him—a corporal, the yellow chevrons bright and new on his blouse, his chinstrap fastened, his shape bulging with carbine sling and saber and rolled blanket and picket pins and ration bags and pistol. Burduck pulled Sally down on her haunches and took secret pleasure at the surprise in the man's face as he saw the shoulder straps. "What the hell is all this?" snarled Colonel Burduck. "Who set this fire?"

"Lieutenant von Arnim," said the man. "He—"

But Burduck was already pushing past him, down the road, past the immense negro woman wailing in the yard, past the Citadel of Djibouti that was now a glowing framework of charred timbers, toward the knot of men struggling through the mud, their muskets slung across their backs, the blanket they carried weighed down with a burden too heavy for anything but simple physical strength to bear.

✦　✦　✦

AS HE PUSHED through the underbrush (the wet leaves made a silent passage, thank God), Gawain Harper unaccountably thought of Morgan and what she would say when she learned that Old Hundred-and-Eleven was sweet on her. She would not laugh, not Morgan. It would sadden her, and she would try to make it right somehow, worrying until she did. Gawain loved her for that—for something that hadn't even happened yet. He wished he had gone to see her today, and maybe he wouldn't be creeping through the woods, his mouth dry, his heart pounding in his chest, the pistol heavy in his hand. Right now they could be sitting on the garden bench in the scent of wisteria and sweet-shrub, and he would tell her how pretty she was, and how he wouldn't let her go to Brazil nor even to Yalobusha County—

I won't have it, won't let you get away again! he would say, rising from the bench and planting his feet firmly on the overgrown bricks of the walk.

Oh, Gawain, how long have I waited! she would say, and rise, and throw herself into his arms—

But, no, here he was on the scout, and all because he had been beguiled by pride again, and old Priam had found him and brought the news that some peckerwood was lurking in the bushes with a rifle, and he, Gawain, with nothing but a pistol he had never fired.

He passed under a cedar tree and brushed against a glop of orange fungus such as cedars sported in summer. He could hear Uncle Priam and Old

Hundred-and-Eleven carrying on like a couple of drunks in the broomsage field, just as they had planned, and he hoped the boy had stayed down in the cut like he told him to. Then, suddenly, he was looking at a horse; the animal was rolling its eyes at him and tugging at its tether, and the sight of him snapped Gawain back to the moment at hand, which included a strange man crouched in the brush with a rifle across his knees. Gawain swung wide around the horse, keeping his eyes on the man's back, and in an instant the man was a stranger no longer but one whom he knew well. What was about to happen burst full upon him, as clear and complete as a memory he had gathered only yesterday.

✦   ✦   ✦

AGAIN, AS AT morning, the upstairs hall of the Carter house was diffused with a light that seemed to grow from the plaster itself, as if behind the walls were a lamp that time turned up or down in its passing. The light belonged to time, Morgan thought. It had always been here, unchanging as the air that held it, and, if a person might only suspend for a moment the tyranny of the present, he might see in the light and air other shapes that dwelt there: a man and woman dancing, a figure risen from sleep to pace in the moonlight, a schoolboy standing on the gallery, watching the yard as though he might actually see the dreams he carried in his head.

She stood just inside the door to the Carter boy's room. The light in there was different, painted by the evening sun that streamed through the oaks outside. Still, in the composition of melancholy sunlight and moving leaf shadow, and in the sounds through the open window—cicadas, a mockingbird, somewhere a calf bawling—Morgan could read the signature of time. She understood that this moment, too, was already being absorbed into the memory of the old house, to be awakened some time in its dreams and perceived by other watchers perhaps, who would feel a shudder they could not explain, then turn gratefully into life again.

The visitors had gathered in the upper hall for reasons Morgan neither understood nor questioned. Her father had not wanted her to stay, but she insisted. The men seemed angry, more at themselves than anything outside, and scared, too: scared of something beyond whatever it was they had done. Captain Stribling had gone to hide his horse in the shed; when he returned, the men grew silent and looked to him.

"Boys, we are in a tight place," Stribling said.

"You don't know the half of it, sir," said Carl Nobles.

The man they called Thomas stood up then and waved his hand. "Tell em," he said. "Go on, tell em."

When Nobles began to speak, he evoked for them a dark landscape of vanity and menace, illuminated by a single name: Gault. Nobles told it without apology, a simple story, predictable even. It began when he arrived in Cumberland on the last day of May, under a noon sun that sent worms of sweat crawling under his clothes. He stood in the churned mud between the shell of Jenkins Hardware and the Old State Bank, smelling the reek of wet ashes, and realized for the first time that, in the two months since he had escaped the Federal encirclement at Hatcher's Run, Carl Nobles, like many another, had sustained himself with the belief that the wastelands through which he passed had no application to him—that if he could just reach home, he would find it magically unchanged, the same people walking about the streets, the ground ready for the plow, mail waiting for him at the post office. And not only that, but he had expected to find himself there, perhaps lounging on the gallery of Frye's Tavern or on a courthouse bench, and whatever he had become would be gathered at once into that which he had been before, and the memories he carried now would vanish forever. The scope of his delusion struck him like a physical blow, and he staggered to the side of the road and sat down among the ashes and wept without shame.

Gault found him a few days later at the Citadel of Djibouti. Nobles had never cared for the planter, but the man had a design, and Nobles grasped at it.

"It was supposed to be a stand-up fight," Nobles said. "Some boys in Marshall County were to strike the Federal depot up there, burn supplies, make noise generally so as to draw the yankees off. Gault figured he could have a hundred fifty, two hundred rifles from the county, and we'd strike hard, take the artillery first. Then—"

"And *then*," Thomas said, rising to his feet, his voice ringing in the hall, "the cavalry routed, the guns captured and turned on the dazed and bleeding foe, a moment when all hangs in the balance, the brave rebels standing alone on the brink of destiny. And *then,* at the last possible moment, out of Yalobusha comes the promised two hundred, three hundred embattled farmers to swell the ranks—the electrifying news spreads over the countryside like a brush fire to every hamlet and town—loyal men flock to the colors, and *behold!* The Rebellion renewed! The oppressor at bay! And we—" He stopped, waved his hand. "And *you,* I mean, get to do the whole thing over again, and maybe even do it right this time."

"*That* was the design?" said Bloodworth. "Jesus, Carl, why'd you buy such a broke-down horse as that?"

"But then he couldn't wait, and sent Stutts to murder the boy," said Stribling. "And the man today—that is part of it, too, ain't it?"

"Not the part I signed up for," said Nobles. "But, yes—the sergeant knew what got him—a Henry rifle, like the one Gault carries. It's a wonder he didn't drill Mister Wooster here while he was at it."

"Only it wasn't Gault this time either," said Stribling. "It was Wall Stutts again."

"I expect you can skate on that ice," said Nobles. "Gault wouldn't do the thing himself."

"But why?" asked Craddock. "Why stir em up, for God's sake?"

Thomas snorted. "Because he wants em that way. It'll look better in his memoirs. But look here, Stribling—how do you know it was Stutts?"

"Molochi Fish saw him kill the boy," said Stribling.

"Molochi *Fish*?" said Craddock. "*He* is your witness?"

"It was *supposed* to be a stand-up fight," Nobles insisted. "But the boy was too many for me, even without that fellow today." He moved to the gallery and leaned on the doorframe; in the evening light, his face was the color of rust on an apple. "Now look at us," he said. "Mister Bloodworth, to answer your question, I was a goddamned fool—beg pardon, Miss Rhea. I can't put any other light on it."

Bloodworth rubbed the back of his neck. "My God," he said. "I dream of dead men every night."

"Who don't?" said Craddock.

✦   ✦   ✦

"WELL, I'LL BE damned," said Wall Stutts. "You just the feller I was lookin for." He had risen and turned all in one movement, and found Gawain watching him a half dozen paces away. He grinned and straightened slowly, the rifle across his chest. "Aye God, you look just the same as you ever did."

Gawain said nothing. He was thinking *It won't fire, I know it won't*—

"You sure got the bulge on me," Stutts went on. "Warn't for that goddamn crowbait yonder, I'd of never heard you atall. That was a good trick, sendin them fellers out in front. Well, I'm glad you're here—my, ain't the muskeeters bad?"

"What you want with me, Wall?" said Gawain. He took a step, then another, closing the distance.

The man grinned again and spat into the leaves. He nodded at the pistol in Gawain's hand. "You don't need that."

Gawain took a step. "What business you got with me?"

Stutts glanced over his shoulder. The two men in the field had stopped and were looking toward the woods. "Well, shit," said Stutts, turning to Gawain again. "Everything got to be complicated."

He snapped the rifle up and fired so quick that the ball was humming away in the trees before Gawain realized what had happened. Through the smoke, he could see the look on Stutts' face, a mild irritation as if the man had just been told a bad joke. *It is a Henry, he will have to jack another round in,* Gawain thought. He raised the pistol, cocked it, thinking *It won't work, it won't—* and pulled the trigger just as Stutts closed the breech on the rifle.

◆   ◆   ◆

MORGAN RHEA LISTENED to them talk, and she watched her father where he sat on the edge of the settee, his elbows resting on his knees. He had said nothing, only grew paler and seemed to shrink before her eyes. Now and then he ran a hand through his thinning hair and shook his head. For her part, Morgan felt like an eavesdropper, as though she had intruded on some mystic cabal of lunatics.

"Gault," Stribling was saying. "He had the boy killed, and then—"

"Stop it!" Morgan said, her own voice shocking her. She raised her fists. "Will you please stop it? How many times do you have to say it?"

"Now, Morgan," said the Judge, rising unsteadily to his feet, his hand out. "Come sit by me."

"No!" she said. She stepped out into the hall. The men who were seated rose, even Peck, who had to struggle with his crutch. Professor Brown remembered the afternoon years before when he had made Morgan Rhea's image, one of his first ambrotypes. He wondered where it was now.

For a moment, Morgan seemed to stand in a vacuum in which the only sound was the blood in her ears. When she spoke, it was to Stribling. "Why have you brought this on us—brought these vile names into our house. And you have put Alex in harm's way. How dare you, sir."

Stribling narrowed his eyes. "We had to go somewhere, Miss Rhea," he said. "I considered the fact that you all might have a personal interest in this."

"Oh, did you?" said Morgan. "Well, I am grateful for your concern. I am sure the yankees will keep that in mind when they tear the house apart."

"Morgan—," began the Judge, but she raised her hand and silenced him.

"Forgive me, Papa," she said. Then she turned, just as Thomas had, only she looked into the eyes of each of them where they stood in the hall, and was neither surprised nor gratified when they looked away. "Listen to yourselves," she said. "All this madness, this insane talk of insurrection, Gault this and Stutts that, as if they were some irresistible flame and you so many stupid, bumbling moths. Talk, talk, talk—I am sick of hearing about Solomon Gault."

"Now, Miss Morgan," protested Nobles. "I have already admitted—"

"Murder, tavern brawls, intrigue—you sound like boys playing Ben Jonson!" she went on. " 'A stand-up fight' indeed, as if that were something to be longed for. Oh, gentlemen, what a sorry thing you have made of your deliverance. No, sir—" She stabbed her finger at Nobles. "Just naming yourself a fool ain't enough by half, for you are guilty of a greater crime than that, sir—you and all these gallants."

"Morgan!" snapped the Judge. "That is sufficient."

"No, Papa," she said. "No, it is not. All my life I have watched you butt your head against towers and walls you built yourself. You helped to build this one too, course by course—don't shake your head at me—and when the wall didn't stand, what was the only thing you could think of? To run, leave it all behind and let somebody else clean it up, sweep up the ashes, bury the dead, even your own. Captain Stribling here told me once that he don't blame anybody. How generous, how Christian of him. But maybe it's time he did. Listen to yourselves, to your stupid talk—that's a good place to start—"

She stopped then. Horsemen were passing on the road in the direction of the cemetery; they could hear the hooves and the jingle of accoutrements. After a moment, Nobles ventured out on the gallery. He returned, shaking his head.

"Bravo, Miss Rhea," said Thomas. "Go on—you were doin good."

"Excuse me?" said Morgan, turning to the man. "Excuse me, sir—are you the one who has the gin mill, the what-you-call-it?"

"I am he," said Thomas.

"Do not condescend to me, sir."

"I didn't mean—"

But she was bracing Stribling now. "You told me something else the other day," she said. "All that vainglory about a strange country where you all had been, how you could never leave it, any of you. Oh, I agree, sir—you not only never left that place, you brought it with you into this one, because you *like* it!" She laughed then, and turned on them all. "Vanity!" she said. "All your talk of nightmares, all your striking of poses, the defeat you wrap around you like some sacred garment—you *like* it! You must, else you would have been home today instead of sitting around feeling sorry for yourselves in a two-bit barrelhouse. What were you looking for that you thought you could find in Gault's company—" She leveled her finger at Thomas. "Or with *him*!"

"Whoa," said Thomas, and shook his head, and stalked out onto the gallery.

"I'm done," said Morgan then. "I will go and see about supper." She started for the stairs, but Stribling touched her arm.

"Miss Rhea—," he began.

"No," she said. "I am sorry, and not sorry, all at once. You have been kind to me, and I wish I could repay you with the same, but I can't. Not today. Look to yourself, sir." She started down the stairs; on the landing, she stopped and raised her face to Stribling again. "Where is Alex?" she said. "And where is Gawain Harper? Why do I always have to ask you that?"

✦　✦　✦

THE PISTOL WORKED, all right. It worked once, again, again, Gawain firing into his own smoke, and the men in the field running, and Wall Stutts roaring like a bull and swatting at the air as if he were swarmed with bees. Four, five, six shots, and among them Stutts got off one of his own, the ball once more rattling away through the treetops. When the pistol snapped empty, Gawain lowered it, stepped aside and waved the smoke away to find Wall Stutts still standing, still holding the rifle, the front of his shirt wet with blood. He laughed, and a red bubble popped on his lips. "You little son bitch," he said, laughing.

Gawain backed away, and the other came toward him, placing each step carefully in the leaves. His breath gargled deep in his throat; he spat tobacco and blood, shook his head.

"Wall!" said Gawain. "Stop it, Wall! Leave me alone!"

"Aye God," said Stutts, "I'm a dead man. You hear them dogs?"

"No," said Gawain. "Get away from me."

"*I* hear em," said Stutts. "They been after me a long time, and now they comin. They'll get us both, boy. I ain't goin by myself." He wavered, caught himself, moved another careful step, and another, then stopped again and tried to raise the rifle, but his strength was gone. Uncle Priam came up behind him and lifted the weapon from his hands. But Stutts was not finished. The demon that had driven him all his days, and sent him down corridors illuminated by smoldering fires, was busy yet. "Git away from me, nigger," he said.

"Let him be," said Old Hundred-and-Eleven. "Let him travel."

Stutts looked at Gawain and grinned, and in his eyes Gawain saw the dark spirit and knew that it would live forever beyond the flesh it was about to leave. Stutts fumbled in the pocket of his sack coat and produced a stained muslin bag tied with string such as the soldiers kept coffee in. He dangled the bag from his fingers, then flung it at Gawain's feet. "Give 'at to the Judge from his darlin Lily," he said, and laughed. "Been good luck up to now. He'll recognize it—it's still got her ring on it."

Gawain backed away from the thing. "Aye God," said Stutts, and laughed again. Then a tremor seized him, and he stumbled sideways against the rump of his horse. The animal stamped in the leaves, and Stutts turned toward the sound. "Hey, hey, hey, easy," Stutts said, and put out his hand. "Watch it!" cried Uncle Priam, and dropped the rifle and grabbed at the man, but too late. The horse lashed out with both hind legs and caught Wall Stutts full in the chest and stopped at last the futile beating of his heart.

✦ ✦ ✦

MORGAN RHEA FOUND her mother sitting in the parlor with all the shutters drawn, the evening sun slanting through the jalousies. At first she thought the old woman was asleep, then she saw the eyelids flutter, and the eyes, unfocused but waking, rove about the room as if searching for a forgotten thought. At last they settled on Morgan. "Oh, I was dreamin of Lily," the old woman said. "Is your father here still?"

Morgan crossed the room and knelt by her mother's chair. "He is upstairs with some gentlemen," she said.

"Ah, yes," the other said, and raised her hand, the fingers twisted with arthritis. "I remember they came. I don't want to know what's happened."

"Nothin's happened, Mama. Just some men talkin, is all. Do you want some supper?"

The old woman made no reply, only closed her eyes again and turned her face away. Morgan took her hand and held it for a moment, then rose and left the room, closing the door behind her.

The house was quiet. She could hear the hall clock and the voices of the men upstairs, but the clock and the voices seemed only a part of the silence, as a dog's barking is part of the stillness of night. In the hall was a lofty mirror in a frame like a cathedral window. She could see her whole image in the glass; it gazed back at her, faintly illuminated, and Morgan had the feeling that someone else was watching there, trapped in a moment of her own. Morgan raised her hand, touched the fingers of the other in the glass. For a moment they stood there, looking into each other's eyes. Then she heard the stair creak. She turned away from the mirror and found her father coming down, holding to the banister with both hands. She watched him descend into the silence one step at a time; at the foot of the stairs, he steadied himself on the newel post and raised his eyes to her. "Papa," she said, and went to him, pressed her face against his damp shirtfront, her fingers grasping the lapels of his coat. She could feel him stiffen, hear the rasp of his slow breathing, and thought *I will not ask any more of you than this* and said again, "Papa." Then she felt the tentative stroke of his fingers on the back of her head, then the press of his palm. At last, he circled her with his other arm and tightened his fingers in the fabric of her dress.

"I want you to know," he said, "that I have tried to do the best I could."

She made no reply. From the corner of her eye, she could see the mirror; the silent figures beyond the glass seemed to be clasped in a moment of intimacy unlike any she had ever known. She envied them, wondering if they, too, wherever they were, had to make do with empty words.

"The . . . agreement with Gawain Harper was my doing, not his," said the Judge. "While you are seeking whom to blame, you should not touch on him."

She winced at that, and felt a flash of anger. "I won't, Papa," she said, and tried to push away, but he held her fast, and she was surprised at the strength in him.

"Don't mistake me," he said, his voice hovering somewhere above her. "I did not come to scold you, any more than to beg forgiveness. Only to tell you that you and the Harper boy are free to do as you will; he is released from all obligations; I will try to amend—"

"Papa, you cannot face down Solomon Gault," Morgan said, pulling back gently now. "What I said up there—I was wrong, it wasn't fair, I can't know what it's like to be under the hand of what you all name honor. Let us go to the yankees, tell them about Gault, let them fix it."

"Tell the yankees?" said the Judge, smiling. "Now, there's a novel idea."

Morgan went on. "Then after, if you still want to go to Brazil, I'll . . . I'll go with you, at least for a little while—"

"No," said the Judge. He sat down on the bottom step, and Morgan knelt beside him, taking his hand, rubbing it. The Judge touched her forehead, brushing aside the wayward strand of hair that always hung there. "When I first came to this country," he said, "there was still an Indian village where the courthouse is—was, I mean—and old man Frye's tavern, and that was all except for some tents and shanties where the white people lived. Wasn't any nigrahs, wasn't even a road then, just a track in the woods, and you dare not go past Leaf River unless you traveled in a bunch, armed to the teeth—and even then there wasn't anyplace to go unless it was Natchez. The first client I had was a man who butchered a whole family for whatever he thought they had in their wagon, which was nothing but some furniture, as it turned out. I lost the case, of course, and the boys got the fellow drunk and had him tell the story one more time—he made a lively account of it, throwing in some details he'd left out before—then we hanged him from a red oak tree in the yard. Wasn't anything else to do—no jail nor penitentiary in the whole territory—and the fellow under-stood that and said he had no hard feelings. That's how it was then, in the new country, and I was a young man and gloried in it."

The Judge was silent for a moment. Up above, the men's voices went on, arguing now, and the clock chimed seven times. The light was fading now, this Sunday falling away to join all the others that had passed since a nameless and forgotten family was slaughtered in the night, and a man swung from a red oak limb in the tavern yard, and before that to a time when there were no Sundays at all, only the green canopy of the wilderness stretching away. "It was fun then," said the Judge at last, "and the closest I ever came to freedom. We made up the rules as we went along, and every-body thrived on possibility—what we could make of this place, what it might become—and God's will seemed to match our own so perfectly that we applauded Him for His good judgment. Well"—he waved his hand toward the door where the light was graying—"there it is, risen and pros-pered and fallen again, and I have seen it all, and take pride in most of it. But it grew up mighty fast, and maybe I got spoiled and forgot what it was like to believe in possibilities, or listen to any will but my own." He shook his head. "I am too old to go looking for God's country again, and your mother is too sick—did I ever tell you how she first came here? Riding behind the wagon on a black mare like a man, with a flintlock musket over the saddle bow?"

"No, Papa, you never did," said Morgan, and thought of the woman sleeping in the parlor, dreaming of her daughter dead and gone.

The Judge stood up then, too quickly, and it was a moment before he could clear his head. Morgan rose, too, and steadied him. "Where is she?" said the Judge finally. "Where is Mrs. Rhea?"

"She is in the parlor," said Morgan, "waitin for you."

"Ah," said the Judge. "In the parlor, of course." He looked at Morgan then, and touched her cheek. "You nearly died of the smallpox," he said. "You and Lily both. Your mother had it too, but wouldn't rest, wouldn't leave you, even in the fever."

"I know, Papa."

"You must not let Mister Harper get away," said the Judge. "He is not much account, but you can work on him. You must believe in possibility. Now, I must go and see your mother. Sometime I'll tell you about that first day I saw her." He laughed. "My God, that was a day all right."

She let him go then. He walked slowly up the hall, tapped gently on the parlor door, then opened it. He looked back at her once, then went in, clos-ing the door behind him.

Morgan had believed in possibility once, on another planet that had long since spun away in time. Then, betrayed, she had abjured it and withdrawn into the shuttered room of her widowhood, surrendering to a long twilight that could only end in night. Then Gawain had noticed her, or she him, and she had breathed the free air again, and brought out her white dresses and straw hats, and went to bed at night with the assurance that morning would come at its appointed time. One morning, there was the War, and she saw in it the possibility of great deeds, the elevation of the spirit, an axis around which all their lives would turn, haloed in honor and accomplishment. In short, she had learned nothing. So this time she betrayed herself, sent Gawain away as her emissary to purchase for them both the right to say *This is what we made out of sacrifice and courage—yours and mine both.* When she thought she had lost him, when her folly came at last to walk with her every day through the ruins, she retreated again (*Oh, Papa,* she thought, *what I have accused you of, you might well have learned from me—*) into a room more tightly shuttered than any, where she believed nothing could ever touch her again. Only, Captain Stribling had found her there, bearing the news that her betrayal had been forgiven, or overlooked, or ignored, and in the space of two short days, she had been brought to the edge of possibility again. Morgan shook her head. She understood how a soldier must feel when he discovers that, in spite of everything, he is doomed to live after all.

She was about to turn away and hunt up some supper when she heard Carl Nobles' voice from the gallery: "Harry, yonder comes the boy, and he's got Gawain Harper with him." Morgan watched the door, willing it to open. Nobles spoke again, something about a rifle; she couldn't catch it. Then she heard Stribling's boots on the stairs.

· XVIII ·

All things followed time, and all persons followed time. Uncle Priam went home to tell the news to Aunt Vassar, taking Wall Stutts' horse with him. The horse went peacefully, as if he'd finally used up all his meanness and could rest now. Old Hundred-and-Eleven went down to the boxcar jail and found Dauncy and Jack playing marbles in the dirt. He took them back to the woods above the Harper place, and there they hid Wall Stutts' body in a shallow grave. They finished as night was closing down and the whippoorwills began calling in the fields. Fireflies rose about their feet as they walked back to the jail through the broomsage, Dauncy and Jack carrying the shovels, all of them silent.

Gawain and Alex did not return to the Harper house. The last thing Gawain wanted right now was to face Aunt Vassar, even though he suspected she would approve of the afternoon's events. Carrying the Henry rifle and his father's Colt, he felt as conspicuous on the daylight streets as a brass band, so he and Alex made their way through back lots and the old Academy grounds to Carter's. Alex wanted to know all about the adventure in the woods, of course, and kept up a steady stream of talk until Gawain told him bluntly to shut up. To Gawain Harper, who had just killed a man, the boy's innocence was unnerving. Though Alex was offended, he felt better when they had to hide among the buildings of the Academy, then again in the weeds by Holy Cross church, while citizens passed on the roads.

At Carter's, Gawain did not knock but came in the door shouting Stribling's name. He stopped when he saw Morgan in the hall. Alex ran to his sister and began, "Mister Harper has—"

"No!" Gawain shouted. "Don't you say it!"

"What do you mean?" said Morgan. "Don't you be talkin to this boy—"

"No!" Gawain said again. He flung the rifle down in the hall and crossed to her. By this time, the others had come down the stairs, and Judge

Rhea burst from the parlor. Gawain looked at them in surprise, but only for an instant. He shoved the boy aside and took Morgan by the shoulders and spoke to her as if no one else was in the hall. "I killed Wall Stutts," he said.

Morgan's eyes grew wide and filled with tears, and she pulled away. "No! Don't tell me that! Don't come in here and tell me that!"

Gawain followed her. He pushed through the men in the hall, pushed her father aside. He caught her arm, but she pulled away again and was out the back door and gone, and Gawain let her go.

"What?" said Stribling. "Tell me, boy."

Gawain turned back to the hall then and looked in the faces of the men gathered there. "What are you all doin here?" he said.

Stribling came forward, took Gawain by the arm and led him to a set-tee in the hall. "Now, you tell us," he said. So Gawain told them, and in a little while understood in his turn that they had all come a long way since morning.

When he could, Gawain slipped out into the yard and found Morgan on the garden bench. She was not crying now, and she would not look at him when he approached. He sat beside her in silence for a moment, wonder-ing if she could smell the death on him. Finally, he started to speak, but she hushed him. "Don't tell me," she said. "Don't apologize, and don't expect me to cry."

"I take no joy in it, if that's what you think," he said.

"Are you sure?"

No, he thought. *I am not sure.* He said: "What do you think?"

She looked at him then. "I think you must do what you must. I think I want it to be over with, so we can start again."

Gawain nodded. After a moment, he said, "Well, ain't you goin to cry just a little? I was in dire peril, after all."

She lifted her face to him then. "You are all right? He didn't hurt you any?"

"Why, no," said Gawain.

"All right, then," said Morgan. "And no, I am not goin to cry."

He took her then, and gathered her hard against him. Pressing his face against her hair, he noticed for the first time a gray strand, coursing through the dark like the delicate skein of smoke from a snuffed candle.

After supper, it was decided that everyone but Thomas and Stribling would go home before the moon rose, then return at daybreak. "The yan-kees don't know who was around the tavern, except for Thomas here," said Stribling.

"Mister Wooster knows," Nobles pointed out.

The correspondent, who had taken a seat in a commodious armchair, smiled and tapped his notebook. "It's all right here," he said. "An account that will enthrall even the jaded readers of Cincinnati, Ohio."

"Well, I reckon that means we will have to kill you," said Bloodworth.

"On the contrary," said Wooster. He flipped through the pages and licked the point of his mechanical pencil. "By the way, how *do* you spell your name, sir? Is it Bloodwort? Bloodsworth?"

Stuart Bloodworth spelled out his name. "It's Welsh," he added.

"Capital!" said the correspondent. He looked around as if everything was decided.

Professor Brown cleared his throat in the silence that followed. "Clyde," he said, "I think we might require of you a pledge of confidentiality."

"Ah, I see," said Wooster. He shifted his great bulk in the chair. "Gentlemen, be at ease. You forget I am your alibi." He smiled and lifted the notebook. "Besides, the story ain't over yet."

"Oh, Henry is all right," said Thomas. "He is a journalist and must let the thing play out to its gaudy conclusion. Ain't that right, Henry?"

"Well put, sir," said the correspondent. "I am a model of objectivity. Merely an observer of the passing scene."

"The profession has changed since I was in it," said Stribling.

Soon after, the men slipped away into the growing darkness. When they were gone, the house was quiet. Stribling, Gawain, and Thomas went up on the gallery to smoke. They had been there half an hour when Nobles returned. "The Citadel is burned to the ground," he said. "The yankees did it for spite." He stood in the candlelit hall, his hat in his hand, his face glistening with sweat. "Ben Luker is caught. He told on everybody that was there. I got to go warn them others, if the yankees ain't snatched em up already."

"I should have killed that son of a bitch when I had the chance," said Stribling.

"Sir!" said the Judge. "You forget yourself."

"It's all right, Papa," said Morgan.

Stribling blushed and turned to Morgan. "Beg pardon," he said. "After this day, I would not blame you if I were lowered in your eyes."

Morgan shook her head. "We are all tired, Captain," she said. "Tomorrow, I will have forgotten everything but your kindness."

In a moment, Nobles was gone, and Stribling with him. They passed into the pale light of the waning moon, then parted, Nobles to find Craddock and Bloodworth, Stribling to seek out the professor in his tent. Toward midnight, Stribling returned alone, exhausted, his eyes empty.

"They are in the boxcar," he told Gawain. "Every one of em, Nobles too. And von Arnim ain't foolin around this time."

✦   ✦   ✦

WHEN L. W. Thomas heard the news about the Citadel, he crept back upstairs and went out on the gallery again. Beowulf followed and lay down at his feet, watching him. The moon was rising through a few feathery clouds, and Thomas noted there was a ring around it. He looked out at the yard, with its shadows just beginning to coalesce out of the darkness, and the sprinkle of fireflies among the trees, and he wondered how he had come to be here. He could, if he wished, trace the actual events that had brought him to this gallery, but choices and turns and missteps were not all of it. In his thirty-eight years, or at least since he was old enough to ponder such things, he had searched for that element within him that made the choices, made the turns, willfully, already knowing what would happen— and he had never found it, never isolated it long enough to anticipate what it might do. Choosing to leave the valise under his bunk was a perfect example, he thought. *He* wanted to take the money, run for the depot, disappear up the railroad toward the Planter's Hotel. But that other part, the one that always prevailed at such moments, whispered *atonement atonement atonement* and he had abjured money and safety and freedom for— what? Atonement for what? he asked himself. There was so much to choose from.

Thomas' hands were shaking. He gripped the balustrade and listened to the murmur of his soul. He was afraid. These days he was always afraid, not of any solid shape or form—not the yankees, for instance, nor even Solomon Gault—but of some indefinable presence that always seemed to be watching, judging, ready to destroy him if he should slip up. Long ago, he had read the stories of Arachne and Niobe, how they had challenged the gods and suffered for it, and it had occurred to him that the origin of his fear might dwell in the ancient, mythic memory of his race. He feared God, of course, but figured he might have some show with Him. The old gods were different, even if you didn't believe in them: they laid for you in the dark.

In Baltimore, the summer after the riot, Thomas had been working under a shadowy character he knew only as "Burke." This Burke had any number of lines running into Washington, and had discovered that a Mister Danforth, one of the most ardent secessionists in Baltimore, was in reality a Pinkerton operative with lines of his own, all of them converging at the office of the Federal secret service. Someone higher than Burke—

Thomas neither knew nor cared who it was—decided that Danforth was dangerous and must be eliminated.

"There will be a bonus, of course," said Burke as they sat together on a bollard by the inner harbor. "Two hundred dollars Federal."

Thomas was surprised at how little he would take for snuffing a man's candle—but it was war, after all. That night, late, he found the man's house on Madison Street. An alley ran behind it, and there Thomas waited in deep shadow. He heard no whispers in his head; he did not know about the gods yet.

Presently, the lamps winked out, and the house was in darkness save for a single window on the ground floor. Thomas crept across the yard (there was no dog; he had determined that already) and up the wooden back stairs. He tried the door and found it unlocked. In a moment, he was in a pantry that opened onto a hall. He drew his pistol and moved soundlessly toward the rectangle of gaslight that would be the parlor or library.

Rupert Danforth, wrapped in a silk robe, was seated at his desk in the green glow of the lamp, writing a letter to the governor of the State of Maryland, arguing for secession. He heard the floor creak and looked up to see the man standing in the doorway, his face obscured by the glare of the lamp. Danforth shaded his eyes and peered into the dark. "Who is it?" he said. "Caspar?"

"You know better than that," said Thomas.

Danforth moved the lamp aside, at the same time sliding his hand toward the desk drawer. "Don't," said Thomas, raising his pistol and moving into the room.

Danforth sat back. "Well," he said. "I suppose I am to be killed."

Later, Thomas cursed himself for letting the man talk. He should have done the thing right then, but he hesitated. He admired the man's brass, he told himself later. That was the only reason.

Danforth let out a great sigh and ran his hands through his hair. "I don't suppose you are a Freemason?" he asked.

"No," said Thomas.

"Ah, well," said Danforth. He was about to speak again when his eyes shifted to Thomas' left. "Toby!" he said.

Thomas half-turned. The door was three or four paces away, and in it Thomas saw a boy, about twelve, in his nightshirt and slippers. With both hands, he held a single-shot Dragoon pistol, the kind with a swivel ramrod and a barrel band and a muzzle as big as a railway tunnel. "Whoa, now," said Thomas.

The boy's hands were shaking, and when he spoke, it was barely a whisper, dry and trembling. "You better leave us alone," he said.

"Toby," said Danforth. "Bring me the pistol, son."

"No," said Thomas. "Lay it on the floor. You're too young to be killin people. I'll be in all your dreams if you do."

"Papa?" said the boy.

"Bring me the gun," said Danforth. "This man fancies himself an assassin, but he won't hurt you."

"Don't do it," said Thomas.

"Come on, boy."

The boy Toby looked from one to the other. Thomas saw that the hammer on the pistol was back, the lad's fingers tight on the trigger. *All right,* he thought, *tomorrow's another day.* He moved then, thinking he would make the door, knowing the boy wouldn't shoot—

"Toby! Shoot!" shouted Danforth, and the boy jumped at the sound and pulled the trigger.

The pistol, apparently, was double-charged. It bellowed and leapt backward, and the hammer struck the boy in the forehead, opening a deep gash and knocking him through the door. Meanwhile, the .54-caliber ball passed through Thomas' right side, through Rupert Danforth's open, shouting mouth and out the back of his head, shattering the window behind him. Thomas, gasping in pain, turned in time to see Danforth stagger backward then slide down the wall, leaving a streak on the damask wallpaper.

Thomas' ears were ringing from the shot. He stumbled to the door and saw the boy lying in the hall, his face marbled with blood. At the top of the stairs, a woman in a nightgown was shrieking for help. Thomas knelt by the boy, lifted his head and whispered fiercely into his ear. "Toby didn't shoot his papa," he said. "Toby didn't shoot his papa. The bad man shot his papa." Then he stood, crying out from the pain, and found the woman lurching at him, her hands clawed. He pushed her aside and ran. In the pantry, he collided with a screaming house servant and knocked her down. Then he was gone, out the door, staggering across the yard and down the alley while dogs barked and men's voices rose in the darkness around him.

That was a long time ago, and the wound was still with him and always would be. He had thought the great physicians of St. Louis might fix it, but he understood now that the notion was only another way of delaying the hard truth. L. W. Thomas would have to heal himself, if he was ever going to be healed at all.

So the money was gone; he would have to give that up for Tom Kelly and Rafe. But the wound was still with him, and if the gods were watching—as he supposed they were—he thought he might know what they expected. He still had his Remington, capped and loaded. It wasn't much, but it would answer when the time came.

✦   ✦   ✦

ALL THINGS FOLLOWED time, and all persons followed time. Shortly after moonrise, Henry Clyde Wooster arrived at the Shipwright house. He had made his way through curfew with a pass—an old one signed by General W. T. Sherman, whose signature impressed examiners so much they rarely looked at the date.

In Shipwright's yard, an orderly stood by his horse, and soldiers lounged on the porch hoping for gossip. Inside, the house was full of cigar smoke and officers. The latter draped themselves over furniture or stood talking in groups, all in their swords and muddy boots and old blouses with the corps badges still pinned on. The scene had a painful, strangely comforting familiarity to it; Wooster felt he had been removed to the war again.

Von Arnim was there, antic and restless, his eyes glittering. He spied Wooster right away and, before the correspondent could speak, had him roughly by the arm and pulled into a corner. "Damn you, sir," said the provost, "you have been consorting with rebels!"

"Take your hands off me," said Wooster, aware that everyone in the room was watching. "What do you mean?"

"That dog Luker has been barking," said von Arnim, jittering with excitement and rage. "It was that or be hanged, and I may hang him yet, along with the rest of those buffoons in the jail. Their goddamned comic opera of an insurrection—pah! But they have named you as their advocate—do you care to explain how that could be?"

Wooster was dumbfounded. He had come here, in fact, to speak for Nobles and the rest regarding the shooting, and nothing more. He had hoped to avoid the subject of insurrection.

Von Arnim punched the correspondent in the chest with a forefinger. "You were at the tavern. You must have seen Deaton killed. Your duty was clear, yet you fled with the others—ran away, sir! That tells me you are guilty of conspiracy, sir; to what degree is irrelevant."

"Oh, let him up, Rolf," said Captain Bloom of the infantry. "He just pissed on his shoes, that's all."

"Lieutenant von Arnim," said Wooster, collecting himself. "These men . . . I have proof, sir, that they—"

"Damn your proof," said the provost. "What are you doing here, anyway?"

"I came to tell Colonel Burduck of the . . . developments," Wooster lied. "I meant to exonerate these good men. They have recanted. You can't—"

"Too late," said the other. "Did you know I burned the Citadel? Burned it personally, sir—and do you know what else? It was great fun. Great sport, sir, like in the old times!" Von Arnim gathered Wooster's shirtfront in his fist. "Now where is that traitor Thomas? You know, don't you! Give him up, and maybe I won't clap you in irons."

"Lieutenant von Arnim!" It was Captain Bloom again. He crossed the room, closed his hand on the provost's wrist and shook it until the man released his grasp. Von Arnim glared at the Captain with bloodshot eyes.

"Leave off that," said Bloom amiably.

"I . . . I want to see the Colonel," said Wooster.

Von Arnim turned and stalked out of the room. When he was gone, Bloom straightened the correspondent's shirtfront and patted his shoulder. "Do not mind the provost," he said. "He's had a busy day."

"I want to see the Colonel," said Wooster again.

In a moment, the officer of the day rapped timidly on Burduck's door, stuck his head in, spoke some words, and withdrew. "He will see you, sir," he said to Wooster.

The correspondent went to the door, knocked once, and stepped inside. The room was lit by a pair of candle lanterns that wavered in the breeze from the window. Burduck was at the window, his back to the room. In the middle of the floor, on an unhinged door propped between chairs, lay the uncovered body of Rafe Deaton, his tunic buttoned, hands crossed on his breast.

"My God," said Wooster before he could stop himself.

Burduck turned then, and Wooster had another shock. The man seemed to have shrunk since Wooster last saw him. His eyes were hollow, his face drawn and pinched with anger—and something else. *Shame*, thought the correspondent.

"Yes?" said the Colonel, steepling his fingers on the table.

"Colonel, I—," Wooster began. Then, before he could stop himself, he gestured toward the body and said, "If I may say so, sir—that is a ghastly sight, unbecoming a brave soldier."

"I am not interested in your opinion," said Burduck. "If I were, it would still be none of your affair. You have already presumed too much, so state your business and be gone."

"Sir," Wooster persisted, "Sergeant Deaton—"

"What the hell do you know about Sergeant Deaton?" snarled Burduck.

"A great deal," said the correspondent, and plucked at the sleeve of his frock coat. "I've got his blood on me."

Burduck's head snapped back as if he'd been hit. He opened his mouth to speak, then shut it again. He sank wearily into his chair and waved toward the settee. "Take your seat, sir," he said. "I have no quarrel with you."

Wooster settled uncomfortably on the settee, which groaned under him. He told the Colonel of the events leading to the shooting, embroidering here, editing there, moving Harry Stribling up into the footlights. He told how Deaton was shot, the reactions of the men, their subsequent flight—"Which is understandable, even if it was poor judgment," said Wooster. "They were afraid of the very consequences which have befallen them."

"Indeed," said Burduck. "And you, of course, went along to make sure they didn't escape."

Wooster blushed, but ignored the remark. He pulled the notebook from his pocket. "I have a transcript of their conversation at . . . at the house we went to. If you will allow me to read it, you will see—"

"Never mind them now," said the Colonel. "I will try to keep the provost from hanging them before morning. What do you know about this man Gault?"

Wooster related the tale he had heard Nobles tell in the hall of the Carter house, wondering as he spoke why he believed it so completely, and if it sounded true in the telling. No matter, Wooster thought—it *was* true. His instincts had never failed him. Nevertheless, he skirted around Thomas' role for the moment, believing it too incendiary for this delicate stage of the discussion. He did not think the Colonel would ask for his notebook; even if he did, it was unlikely Burduck could read Pitman shorthand. Then the correspondent played what he thought was a good card. "Sir, I have it on reliable evidence that Solomon Gault ordered the killing of Kelly and Deaton."

"Yes," said the Colonel. "Luker told us."

Damn, thought Wooster. But that was all right; that added credibility. He said: "Ah. But not only that, I have learned the very man who was assigned the task."

"Yes," said the Colonel. "Wall Stutts. Luker told us. Fire again."

Damn Luker, thought the correspondent. Credibility was all very well, but he did not like being trumped. Still, he had one more card, maybe the best of all, and he played it now. He leaned forward. "You won't have any more trouble out of Stutts," he said. "He was shot dead this afternoon, trying to bushwhack Mister Gawain Harper, the associate of these same men you accuse of conspiracy."

The Colonel sat up, his eyes bright for the first time, as Wooster told the story he'd heard from Gawain. Again, he wondered why he believed it, and decided that he believed it because it was true. It had to be.

"Well, this throws a new light on things," said the Colonel when Wooster was finished. "Where is the man Harper?"

Wooster hesitated.

"I retract the question," said the Colonel. "Let us see where our conversation leads. Did you know von Arnim and a company of cavalry paid a call on Gault this evening?"

"I did not."

"He wasn't home, naturally, but he left this where we would find it." Burduck pushed a folded sheet of paper across the table. "It bears the same watermark as the note left with Kelly's body." Burduck snorted in disgust. "I sound like a goddamned Pinkerton."

Wooster heaved himself up from the settee and crossed to the table. He looked at the paper.

"Go on," said Burduck.

Wooster took up the paper, unfolded it, and held it to the candlelight.

Col. M. Burdick, Cmndg
United States Troops
Cumberland, Miss.

Sir:
If you are reading this, it is because you have discovered the true nature of our relationship. Of course, I knew it all the while, which is an excellent joke on you. I spared you today. Next time we meet, I will collect the debt. Perhaps we can talk first. I would be interested to hear what you have to say on the subject of mortality. Your own, I mean. You may think me mad if you wish, but do not allow that to cloud your judgment of

Yours Respectfully, &c.
Solomon Gault, Capt., PAC

Wooster lowered the paper and found the Colonel watching him. He let the note fall on the table. "What does he mean by—"

"Sparing me?" said the Colonel. "Oh, Mister Wooster, Gault and I are old chums. If only you could have seen us this afternoon, chatting away at the Wagner place. Of course, I did not know until I returned whose company I'd been in, but . . . " His voice trailed off then, and he waved his hand vaguely. "But never mind. Try to resist putting that in the papers, however difficult it may be."

Wooster turned his head away, stung by the remark. "It's an empty threat, sir," he said.

"That's what von Arnim said," replied the Colonel. "But I don't think so."

Again, before he could stop himself, Wooster said, "You think Gault will come?"

Burduck glared at him. "Come? Come! Like some avenging spirit, leading a horde of inflamed patriots under the banners of righteousness? Good God, sir—do I appear to be cowering in a bomb-proof? I wish the arrogant bastard *would* show his face."

"I didn't mean—," stammered Wooster.

"Well, what the hell *did* you mean?" snapped Burduck.

Wooster collected himself again. "Colonel Burduck," he said, "you have been candid with me, and you have my pledge of confidentiality. May I be candid as well?"

Burduck had folded again, as if he could sustain anger only so long before it sucked him dry. "Feel free," he said.

Wooster pressed his palms together and looked at the Colonel. "Sir, Solomon Gault is mad, and so he is still out there in the dark, believing fervently in his design. I know you have nothing to fear from him, but . . . but fear isn't the issue. He has made a fool of you. Isn't that it?"

Wooster expected an outburst. Instead, the Colonel merely nodded. "In a word, yes," he said. "It is personal now, would be so even if it were not for that boy and—" He stopped, shaken, and Wooster suddenly understood why Deaton's body was laid out in plain view.

"If he comes, what do you think will happen?" the correspondent asked.

The Colonel sat back, and Wooster, veteran of a thousand interviews, knew that this one was nearly over. They had come as far as they could on the trust that Burduck could allow himself. He also knew that just beyond that limit was something the Colonel wasn't going to give him. He was about to rise and go when the Colonel surprised him by opening another door, one that Wooster would just as soon have remained shut.

"You have made a good case for these yahoos," said the Colonel. "You seem to have left out Mister Thomas, though."

Wooster shifted uncomfortably. "Sir, Gault used him like he did the rest."

"You think so, do you?" said the Colonel. "Mister Wooster, L. W. Thomas was a spy in the Confederate service. Since the surrender, he has passed information of a delicate nature to aid an avowed enemy of the United States. He is guilty of treason. He will hang, and nothing you can say will save him. Do you know where he is? If you do, and fail to speak, you'll hang with him."

"Colonel, the information he gave Gault was such that anyone—"

"Answer the question, sir. Do you know where he is?"

Wooster fidgeted, already feeling the noose around his neck. Outside, someone threw a log on a fire, and sparks swirled skyward. "Colonel," said Wooster, summoning all his dignity, "how can you put me in this position? I—"

"You put yourself in it when you left the tavern this afternoon," said the Colonel. "Do you want me to call the provost?"

Henry Clyde Wooster rose from the settee. "Call him," he said.

Burduck pushed his chair back and stood up, his jaw twitching. "Sergeant of the guard!" he said.

A beat of silence then, while the two men glared at each other across the table. Wooster could hear his own pocket watch ticking, heard the sizzle of a doomed moth in one of the lanterns. When the door opened, Wooster had to keep himself from crying out. "Sir!" said the sergeant of the guard.

"I want—," Burduck began, and stopped. He leaned forward, hands flat on the tabletop, his eyes fixed on a point above Wooster's head. Wooster could see the sweat on the Colonel's forehead, as if he were struggling physically with a great weight. The Colonel's eyes, narrowed now, came back to Wooster's face and remained there while he spoke in a level, almost amiable voice. "I want you to call Captain Bloom, have him come in here."

When the sergeant was gone, the silence only deepened in the room. Wooster had to look away from the Colonel's eyes when he spoke. "It is all right, Colonel," he said. The other made no answer. In a moment, the door opened again, and Captain Bloom entered with his cap tucked under his arm. "Sir," he said, and glanced at Wooster.

Burduck tapped his finger on the tabletop. "Captain, I—" He stopped again, the muscles in his jaw working. His hand moved across the table as if he were trying to grasp something there. Finally he looked up. "Captain, parade your company at first light for burial. Have the provost . . . have him engage the usual party for the grave, the digging, I mean." The Colonel struggled with his thoughts a moment before he spoke again. "Now . . . now, Captain Bloom, you must take morning call. In the orders of the day—" He stopped and half-turned toward the window, as if someone had spoken his name. The Captain exchanged a glance with Wooster. In a moment, Burduck turned back again and looked at the Captain with surprise. "What?" he said.

The Captain smiled uneasily. "You were about to say something, sir."

"Yes, yes, of course," said Burduck. "I was about to say—" He waved his hand. "About Deaton. He is a good man. Have . . . ah . . . have the first sergeant show him in hospital on the morning report. There is no need to disgrace him."

Wooster turned away, studied a print of Arundel castle hanging on the wall. Behind him, he could hear the Captain's palpable hesitation, heard him say "Yes, sir, Colonel" then back away out the door. When the latch clicked shut, Wooster turned again. The Colonel was looking out the window, his fist pressing against the frame. "Get out of here, Henry," he said.

But Wooster didn't leave. He stepped to the body of Rafe Deaton. From it rose the smell of blood, and a fly was crawling across the eyes. Wooster brushed it away. "Thomas is dying," he said. The Colonel was silent. Wooster went on. "He tried to get Deaton to go home today. He didn't want to run when all the others did. He let the money Gault paid him burn up in the tavern when he could of got it out. He looked after your boys, Colonel."

Burduck turned his head. In the lantern light, his face seemed lifeless as Rafe Deaton's.

"The war has to end, Colonel," said Wooster, but the other had already turned back to the window.

On his way out, Wooster stopped on the gallery to talk with the soldiers who were smoking there. No officers were around, so the correspondent broached the subject of Solomon Gault, thinking to tap the deep waters of rumor that always ran beneath an army camp. He was not disappointed.

"Son of a bitch ought to come if he's comin," said a lean corporal. "Somebody said they was a riot up in Memphis, the niggers and the whites. Washburn called all the cavalry back this evenin, nothin left but the headquarters guard."

"Cap'n Bradley's company, too," said another. "They left on the cars 'bout six o'clock."

"Well, well," said Wooster. He lit a cigar and listened to the thunder, and watched the fireflies rising from the grass.

✦   ✦   ✦

THESE, TOO, FOLLOWED time:

In the rays of the falling moon, Morgan Rhea dreamed of the sunlight that had come through the windows of the Carter boy's room and the strange, suspended ambience of the hall where the men had gathered. They were all there in the dream, but silent, sitting against the wall like schoolboys while another man paced up and down, gesturing, talking, though he made no sound. She could not see his face, but she knew who it was, wanted to warn them, tried to speak but couldn't. She struggled, trying to shape the name, and when she almost had it, she found them all turned to stone: gray headstones mottled with moss, leaning obelisks, tombs sealed by iron doors. And among them a lady passed, carrying a basket of flowers. Lily. Her sister turned, plucked a dark flower from the basket, held it out to Morgan and spoke the name—

"Gault!" cried Morgan, and sat upright. She was sweating, the sheet twisted around her feet. The bed, the room, was painted with moonlight and writhing with shadows.

"Gawain Harper," she whispered. She said it again and again, like an incantation, until it crowded the other name out of her mind. Then she shut her eyes and prayed: *Forgiveness, mercy, compassion, courage, all these, O Lord, and make us instruments of thy peace and fill us with thy grace and save us from evil and shame, amen.* When she opened her eyes again, the shadows were gone.

"Thank you," she whispered, and composed herself on the pillow again, listening to the whippoorwill and the soft breathing of Alex on his pallet and the snoring—

She sat upright again. Snoring? She crept to the edge of the bed and saw Alex wrapped in his cotton coverlet in the moonlight. As she watched, the coverlet stirred in a peculiar way, then was still. She sniffed the air. It smelled of midnight, of privet and oak leaves. It smelled of dog.

"Alex Rhea!" she hissed.

"I ain't done nothin," came the muffled reply. And not only muffled but sullen, a fair indicator that he had, indeed, done something.

Morgan slid off the high bed. In the pale light, she saw Beowulf's tail slide out from the edge of the coverlet like a scabrous worm. It thumped twice and lay still. "I told you—," Morgan began, her hand on the coverlet to lift it. Then she stopped, and raised her eyes to the window and the night beyond. To the west, where the Great River lay and whence their weather always came, she heard the growl of thunder. The leaves outside shuddered as if in answer. The moonlight dimmed as a cloud wandered by, then filled the room again, and the whippoorwill called without ceasing. Morgan lowered the coverlet and crawled back into the Carter boy's bed and moved her legs across the cool bottom sheet. In a little while she slept, and this time she did not dream.

Though Thomas did. He moaned and thrashed in his sleep, and moved his hands, and muttered lines which Gawain and Stribling agreed were from *The Merchant of Venice*. The three of them were bedded down in the barn with Zeke.

"I'm damned if I bunk with him again," said Stribling, his hands behind his head. "If he ain't snorin, he's quotin Shakespeare. Good God."

Gawain had been awake anyway. His head hurt worse than it had at morning, and he had wrapped it in a wet rag. In the moonlight slanting through the cracks, the rag glowed like some obscene cave-dwelling fungus. "I hear thunder," said Gawain. "It's gon' rain again directly."

"I expect it will," said Stribling. He propped up on one elbow. "Listen, you don't fret about Wall Stutts. You hear me?"

"I ain't," said Gawain.

Zeke stamped in his stall. A swallow chittered restlessly in the eaves of the barn, as though in protest at these noisy intruders.

"I hope there ain't any spiders in here," said Gawain after a moment.

"I seen a big one a while ago," said Stribling.

"Damn you and your spiders both," said Gawain, and groaned. "My head is killin me."

"You want me to get you some coffee?" asked Stribling.

"That's a lot of trouble," said Gawain.

In a moment, Stribling was creeping in his stocking feet across the dew-wet yard, heading for the shadowy bulk of the cookhouse. Midway he stopped and looked up at the moon. It was pale and watery now behind a brush of clouds, and the stars were gone. He remembered one such night when he and Zeke rode out to check the vedettes. They topped a ridge, and below them lay a broad valley cloaked in a ghostly light that did not seem to come from the fading moon. In the distant treeline burned the fires of the enemy, orange pinpricks against the dark trees, warming strangers who would kill him if they had the chance. Yet, as he watched, Stribling felt no sense of danger or harm, nor any rancor toward the travelers over there. Yonder was the valley, and beyond the invisible hills, and beyond them the whole country stretching away to the sea. And the sea itself, heaving and tossing under the same moon, bearing eastward and westward the little ships, their masthead lights winking with infinite trust in tomorrow. The world is too big to worry about sometimes, Stribling told Zeke that night, and in a little while they moved off into the valley, toward others like themselves waiting for dawn. Now, in the yard of the old Carter house, Stribling said it again, to himself this time. "The world is too big," he whispered, nodding at the moon. "It will be all right."

He lit a fire on the hearth of the cookhouse. In the cupboard, he found a sack of coffee, and a blacksnake that had swallowed a rat. That was all right, too, he figured.

✦ ✦ ✦

MORGAN WOKE TO a sharp clap of thunder and the rain blowing through the open windows. She scrambled out of bed and pulled down the sashes, and the sound of the rain diminished. Her feet were wet now, and the front of her nightdress, just that quick. She looked at the pallet where the boy and the dog lay, and saw that it was dry. Beowulf, his head out of the covers now, regarded her with friendly curiosity.

"Go back to sleep," Morgan said, and the dog's tail thumped under the sheet. "You wake that boy and I'll strangle you," she said.

She sat on the edge of the bed and discovered she was thoroughly awake. She thought of Gawain, and wished it was Tuesday. Morgan Rhea took a bath every Tuesday and Saturday, no matter what—no matter war nor conflagration nor death in any form. Her father thought it excessive, her brother believed it insane. Still, she bathed, and took her own time about it. If it was Tuesday, she would smell clean now, like the lye soap she used, and smell of rose water, and Gawain would breathe in the hollow of her shoulder and say how sweet it was. She blushed at the thought. Then she remembered that she hadn't any rose water for two years now. But if it was Tuesday, she would smell clean anyhow, and maybe he would put his face against her breasts and say how sweet it was. *This won't do,* she thought, so in the flickering dark, with the rain hammering outside, she tried to remember all the interesting facts she'd learned recently. A brick laid vertically with the broad side out was called a sailor, with the narrow side, a soldier. Gawain was a soldier, years gone into the dark and smoke, and he knew things she could not imagine. *No,* she told herself, and thought about old Mister Carter in the garden one afternoon, and she asked him why he always tied up gourd vines instead of letting them travel on the ground, and he said for the martins. A martin gourd wants a straight neck for hanging, he said, and if you let them travel on the ground, the necks will be crooked. That was an interesting fact. A martin gourd's neck was thick and straight for hanging. Gawain Harper—

"Oh, hell and damnation," she said aloud. She rose then and moved across the room and out the door and down the stairs, just as she had done on the night Gawain Harper returned. No one was in the parlor now; the house was deathly still, save for the tick-tock of the hall clock where it kept vigil, its wheels and cogs moving by tiny increments, its little brass hammer waiting to strike. And strike it did, three times, just as she opened the back door onto the storm.

The gallery roof was pouring a perfect curtain of water, and the yard was lit by lightning. Morgan took a deep breath and plunged through the silver curtain, the rain shocking cold on her back, her head. She splashed through the yard, laughing to herself, until she stood under the eaves of the barn. Her hair was soaked, and her nightdress wringing wet, and her feet muddy. The barn door was open a crack, and she slipped through into the sudden dryness, the ammoniac smell of horses and the sound of men sleeping. Zeke whinnied softly and stamped a hoof. "Easy," Morgan whispered. She could see Thomas where he lay tangled in his blanket, and Stribling lying in his long underwear, an arm thrown across his eyes. And Gawain. Morgan moved silently across the barn floor, over the old cornhusks and damp straw, and stood over the place where Gawain Harper lay. He was propped up on Stribling's saddle, breathing softly, his face composed like one who had no troubles in the world. *He shot a man today,* she thought. *How many does that make?* And again she wondered at the knowledge that lived in him that she would never reach if she lived a thousand years. A sadness wrapped around her then, and, soft, she pulled aside the rough blanket and lay down beside Gawain Harper and pressed her head against his thin naked chest, breathing the smell of him—the sweat and tobacco and horse smell, but nothing of death or remorse.

Gawain woke then, and moved against her, and she felt his hand on the back of her head, and maybe he was dreaming, she thought.

"Are you dreamin?" she asked, and Gawain started, his hand groping for the pistol until she spoke again. "It's Morgan," she said. "Don't be scared."

"Aw, me," said Gawain. "What are you doin, child?"

"I'm damned if I know, sir," she said into the warm skin of his breast. "What's that thing around your head? You look ridiculous."

"It helps my head when it hurts," he said.

"Oh, is your head hurtin?" she said, and let her lips brush his neck. "Poor darlin."

"Well, not so much as it was," said Gawain, and unwound the rag and tossed it aside and laughed.

"Does a Jew not bleed?" Thomas muttered in his sleep, and threw his arm over Stribling, who stirred and muttered.

"Damn, I wish the boys was elsewhere," said Gawain into the wet tangle of Morgan's hair.

"What if they were?" said Morgan.

"Well, I will show you," said Gawain, and he did.

✦   ✦   ✦

MOLOCHI FISH WAS awake; he could never sleep when his mother was in the yard. She was out there now, howling, stalking back and forth with her winding sheet dragging behind, tearing at her hair. The cabin was stifling with the door closed and the window boards down, and it was dark as pitch. He could hear the dogs moving in their pen, made restless by the old woman. But there were no children tonight, nor any niggers. That was good. That meant he could go outside, even cross the river if he wanted to.

He thought about whether he should go or not. He had gone over the river yesterday, early in the morning, and found himself in the willows by the railroad. The soldiers were burying somebody in the graveyard, and Molochi watched. He could hear words drifting over the morning. Suddenly he shivered, as if an ague had taken him. He looked around, expecting to see the dark birds. Instead, a man was sitting horseback a dozen paces away, the same man who was with the Harper boy up on the big road that other day when the dogs killed the fyce. Molochi couldn't figure how he'd missed him when he came into the willow grove. At that moment, the horse caught wind of Molochi and shied, and the man calmed him, then spoke to Molochi. Molochi said something in return, and the man let him use his spyglass, and there was Solomon Gault. After a while, the man was gone. Molochi never heard him go.

Now, in the sweltering cabin, Molochi's head stirred with a collection of murky images inhabited by figures he could not name. Then another picture came, this one clear and distinct: a wood in moonlight, a stone wall, a dog sniffing at the fresh-turned earth while lightning flickered to the west.

Molochi Fish rose stiffly from the floor where he had been sitting for hours. He felt in the dark for his hat, then groped for the bolt on the cabin door. When he pulled it back, the door swung open on its leather hinges. The moonlight burst upon him all at once and made him blink. He stepped down into the yard.

His mother stopped her howling and looked at him. She was thin and hunched over nearly double, and he could see the black O of her mouth. Molochi picked up a rock from the fire pit and flung it at her; it passed through her as if she wasn't even there. Down the slope, almost to the trees, the Indian woman was watching him. In the trees themselves he could see a moving white line, like a tendril of fog. Those were the dogs, the ones he'd cut their throats and didn't save their blood. He did not give a goddamn about them. Molochi reached in his pocket and took out a leather bag with a dried frog in it. Clutching it tightly in his hand, he moved down the slope toward the trees, the river, the town.

✦   ✦   ✦

MIDNIGHT, AND THE candle lanterns still burned in Colonel Burduck's office. The moon was gone now, lost in the storm. Through the window came the smell of rain, of something blooming, of wood smoke from the soldiers' dying fires. The wind trembled the candle flames; the moving light made shadows on the face of Rafe Deaton.

Deaton's body had been in the hot sun almost an hour that afternoon, and the agents that would return him to dust had got a good purchase. They announced themselves now by a faint odor that persisted in spite of the open window, the cool breeze, the blooming things. Rigor had set in and pulled Deaton's eyes open and drawn his lips back from his teeth, so that he appeared to be grinning at some secret joke on the ceiling. His hands were swelling and had lifted themselves from his chest, as though he were preparing, by infinite degrees, to rise from his couch.

Henry Clyde Wooster lay on the horsehair settee, his hands under his cheek, snoring lightly like a child. Colonel Burduck sat alone by the window, his feet propped on the sill. He was not aware of the corpse, nor of the grumbling sounds its stomach made from time to time. In fact, he was aware of nothing but the rush of the water moving under the keel, the groaning of the shrouds, the clink of a tin lantern swinging from the eave of the deckhouse.

The storm was pushing a wind ahead of it. A gust found its way through the window and ruffled the hair of Sergeant Rafe Deaton and blew out the struggling candles. The wind might have blown Solomon Gault's note off the table, too, had it not been weighed down by the star-and-crescent badge of the sheriff of Cumberland County.

As the wind drove them eastward, the stem of the ship plowed deep into the sea, churning bursts of phosphorus, like liquid stars, from the ink-black water. All around lay the great dark; it seemed so infinite, so immortal in the night watches, yet it too, like all things and all persons, followed time. Soon it would yield, not to light yet, but to a lesser dark illumined by the morning star. Then, sudden and unexpected, a red smudge would flame over the lip of the world, as though a ship were burning there. That would be tomorrow.

· PART 4 ·

Deo Vindice

· XIX ·

The storm broke with a great display of lightning and uproar of thunder—the sharp, cracking kind that jolts a sleeper awake, then reminds him of all his unshriven sins. Rain fell in sheets and wind-driven waves; the creek rose, but there was no overflow this time. Finally, the storm went muttering and complaining off to the east, and behind it the stars winked on again. When the sun rose, people looked at it and said, "Gon' be a hot one today."

The sun had not been up long when a sentry pounded on the side of the boxcar with his musket butt. Another pushed the door back, squealing on its tracks. A contraband set a steaming tub of cornmeal on the sill, then followed it with a clatter of tin plates and spoons. "Eat up, boys," said the sentry, and pushed the door to again, leaving a narrow crack for light.

Within, Marcus Peck sat up in his mildewed blankets and scratched himself. "Goddamn mosquitoes like to eat me alive," he said.

Nobles yawned. "They ain't that many mosquitoes in Miss'ippi," he said. He pressed his temples gingerly. "Mankind, who stole the top of my head?"

Craddock said, "They never brought Luker back."

"Too bad," said Peck. "I was havin fun watchin him shit his pants."

"Lord, I pitied the man," Craddock replied laughing. "Our provost has a sense of humor, don't he?"

Bloodworth sniffed at the tub of mush. "Boys," he said, "if this is our last meal, it lacks some."

"Looks fine to me," said Peck.

Professor Brown crawled out on all fours and examined the tub. He looked at Bloodworth. "Don't be talkin about any last meal," he said. "It gives me the fantods."

"Mac!" said Craddock. "That's the longest speech I ever heard you make."

"Well, just don't you all be talkin about that," said the professor. "Here, give me a dollop."

Stuart Bloodworth dipped a plate of cornmeal for the professor and one for himself, and retired to a corner of the car. He listened to his comrades talk: bravado, and they knew it. Time and again, Bloodworth had heard that kind of talk from men going into a fight. Had talked it himself. But now, as then, they were scared, uncertain, walking into a dark cave. For himself, Bloodworth was not only scared, he was disgusted. Home a week, and already in the jailhouse. They had literally snatched him from his wife's grasp before he had time to explain where he'd been all afternoon. Jesus. If the yankees didn't hang him, little Amy would for sure. He laughed. Bravado again.

Under the boxcar, Old Hundred-and-Eleven stuck his head out of the quilt he had wrapped around him. They'd had a lively time of it all night, with the storm blowing rain in on them and the lightning popping all around. A raccoon had sought shelter among them, had slept on top of Old Hundred-and-Eleven all night and was hissing at him now. The old man poked at the creature with his umbrella until it waddled away. Then he poked Dauncy and Jack. Dauncy pulled his blanket down and peered out. "He gone yet?"

"Who?"

"That coon. Who you think?"

"Get up," Old Hundred-and-Eleven said. He crawled out between the two sentries, stood, and shook himself. He looked at the sun. "Gon' be a hot one today," he said, and opened his umbrella.

✦ ✦ ✦

IN THE BARN behind the Carter house, Gawain was dreaming of Morgan Rhea. Specifically, he was dreaming about her legs; they were all stretched out on a featherbed white and billowy as a cloud. The room was full of sun, and a wren caroled just outside the window, and way back in the trees a redbird was saying *Free*-dom! *Free*-dom! *Free*-dom! and Morgan moved her legs on the featherbed. Gawain smiled. *She won't mind,* he thought, and put out his hand, thinking to touch her ankle, when she prodded him in the ribs. *Hey,* she said. Gawain opened his eyes.

"Hey," said L. W. Thomas again. "Get up." He was standing at the wide door now, peering through the crack. His face was gray in the shaft of light, his eyes puffy. In the stall, Zeke was whickering and moving restlessly.

"What is it?" said Stribling, rising from his blankets, Luker's Navy Colt in his hand.

"Better put that away," said Thomas, backing up from the door.

Gawain rolled over and put his eye to a crack in the boards. All he could see were the fetlocks of horses. "Oh, my God," he said.

"Yep," said Thomas.

As they watched, the door creaked open and filled the barn with sunlight. Lieutenant von Arnim strode in rubbing his hands, two cavalrymen flanking him with carbines. "*Good* day, lads," he said brightly. "Better get dressed, and make it fast. Ah, Thomas—there you are, you slippery devil, you."

•　　•　　•

AT THE SHIPWRIGHT house, Colonel Burduck rested his hand on the blanket-shrouded form of Rafe Deaton. He wondered if Wooster had covered it sometime in the night, or if he had covered it himself. In any case, it didn't matter. Wooster was gone, and morning had come. Burduck looked up at the two privates standing just inside the door. "All right," he said. The soldiers unrolled their litter and set it beside the makeshift bier. When they lifted the body, it sagged between them and groaned, but the men were veterans and had seen worse than this. In a moment, they had maneuvered the litter out the door and were gone.

The Colonel turned to the window. At the creek, two negro boys were preparing to fish, their long cane poles waving in the air. A soldier stood with them, giving advice, his frock coat open and hands thrust in his breeches pockets. "Too much fresh water," the soldier was saying, his voice drifting through the window on the morning breeze. "You'll want to go deep." On the ruined carriage, a mockingbird was flicking its tail. Old Mister Shipwright wandered through the yard, and the mockingbird flew away. The old man stopped, looked at Burduck a moment, then shuffled on around the corner of the house.

I could have told them, thought Burduck, his hands gripping the windowsill as the ship took a long roll to larboard.

•　　•　　•

WHEN MOLOCHI FISH awoke, he was lying at the foot of the stone maiden in the cemetery. He had been there throughout the storm, huddled against the base with his knees drawn up while the lightning slashed around him and filled the air with that peculiar smell that Molochi could put with no other thing he'd ever known. From time to time, he would look up at the figure above him; blinded with the rain, he could still see the woman's face by the lightning flashes, the water streaming from her outstretched arm. She seemed to be leaning into the force of the wind, her garments swirling around her legs, eyes searching the ground as she struggled through the dark.

When the daylight came, it brought the blackbirds. The figure was still now, gone to stone again, and the birds lit on the arm and the crown of the hair and the bare shoulder, and they croaked at Molochi and watched him with cocked heads. The skin of Molochi's hands was shriveled like a drowned man's, his clothes soaked and clammy. The sun, when it rose at last above the trees, hurt his eyes and made him creep to the shadowed side of the great stone shaft. Presently the birds rose in a cloud; they circled aloft for a moment, as though taking their marks, then settled down on the iron archway of the gate where they jostled one another impatiently. Molochi rose then, and made his way to the road, the birds flying ahead. In a moment, he was passing the Carter house. Two cavalrymen sat their horses in the front yard, their carbines unslung and resting on their thighs. One called to Molochi, but Molochi went on, following the birds.

✦   ✦   ✦

THE TROOPERS IN the yard of the Carter house were part of the headquarters guard left behind when the cavalry was pulled back to LaGrange. All of them were glad to be in the saddle, having grown weary of peace and garrison life. In fact, many of them had not been in the war at all and figured the closest they would ever get to any real action was tracking down fugitive rebels as they were doing now. They envisioned exciting chases, bloodhounds straining at the leash, ambushes, desperate gun battles. They saw themselves jumping their horses over back-yard fences in pursuit, rescuing loyal citizens, bringing down swift justice on the heads of traitors. And while some of those adventures might actually befall the troopers in the next few years, they were not going to experience them this morning. Instead, they slumped in their saddles in the humid dawn while an old man still in his nightshirt moved among them, touching the flanks of the horses, touching the legs of the young riders and looking into their faces. "Gentlemen, gentlemen," the old man intoned. "Gentlemen, please." Another old codger, this one in frock coat and cravat, stood on the back gallery and glared at them fiercely and twisted his hands on the knob of his walking stick. As for the rebels themselves, they turned out to be a great disappointment, at least to those who had never seen an actual rebel before. Von Arnim led them shuffling out of the barn and into the lot where they stood sullenly, blinking, yawning, hatless, coatless, straw clinging to their hair.

The only real excitement came when the back door of the house slammed open, and a barefoot woman in a nightdress swept into the yard, her hair falling in a dark cascade, ankles flashing for all the boys to admire, a sweet thing to see in the early morning but for the frying pan she carried.

"Great God! Dismount!" laughed one of the boys.

"Horse holders to the rear!" cried another.

They all laughed then, and the woman's face reddened, and she swung the frying pan at the rump of the nearest horse. "Out of my way, damn you!" she cried, while the old fellow on the gallery came hustling down. One of the troopers made a snatch at her, but she bounced the flat of the pan off his knee; he yowled and grabbed his leg, and the soldiers made way, laughing.

"Morgan, for God's sake!" cried the gentleman in the frock coat, but she beat him to the front and drew up short at the sight of the prisoners. The soldiers heard her say only a single word: "Gawain?"

"Here now!" said von Arnim. The troopers did not much like the Lieutenant for his being an infantry officer—and they were no longer taking this business very seriously anyhow—so they cheered and whistled when the prisoner broke away and gathered the woman up. She dropped her frying pan and flung her arms around the man so that both of them nearly fell to the ground, then as quickly broke away and pointed her finger at the fellow some of them knew as the tavernkeeper. "This is your doin!" the woman cried, and the man ducked his head as if he'd been slapped, and the old gent came up at last and tried to pull her back, and von Arnim said, "For the love of Jesus, you people settle down, can't you?" and the soldiers laughed.

"I belong to this house!" said the woman.

"I am sensible of that, Miss Rhea," said von Arnim.

The sound of her name seemed to surprise the woman. "Well," she said. "Well, anyhow, these men are our guests—how dare you—"

"Singular guests!" said von Arnim. The Lieutenant was carrying three confiscated pistols and a Henry rifle. He dropped the pistols and thrust the flat of the riflestock under the woman's nose. He tapped on the brass plate inlaid in the wood. "Look at that, Miss. Read the name!"

She read it. The troopers watched her shoulders sag, heard her say, almost in a whisper, "Oh, of course. Of course it would be his."

The Lieutenant turned to the old gentleman. "You will be Judge Nathaniel Rhea, I presume?"

"How do you know me, sir?"

"Only by reputation, sir," said von Arnim. Then, to the troopers' amusement, he swept off his cap and made a little bow to the woman. "And you are Miss Morgan Rhea."

"And how do you know *me,* sir?" Morgan snapped. "My reputation is hardly the sort that *you* would have any knowledge of!"

The troopers guffawed at that. Von Arnim replaced his cap and glared at his men. "It is my business to know things!" he said to Morgan. "For example, I know of your father's rabid sentiments which, fortunately for you, lie outside this morning's affairs. I know all about the man who owns this rifle, and how he brought grief to your family in addition to his other sins. I know also, even without your bold demonstration, that you and this fellow"—he pointed at Gawain—"who but lately had this rifle in his possession, are . . . may I say, intimate?"

"Now, see here—," began the Judge, but his daughter hushed him. "You may say that, sir," said the woman. "More than that, we are . . . we are soon to be married!"

The three prisoners and the old Judge dropped their jaws in astonishment.

"Ah," said von Arnim. He lowered his voice, and the soldiers had to strain to hear him. "Well, at any rate, I am very much interested in all these matters," he said. "The complex permutations of life, you know, and how things come to be the way they are. Perhaps you and the good gentleman would care to explain—just for my own curiosity, understand—how Thomas, a traitor and a spy, came to be in your barn?"

"Sir," said the Judge, "I would see your commander."

"No, sir," said von Arnim. "He has enough to think about at present." He turned to the sergeant of the escort then. "Get your picket ropes," he said.

"You can't!" shouted the woman.

"I can!" returned the Lieutenant, red-faced. "Now, my advice to you is to gather up these old gents and get back in the house, and be damned glad I don't burn it out of principle!"

"Old gents!" protested the Judge.

"Quiet, sir!" said the Lieutenant. "Now tie these men and get em to the graveyard."

The prisoners' hands were tied with lengths of picket rope. Thomas, his face gone the color of ash, was sick in the yard. The sergeant stepped back until he was finished, then tied his hands. The one called Gawain kept his eyes on the woman. She tried to go to him, but this time her father held her back. Only the third man spoke. He flipped his long hair out of his eyes and addressed the Lieutenant. "Sir, Harper was not at the tavern. He killed Gault's man is why he has the rifle. You shouldn't—"

"Quiet, sir," said the Lieutenant. "You have been trouble since you arrived. Mister Harper needs to be more selective of his bedfellows."

In a moment, the prisoners were led away, shuffling awkwardly between the files of horses. Harper watched the woman over his shoulder as long as he could. The old fellow in the nightshirt followed them down to the road, still pleading, "Gentlemen. Gentlemen, please," until one of the troopers stopped and led him back again.

✦   ✦   ✦

THE PEOPLE EMERGED from their tents and shebangs, or stopped in their morning work, to watch silently as the column passed. Children and dogs ran along beside, trying to scare the horses, until the cavalrymen chased them off. Still they followed, but at a little distance, throwing mud clods and making up rhymes:

> *Lucy, goosey, puddin and pie,*
> *Hang by the neck until you die.*

The horsemen rode in two files; the prisoners walked between them, pulling at the foul mud that weighed them down. Gawain Harper tried to keep his distance from the horse next to him, expecting to be kicked or stepped on or bitten any minute. He could hear Aunt Vassar: You get too close to horses, they'll knock you in the head. Gawain's face burned with shame and anger, and he was glad there were no goddamned redbirds singing of freedom in the trees, as they had sung once on the road, and again in his waking dream.

Gawain's mind went around and around, and his stomach churned with hunger and the bitter knowledge that he ought not to be here at all. He watched Stribling and Thomas stumbling along ahead, and for the moment he hated them. Morgan was right—the man Thomas had brought him to this pass, drawing him into a circle of doom that had nothing to do with Gawain Harper. And why did Stribling have to be such a busybody, poking his nose into places it did not belong? Damn them all: Gault and Stutts and Stribling and Thomas and Nobles—and the journalist Wooster, too, who had surely betrayed them just as Ben Luker had. Gawain wanted to be shut of them all; he wanted to be among the citizens by the roadside, who would return to the business of life after this shabby procession had passed. Of course, Gawain despised himself, too, for thinking of his comrades, and even his enemies, in such a light. He felt small, selfish, cowardly; he imagined his features turning ratlike, snoutish, his hands curling into little claws. His voice, if he tried it, would be a vile squeaking, so he remained silent, letting his thoughts turn where they would.

Morgan! Was that a dream last night? What was all that about marrying, he wondered. Where did it come from? He decided not to think about marrying, not now. Then, the more he tried to put the idea away, the more it mocked him, and wove itself into the whole garment of emotion that was smothering him. He held up his bound hands; the picket rope seemed coiled around his vitals too, his heart and lungs and soul, constricting them like a rat snake. *I can't stand this,* he thought, stumbling along beside the horse while the citizens watched. *I can't stand it—*

Gawain had always said he would never be captured, swore an oath that he would die before he was put into a prison hole like an animal. The gods heard, and so, at Stones River, Gawain and three others were surrounded and taken in the first charge of the morning. Gawain threw down his rifle but kept his bayonet; in the killing, in the yelling and the smoke (the countercharge was just beginning to roll over them) nobody noticed. It was sleeting, and Gawain, terrified, could hear the ice needles pattering in the cedars, even among the iron rain of the case shot bursting overhead that killed the other three prisoners and left Gawain cowering against the wet bark of a cedar. He squatted there, hands over his head, while the Federal line swept past, yelling. Gawain wept and pleaded, choking on his own phlegm and the blood running from his nose. When he raised his eyes at last, he saw that he was alone. Around him lay the darkness of the cedar grove, the deep shadows full of dead men, and he knew that he could hide among them until he was forgotten, until he was free. The idea of deliverance opened like a flower in his mind. Gawain's heart was beating louder than the guns now; he was about to move when a boy soldier came back—young, his smooth face black with powder, in a frock coat too big for him—yelling at him No, you don't, goddamn you! in a flat Hoosier voice that trembled with fear and rage. You my pris'ner! Git up! Gawain, squatting, moved his hand to the socket of his bayonet as the boy jabbed him with his own, shouting not words now but only sound, his eyes wide, chest heaving for air. The boy would shoot him, Gawain knew, but that was all right—he had sworn an oath, and the gods reminded him of it now as he rose, drawing his bayonet in the same motion, the boy watching him in disbelief. Then the boy's eyes went all white as Gawain drove the bayonet into him, pushing with both hands, and when the boy fell, Gawain was on top of him, leaning into the bayonet, hating himself, hating the proud gods who had made this little joke on them both. Then Gawain put his hand over the boy's face and squeezed until he believed he could feel the soul passing through his fingers, loosed and free as he was now—

Gawain strained at the rope that held him, the panic rising in him like a foul smoke, choking him. They were crossing the square now, and Gawain could see the steps of the Presbyterian church rising into nothing, and the thought came to him that if only he could make the steps and climb them, he would pass into nothing, too. Better than hanging. Better than prison, where it was said men did dreadful things to each other, and where you couldn't walk out in the air and light whenever you wanted, nor lift your face to the rain. *I can't stand it,* he thought again, wanting to speak but afraid of the voice he might hear, and he gathered himself and was about to run when Stribling tripped him, and he fell face-first into the mud. Then Stribling was kneeling beside him, pulling at him with his bound hands, whispering, "Don't you even think about it, goddamn you, Gawain Harper." Then Gawain was spluttering, spitting mud, while the column halted and a soldier dismounted and jerked him to his feet. The soldier wiped Gawain's eyes with his own handkerchief. "It ain't far now," said the man.

Then, where the southerly road entered the square, they were met by a mounted officer. The column halted while the officer spoke to the sergeant of the escort, then moved again, taking the Oxford road now. As they crossed the bridge over Town Creek, Gawain speculated that maybe the yankees had decided to skip the trial and get on with the hanging. He felt his throat tighten; again he wanted to speak, never mind the voice, but he couldn't now. Instead, he began to cry, unashamed, sorry that the long road had come to this. He remembered sitting in the hot summer field with the little fyce, making coffee, breaking the good biscuits while the dog watched with his bright eyes. Why couldn't he be there again? It was only just a little ways back, and he could start over again—sit there a little while longer, let Stribling get on down the road so that they would never meet. Then he would go straight to Aunt Vassar's and climb in his old bed and pull the counterpane over his head.

"You can't go back," said Stribling, and Gawain looked at him and thought that, if he had a bayonet again, he would shut Harry Stribling up for all time. But the other only smiled. "It's all right," he said. "It ain't our funeral we're goin to."

And it wasn't. Instead, it was the funeral of Rafe Deaton, the old soldier whom neither Indians nor rebels could kill, who was shot down drunk in the yard of the Citadel of Djibouti. The column passed through the Federal camp, where the cooks and contrabands watched them in even deeper silence than the citizens had. Queenolia was there, and she spoke to Thomas, but Thomas staggered on, his eyes on the ground before him, and

the old woman set up a keening in their wake. Then they were at the soldiers' burying ground where Captain Bloom's company was again formed
in a hollow square around the grave of their comrade. Old Hundred-and-
Eleven was there with Dauncy and Jack; the old man waved at Gawain and
Stribling, grinning under his umbrella. "Hidy, boys," he called, and would
have said more had not an officer cursed him silent. Wooster was there,
too, a dozen yards away, his notebook open.

Gawain wiped his eyes on his sleeve and looked around carefully for
any sign of a gibbet. Then he thought *What if they mean to shoot us
instead?* and cast around for open graves, but the only one he saw was the
Federal sergeant's. The sight of so many armed Federal soldiers, and the
drummers standing with their sticks under their arms, was beginning to
make him sick to his stomach. The national flag floated out on the morning breeze beside the blue regimental colors, and Gawain thought of those
two banners, always together: how they waved frantically in the smoke of
an engagement, and how beautiful they were. He wanted to huddle
beneath them, wrap himself in them, kiss them if necessary, if it would
allow him to get back in the world again. Then, oddly, he remembered the
sergeant at the Citadel of Djibouti, the one with the clever pipe, and
Gawain wondered if this was him they were about to bury.

"Say," said Stribling, nudging Gawain with his elbow. "Look over yonder, in the willows. Is that Molochi?"

Gawain peered into the bright sunlight and saw Molochi Fish standing
in plain sight with his arms at his sides, his face shadowed by the wide
straw hat. But Gawain was not interested in Molochi Fish just then, and
his irritation with Stribling flared anew.

"Well, ain't it?" asked Stribling again.

"Yes, dammit," said Gawain. "So what? So *what*, Harry?"

Stribling looked at him. He started to speak, then turned away.

In a moment, the three comrades were joined by Nobles, Craddock, and
Bloodworth. They, too, were bound, and accompanied by a detachment of
infantrymen with fixed bayonets. "Well," said Nobles, his face gray, eyes
baggy with his hangover. "I was afraid they'd catch you."

"It was Wooster, wasn't it?" asked Gawain. "He told."

"I don't know," said Nobles. "I expect he did, but I'm not sure what it
means."

"It means he's a goddamned lying son bitch," said Craddock.

"He got them to let Brown go," said Bloodworth hopefully.

Before Gawain could reply, the guard came to attention in that shuffling, self-conscious way that signals to all old soldiers the unhappy news

that an officer is approaching. Unconsciously, Gawain drew himself to attention too. He smelled the grass, the wood smoke from the camp, the damp wool of the soldiers and the stink of fear and sweat and sleeplessness that rose from his own body, and he had but to close his eyes to imagine himself in the ranks again. Then he heard one of the soldiers say, "These are the ones from the barn, sir."

Gawain opened his eyes and found himself looking at a tall officer—a Lieutenant Colonel by his shoulder straps—bearded, in full dress uniform with sash and white gloves, watching them with nothing in his face at all, neither anger nor curiosity nor compassion. Gawain expected the man to make a speech of some kind, but he only looked at them, then turned and stalked away, his gloved hand on his sword hilt.

"That's Colonel Burduck, the commander," whispered Nobles. "He is a wheelhorse, sure."

"Quiet," said one of the guards.

In the course of his campaigning, Gawain had seen any number of military funerals: some furtive, some hasty, some full-blown with the rigid decorum and propriety that only the military can bring to such rites of passage. He had seen men buried in snowstorms and rain, in dark of night, under fire, under bright skies where buzzards circled and feral dogs watched patiently from the woods. He had even presided over a few, where Masonic rites had been called for. But he had never seen the yankees do it, and for a moment, he forgot his fear and watched as the troops came to present arms, and the white gloves of the officers rose slowly in the hand salute. Then the command for shoulder arms was given, and the white gloves moved slowly out and downward, leaving on the eye a trail like the arc of a falling star. Gawain listened to the little Methodist minister, whom he'd known since childhood, recite the Twenty-third Psalm and the verse from Ecclesiastes where man goeth to his long home, and the mourners go about the streets. Then "Present . . . *arms!*" and the rifles came up, bayonets rattling, and the white gloves slowly rose, palms outward, and five riflemen stepped out to the grave, their officer's sword flashing, and fired three volleys by the beat of the drum. Each volley was a perfect clap of sound like the discharge of a single rifle; in the intervals, the ramrods flashed and rang in the bores, while the smoke drifted away on the morning breeze and wreathed the colors like a benign ghost. Then, at the last, the square broke up into columns of platoons, the men went to right shoulder shift, bayonets bristling, and the company moved off to the quick march, drums beating and fifers playing "The White Cockade." And Gawain Harper stood at attention with tears in his eyes again, thinking this was not such a bad end to the journey, and how it would be denied him and his comrades, who had fought so long and honorably, but who were now prisoners and rebels and traitors.

A carriage wheeled toward them over the broken, soggy ground. It was a little hack with an enclosed bed like an army ambulance, drawn by a single bony mare in blinders. On the side of the box, in faded gold leaf, were the words

ATELIER BROWN
Cumberland, Mississippi

All Work Guaranteed

The professor brought it over the ground creaking and groaning on ungreased axles and reined up in front of the prisoners.

"As I live and breathe," said Peck, grinning down from the seat. It was not a long seat, and Peck and Wooster crowded the professor, who sat hunched up over the reins, his shoulders pushed together like a vulture's.

"Climb aboard, lads," said Wooster expansively, as if he were the steward of the Queen's coach.

"I ain't ridin anywhere with you," said Gawain.

"Me neither," said Craddock.

"Oh, it's not so bad," said Peck. "A little like fallin downstairs on your ass, but better than walkin."

Gawain noticed that Peck's hands were not tied. Had he sold them out, too? Impossible. Still, the man's good humor galled him. And Wooster's. How dare he mock them.

Stribling, quiet up to now, said, "Henry, maybe you ought to explain yourself. I mean, before I jerk you off that seat and cut your balls off, if you have any."

Wooster's face lost its color, then flushed pink. He opened his mouth, then shut it again. When he found his voice, it had lost its buoyancy. "Sir, I . . . I understand how it must appear, but—"

Before he could go on, a fresh Second Lieutenant, the gilt of his shoulder straps still bright, approached the group. "Get in the wagon," he said.

Thomas lurched forward and put his bound hands on the brake handle. He looked up at Wooster. "I want to know—," he began, and stopped. He turned to Gawain, a puzzled look on his face. "I want . . . I just want—," he said, then his eyes rolled up into his head, and his knees buckled, and Gawain, his hands tied, had to watch helplessly as he hit the ground.

The guards had to help them aboard. Moments later, the carriage was trundling and swaying through the Federal camp, then out on the Oxford road, the three men on the seat, the other six crowded into the back. Gawain figured they were going to the Shipwright house now, where the Federals had their headquarters. L. W. Thomas was out cold, his head in Gawain's lap, his body in Stribling's, his feet in Craddock's. As they rattled over the Town Creek bridge, Stribling turned to Gawain, his face barely visible in the gloom of the former traveling studio.

"How you feelin now?" asked Stribling.

"How the hell do you think?" snapped Gawain. Then, softer, "Oh, I am sorry to be such an ass."

Stribling patted Gawain's leg. "Never mind," he said. Then: "You know, he was in the willows, where I was yesterday."

Gawain shook his head. "All right," he said, "I will play. *Who* was in the willows? Molochi? I saw him."

"No, Gault," said Stribling. "I saw the sun glint on his field glasses."

"How the hell do you know it was Gault?" asked Gawain. Stribling was about to reply, but Gawain shook his head. "Never mind," he said. "I am sorry I asked. If we live through this, you and me are gon' find us some horse races. I'll provide the dash and personality, and you can conjure. We'll be so rich we can start our own church."

Stribling grinned. The carriage bumped and swayed, and in a moment turned down the southerly road.

· XX ·

Solomon Gault rode all Sunday night. He welcomed the storm when it came: not only did it keep people off the roads, but the wind, the thrashing trees, the cold, lashing rain seemed an appropriate backdrop for his mission. From time to time he'd imagined himself as the rain must have seen him, or the creatures huddling in their burrows. He made a fearsome messenger, he thought: illumined by lightning, poncho flying behind, silver water streaming from his downturned hat brim, the horse blowing flecks of foam as it galloped, hooves throwing mud and water from the road, or exploding over bridges. Along the way, in the yards of certain cabins, Solomon Gault called out, then waited in the lightning and the steady hammer of the rain, dogs roiling and barking around him. Soon, a figure would appear on the porch, against the candlelit rectangle of the door, always with a pistol or shotgun, and hush the dogs, and call into the darkness. In a little while, these, too, would be galloping through the night, spreading the word as in the old days.

At one such place, long after midnight, the door opened just a crack, a thin black line against the rain-streaked wall. Gault held his pocket pistol under the poncho and watched carefully, remembering the man behind the door. "Bill Huff!" he called. "It is Captain Gault!"

The door creaked a little then, and from it a voice growled the names of a half dozen dogs, and the dogs went silent and slunk back under the cabin. "Hell of a night, Cap'n," said the voice then. Gault could see no one, but he knew the man: shaggy, bearded, with the tiny, unblinking eyes of a feral hog.

"You remember what we talked about last time I was here?" asked Gault.

"Aye."

"Tomorrow, then. The Wagner place by daybreak."

A long silence followed. In the flicker of lightning, Gault could see the half-opened door, the littered yard, the shingled roof dripping water. Finally, the voice came again: "Daybreak comes mighty early, Cap'n. By the way, Ben Luker was here a while ago."

"Don't say," replied the Captain calmly, as if he'd expected that news. "A social call?"

"Oh, he wanted to stay the night," said the other, "but you know how it is."

"Surely," said the Captain, though he didn't. Another silence followed. Gault was tired and cold and wet, but he kept his impatience in check. "What'd Ben allow?" he said at last.

The other laughed. "Said old Wall's been active—shot a man this afternoon over to Cumberland."

Gault tightened his hand on the pistol and waited. At length, he spoke again. "What else did he say?"

"Said the cat's outen the bag, Cap'n. They run him out of the state tonight—why you reckon they didn't hang him?"

"I don't pretend to know," said Gault.

"Sure you do," said the voice. "He traded you for his own hide—you and Wall both, and the whole plan. They'll be expectin us now."

"Maybe," said Gault, "but they won't believe. The harder they look, the more surprised they'll be. Think of the sport of it. You ain't crawfishin, are you, Bill?"

"Oh, not me, Cap'n. No, indeed. Only, maybe the wages is gone up."

Gault ground his teeth. "Come out where I can talk to you," he said. "Or let me come in."

The door swung open then, and the dim light of a candle flared inside. Gault dismounted and splashed across the yard to the cabin, the pistol in his waistband now. He stood just inside the door, letting the water run off him, and looked around in the candlelight. The man Huff was standing by the hearth, a shotgun in the crook of his arm. He was naked from the waist up; his body was shaped like an enormous pear, and covered with dense black hair. A table and two rickety chairs, the only furniture in sight, stood in the center of the room. On a pallet in the corner, a woman and child huddled, blinking in the light.

"Who was it Wall shot?" asked Gault.

The other grinned. "Why, Cap'n, I thought you'd know. A Fed'ral soldier it was, in the tavern yard. That was real smart, Cap'n—that really got their attention."

"What makes you think I—"

"Aw, bullshit, Cap'n," said the man. "But never mind—what you do is your own business, at least 'til they start hangin folks. Tell you somethin else Ben found out. Stutts is dead. Frank Harper's boy caught him in ambush and hauled his freight. Now guess who's got your Henry rifle?"

At this revelation, Gault could not conceal his shock. He pulled a chair away from the table and sat down. "That damned fool," he said.

"Don't take it so hard," said Huff. "You still got me."

"What do you want?" asked Gault.

"Question is, what do *you* want, Cap'n?" said the other.

Gault looked at the floor, his mind racing, bringing together the things he'd learned in the last few minutes. Stutts was dead. Good. Harper had killed him. Irony, but no harm. Luker was gone. Good. A Federal soldier had been killed. Gault took that knowledge and turned it every way he could, and as he studied it, the thing began to glow with the light of possibility. Finally, Gault smiled and looked up at Bill Huff. Slowly, he drew the pistol from under his poncho and laid it on the table. Huff watched with his little eyes. "I'll tell you what I want, Lieutenant," said Gault. "In six hours, I want a hundred men, armed and mounted and ready to go, in the woods by the old Wagner place. I want a skirmish line to the north along the old fence line. I want an ambush, say twelve men, along the road just below the Leaf River bridge. Then I want to kill yankees. Now, what do *you* want?"

"Lieutenant's fine," said the other. "That's real good for a start. But all that's a tall order—and maybe you won't want me to mention to the boys that you got the yankees stirred up like goddamned ball-face hornets."

"Some things only we officers need to know," said Gault amiably.

"It's a heavy burden," said the other.

Gault nodded. "Maybe two thousand U.S. would lighten it some."

"How 'bout five?"

"How 'bout thirty-five hundred," said Gault, "payable when the fight is over."

Huff grinned and leaned the shotgun against the wall. He crossed the room and prodded the woman with his foot. "Git up, Addie, goddamn you, and gather some rations. Me and the Cap'n got a long ride ahead."

Later, in the last moments of night, the stars appeared. When daybreak came at last, the sky was pale with no red in it. The trees dripped water, and the air was fresh and clean as the first day in Eden. In the old Wagner cookhouse, Solomon Gault dozed in a corner. Huff stood by the open door in his rain slicker. He had just dropped a cricket in a spiderweb and was watching the insect struggle. In a moment, the spider looked out from his crevice in the doorframe. "Breakfast," said Huff. The spider leapt on the cricket, and Huff brought his fist down on them both. The noise woke Solomon Gault. "What!" he said.

Huff wiped his hand on his slicker. "Nothin," he said. "Not a god-damned thing."

Gault rose stiffly to his feet and peered out the door. "It's just now day-light," he said. "They'll be here."

"Sure," said the other. "But what if they ain't."

"They'll be here," said Gault again.

"Cap'n," began Huff, "do you really believe—"

Gault held up his hand. "Quiet," he said. "Listen."

There was a ground fog lying in the trees. It swirled through the under-brush and around the rain-darkened trunks. The voices in the grass were desultory; in fact, there was only the thin, reedy sawing of a single cricket, and of all the birds, only a mockingbird was awake. Then it came again: the squelching of a horse in the mud, and another, and another. A squirrel set up a fuss in the trees, then the voices of men, flat and toneless in the heavy air.

The shapes that emerged from the fog were those of horses and men. The riders carried no watches, but measured time by the sun, and the sun was drawing them to this place now. They rode by twos and threes, some bareback with rope halters, some on mules, some on good horses and some on bad. They brought with them weapons of every description, and they wore the sack coats and slouch hats and jeans breeches of farmers.

King Solomon Gault walked out in the clearing and watched them gather around, more coming all the while. He watched them dismount in silence or sit their horses with the air of men who did not give a goddamn what was about to happen to them. A few nodded in greeting, none of them spoke, all took their places and waited.

Solomon Gault had been around these men all his life, and had led them in the war, yet he had no idea what they were thinking. He had often tried to imagine what they thought, what they talked about, in their lonely cab-ins among their worn-out, slatternly wives and snot-nosed children. Their lives eluded him, as if they were inhabitants of some dying star, and he despised them for their blind and narrow passage. Yet he knew this about them, had seen it proven over and over again: they were capable of any violence, without premeditation, often without reason, and they seethed with a sullen, illogical pride that nursed every insult, every affront, as if it were the most important thing life could bring them. So Gault moved among these strange, silent men, touching their stirrups and the necks of their horses, speaking their names—John Surrat, the Pointer brothers, Pony Herrod, Log String and old Ivy Luker, W. B. Snell, Green Stanley, Frank Stutts—Here we are, boys, he said. It's a new day, Jasper. Here's old Gus Sewell—where'd you steal that horse, Gus? Ivy Rinkle, Carl Paice, Joe

Wamble and the Wardlow twins, Doc Mangrum. They filled the ghostly wood. Hey, Cap'n, they said. We gon' smite em today, Cap'n? We surely are, Nelse, said the Captain. Remember the Tallahatchie, Nelse? Remember the fight at the river, Sam? Remember how they tricked us, how they hanged those gallant boys? Remember them? *Remember. Remember. Call back the way people looked at you in town, how the girls laughed at you, and the house niggers sent you to the back door with your wood. Remember what it's like to suck hind tit, boys. How many carriages you ever ride in? How many niggers you got to plow and harrow, to chop and bust middles and pick while you sit in the shade on a fine horse? Remember, boys—remember every spring when you had to buy your seed on credit, every fall when you came up short again, every winter when the ague racked you. Where'd your teeth go, boys? Why do you look so old? And this, too: remember how they hunted you like foxes, burned you, hanged you. Remember these things, and rise up from the terrible plain where they left you to burn and suffer forever . . .*

Gault paraded them in an overgrown pasture behind a screen of trees. He counted eighty-one men and boys, eighty-one horses and mules, and fourteen mangy, rack-sided dogs. He split them into two companies, appointed sergeants (he knew better than to turn this rabble loose on an election), and delivered a short oration on their glorious past (*Remember, boys, remember*) and the deprivations wrought by the invaders. Then he left Bill Huff in charge and carried fifteen men as far as the Leaf River bridge. These were spread out in the woods on the west side of the road and told that, if they would only be patient, their Captain would fetch some yankees directly.

A little while later, Solomon Gault was hidden in the willows by the railroad. As he expected, the yankees were wasting no time burying their dead. He studied the scene through his field glasses and was impressed once more by the splendid discipline of the Regulars, and again he felt the old burn of envy. But that was all right. For all their discipline and strength, for all their victory, the Federals were at this ceremony because he, Solomon Gault, had willed it. All this—the troops, the open grave, the crude casket, the drums and unfurled colors tassled in black—were *his* doing, all set in motion by a few words spoken in the quiet of a Sunday afternoon. When the volleys were fired, and the wind brought the acrid smoke drifting thinly through the willows, Solomon Gault took it as an offering, like incense lifted in the temple of his namesake.

The horse, tethered in the trees, moved restlessly. The animal was tired and needed forage, and Gault himself was weary beyond belief, and his stomach gnawed with hunger. Gault had grown soft over the last few months, and the night's business told on him more than it would have once. But there would be plenty of time for rest when the thing was done. Maybe forever. That would be all right, too.

Presently, the yankees formed up and marched away, and only the old lunatic and his niggers were left at the grave. A little rise separated the burying ground from the Federal camp. Over it, Gault could see the tops of a few Sibley tents and the flagpole where the national colors waved. The field was empty, the sky blue and cloudless and serene, as if the affairs of men had shifted elsewhere all at once. Gault returned his glasses to their case and mounted up. He moved to the edge of the willows and looked out over the field. Already the niggers were filling the hole; the breeze was blowing away from camp, and Gault could hear the chafe of their shovels in the earth and the splash of the clods in the water-filled grave. Suddenly he was grinning and no longer felt his weariness. He touched his spurs to the horse and walked out into the sunlight, into the sibilant grass that stretched away toward the grave.

✦   ✦   ✦

MOLOCHI FISH HAD seen the buzzards circling over the wood near the Harper house. When he began to move in that direction, he found that the other birds had gone away, as though the sky had drawn them up. He knew they were there, watching to see what he would do.

Molochi did not care for buzzards. Years ago, on a summer afternoon, before he understood what they were, Molochi had shot a big turkey vulture out of the sky. It landed in a heap in the middle of a watermelon patch; when Molochi approached, the thing lifted its pimpled, naked head and watched him, its eyes burning with malice, until Molochi prodded it with his foot. Then the great bird stretched its wings and vomited its gorge over Molochi's bare feet. When it died, the creature's eyes were still quick with a hatred that seemed to embrace every living thing. Now Molochi followed the buzzards where they led, where they planed and sailed on their broad wings, swirling in a tall, airy funnel whose apex was death itself.

On the way, Molochi had to pass through the yard of the Harper house, where he had come once with his dogs to pick up the scent of the runaway nigger boy. He had not been here since that day, but the image returned to him—not as memory, but as a dim awareness, like wordless voices heard amid the din of a sawmill engine:

Winter, and the trees bare and creaking, horses and men and dogs breathing smoke. Constable John Talbot on his mule, old John Talbot with a patch over his lost eye and his beard tucked inside his overcoat, and Frank Harper mounting his big roan horse, and the boy on the gallery with

*his mother and the aunt who always looked at Molochi as if he were a bug
or a garden snake.* You, boy, *said Harper.* Get up here behind. *And the
aunt pulling the boy to her, saying* He don't need to go. Don't make him
go. *And old Harper:* Get that boy down here, I don't want to have to come
get him. *The boy was crying now, but he came down the steps without a
word, and old Harper jerked him up by the collar of his jacket and set him
on the rump of the horse, and the boy wrapped his arms around his
father's waist, and the chase began. The dogs had their noses full of the
nigger's smell from a pair of breeches he'd left behind; they strained against
their leashes, and finally Molochi let them go. The boy pressed his face
against his father's back, his legs gripped tight on the horse's flanks.*

Now old Harper was in the yard again, sitting in a rocking chair in the
sunshine, a shawl wrapped around his legs, his long, spidery hands folded
in his lap. He was watching the buzzards, too. Behind him, the house rose
paintless among the oaks, silent, intersticed with shadow. Molochi could
smell the breath of the house, an exhalation like rotten leaves in the wintertime stirred by the passage of horses. Molochi could smell the old man
too, and wondered if the buzzards could. As if in answer, one of the great
birds broke away from the circling flock and glided over the intervening
field, dipped behind the oak canopy a moment, then reappeared over the
yard riding sideways on the breeze, so low that Molochi could see the separate feathers of the wings and the eye tilted toward them. The shadow of
the bird passed over the yard and fled away toward the wood again.

"Who is that?" old Harper said, squinting at Molochi.

*Men on horseback always seemed to think that, if they didn't gallop and
jump fences, it wasn't a chase. Molochi knew better: they need go no faster
than Molochi himself could trot on foot. The men urged him on, fumed at
him, cursed, but Molochi jogged along, his truncheon in his hand, through
woods and plowed fields and ditches, following the dogs, though they
made no sound.*

"Here, I say!" croaked old Harper, tilting his head like the buzzard.
"You keep away from me!"

*They had him in an empty corn crib; when Molochi came through the
door, he could see the little nigger balled up in the corner among the blood-
spattered shucks and rat droppings, the dogs feinting at him, slathering,
silent as the shadows that filled the crib. Molochi could hear the click of
their teeth, and the crib stank with their breath. As Molochi watched, one
of them, the young bitch whose blood Molochi would one day keep in a
bottle, jumped in and took the boy by the shoulder where his shirt was
gone. The dog worried the flesh until she had a piece of it, jerked her head
so that a gobbet came away and the bone showed white and glistening, and*

all the while the nigger never made a sound. The dogs were all over him then, still silent but for the rasp of their breathing. Then Harper was there, dragging his boy by the arm. The boy stumbled and landed on his hands and knees; he scuttled back and pressed himself against the wall of the crib while Harper raged at Molochi: Get em off! Get em off, goddammit! *he said, and Molochi looked at him and said* You get em off, he's your nigger. *Then another sound, a high wailing like rabbits made when the dogs got them, and it should have been the nigger, but it was the white boy, pushing himself against the wall, his hands full of corn shucks, his face wet and smeared with dirt. And Harper:* Shut up, damn you, can't you be a man one time, just one goddamned time *and snatched the truncheon from Molochi's hand and raised it at the boy, his face twisted in fury and in a pain Molochi neither understood nor acknowledged, but that the boy seemed to recognize so that he stopped his wailing. He hid his face in his hands, his stomach heaved, and in a moment, the sour bile was running through his fingers. Then Harper turned the truncheon on the dogs; it rose and fell among them until they slunk away, while the nigger boy watched with eyes that were already dead.*

"Ellie!" cried old Harper. "You sent him, didn't you! Call him back, damn you, Ellie!"

Molochi went on then. Behind him, in the warm, sweet morning that smelled of grass and sunlight and rain, old Harper cried and cried.

Presently, Molochi came to a low stone wall. He recognized it right away as the place he'd seen in his vision, back at the cabin before the storm. When he raised his eyes, he looked up through the funnel of buzzards; so many, and not a sound from them. All the sound was behind the stone wall. Molochi touched the gris-gris bag in his pocket and peered over a clump of honeysuckle and morning glories humming with bees.

The neighborhood dogs had evicted Wall Stutts from his shallow grave; he lay now under a shoving crowd of birds, their shiny black backs humped as they jostled for position. They squawked and croaked at one another, their hooked beaks tearing. Now and then one would lift its head from the mass with a rubbery strip of meat dangling from its beak. He might throw his head back and gulp it down, his long neck working, or another might snatch it away. Here one hopped awkwardly around the fringes, there one spread its great wings and went aloft, feathers whisking.

The dogs slunk around outside the huddle of birds, or lay gnawing on a prize held in the forepaws. These lucky ones snarled and snapped at the birds when they hopped too close, or at their comrades who crept by them with lips pulled back and hackles raised. The dogs lunged at the birds and fought with one another. Their muzzles were bloody and their legs were caked with mud. There were six of them; the seventh, a terrier with a blue ribbon around its neck, lay dead, attended by its own party of birds.

In the air, and along the ground among the leaves and trampled grass, moved the lesser guests: gnats, butterflies, dung beetles, carrion beetles, wasps and bees, iridescent blowflies, marching ants. So many there were that the ground itself seemed to move, and the air buzzed with them.

All these creatures ignored Molochi Fish—all but the flies, and the gnats that swarmed around the rheum in the corners of his eyes. Molochi waved them away with the rag he carried for wiping his eyes. He watched without curiosity, waiting for whatever it was the scene would reveal to him. Finally, the dogs made a concerted rush and drove the birds off a portion of the corpse, and Molochi caught a glimpse of the ravaged face. It was picked nearly to the bone, but Molochi knew whose face it had been once. He thought *The injun will have him now,* and the notion caused him to nod his head. Maybe she wouldn't come around so much after this.

In a little while, Molochi turned away. He didn't go back by the Harper place but went through the broomsage toward the railroad cut where the blackberries rambled and copperheads sunned between the rails. Presently, he passed the depot and came in sight of the willow grove. There, bending the lithe branches, his own dark birds waited for him once again. As he moved toward them, he saw a man on horseback emerge from the willows and move out across the field.

✦　✦　✦

OLD UNCLE PRIAM, hunting squirrels in the fall, would come upon the last remnants of Wall Stutts: his boots, a belt and buckle, a few rags of clothing and a jawless skull where a field mouse was building his winter nest. Uncle Priam would lean his shotgun against the stone wall and light his corncob pipe and remember the hot afternoon when Gawain Harper killed Stutts with the Colt revolver. In the melancholy light of October, all that would seem alien and distant; were it not for the evidence, the old man might think it was a memory he had made himself from the fragments of dreams.

Old Priam would ponder what Molochi could not: how Gawain had freed the wasted shred of the man's soul, loosing it from all meanness and harm; how Wall Stutts, when he died in this place, made something good at the last, turning back to the ground what he had taken from it all his years. When the field mouse poked his whiskered nose out of one of Wall Stutts' eyeholes, Old Priam showed his yellow teeth and laughed. Then he went on his way, through the cool umber shadows and under trees gone scarlet and gold.

The leaves of that fall would cover the graves of Tom Kelly and Rafe Deaton, and the ashes of the Citadel of Djibouti, and drift in silent courses over the relics of Wall Stutts. The field mouse would sleep, waking on warm days to forage, and that summer would raise his family where once a man's thoughts made bitter passage. When the next October came, he would not return, nor any of his kin. And while all persons and all things followed time, living out their moments to good or ill, the leaves would fall and cover what they left behind.

✦　✦　✦

OLD HUNDRED-AND-ELEVEN WAS standing in the shade of his umbrella, his tattered Bible under the crook of his arm, thinking about Miss Morgan Rhea. He had never found any ginseng for his love potion; in fact, he had not had a chance to search for any since the events of yesterday. The memory irritated the old man. He'd thought, since Gawain Harper seemed to know the lady, that an introduction of some kind might be arranged. Then the man Stutts had interfered, and the rest of the day was taken up with killing and burying him. From the swirling kettle of buzzards to the north, Old Hundred-and-Eleven deduced that they had perhaps buried Stutts a little too hastily. Well, it served the bastard right.

Now here was another interruption, in the shape of the rider approaching from the railroad. He was a civilian, a gentleman by the look of him, though a little frayed around the edges. Old Hundred-and-Eleven rattled his umbrella and frowned. "Boys," he said, "here is a man oozing curiosity. I think I know him."

Dauncy peered into the bright sunlight. "Ain't that the gentleman farms without niggers?"

"If you mean Solomon Gault, I believe that's him," said Old Hundred-and-Eleven. "You all run fetch Gineral von Arnim."

As Dauncy and Jack clambered out of the hole, the rider spurred his horse. "Hold on, there!" the man said, and the two men stopped and removed their hats and stood waiting. Old Hundred-and-Eleven looked at them. "Didn't I tell you to go fetch the Gineral?" he said.

"Yes, sir, you sure did," said Dauncy. He shifted uncomfortably but didn't move. Before the old man could say more, the rider drew up, his tired horse blowing from the short canter.

Whatever notion of freedom the two brothers might have had, it did not include running when a white man said not to. True, Old Hundred-and-Eleven had ordered them to go, but he'd been countermanded now. In the blood-deep social code of the region, Solomon Gault, a gentleman, had taken charge. Now he sat his horse and looked down at them with the customary, assumed superiority (to which all classes agreed and acquiesced) of a mounted, well-dressed man of polished speech and property. Old Hundred-and-Eleven understood this too, and it rankled him. "Well, if it ain't Mister Solomon Gault," he said. "I believe I heard Gineral von Arnim mention your name just this mornin."

"General, hell," said the horseman. "Anyhow, what is it to you?"

"Well," said the old man, "I expect your hide would bring at least five dollars on the northern market about now."

Gault laughed. "Hell, I can beat that," he said. He dug into his waist-coat pocket and produced a twenty-dollar gold piece. Jack and Dauncy stared wide-eyed at the glittering thing. Gault flipped the coin once in his palm, then flung it down at the old man's feet. "There's the five dollars for my hide, and fifteen to keep your goddamn mouth shut while these niggers open that coffin yonder," said Gault. "Be quick—I don't have much time."

Dauncy and Jack looked at the horseman, then at Old Hundred-and-Eleven. The old man nudged the coin with his bare toe. "Naw," he said, "we ain't openin any coffins today." He looked at the brothers. "You boys run along. You ain't workin for him."

During his long night ride, Solomon Gault had carried a big Dragoon Colt in addition to his pocket gun. The Dragoon was kept in a saddle hol-ster by his right knee; he drew it now and laid the long barrel across the pommel. He looked at Dauncy and Jack. "Boys," he said, "you get down in that hole and prize that lid. I want to look on that man's face."

"Now, see here," said Old Hundred-and-Eleven. "That was a good man in there. I won't have you—"

"I am speaking to your niggers, sir," said Gault. "Now do like I say, and be quick."

Jack bent and picked up the spade, but Dauncy stepped forward. "I knowed Mister Rafe Deaton, sir. Please don't ask me to do that."

"Well, by God," said the horseman. He raised the pistol. "You don't have but a minute now."

It was bright morning in a season when all things grew into life; in the veins of young men, the blood ran hot and joyous, aching with every pos-sibility save that of death. But not for Dauncy. Death was there in the box that still smelled of fresh-milled pine, lying in the water at the bottom of a hole. And Death had come riding across the grass, meadowlarks rising before the horse's hooves, under the good sun that warmed them all. Dauncy thought there might be more of Death than anything else in that bright landscape, and maybe that was where freedom was. Or maybe that was the test of it, if what Old Hundred-and-Eleven had read them from the book was true. Dauncy couldn't say; he only knew that it was the Year of Jubilo, and if he was ever going to be a man, this was the time. He moved close to Jack and took him by the arm. "No, sir," he said. "We goin now."

Solomon Gault nodded. "Well, by God, times have changed, make no mistake. But I reckon I'll always be a little old-fashioned in a lot of ways." He cocked the pistol; the cylinder made a loud racheting in the morning air. "Which one of you insolent chattel shall I shoot first? I'll let you choose."

Old Hundred-and-Eleven dropped his umbrella. "No, now, wait a minute. Wait, we'll—"

"Too late," said Solomon Gault. "Which one."

"Lord Jesus, Dauncy," said Jack, twisting his hands on the spade handle.

Dauncy dropped his brother's arm and stepped away. "You gon' be in hell a long time, you shoot us. But if you do—" He pointed to Jack. "Take him first. I don't want him to see me die."

"All right, then," said Solomon Gault, and shot Dauncy in the chest.

Out of the roar of the big Dragoon rose a scream of rage and unbelief that seemed to split the day into fragments—not Dauncy, who lay jerking in the grass, but Jack, running, screaming, the spade upraised, already beginning his swing when Gault shot him. The momentum of his charge brought Jack hard against the horse's flank; Gault slipped his foot out of the stirrup and pushed the boy away, and he fell across his brother's body, hands reaching toward the sky he could no longer see. Then it was Old Hundred-and-Eleven, running at Gault with the Bible raised in both hands. Gault waited, and at the right moment kicked out with his boot and caught the old man squarely on the nose. The Bible flew up and landed with a splash in the open grave. Old Hundred-and-Eleven reeled backward, his eyes crossing, then collapsed in the grass, blood pouring from his nose. "Oh, the meanness!" cried the old man. "Why'd you shoot them boys! They wan't any of your niggers!"

"They are now," said Gault. "I gave you fifteen dollars for em."

The other struggled to his knees, his right hand pressed to his nose. "Whyn't you shoot me, too!" he wailed. "Go on—see can you do it, god-damn ye!"

But Gault wasn't listening to Old Hundred-and-Eleven now. His heart was pounding, pushing fire through his veins. The act of killing, whether of a rabbit or of a man, infused Solomon Gault with an electric, almost sexual, love: not for the life taken, but for himself, as though he were suddenly burning with a radiance other men attributed only to God. At such a time, Solomon Gault felt the world order itself around him, no longer spinning on its own but hushed and waiting to see what he would do. And he could do anything, whatever he wanted.

He slapped the spurs to his horse, and the animal, jaded though she was, gathered herself and leapt forward, almost trampling Old Hundred-and-Eleven where he crouched in the grass. Gault laughed and drove the horse at the cemetery fence; they cleared it and lit running, the horse's ears laid back and her tail streaming, her heart in the race now. They topped the rise at full gallop, and Gault could see the camp swarming with men, officers shouting, drummers beating the long roll, all just as he'd known it would be—for King Solomon Gault had created this moment; it was his alone, shaped of his will, and from it there could be no turning.

The sentries cried Halt! Halt! and fired their muskets, the smoke snatched away on the breeze. Gault flattened himself on the horse's back and emptied the Dragoon at them with no more success than the riflemen had. Then he was inside the picket line, and not a moment too soon, for a company was forming up, grabbing at their stacked muskets—if they got off a volley while he was in the open, it would be too bad for Solomon Gault. But in an instant he struck the main company street and charged right down it; he was among the tents and fires now, faces flashing past, open-mouthed. The horse leapt a fire pit, scattering kettles and pans, and the air was filled with shouting. Then Gault could see the end of the muddy street, and beyond it the Oxford road, and something else, too: a line of men formed across the width of the street, their bayoneted muskets at guard-against-cavalry. As the distance closed, Gault could see their faces, the points of their bayonets steady as if at drill. *They cannot shoot,* he thought. *Not down the middle of camp.* Then, at the last moment, he wrapped his hands in the horse's mane and sank his spurs deep enough to draw blood.

In a lifetime of riding, Solomon Gault had never made such a jump. He almost lost his seat when the horse left the ground, forelegs tucked under her, neck extended. The soldiers scattered—all but one, who held his ground and thrust with his bayonet, driving the steel into the horse's belly. But the hind hooves struck the man a solid blow; he dropped his musket and reeled away holding his head, and again the horse landed at full stride, squealing in pain but still running. Gault clawed himself back upright in the saddle and struck the Oxford road; looking back, he saw a half dozen cavalrymen pounding out of camp behind an officer with a drawn pistol. *That's right!* Gault cried to himself. *Now let it commence!* In an instant, Captain Solomon Gault clattered over the Town Creek bridge, flogging the horse with the barrel of his Dragoon Colt. He flew along the south side of

the square, scattering citizens, and a moment later galloped past the surprised sentries at the Shipwright house. He waved at them, wishing the
Colonel was in the yard. Then he was gone down the southerly road,
laughing, hoping the yankee cavalry could keep up, hoping the horse
would live to make Leaf River.

✦   ✦   ✦

MEANWHILE, OLD HUNDRED-AND-ELEVEN, weeping from his broken nose, had crawled to the place where Dauncy and Jack lay. Dauncy
was still alive, the blood bubbling from the hole in his shirtfront. But he
was peaceful, his fingers moving lightly over his breast, his eyes glazed
with shock.

Old Hundred-and-Eleven rolled Jack's body over and saw that the boy
was dead. Then he got to his knees and bent over Dauncy, pressing his
hand to the wound. "Oh, they ain't no good in that," said Dauncy, and the
old man knew that it was true. So he sat back, one hand holding his nose,
the other on Dauncy's shoulder. "I tole you to run," he said. "Why didn't
you?"

"Wisht we had," said Dauncy. He coughed blood over his chin, and Old
Hundred-and-Eleven wiped it away. In the silence that followed, the old
man thought the boy had gone, but in a moment, he opened his eyes and
raised his head a little. "Jack?" he said.

"He is waitin for you," said Old Hundred-and-Eleven, patting the boy's
shoulder. Dauncy's head dropped back again, and he looked at the old
man. "You was always decent," he said.

"Well, well," said Old Hundred-and-Eleven. "We had a nice time."

"You gon' bury us, ain't you?" said Dauncy.

"Surely," said the old man. "I'll see you're put outside the fence yonder,
with them nigger soldiers—would you like that?"

"With the soldiers?"

"Yep."

Dauncy nodded, gasping for breath. His hand closed on the old man's
wrist, and in a moment, he was gone.

Old Hundred-and-Eleven sat by the brothers for a while, waving the
flies away. At length, he rose unsteadily and lay them side by side and
crossed their hands on their breasts. Then he looked for his Bible, and
found it in the bottom of the open grave in the water and mud, wedged
between the coffin and the wall of earth. Old Hundred-and-Eleven knelt at
the edge of the grave for a moment, then lowered himself into the hole. He
lifted the book, soaked and wrinkled, and sat cross-legged on the mud-
covered lid of the coffin and began to turn the thin pages one by one, care-

ful not to tear them, though the blood from his nose dripped on them. He was halfway through Genesis when a shadow fell across him. He looked up, red eyes blinking in the brightness, into the peeling, rheumy face of Molochi Fish.

"In the New Bible," Old Hundred-and-Eleven said, "we ere called to love and forgiveness." Molochi watched the old man from under the brim of his hat. Old Hundred-and-Eleven lowered his eyes and went on, as though speaking to himself. "So I forgive Solomon Gault. I forgive him for murderin these boys, that never did harm to nobody, and I promise to love him like a brother and pray for his immortal soul, amen."

Molochi Fish nodded. He spat once, then turned and looked back toward the camp. "Some of them soldiers might come over here," he said.

"But they's the Old Bible, too," said Old Hundred-and-Eleven, and tapped the book with a horny nail. "It ere stained with blood, and the blood calls out."

"Somebody gon' have to bury these niggers," said Molochi. "Otherwise, they gon' be out roamin around."

Old Hundred-and-Eleven struggled to his feet and pulled himself out of the grave, shoving the open book before him through the trampled grass. Molochi moved back to make room, and watched as the other rose to his knees. "They's blood all over it," the old man said, "and water, and earth, and all of em's cryin out."

"We could put em in this hole," said Molochi. "It's already dug."

Old Hundred-and-Eleven rose again, more swiftly now, and steady. His skin, painted and smeared with blood, was almost translucent in the sunlight. His pink, browless eyes were wide, and his white hair tangled and matted. He lunged at Molochi and wrapped his claws in the other's shirt and pulled him close so that their faces were almost touching. "No!" he said, his voice and his breath hot on Molochi's face. "We got to bury em outside, with them nigger soldiers, like I said I would."

Molochi grasped the old man's wrists but couldn't break his hold. "I ain't buryin nobody," he said.

Old Hundred-and-Eleven shook Molochi, pushed him and shook him. "Oh, yes!" cried the old man. "Yes! And that ain't all you gon' do!"

Molochi drew his knife, held the blade up where Old Hundred-and-Eleven could see it. The old man laughed and closed his hand over the knife blade. "Shit," he said. "Go ahead, jerk it out. See can you make me bleed." Molochi's eyes began to bulge, and a strand of drool dripped from the corner of his open mouth. Old Hundred-and-Eleven laughed again. Still grasping the blade, he drew it through his hand. The blood dripped from his closed fist then, and when he opened his hand, it was cut deep through the palm. "I know you, Molochi Fish," he said. "I ken how the spirits hunt you of a night, how you see the dead. Well, you go ahead and cut my th'oat now if you want—maybe you'd be doin me a favor. But I'll tell you—if ye do that, you ain't seen no spirits yet. If you got a soul, I'll find it, and gnaw a hole in it like one of them birds yonder, and I'll fill it up with dreams even *you* ain't thought of yet!"

Molochi stared at the old man's bloody hand open before him. He let the knife fall into the grass. "What you want with me?" he said.

Old Hundred-and-Eleven showed his yellow teeth. "You he'p me get these boys in their grave—then you swear by this blood that you'll he'p me put Solomon Gault in one of his own before tomorrow sundown."

"I ain't got nothin against him," said Molochi.

"That ain't ever stopped you before," said the other. "You want me to turn these boys' spirits loose on you? Nigger ghosts is way worse than any, you ought to know that."

Molochi brought out the bag with the dead frog. "I got this—," he began, but the old man snatched the bag and worked it open and peered inside. Again he laughed. "Aw, delusion," he said, "you call this a conjure?" He lifted the frog by a withered hind leg and popped it in his mouth, chewed once, and swallowed. "Now, by God, you swear," said Old Hundred-and-Eleven, and raised his hand again. Molochi backed up a step. "Swear!" roared the old man. "Put your hand to it!"

So Molochi Fish pressed the palm of his hand against that of Old Hundred-and-Eleven, sealing himself in a bargain to which, for the first time in his life, he addressed a question he hardly knew how to frame. "Why?" he said.

Old Hundred-and-Eleven grinned and picked at his front teeth with a fingernail. He spat. "To save you," he said. Then he bent and picked up the twenty-dollar gold piece. It lay in his bloody palm like a fragment of the sun.

When Professor Brown's studio wagon arrived in the yard of the Shipwright house, it was met by Colonel Burduck and Lieutenant von Arnim and a dozen infantrymen with fixed bayonets. Getting out of the carriage was easier than getting in; when the prisoners were on the ground, they were told by a corporal to fall in on the tall one, meaning Stribling. Gawain, in spite of everything, took secret pride in knowing what the corporal meant. However, the sight of the officers was enough to make Gawain's dawning hope blink out again, and the riflemen were almost more than he could bear. They watched as Thomas was carried into the house, followed by Wooster and Brown. Then von Arnim approached, while the Colonel stood silent, his hand on his sword hilt.

"Now, look here," said the provost. "I am goin to have these bonds taken off, and you will all get some rations. If you try to run, I will truss you up like a runaway nigger. Any questions?"

"I want my mama," said Craddock.

Von Arnim ignored him and turned to the corporal. In a moment their hands were loosed, and the corporal led them around to the back yard where a contraband, smoking a corncob pipe and wearing an old surgeon's apron (Gawain tried not to look at the dark stains down the apron's front), was squatting by a fire. In his hand was a wooden ladle; on the coals were blackened pots and a tin coffee boiler.

Gawain had just begun to believe that they were really to be given breakfast when shouts arose in the front yard. Men ran in that direction. In a moment, one returned, and another hailed him. The man shook his head. "Feller just charged the camp," he said. "Went right down the company street. That was him goin by just now, and milord's household cavalry all hell after him." The man made a little limp-wristed pirouette in the yard, and the soldiers laughed.

Gawain looked at Stribling. The other shrugged. "Told you," he said.

They ate from tin plates—bacon and bread and a concoction of white beans and onions—and drank coffee from tin cups. They squatted in a circle around the cooking fire, the smoke stinging their eyes, and around them were the old familiar sounds of an infantry camp, and the smells of damp wool and canvas and rancid grease they knew so well. The guard (doubled now) was drawn up for inspection by a bespectacled officer, who moved from man to man with the sergeant of the guard a step behind. A wood detail was coming in, a musician was drying the head of his drum over the coals, an awkward squad drilled at the manual of arms. Just to the south, in the open side yard, a farrier had set up his portable forge, and his hammer rang across the morning air like old Miss Chastain's school bell used to do.

Gawain, his stomach full for the first time in recent memory, poured his third cup of coffee and marveled at the perversity of his heart. The war had brought him to this sorry pass, yet Gawain Harper, kneeling by the smoky fire, found himself longing for the war again, for the things he had found there that he knew could be found nowhere else, not ever again. He looked at the faces of the men around him, listened to their talk, watched the movements of their hands and the way they stood or sat or stretched themselves, and he understood once more the singularity of what he'd been given, and that he wouldn't trade it for any memory of peace.

Gawain smiled, and chided himself a little. Just a while ago, he had hated his comrades in their humiliation, and despised himself even more. Now he wished that somehow they could be borne back together to some arduous field, and rise to the long roll of the drum, and fall in, jostling and complaining under the old whisking flags, and ahead the long march, and the striving, and the eerie cry awakening in the smoke as they lowered their bayonets and charged. Madness, he knew. And he knew as well that he would not go back, even if he could. But he was glad to have done it once, even for all the ruin and sorrow and violence—glad it was over now, so that it could be his forever. In that moment, he missed Sir Niles terribly, and all the other lads with whom he had walked in the valley of dry bones.

And it all had to mean something. He insisted on that. He wanted badly to live past this moment, this day, and swore to live and die insisting that the process had meaning, though what it was, he supposed he would never discern. But no matter. He thought of old Uncle Priam, who asked so little of the world in which he lived and suffered and found gladness. Old Priam would agree that the faith was enough, even if the answers never came. It had to be that way, else Sir Niles, and young Fitter, and Bushrod Carter, and Tom Kelly, and Rafe Deaton—even Wall Stutts, in his way—had striven in vain, and the lives they offered had been lifted up to nothing. He would not believe that, would never accept that. All men dreamed their lives, and even the small ones, the defeated ones, the lost and ruined ones whom chance never visited and never would—even these refused the notion that a journey so complex, so filled with light and noise and movement, would come to nothing. It was not vanity or delusion, Gawain thought: it was a simple lesson in astronomy. No sun, no galaxy nor constellation stood at the center of the universe; rather, every man's soul burned there like a cloudy spray of stars, and offered a light no meanness, not evil itself, could extinguish. Thus did every man have his dignity, and every one a portion of immortality.

"What are you thinkin about so hard?" asked Stribling.

"I was just wishin I had some more of that good possum," Gawain replied.

"My God," said Stribling.

"Harry, you saved my worthless ass again, back yonder by the church. I was fixin to run. I couldn't stand bein trussed up like that."

"Oh, they prob'ly wouldn't have shot you much," replied Stribling.

"Well, anyhow," said Gawain, and let the subject slide away into that place where dwelt the things men didn't talk about.

All this time, a youth of about seventeen stood guard over them, more or less. The sleeves of his coat, too long, were rolled back over his bony wrists, and he gripped his musket with slender fingers, the nails bitten to the quick. Gawain couldn't look at him; the boy was too much like the one at Stones River. For his part, the young soldier stared at Gawain and his comrades in wonder. Marcus Peck, who was seated on an ammunition box and swabbing his plate with a hunk of bread, noticed him.

"See here, young fellow," said the gunner. "What're *you* lookin at?"

The boy swallowed, his Adam's apple bobbing in his long neck. "Why, nothin, sir," he said.

Peck jabbed a finger at Carl Nobles. "You wasn't lookin at *him,* was you?" Nobles scowled at the boy and scratched his beard.

"Oh, n-no, sir," said the boy.

"Oh, *well,* then," said Peck. "Maybe you don't know who he is. Maybe you ain't been informed. Maybe you think he is just some *ordinary* hairy-assed, uncouth, ugly—"

"Here, now," protested Carl Nobles. "You leave that boy alone."

"Just don't get him riled," said Peck. "God, I hate to think of it."

"Tell him how you lost your leg, Marcus," said Stuart Bloodworth.

"Oh, I can't. The memory's too bitter."

"How *did* you?" asked the boy, keeping his eye on Nobles.

Peck gobbled up the sopping wad of bread and wiped his mouth on his sleeve. "Oh, my Lord," he said, pressing his fingers to his forehead.

Craddock knelt beside the one-legged gunner and lay a hand on his stump. "There, there," he said. "I know it's painful for you."

"*You* tell it," said Peck, his voice breaking.

Craddock rose and walked around the fire and draped an arm over the youth's shoulder. The boy shifted uncomfortably and tightened his grip on the musket. "I suppose you were at Franklin?" said Craddock. The boy shook his head.

"Well, no matter," Craddock went on. "There we was, in the hottest part of the fight—"

"The very hottest," said Peck.

"Quiet," said Nobles. "I am all a-tremble to hear this."

"Thank you," said Craddock. "There we was, the Minié balls so thick you could catch em by the bucketful, if you had a bucket, and it was desperate—*desperate,* sir—and at the moment of crisis, who should appear but our gallant General there—"

The boy looked at Peck in astonishment.

"Oh," said Craddock, "you didn't know Marcus was a General? Well, he ain't now, but he was then, and the heat of battle was on him. Oh, granted, he don't look like much *now,* but he was solid inspiration *then,* and he leapt from his great warhorse, and I'll never forget his words, heard through the din of the fray. He said . . . he said—"

"Over you go, boys!" shouted Peck. "Cap'n Stribling and me are right here behind you!"

"They was his very words," said Stribling.

"Jesus, what a fight," said Craddock. He was about to go on when he noticed three Federal soldiers who had gathered to listen to the story. They stood loosely, one smoking a pipe, all with hands in their pockets, watching. Craddock looked at them, his mouth open, hand upraised, his left arm around the boy's shoulder. The yankees studied the ground at their feet. Of a sudden, beads of sweat appeared on Craddock's brow and began to roll down his face. His hand began to tremble; he lowered it, and stared as if something unspeakable lay in the palm.

A silence lay upon them all. Beyond the fire, the sounds of the camp— the drill, the guard mount, the ring of the smith's hammer—went on, and beyond that the world busy at making or unmaking itself, as if there were no memory, no old dreams to twine like smoke around the lives of men. At last, Craddock found his handkerchief and mopped his face. He patted the boy's shoulder, then let his arm fall away. The boy looked at him, puzzled.

Craddock smiled and shook his head. "It was a hell of a fight," he said, and the silence passed, and they were all right again.

The three yankees came and knelt by the fire. One borrowed a cup from Bloodworth and poured some coffee from the tin boiler. "What regiment was you?" he asked.

"Twenty-first Mississippi," said Bloodworth.

"Don't remember it."

"You would if you'd ever met us," said Craddock.

"How about you all?" asked Bloodworth quickly. "Ain't you Regulars?"

"Fourteenth U.S., one of Uncle Billy's own," said the drummer. He thumped the head of his drum to test its tightness.

The Twenty-first had indeed met the Fourteenth, at Stones River and again on the Atlanta campaign. Gawain remembered the acorn corps badges on the dead.

"What you boys doin here?" asked another soldier, a piece of bacon dangling from his hand. "Come to enlist?"

"Oh, no," said Peck. "I think they mean to hang us for treason."

"Don't say?" said the soldier.

The boy with the musket shifted his feet impatiently. "Well," he said, "ain't you gon' tell me how the Gin'ral lost his leg?"

Craddock rocked on his heels. "Well, to continue," he said. "It was in this wise. You see, a big cannonball come and landed so far behind that it found the General and mangled his leg somethin awful; it was all a-welter with blood and the bones stickin out everywhere."

"My!" said the boy.

"Yes, indeed," said Craddock. "He was squallin and carryin on so, and makin such a big thing of it, and causin such havoc with the boys' spirits, as it were, that somethin had to be done, and of course it was."

"What?" asked the young soldier.

"Well, there ain't but one thing," said the drummer.

"That's right," said Bloodworth.

"Well, what was it?" asked the boy.

"Why, gnaw it off," said Craddock.

"Gnaw it off?" said the boy.

"Yep. They sent for Nobles, and he done it. He always did the gnawin in the regiment."

"Aw, hell," said the boy.

"I sure did," said Nobles. "Tasted like shit, too."

"Here, now!" said Peck, while the others looked solemnly into the fire.

"It was hell on campaign," said the Federal with the coffee, and every man nodded in agreement.

✦   ✦   ✦

FOR KING SOLOMON Gault, it was the most exhilarating ride of his life. First the charge through camp, then the Shipwright house boiling like an ant hill behind him, cavalry in pursuit, his name on every tongue—if only the Colonel had been in the yard! But no time for that now. He expected to see the road ahead filled with cavalry, but there was none—only the troopers behind, pushing their big horses to their doom like the French knights at Agincourt. Excellent image, he thought, and filed it away for his memoir even as he wondered where the swarms of Federal cavalry he'd expected had got to. He could not dare to hope that they were pulled back north, but he knew somehow they were, as if he himself had given the order.

The muddy road reeled beneath him, the sunlight flickered on his face. The horse was fast, but she was flagging, and he could hear the huffing and pounding and jangling of his pursuers. They did not fire—excellent discipline! thought Gault—for they could see the blood hosing from the horse's belly and knew the chase was almost run. Gault holstered the Dragoon and, awkwardly, in a movement that nearly unseated him and that cost him a yard or two, he fumbled in his pants pocket for his clasp knife. He opened it with his teeth and jabbed the blade into the horse's withers. She squealed and leapt forward. The trees blurred, and the open fields, and in a moment there was the bridge and the road beyond, all lying quiet in the shadows as if nothing would ever happen there. *Now we will see,* thought Gault, and closed his mind to everything but the picture he had created for this moment. Should I have put them on both sides of the road? he thought. No, the damn fools would only kill each other. The horse hammered over the planks of the bridge, nearly stumbling. Gault plunged the knife again, and the horse twisted her head, her teeth clacking over the bit, her foam pink with blood, and Gault saw them in the trees. *Wait! Wait!* he demanded, *Not yet!* and now the horse fell, all her strength gone, and Gault hit the soft mud rolling, losing his knife, crying *Now! Now!*

The cavalrymen reined their horses, shouting Halt! Halt!, horses pulled down on their rumps, heads thrown back. One fell on its side, pinned the rider, the muzzle of his carbine driving into the mud. The trooper pulled it loose, pushed with his free leg against the saddle as the horse struggled to rise; then he was free and crawling toward the roadside, and so he was the first to die. Second was the officer, who died cursing his men for opening fire without orders, only the fire was not theirs. Another man fell, foot caught in the stirrup, before the survivors realized they were being shot to pieces; they dismounted, raised their carbines, backed toward each other for mutual support, but too late. In a moment, the image Gault had created for this moment was complete and three-dimensional: six dead cavalrymen tangled in the churned road, horses with empty saddles and stirrups flapping, the scavengers swarming from the woods in feral joy. The dead were sprawled in their boots (already being yanked off) and blue fatigue blouses (pockets to be gone through), leaving behind their six Spencer carbines and cartridge boxes full of ammunition. The quickest assassins snatched these up and immediately had to defend their prizes from the others. Gault registered all of this as he stroked the nose of the officer's big gelding. The animal's nostrils were flaring from the scent of blood; he quivered, and his eyes rolled white. Gault calmed him, noted with satisfaction that a saber was strapped to the saddle. He drew it and, leading the horse, waded into the ragged scavengers capering in the road, struck them with the flat of the blade, cursed them, and in this way calmed them as well. *Get these men out of the road,* he said, his voice serene, steady now. *Catch those horses.* Finally, he sheathed the saber and mounted the skittish gelding, patting its withers, speaking to it. He pushed the big horse over to the side of the road where Joe Cree, a scrawny, red-bearded man with plaited hair, was scraping mud from his new carbine. *Give it to me,* said Gault, serenely, his hand out. The man looked at him, but only for an instant before he put the weapon into Gault's hand. *The cartridge box, too,* said Gault. In a moment, the road was empty. Gault remained long enough to dismount and retrieve his saddlebags from the dying horse that brought him here. He left the Dragoon. Then he, too, was gone, back toward the Wagner place, leaving only a thin haze of smoke rising to the trees.

✦　✦　✦

GAWAIN WOULD HAVE liked to sit in the camp all day and listen to the soldiers and watch the goings-on, for he had decided that soldiering was an interesting trade when you didn't have to do it yourself. Suddenly there was excitement in the yard: sergeants shouting, men running for their stacked arms and accoutrements. The Federal soldier returned the tin cup to Bloodworth and rose wearily with his comrades. "Sure you don't want to enlist?" he said. "We can fill out the papers in no time."

The drummer was collared by von Arnim. "Sound the long roll," said the provost. The drummer grinned and tightened the ropes of his drum and in a moment was beating the call that Gawain Harper could not hear without a painful quickening of his heart. The young guard grew more nervous

than ever, and Gawain shook his head at the notion of how easy it would
be to get the musket away. He looked at Craddock, who was likely to
make a grab if anybody was—that wouldn't do, and Gawain was ready to
stop it if he could. But Nobles was beside the boy now, talking to him, and
anyhow von Arnim was approaching again. The provost seemed almost
happy. "*All* right, lads, let's get on with it," he said. Von Arnim led them
into the Shipwright house. Gawain caught a glimpse of old Mister
Shipwright lurking at the top of the stairs, and he remembered when he
used to tangle with the Shipwright boys, Elmer and Ernest, his boyhood
enemies. They were both older than Gawain, and longer of reach, and
meaner, and regularly trounced him, and once nearly drowned him in
Town Creek. Elmer and Ernest had ended up in the Virginia army, and
Gawain wondered where they were now, and if they were coming home.

In Colonel Burduck's office, the atmosphere grew chilly. The Colonel
himself stood with his back to the room, peering out the window toward
the creek. Two guards flanked the door with the usual bayoneted rifles,
and Gawain wondered if these yankees ever unfixed their steel. L. W.
Thomas sat on the horsehair settee between Mac Brown and Henry
Wooster. Brown sat meekly with his hands in his lap; Wooster seemed
excited, his notebook open on his knee. Thomas looked feverish; his jaw
was slack, and his eyes seemed empty and unfocused, as if they could only
see inward now. Gawain had seen that look on men's faces before. He had
seen it on his mother's face. In that moment, a peregrine thought wandered
through Gawain's mind: he wondered if anyone would ever erect a monument to the Great Confederate War. He could see, as in a vision, vast
crowds swarming around a megalith of granite, upturned faces outraged,
wondering, their hands waving, shouts of Take it away! Cover it up! and
the monument itself atop the stone, out of their reach, burnished in the
light of dawn—two bronze figures, nude, in heroic proportion: one mas-
culine, seated, hands between his knees, head bowed; the other feminine,
standing behind, her face in anguish but fixed defiantly on the crowd, her
graceful arm raised, and in the hand a frying pan of polished copper gleaming in the sun like a torch—

Von Arnim lined them up before the desk. Still, Colonel Burduck stood
at the window, his hands clasped behind his back. "Damn," Stribling whispered to Gawain, "I feel like the twelve fellowcraft."

"Mea culpa runneth over," said Gawain, and took his rosary into his
hands.

"Quiet, you men!" said the provost.

✦　　✦　　✦

HENRY CLYDE WOOSTER sat back on the horsehair couch and observed the prisoners. Thomas had looked bad when they brought him in, but he had rallied at the news of Solomon Gault's mad charge through the camp. *South,* he had said. *They will come from there.* Von Arnim had cursed him, called him a liar, but Burduck said *No! I have seen him there. Is that the meeting place?*

South, said Thomas. *They will come from the south.*

So Burduck had ordered Captain Bloom to establish a line to the south, and called for a gun to be brought to the Shipwright house and two more to be held in reserve. Now the Colonel was at the window again. Wooster thought the Colonel must know the yard pretty well by now.

Last night, after his interview with the Colonel, Wooster had left the porch and crept around the back of the house, the thunder rumbling and the trees along the creek shuddering in the wind. When Wooster stepped up to the open window, the Colonel was sitting with his chin on his breast, his eyes closed.

"Colonel Burduck," said Wooster softly, trying not to startle the man. But Burduck didn't move nor even open his eyes. "Go away, Henry," he said.

"Colonel, I know where Thomas is hiding," said the correspondent, his heart hammering now that the actual words were out.

"I know you do. Now, go away."

"Colonel, your cavalry's gone, ain't it. And a whole company of foot."

Burduck raised his head then. "Of *foot?*" he said. "This is not the British army, Wooster."

"Call em what you will, they are gone, ain't they?"

Burduck leaned forward, his elbows on the windowsill. "Yes," he said. "I have one reduced company, a section of guns, and a dozen . . . *horse.* Now you know. What of it?"

"If Gault strikes—"

"Sir, if Gault strikes, he is a goddamned fool, and I will whip his ass. That is not bravado, sir—you may quote me in the Cincinnati papers. Now begone." The Colonel rose and put his hand on the window sash, but Wooster lay his own hands on the sill. "No," he said.

Burduck sighed and sat down again. He pinched the bridge of his nose. "Wooster," he said finally, raising his eyes, "you have followed this battalion since the Chickasaw Bluffs. You have always been a discreet and loyal and steady man, and I wonder what has come over you now. These goddamned rebels—"

"They are not rebels, sir," said Wooster. "They have taken the oath."

Burduck leaned on the windowsill again. "Henry, no doubt there is a place for you in the government somewhere, but do not split hairs with me, sir. Do you think Thomas ever took the oath?"

"No, Colonel, but he might."

Burduck laughed. "Are you so innocent to believe that the goddamned oath means anything—that it can change the way a man feels about—"

"No," said Wooster, stung. "I know better than that."

"Then what do you want, sir? You want me to turn my head while a traitor—"

"I want you to end the war, Colonel," said Wooster. "Before it kills you."

Burduck sat back then, and propped a foot on the windowsill. He pressed his temples, and Wooster knew that the wolves were gnawing in the Colonel's head again, but he went on. "How many times you been out of time lately, Colonel?" he asked. "Deaton told me all about it, the night after the tavern fight, the night Kelly was killed. The old men know it, sir. They remember."

"You are out of line, sir," said the Colonel.

Wooster shook his head. "No, sir, I am not. You always thought you could hide it before, in the general madness, in the days when everybody was wrung out. But you couldn't hide it then, and you can't hide it now, Colonel. Tell me why you never made brigadier? Can you tell me that? What do you see out this window, sir? Why do you have Rafe Deaton laid out like a shrine—"

"That's enough!" bellowed the Colonel, and men in the yard turned from their fires to look. A sentry came up, his accoutrements creaking. He looked at Wooster, then at the Colonel. "Everything all right, sir?" he asked.

"Yes, yes," said the Colonel. "Go back to your post."

When the man was gone, Wooster tried again. "You won't be the last casualty, Colonel—there'll be plenty more in the years to come. But you don't have to be one at all. You want to know where Thomas is hid? I'll tell you. You can go get him anytime you want. But you have a choice. You can give him the oath, you can make believe it means something, you can at least pretend that peace is more than the arbitrary mouthing of politicians. Or you can hang him, and let the poison boil in your blood if that's what satisfies you, and maybe in a little while you'll go out of time and stay there, wherever it is, where there ain't anything but the cold dark. Is that what you want, Colonel?"

For a long time, Colonel Burduck sat in silence. The wind was whipping the smoke around the abandoned fires now, the men gone to their tents. Presently, the first drops of rain began to fall: fat drops, striking the earth like ripe fruit. Wooster turned up his collar and waited. At last the Colonel sat upright and looked around as if he'd just awakened. "Wooster," he said. "Damn you, Wooster. Come inside out of the rain."

Wooster crawled through the window then, no easy task for a man of his bulk, and in time he fell asleep on the horsehair couch. Later, deep in the night, Wooster was roused from sleep. He was stiff, and a mosquito was humming in his ear, but he was still in that stage of waking where movement, if not impossible, is not yet a priority. The lanterns were out now, the shutters pulled against the blowing rain. Yet through the jalousies filtered a strange, ambient light, like starlight or the glow of phosphorous. Through this light, Colonel Burduck paced up and down before the body of Rafe Deaton. Wooster watched him move across the shuttered window, then back again, his head down, murmuring in a language Wooster did not at first recognize. Then Wooster's mind passed through that region of clarity that comes just before the intrusion of full consciousness with all its noise and sensation, and the words began to shape themselves in the mysterious light. *Requiem. Requiem. Requiem aeternam dona ei, et lux perpetua luceat ei.* Then, at last, the pacing figure stopped, and for a long while, Colonel Burduck stood absolutely still against the pale interstices of the window. Wooster sat up, hardly daring to breathe. The drip of water from the eaves. The thunder, barely audible now. The croak of a night heron hunting at the edge of the swollen stream. *Come back,* pleaded Wooster in the perfect stillness of his mind. *Come back and end it and you won't have to go again, not ever again, and the morning will be pure, and all of us cleansed of it forever.* And as he pleaded, Wooster saw a word stir in the deep bronze well of his memory, and then another, then both rising on his own voice as it was thirty years ago, in his schoolboy Latin: *Vita. Animus. Vita. Animus.* Then, as if the words had nudged him, Burduck trembled. He crossed himself slowly, then, slowly, turned and passed into a deep shadow of the room. When he emerged again, Wooster was startled by the impression that he had grown wings, the vast, white pinions of an archangel. But the white blur was a blanket that the Colonel held before him, that he spread over the body of Rafe Deaton and smoothed with his hands. Then, wearily, like a man whose long vigil is ended at last, Burduck returned to the chair behind the table and sat, and leaned forward until his head was resting on the windowsill, and began to weep. Only then did Wooster understand the source of the uncanny light that diffused in the room, that seemed to grow with every moment now. There was no mystery to it at all. It was only the dawn, only tomorrow.

✦   ✦   ✦

WHILE THEIR MOUNTED comrades were being massacred on the southerly road, a squad of soldiers, observed by a sergeant, were filling the grave of Rafe Deaton. The sergeant was smoking the fanciful pipe that had lately belonged to the departed. The sergeant had known Rafe Deaton since the Indian-fighting days and had taken the pipe from the man's effects to remember him by.

A little way distant, beyond the paling fence, four contraband, observed by Old Hundred-and-Eleven, were digging another grave, this one to receive the blanket-shrouded figures of Dauncy and Jack. Their grave was adjacent to a pair of rain-eroded mounds, each marked by a barrel stave:

Unknown Colored Soldier
U.S.C.T.
March 1865

Like all unknown soldiers, the men who lay in these graves had been known by *somebody*, but not by the men who buried them. Neither had they coffins; by now, the blankets that wrapped them were rotted, and all they had been was now indistinguishable from the earth that held them fast.

The burial place had once been pasture, and only a single tree had been left to shade the cattle who once lived here. It was a big white oak, perfectly formed, its trunk crawling with poison ivy. The soldiers, always ravenous for wood, had left it uncut because Bloom, the senior Captain, liked to sit under it in idle, contemplative moments. Sitting under it now, his back pressed against the poison ivy, was Molochi Fish.

The soldiers had come to investigate the gunshots that had been heard just before the wild horseman charged the camp. Old Hundred-and-Eleven had identified the man and told how he murdered the two boys, and of the promise made to Dauncy before he died. The soldiers had rounded up contrabands and shovels, and now all the dead were being hurried under the ground, away from the sun that was growing hotter by the moment.

The men looked with curiosity upon Molochi Fish. For his part, Molochi ignored them, sitting under the tree with his eyes closed, apparently asleep. Old Hundred-and-Eleven made no effort to explain Molochi's presence.

Deaton's grave was almost filled when word came that the infantry were to pack up and be ready to move. The sergeant gave his orders: the blacks would finish the graves, Old Hundred-and-Eleven and the strange man under the tree would come and talk to the Captain.

"Like hell," said Old Hundred-and-Eleven in reply to the sergeant's directive. "You talk to him."

But orders were orders, and in a few moments, the two civilians were being prodded by bayonets toward the infantry camp.

✦   ✦   ✦

AS QUICKLY AS she could dress herself, Morgan Rhea had gone to see Aunt Vassar Bishop. She wore a green dress trimmed in black, and net gloves, and a straw boater with a green ribbon. She swept through the morning without seeing it, past Holy Cross church where the priest was painting the door; past children playing in the dirt; past negroes with bundles of laundry on their heads, laughing and calling to one another on their way to Town Creek. She made no answer to friends who greeted her, nor gave any thought to ghosts.

"I thought you might come," said Aunt Vassar in the cool, dim hall of the old Harper place. "I was hopin you would."

"You don't know me well," said Morgan. "I was not sure if you—"

"Oh, honey," said Aunt Vassar, taking Morgan by the hand. "I know everything about you I need to. Now come in the parlor and tell me what's happened to my no-account nephew since he shot Wall Stutts yesterday."

In a little while, the two women were walking beside the muddy road toward the square. Aunt Vassar wore her usual rusty black and carried an umbrella and a fan, and a reticule into which she had slipped old Frank Harper's Remington pocket pistol and her *Book of Common Prayer*. She wore a broad straw hat with a black ribbon.

"Did you ever take laudanum?" asked the old woman as they marched along.

"Only once, ma'am," said Morgan. "When I was birthin."

"You ain't got any now, I suppose?" Aunt Vassar said.

"No, ma'am. I liked it too much to keep it around."

"Well," the old woman said, "I'll be glad when things are civilized again and we get a proper apothecary. Old Mister Lloyd promises me he'll rebuild, and restock as soon as the roads are dry. I am tired of chewin that St. John's wort; those little flowers never did a thing for me. How do you feel about Gawain killin Mister Wall Stutts?"

Morgan thought a moment. "Well," she said at last, "I can only say that it seems . . . appropriate."

"That is a good answer," said Aunt Vassar. "You have your sights on him, I suppose—Gawain, I mean."

Morgan blushed. "I suppose I do," she said.

They passed a man whose mule was bogged down in the muddy road. He was cursing the animal and beating it with a charred board. Aunt Vassar berated the man until he stopped, breathless, embarrassed. They watched while the mule pulled itself out of the mire, then went on.

"How did you meet Nephew?" asked Aunt Vassar as they entered the square.

"At a barbecue, down by John Walker's," said Morgan. "I thought he was pretty hateful that day."

"Oh?"

"Yes, indeed. He read from *The Lady of the Lake,* and I fell in love with him right away—but do you think he would talk to me?"

"No?" said Aunt Vassar.

"No!" said the younger woman. "He excused himself with a headache."

"Well, he gets those now and then," said Aunt Vassar, "especially in social situations. He is a peculiar boy—takes that from his father's side, you know. All the Harpers were lunatics."

"That is a comfort," said Morgan.

They were nearly to the Shipwright house now. Just west of the road was a brick structure, the old Brummett livery which the yankees used as a magazine. A pair of twelve-pounders, hunched like sullen beasts between their high wheels, were being set up in the yard, pointed south. As the two women passed, a group of soldiers standing in ranks beside the road were suddenly overcome with coughing fits.

"Whatever is wrong with those yahoos?" asked Morgan.

"Oh, that is for you, darlin," said Aunt Vassar behind her open fan. "It is the soldierly way of showin . . . appreciation. They all do it."

"Hmph," said Morgan. "I wish they'd appreciate themselves back to wherever they came from."

"Lord, don't we all," Aunt Vassar said.

When they came to the Shipwright yard, with its soldiers and orderlies and now a gun and limber sitting by the road, Aunt Vassar stopped. She turned to Morgan and brushed a strand of hair from the young woman's forehead. "You are a pretty girl," she said, "and wise enough to know that every person carries yesterday with him all the time, these . . . these boys more than most perhaps."

"Yes'm," said Morgan.

"You will need a lot of patience," said Aunt Vassar. "A lifetime of it, probably."

"I know, Miss Vassar."

The old woman smiled. "Yes, I expect you do. Now let us go and pluck young Gawain from his folly."

✦   ✦   ✦

WHEN THE FEDERAL Colonel turned at last from the window, he did not bother to introduce himself, and delivered his remarks as he paced up and down before the six former rebels. What followed lasted only long enough for Gawain to say a decade of Hail Marys on the beads he held behind his back.

"I am aware that some of you are more guilty than others," said the Colonel, his glance singling out Nobles and Thomas. "However, you have all been a great deal of trouble, and some of you—" He paused before Nobles and fixed him with a hard look, which Nobles returned in kind. "Some of you have conspired against the national government in violation of your parole." He began to pace again, unbuckling his sword belt as he walked. "I don't care for your ways," he said. "They are cowardly and stupid." He laid his sword and pistol on the table and began to unbutton his double-breasted uniform coat. "I take them personally," he said, and removed the coat and laid it on the table. "You see me now stripped of arms and rank," said the Colonel, holding out his arms. "Any one of you, or any combination, who care to pursue this matter will find me just this way at sundown behind the ruins of Mr. Thomas' late tavern."

"Why wait, Colonel?" asked Craddock.

The Colonel smiled. "What's your name, sir?"

"Louisa May Alcott," said Craddock.

"I see," said the Colonel. "Well, Miss Alcott, I am waiting because I choose to—being a woman, you should find sympathy with that."

Craddock's face reddened. He was about to speak again when Nobles elbowed him. The Colonel went on, speaking to them all now. "You have shamed your honorable service. You have shamed your people. The colors you followed, though tainted with treason and enslavement, deserve better of you, for no other reason than that they are bathed in the blood of brave men. Now you would shame that blood by spilling more of it. I should think you'd have lost your stomach for fighting by now, but if that is what you want, I shall be happy to oblige."

"What if we won, sir?" asked Craddock. "I mean, what's the point?"

"You won't win," said the Colonel. "But if you did, the results would be exactly the same as your insurrection—that is, nothing—but with a whole lot less trouble to everybody."

"Colonel," began Stribling, "if I may—"

"You may not, sir," said the Colonel. "Lieutenant von Arnim?"

"Sir?" said the provost, straightening at the mantel.

"Do you have a copy of the Oath of Allegiance?"

"Ah, regrettably, sir—"

"Then make one up, sir," said the Colonel. "We will see who'll take it again. Now, raise your right hands, you men."

This seemed promising to Gawain, and he shot his right hand up, along with Peck and Bloodworth and Stribling. Only Nobles and Craddock hesitated, which Gawain found irritating. A long moment passed. Gawain began to detect the first signs of a call of nature, and he wished he hadn't drunk so much coffee. He wished he could be more honorable, but the fact was, Gawain Harper was ready to take any oath—willing to declare himself a citizen of Rhode Island if necessary—if it got him out of the Shipwright house. He admired his comrades, but wished they would cease this foolishness. After all, they could *lie* to their grandchildren if they wanted to.

"All right," said the Colonel at last. "Lieutenant?"

And at that moment, the demands of honor satisfied, Nobles and Craddock raised their hands.

The provost stepped forward. "Do you solemnly swear to uphold the laws of the United States and to not take up arms against her anymore and to return to your homes, there to dwell in peace and harmony?" he said.

The six ex-rebels signified that they would do these things, and once more they were bona fide citizens of the United States—all but Craddock, who crossed his fingers behind his back. Later, when he was old enough, and the world safe enough, Craddock would maintain that he was still a rebel and would die one—a dash of theatrics that would help make him a U.S. senator in the Hayes administration.

"Citizens," said the Colonel, "you have once more pledged your loyalty to the national government, and it damned well better take this time. You would be on your way to the city jail in Memphis right now were it not for Mister Henry Wooster here, who seemed to think you were worth saving. Do not forget that, nor what you owe him."

"Good," whispered Stribling, and Gawain, too, was glad. Though he hardly knew the correspondent, Gawain, who always wanted to believe the best of everybody, did not want to think badly of the man. So, Gawain thought, perhaps they were going to get out of here after all. Yet Gawain understood that the absurd and unexpected melodrama of his homecoming was not over. Gault was still alive—the yankees might get him now, but they might not, and in that case, Gawain would still owe Judge Rhea a life. Also, there was the matter of L. W. Thomas. Gawain did not know him well either, but Thomas had joined the circle of those with whom Gawain had known fear, and that called for loyalty, no matter what the man had done.

"Now get out of here," said the Colonel. "And do not let me hear from you again, unless you intend to be at the tavern at sundown."

"Sir," said Stribling, "what about Thomas there?"

"That doesn't concern you, sir," said the Colonel.

"Yes, it does, sir," said Stribling.

"Who are you, anyway," asked the Colonel.

"That is Harry Stribling," said Wooster. "The one I told you about."

The Colonel looked closely at Stribling. "Yes, I have heard all about your adventure at the tavern, how you assaulted a sworn officer of the law and so on. As it turns out, the man Luker has been invited to visit his relatives in Arkansas—permanently—and your beloved county is without a sheriff." He turned to the table and took up the star-and-crescent badge and flipped it in his palm.

"Ben Luker never was our sheriff," said Peck. "Julian Bomar was *our* sheriff."

"But he was captured at Nashville," said Gawain. "Brentwood, actually—on the retreat."

"He ain't home yet?" asked Bloodworth.

"No," said Nobles. "I saw Miss Rose the other day, though—she said she had a letter from him posted at Cairo. He was—"

"Never mind," said the Colonel. "Until your Mister Bomar arrives, who will be sheriff?"

"I nominate Harry," said Gawain. "After all, he run the other one off."

"Now just a damn minute," protested Stribling, adding that he was not a registered voter in this state.

"*Nobody* is registered in this state," said Bloodworth. "I second."

Harry Stribling became the sheriff of Cumberland County by the unanimous vote of a citizen's committee appointed by the military governor. The Colonel pinned the badge on Stribling's butternut frock coat. "Now then," said the Colonel, "since you are concerned with this man's welfare, I will let you decide. What about it, sir? Should I let him go with the rest?"

"Let him go," said Gawain, so quickly he surprised himself. The Colonel glared at him.

"I think Harper speaks for us all," said the new sheriff.

"Very well," said the Colonel. He turned to Thomas. "Stand up, sir," he said.

Professor Brown helped Thomas to his feet. Thomas watched them all suspiciously. "What?" he said.

The Colonel approached and crossed his arms. "The other day," he said, "you made me admit that I hated the rebels most when they believed we'd lost. Do you believe we lost, Thomas?"

"No," said the other, "I never did. Fact is, it never made much difference to me either way."

The Colonel shook his head. "Raise your right hand," he said, then pointed to the professor. "You, too, while we're at it."

The provost administered the oath again, embellishing it this time to include the national flag and Almighty God. "Very well," said the Colonel, turning to Stribling again. "I remand this citizen to your custody. Get him out of here. You will find the surgeon set up across the hall; maybe he can stop Mister Thomas from leaking. Now go."

"Sir," said Gawain. "Can I have my pistol back? It belonged to my daddy."

The Colonel shook his head. "It belongs to Town Creek now, along with the Henry rifle. Don't push it. Go."

When the Southerners were gone, and Wooster with them, Lieutenant von Arnim lowered himself onto the settee. His face was long, and his hands busy with themselves. Burduck pulled on his coat again, and buckled his sword belt, his eye on the provost. "Rolf," he said at last.

The Lieutenant looked up in surprise at the sound of his first name. "Sir?"

"Perhaps all that business didn't come out as you'd expected," said the Colonel. He crossed to the chair and put his hand on the Lieutenant's shoulder. "You mustn't think your work was wasted," said the Colonel. "You did all right. I suppose it had to come out that way, else—"

"Oh, it ain't that, sir," said von Arnim, waving his hand. "I am glad to be shut of them with so little trouble."

"What, then? Are you afraid they will recant, go back to their foolish notions?"

"No, sir," said von Arnim. "They are too smart for that." He got to his feet then, walked to the window, walked back to the chair. He did not sit down, but began to rock the chair back and forth on its legs. "Five men left camp with Lieutenant Stanfield, chasing that Gault fellow." He turned to the Colonel. "Where do you suppose they are?" he asked.

◆   ◆   ◆

THEY WERE ALL dead now, dragged into the tall grass by the side of the southerly road. Their beards were matted with blood, their hands closed into fists, eyes turned to the greening leaves where already the crows were gathering, and the greater birds that would have them soon. They did not hear the men in the road, the talk and the cursing fueled by bad whiskey, the snorts and bickering of horses who did not know one another, nor the laughter that passed down the column when one man, drunk and reeling, was unseated by his gray mule. The troopers did not see King Solomon Gault sitting the dead officer's horse, but Solomon Gault saw them. Somewhere in Solomon Gault's mind, the troopers were still alive—not as enemy, not even as men, but as an idea diffused over the faces of the mounted rabble in the road. In this moment, Solomon Gault loved himself, loved the amazing thing he had created, and the dead men rose up to that love and gave it substance. Solomon Gault looked down the raffish, disordered column and saw only the idea of the dead in column-of-fours: bright young faces, dusty uniforms, oiled carbines, sabers strapped to every saddle, musicians with the bells of their bugles pressed against their chests, and above all the silken colors floating, and the guidons in red and white. Gray horses, their heads tossing against the martingales. A section of lancers, weapons erect, a bristling copse pennoned with yellow silk. His wife walked over the sweet grass, smiling though her cheeks shone with tears in the sunlight. She put out her small hand, touched his leg. Her hair was pinned up; a butterfly perched on her shoulder, opening and closing its wings. *You shouldn't be here,* he said, and found his own voice catching, his eyes blurring. He shook it away. *You shouldn't be here, Milly.* She pressed her cheek to his leg, then pulled away, looked up at him. *I will wait for you,* she said. *I will be where it is safe, waiting.* Then she was gone across the grass.

Perhaps the dead men lying in the grass saw her as she passed on her way. Perhaps she stopped, spoke a kind word to them before the green leaves drew her up. Solomon Gault, unashamed, wiped his eyes on his coat sleeve—the gray frock coat he had been saving for this day, with the tarnished gilt bars on the collar. He touched his leg, believed he could feel the burning of her cheek there. Of a sudden, Solomon Gault was consumed with love, with joy. He heard music falling from the sky, beating against his heart. One last time he looked down the eager column, then pulled his horse around. He raised his hand. "Forward!" he said, and touched the horse with his spurs. In a few moments the road was empty, and the birds descending.

✦　✦　✦

WHEN GAWAIN HARPER was free, his first thought was for the sinks. Peck had the same thought, and together they inquired. The sinks were, in fact, the old privy, a commodious three-holer south of the house. They stood together in the evil-smelling gloom, wasps buzzing around their heads, Gawain watching for spiders.

"I always have to piss when I'm nervous," said Peck.

"Me, too," said Gawain. "I can't believe we got off so easy."

Peck leaned on his crutch and buttoned his fly. "Can I ask you somethin?"

"Surely."

"Do you think I can stop feelin like such an ass-hole now?"

Gawain laughed. "I believe you can," he said, and together they walked out into the sunlight.

The first person Gawain saw when he reached the front yard was Morgan Rhea. Aunt Vassar was with her, and Stribling was talking with them both, but Gawain saw only Morgan. She seemed to occupy a space to herself, illuminated by a strange and wavering light as if she had just emerged from the flame of a candle.

"That is your lady?" said Peck as the two men paused in the yard.

"Yes," said Gawain, aware of the foolish grin on his face and not caring. "We are betrothed."

"I danced with her once," said Peck.

Gawain looked at his companion. "Did you?"

"Oh, yes," said Peck. He smiled. "At a barbecue down at John Walker's on the Fourth of July. You were there."

"Ah," said Gawain, his face reddening at the memory. "I think I do recall that afternoon."

"That was a long time ago," said Peck.

Gawain thought that it was, indeed, a long time ago. "No doubt you will dance with her again," he said.

"You reckon?" said Peck, grinning.

At that moment, Morgan turned her head and saw them. Later, Gawain would remember that she called his name.

✦   ✦   ✦

IN THE RUINS of the courthouse, among the ashes and charred timbers, among the blackened deed books and remnants of furniture, sat the old bell. It was cast in Massachusetts in 1840, sent down by ship to New Orleans, then upriver by steamboat to the mouth of the Yazoo. From there it made its way on smaller boats to Wyatt's Landing on the Tallahatchie, thence by the muddy roads to Cumberland. For twenty-four years, it rang the hours in the cupola of the courthouse, signaling quitting time and dinnertime, ringing of fires and death and Easter morn and New Year's. When the courthouse was burned, and the flames reached the cupola, the bell dropped two stories straight down into the fire, landing upside down with a final clang that was heard by no one. Now it squatted in the ashes, its temper ruined, waiting to be hauled away. It was half full of water that, unaccountably, swarmed with minnows; children marveled at their silver flashes as they rose for air.

Had the courthouse not been burned, and the bell still hanging, it would have struck ten o'clock just as Solomon Gault and his men topped the rise at Walker's place and put their horses into a gallop.

· XXII ·

She called his name, then ran to him holding her hat, the shape of her legs in the folds of her green dress and her free hand outstretched. It was the first thing he touched, her hand; he seized it in his own, then grasped her as if they were dancing, and spun her around, and almost knocked Marcus Peck off his crutch.

"Sorry! Sorry!" cried Gawain, laughing, and she kissed him then, in broad daylight, still holding on to her hat. Then she pushed away, and brushed the hair out of her eyes, and put her hands on her hips.

"What do you mean doin that?" she said. "You are too bold, Gawain Harper!"

But he grasped her again, and when she turned her face away, he kissed her cheekbone, and then she wasn't turning away. After a moment, she leaned back and looked at him, her face gone scarlet. "My!" she said. Soldiers in the yard watched in astonishment, having gone a long while—some of them all their lives—without such a display. A few of them coughed vigorously, which made Gawain laugh.

"It's all right, boys," announced Peck. "They're betrothed."

"*Are* we, now," said Morgan, pushing away again. "Since when?"

Gawain scratched his head. "Well, you said back at Carter's . . . didn't you say—"

"Oh, *that*! Well, that was under duress. No, first you have to ask Papa, then you have to ask me."

"Well, I already as much as asked your papa—"

"No, you have to wear your best coat—"

"I *was* wearin my best coat!"

"—and arrive by carriage, and present your card, and—"

"Why, Morgan Rhea," said Gawain. "You are actin just like a woman—imagine that!"

From her place by the front gallery, Aunt Vassar watched the reunion.

"Shameless behavior," she said, smiling. "Have you ever been married, Captain Stribling?"

"Oh, no, ma'am," said Stribling. "I can hardly bring myself to utter the word."

"Why, sir, the institution has much to recommend it!" said Aunt Vassar. She went on talking, and Stribling smiled and nodded, but he wasn't listening now. He was watching the twelve-pounder, the gun crew rummaging through their limber chest, one man walking away toward the creek with the sponge bucket. *Load,* thought Stribling. *Canister.* He cocked his head, listening. He pulled his watch and opened the case. Nine fifty-five. He snapped it shut, and at that moment saw Old Hundred-and-Eleven arguing with a soldier by the road. Behind the old man, his arms pressed to his sides, stiff as a ramrod, Molochi Fish stood blinking in the sunlight.

"Ma'am, you must excuse me," said Stribling, touching Aunt Vassar's arm. He left her by the gallery then. He was walking, still watching the gun, still listening. When he came to the limber chest, the gunners looked up. The sergeant of the crew, a lean man in muttonchop whiskers and shirtsleeves and a floppy bummer's cap, started to speak, but Stribling held up his hand. "Load," Stribling said softly. "Canister."

The sergeant nodded, his eyes on Stribling's face. "Go tell Tom to hurry up with that bucket," the sergeant said to a comrade. "Gabriel, you take the rammer. Load canister." As the gun crew began to move, Stribling went on toward Old Hundred-and-Eleven and Molochi Fish. He had removed the sheriff's badge and slipped it in his pocket; he withdrew it now and pinned it on.

"I told ye," the soldier was saying. "Cap'n Bloom is down with the pickets, and you ain't goin no goddamned place, so be quiet."

"Turkestan!" shouted Old Hundred-and-Eleven. "The Sanhedrin!" Then he saw Stribling. "Ha! Mister Stribling! Come over here straightway!"

"What's the trouble here?" asked Stribling, in his former Captain's, now sheriff's, voice.

While Stribling discussed the situation with the guard, and Old Hundred-and-Eleven capered about waving his Bible, Craddock and Bloodworth were fabricating lies. They stood with their backs to the Shipwright yard; before them was a thick privet hedge, and beyond that, Brummett's livery.

"We will say we were fishin yesterday," said Craddock, "and the yankees—"

"Aw, I ain't been fishin since I was ten years old," said Bloodworth. "Amy Lou will never buy that horse."

"Well, what, then?"

Bloodworth thought a moment. "Well, we can say we were at Mister Boswell's—framin up his house. He'll stand by us, long as Miss Emily don't catch wind of it. Then—"

"Then, they gave us supper, and—"

"And we were goin to send somebody to say we'd be late, but—"

"The yankees caught us after curfew," said Craddock. "Of course, you *were* opening your front door at the time."

"Still past curfew," said Bloodworth. "It was all a big misunderstanding."

"Will she buy that?"

"No," said Bloodworth.

"Nor Carrie. God save us—we may have to tell the truth."

"Let us walk that way and ponder awhile," said Bloodworth.

The former dining room of the Shipwright house was now the province of the Federal surgeon, Dr. J. J. Hammond of St. Paul, Minnesota. The doctor was a large man, florid of face, with a great beard that made him appear to be standing behind a bush. In spite of three years' campaigning in the South, Dr. Hammond had never adapted to the climate; his clothes were always wringing wet, and he fanned himself constantly with a great palmetto fan. He was fanning now as he regarded the shirtless L. W. Thomas, who was slumped on the former dining room table. Brown and Nobles stood by.

"Sit up straight," said the doctor, scowling. He grasped Thomas' chin, turned his face this way and that, worked the joints of his arms, pressed an ear to his chest, pulled down his eyelids and peered within. "What the hell's the matter with you?" he said at last.

"The wound, sir," prompted Professor Brown. "He is shot through and through."

"Oh, yes," said the doctor. He bent down and scrutinized Thomas' gunshot wound. When he poked his finger into the hole, Thomas howled. "You call that a wound?" said the doctor, unmoved. "Nothing to it."

"It hurts all the time," protested Thomas, "and it won't stop running."

"I can see that," said the surgeon. "Laudable pus, nothing more. We'll cauterize. Terence?" A hospital orderly stepped forward. "Where is the ramrod?" asked the doctor.

"Now, hold on a minute—," began Thomas.

"You won't feel a thing," said the doctor, fanning vigorously. "We have plenty of ether— Terence, ain't we got ether? Yes, of course." He pushed against Thomas' chest. "Now lie down, be comfortable—won't take but a minute."

✦   ✦   ✦

IT WAS GLORY, it was movement and madness, headlong rushing. At the trot. At the gallop. They came over the rise, the road unreeling, and found a body of infantry standing in the road. The officer's face turned toward them, he drew his sword, his mouth opened to shape the order, and the men began a left wheel, pivoting on the road. The big gelding, his tail streaming behind, moved heavily between Gault's legs. The saber came out with a ring; in his other hand, with the reins, Gault clutched the carbine. But he didn't need the reins—the horse knew how to do this. "Sabers!" Gault cried, and knew he heard the terrible clang and rattle of eighty drawn blades, and knew they glinted in the air like the teeth of a terrible machine. "Bugler, the charge!" he cried then, and the clear notes rang out in the sunlight over the pounding, over the breathing of horses and the cheers of his men. It is only a moment passed now, an instant, but the horse seems to float through time.

Solomon Gault would strike them in column; the irresistible weight of eighty horses at full gallop would crush the infantry and carry the riders on to the Shipwright house, then a quick wheel into line and another charge into the shambles. The men in the road were firing now, but they couldn't sustain a volley. Too late for them, too late, Gault thought, as the balls hummed past. Then he brought the saber down hard, like a ribbon of silver fire arcing.

✦   ✦   ✦

"LET US FETCH Aunt Vassar and Stribling," said Gawain. "Let us go to our house, and I will brush my coat and slick my hair, then you and I will walk in the garden, and I will ask you, and you will be satisfied, praise God."

"Yonder is Captain Stribling," said Morgan. "And look—it's Old Hundred-and-Eleven. And who is that other strange fellow?"

"Declare," said Gawain. "It is Molochi Fish!"

They were crossing the yard, Morgan lifting her skirts from the mud, Gawain already shaping in his mind the words he would only get to say once, so he better have them right. A little cat had come from somewhere and was parading before them, tail in the air. Suddenly, the cat darted away, vanished as cats will do, and Gawain saw men running and at the same time heard the firing down the road. But his mind refused the implications, accepted only the weight of Morgan's arm on his own, the sound of her laughing at the cat, their steady progress across the yard toward Stribling. But Stribling was moving too, shouting at them, running for

Aunt Vassar where she stood by the gallery. Then Gawain saw the gun, saw all at once the crew in position, the rammer straight up, the lanyard taut, the gunner with his hand in the air—

"Aw, shit!" he cried, and the gun bellowed and leapt back on its trail, and the air was filled with humming and a great wind.

✦ ✦ ✦

GAULT SAW THE gun and drew back on the reins just enough so that the column flowed around him. He was two files deep in the column now, eight or ten riders ahead of him, their horses' hooves throwing great clods of mud, and those eager ones were the first of Gault's men to die. The canister raked them, horses reared or tumbled headlong, men were riven, sliced, transformed. A severed arm struck Gault in the chest, balanced an instant on the pommel, then fell away. Gault was flecked with blood, with bits of flesh and bone; his horse leapt over the fallen, and in an instant, he was among the gunners.

✦ ✦ ✦

WHEN THE TWELVE-POUNDER discharged, Morgan screamed and leapt into the air. Then she was running, bent low, Gawain's arm around her waist. She fell, lost her hat, tasted mud, then up again, Gawain pulling her now, the house floating in a little circle of light as if she were seeing it through the wrong end of a spyglass. *Get in the house,* Gawain yelled into her ear, and pulled her stumbling toward the front steps. They were almost there when Morgan saw Aunt Vassar standing calmly by the gallery, her pocket pistol in one hand, prayer book in the other, the smoke from the gun drifting over her. At the sight of the old woman, Morgan felt the fear rise out of her like a departing spirit, and in its place a rarefied anger of a kind she'd never known before—not hot, as she had thought all anger to be, but clear and pure like cold spring water. She stopped then, pulled away from Gawain, her vision opening until she saw with perfect clarity the house, the running men, the sun going dark with smoke. Then she felt the horses, the pounding of them jarring in her legs, and would have turned but Gawain was pushing her now. *Get Aunt Vassar!* he shouted. *Get in the house!* She fought him, not to turn back but to make him look at her. She took his face hard in her hands and shouted into it: *Gault! It's Gault! You can't stop him, you can't—*

Gawain almost smiled. He took her hands away and kissed her once, hard on the mouth, then spun her around and shoved her toward the house. *Get Aunt Vassar!* he said, and was gone.

At the first rattle of musketry, old soldiers Craddock and Bloodworth turned their faces to the south. When the gun went off, they dove headfirst into the privet hedge and burrowed into the leaves and mulch, then reached back for their cartridge boxes. But they had no cartridge boxes, nor any musket nor bayonet, and they looked at their empty hands in wonder. Then they parted the hedge and saw the horsemen. *Goddamn, it must be Gault,* said Bloodworth.

Well, it ain't Joe Wheeler, said Craddock. *Still, it's a gallant charge for peckerwoods. What'll we do?*

Stuart Bloodworth, who hated all armies, who wanted only to be home with his young wife, who had sworn never to touch another firearm, not even for squirrels—this Stuart Bloodworth, who wrote poems after Milton and read Virgil in the original Latin, nevertheless owned a temper that came at times unbidden, and it was coming now, and he embraced it, breathed deep of it like he would the smell of his wife in the dark night when the dreams woke him. The madness pierced him like a lance, and he cried out at these men who would crumble everything and dare wake the demons again, and all for nothing. *Goddamn the sons of bitches,* he cried. *Let's catch one when they come by!*

Dr. Hammond was just soaking a cloth in ether when the fight broke out. At the gun's report, which rattled all the windows in the house, he paused, looked up, then clapped the pad into a covered jar. *Clear the table!* he cried. *Terence!*

L. W. Thomas was happy to rise from the dining room table. He was rallying, the sickness gone, his mind clear of fever enough to remember that he was free, that Burduck wasn't going to hang him after all. Through the front window, he saw the horsemen pounding through the yard, saw their mud-colored clothes and sorry mounts, saw Gault himself in his gray frock coat, swinging a saber from the back of a galloping horse. Thomas remembered telling the Colonel how Gault would come from the south, and sure enough, here he was. Nobles was already out the door, Brown crowding behind. Thomas made to follow when the doctor grabbed his arm. *No, you don't,* he said. *There'll be hurt men. You must fetch em for me.*

Hell, I am hurt my own self, said Thomas. The doctor grabbed him by the front of the shirt. *You ain't hurt. I can heal you,* the doctor snarled. *You get out there and take up the wounded. Get somebody to help you. Do like I say!*

In the hall, Brown and Nobles collided with Colonel Burduck and Lieutenant von Arnim. Burduck shoved them aside and was out on the porch, his eyes moving over the yard. He saw the gun and the dead men around it, saw horses bucking and wheeling in the mud, their riders shooting into the crowd. An old woman stood by the gallery, her arm out-stretched, a little pocket pistol in her hand. She fired once, and a horseman pitched backward over his mount. Another woman stood beside her, all in green, pointing out targets: *There. That one. That one there!* Now Bloom was to the south; they must have come on him before he was ready. He would be moving in now. Can't shoot until he closes, though. Where was Gault?

Burduck's mind was empty of all but the immediate present. He gave no thought to the way this debacle would appear to General Washburn in Memphis, nor to its repercussions in the faraway halls of Congress. The philosophies of government, ratifications of peace, human slavery, his own mistakes, the day and month and year—nothing of that mattered now. Only the violation taking place before him mattered, and how he might erase it from the earth. Rally the troops then, and find Gault, and kill him.

So when Gault actually appeared for an instant in the swirling smoke, Burduck raised his pistol and took careful aim. Somewhere in his mind lay a burden of shame, of gullibility, and with it the image of Gault in the shadows of Sunday afternoon: his calm arrogance, his certitude, his impli-cations of kinship. In time Colonel Burduck would recall these things and wrestle with them. But not now. For now, there was only the face grinning in recognition, the saber lifted in salute, the flash and report of the pistol—and the empty space where Gault had been. Burduck felt the wrenching irritation of a missed shot, but he was not surprised. He had known the instant he'd pulled trigger that the Ockham's razor of armed combat would not apply to a man like Gault.

Another gun went off, rattling the windows, then another—the guns by the magazine, Burduck thought. Soldiers in the yard firing, loading, firing. Horses screaming. Chunks flying from the porch posts. A man ran by, brushing his elbow: it was Thomas, half naked, galloping down the steps. What the hell was *he* doing?

Lieutenant von Arnim had his sword and pistol out. *Colonel*—he began, and stopped. Burduck heard the ball strike flesh, then the hard slap as it buried itself in the weatherboards of the house. Von Arnim stumbled back-ward, looking down in astonishment at the hole in his frock coat. Burduck caught the provost before he fell, and eased him down to the porch. Von Arnim wore the expression of a man who had just suffered an insult unde-served. *Rolf. Goddammit Rolf—*, said the Colonel. *The very idea,* said Lieutenant von Arnim. *And after all this way—* Then he was gone.

Burduck went down into the yard then. The old woman fired past his ear, and the younger one cried *Colonel!* but before she could go on, the man Stribling came on the run and swept both women up and pulled them into the house past where von Arnim lay. Burduck looked around the yard. Lieutenant Osgood was there, firing his pistol, and Burduck jabbed a finger at him. *Rally these men!* Burduck shouted, waving his hand at the riflemen in the yard. *Form up on the guns!* Then a horse rearing, and Burduck seized the rider, pulled him off, planted the heel of his boot squarely in the man's face. He turned then to see Carl Nobles with an infantryman's musket, saw Nobles raise it, saw the muzzle swing into his face and the foreshortened barrel. Burduck did not hear the discharge but felt the sting of powder, and something struck him hard from behind. Burduck turned again and caught the body as it slumped against him, saw the flash of the knife falling, smelled the stink of whiskey and sweat, and the blood that swelled from the black O in the man's forehead. *Sorry Colonel,* said Nobles, drawing his ramrod, *that was mighty close work.* Burduck nodded, then turned again, sweeping the yard with his eyes: no Gault, no Solomon Gault. But there was Thomas, and for the first time that day, Colonel Burduck felt a nudge of satisfaction.

You! cried Thomas, and grabbed Old Hundred-and-Eleven with one hand and Molochi Fish with the other. *Help me get these men!* The smoke rolled over them, the air humming with balls, hissing with shot. A riderless horse, stirrup irons flapping, nearly ran them over. Molochi Fish had seen the woman, the one like the stone figure from the graveyard, and the old one from Harper's. Molochi wished it were night, even with his mother yowling outside and the gray smoke of the dogs moving in the trees. Nevertheless, he followed the man from the tavern, moving stiffly, his mouth opening and closing for breath. Suddenly, at his feet, a red-bearded man with plaited hair. *Jesus,* the man said. *Jesus Jesus Jesus.* He was torn across the breast, like Molochi's mother was torn by the machinery. Molochi Fish bent stiffly and lifted the man by the shoulders and began to drag him after the others.

Carl Nobles had made Brown go back to the surgeon, and now he was falling in with the troops at the magazine—the balance of Captain Bloom's company and six dismounted cavalrymen from the headquarters guard. Lieutenant Osgood, his sword in his hand, was shouting, bullying them into line. Nobles stood with the Enfield at shoulder arms, in the accoutrements he had taken from a dead Federal soldier in the yard, feeling the old, familiar press of the men to either side as they dressed ranks. The man to his right, sighting down the line, looked at Nobles curiously. Nobles, in his short gray jacket and slouch hat, his accoutrements, his musket, awoke in the soldier unpleasant memories. *Shouldn't you be across the way?* asked the soldier. *Prob'ly,* replied Nobles. *Where'd you come from, any-*

how? the soldier asked then. Nobles grinned at the man. *The Army of Northern Virginia,* he said. *How 'bout you?*

In his years with the army, Henry Clyde Wooster had learned to load a musket. He was loading one now, while Marcus Peck lay prone, firing around the corner of the house. *Hurry up!* cried Peck. *It's a goddamned turkey shoot!*

I can only go so fast! replied Wooster, ramming a charge down the muzzle. Beside him lay the cap box and cartridge box he had snatched from a stack of muskets. Wooster was intent on his work, but in his mind lay a calm center, and there he was busy collecting images. The yard full of horses. The women by the gallery. The yankee rifleman who chewed tobacco. Craddock and Bloodworth emerging from the privet hedge, raising the old cry that used to scare him so. Nobles among the yankees. The man Gault—it must have been he—in the gray coat, whirling, swinging his saber, then vanished as if he had never been at all. The indifferent trees moving in the light breeze, and a redbird flashing overhead, the pinions of his wings stretched out, each one clear and defined against the sweet blue, cloudless sky. The correspondent passed the loaded musket to Peck and took the empty one and fumbled for a cartridge. *Hot damn, it's the judgment day!* shouted Peck in his joy.

Hit's jedgment day! cried Old Hundred-and-Eleven, pawing at the collar of a Federal soldier. *That one's dead,* said Thomas. *Find you another one!* The old man felt the snick of a ball cut his cheek. He put his hand there and brought it away bloody. *Heliotrope!* he bellowed. *Gault, damn you to the fires of perdition, amen!* Then he saw von Arnim lying on the porch.

Molochi Fish, returning from the Shipwright house where he had left the red-bearded man, walked stiffly to another. This man was lying on his back, eyes open. He had been shot in the side, and the ball had passed through his lungs, and when he breathed, a red bubble popped at his lips. Molochi looked at his face and felt the fragile brush of memory, as if just beyond this moment lay another, a different one, hazy with the smoke of woods fires, where the breeze rattled in leaves gone dry as beetle hulls and men rode up from the treeline, their horses raising little puffs in the dust. Molochi heard the man say *Well, it's ripe, but Gah damn if it ain't dry as a corn shuck* though the man's mouth didn't move except to open and close like Molochi's own, popping the little bubble of blood. Molochi heard the man's voice again *Gah damn if it ain't dry* and for a moment thought he was talking about that other day. But no, there was something else, elusive, swirling inside the red bubble. Then he remembered the squaw woman last night, watching him from down the hill, and Wall Stutts' bones gnawed by the dogs, and the great birds. Molochi knew the man then. The man watched as Molochi sat down beside him in the mud and drew his knife.

Had the guns at the magazine been trained a little further to the right, they might have spread Bloodworth's and Craddock's brains across the landscape. As it happened, the two emerged from the hedge just in time to be deafened by the muzzle blast, and to find themselves in a mad shambles of horses and men. Now Bloodworth had a specimen of his own: a big, slit-eyed, mean-looking man whom they had pulled from his horse while he was reloading. Bloodworth drove his fist again and again into the man's face until Craddock stopped him. *Whoa,* shouted Craddock. *Ease up boy. You liable to break your hand on that son bitch!* Craddock was holding a pistol that he had taken from another fallen raider and emptied into the general melee. Bloodworth rose and looked at his bloody hands, and at the man who lay at his feet. *Goddamn you Bill Huff!* he cried, and cursed him for raising the demons again, and kicked him one last time, and was satisfied.

Inside the house, Stribling sat the women down on the horsehair settee in Burduck's office. *You set there now and don't you move and don't give me no argument,* he said.

Captain Stribling, you are such a handsome man, said Aunt Vassar, fanning herself, the pistol lying in her lap.

Find Gawain, said Morgan. *You can do that for me.*

Yes, said Stribling. Then he was on the porch again, and found Old Hundred-and-Eleven, his shirt wet with blood, kneeling beside the provost. Stribling knelt too, and began to unbutton the officer's coat, but the old man stopped his hand. *Ain't any use in that,* said Old Hundred-and-Eleven. Thomas came out of the house, swabbing his body with a bloody rag. *Is he dead?* asked Thomas. Stribling nodded, and closed the man's eyes. *He was all right,* said Thomas. *He was all right,* agreed Old Hundred-and-Eleven, and followed Thomas back into the yard.

Stribling had to go all the way around the house before he found Gawain Harper leaning against a porch post, his legs stretched out in front of him. Across his lap lay a double-barreled shotgun. The rosary was around his neck. At the bottom of the steps lay a barefooted man in a jeans sack coat, his breeches tied with a length of twine. The man had been badly used by the shotgun and was dead, though his right foot still twitched in the mud.

Are you all right, boy? asked Stribling. *Are you hurt?*

Gawain looked at him with dull eyes, as if he had just awakened. *No, I ain't hurt,* he said. He lifted his hand toward the dead man. *I tried to get him to surrender, but he wouldn't.*

Stribling sat down on the steps, rubbed his face. *They won't surrender,* he said. Then he shook Gawain's knee. *Have you seen Gault?*

I swear to God, that's the last one, said Gawain, looking at the dead man. *I swear it to Almighty God.*

Stribling shook him again. *Listen—have you seen Gault?*

I do not give a goddamn about Gault, said Gawain. He sat up then and wrapped his hand in Stribling's shirtfront. *Where is Morgan? Don't be tellin me she is still out there.* He loosed his hand from Stribling's shirt and pressed the palm to his temple. *Dammit, I should not of left her.*

She is safe, and your aunt, too, said Stribling. *I seen to it. Now answer my question.*

For reply, Gawain rose to his knees and took the shotgun by its muzzle. He was about to fling it into the yard when Stribling stopped him. *Not yet,* said Stribling. *Keep it just a while longer.* Then he plucked the sheriff's badge from his coat and pressed it into Gawain's hand. *You want to throw somethin, throw this.*

Gawain smiled then. He cocked his arm and threw the badge toward the creek; they watched it sail in a silver arc and disappear among the trees. Stribling got up and pulled Gawain to his feet. *We got to find him,* he said.

Who? asked Gawain.

✦　　✦　　✦

THOUGH THE CHARGE was heavy, its momentum was quickly spent. Gault's planned movement from column into line, especially under fire, was impossible for men accustomed to the simple tactics of guerrilla raiders. In any event, the guns by the magazine and, after a moment, the volleys of the infantry formed there, broke up the head of the column and turned it back into the yard, and Solomon Gault lost even the illusion of control. Moreover, Captain Bloom's men were moving up from the south in open order, firing at will, choosing their targets with good effect.

Across the road, in a little clump of cedars, Solomon Gault sat his horse coolly. He had long since sheathed the saber, and now he noticed the carbine in his hand. He was curious as to how it came to be there. Certainly he had not fired it, he would remember that. Well, he ought to make some use of it. Too late for the business here, but there was something else just as urgent, something else to be taken care of.

Gault steadied his horse and watched the fight across the road. He was removed from the scene, nothing more than a spectator now, calm and fair in his judgment, nodding his head as if everything was happening just as he'd expected. *You cannot*—he told himself, shaping the thought carefully, *you cannot hope to defeat a great evil with a lesser. The instruments of liberty must be tuned to a higher purpose, must be driven by the hope, not of gain, but of sacrifice.* That was as far as he could go at the moment; he repeated the phrase to get it firm in his mind, thinking it would do to open the epilogue of his memoirs.

A stray round clipped through the cedars, and Gault looked up, irritated. He was tired of the spectacle in the yard, and anyway, it was nearly over. Men were surrendering, throwing their weapons down, raising their hands. Others were fleeing south, hoping to break through the line. Some did, others did not. *Peckerwoods,* thought Gault. *Goddamned yellowhammer trash.* The sight of them filled Gault with disgust, and he cursed again the fate that put him always at the head of such men. You could not sublimate the rabble nor lift them to any plane higher than the urges of their own glands. Well, he was done with them.

Clearly, it was time to go. There was much work to be done if this morning's events were to take their logical place in the design. As an experiment, the attack was a failure; however, it had borne fruit in unexpected ways. The enemy was off-balance. Certainly they were off-balance. *Power, if it is to be useful, must lie in the balance of force and reason. Should the scales be tipped either way, a weakening of morality and will must inevitably—*

A handful of Federal cavalry came around the corner of the Shipwright house and galloped after the fugitives; no doubt they would find . . . Gault blinked, tilted his head. They would find something—what was it? The bridge, of course, and the shadows moving in the road, the smell of dust warm at nooning. There is the river, there the green banks where the wild sweet William grows. No, nothing left to find but silence. Solomon Gault was finished here, finished and done with all of them.

Yet something remained. A gesture. A loose end. Then it came to him. Solomon Gault smiled and shook his head like a man remembering where he left his pocketbook. Of course, of course. He looked once more at the shambles in the yard and pitied the fools who had thought themselves worthy. Then he turned the horse and rode out of the cedars toward town.

· XXIII ·

Solomon Gault was careful to avoid the square where a crowd had gathered, all hats and walking sticks and umbrellas, all abuzz with talk, all careful to stay clear of the southerly road in case a stray ball came traveling up that way. Gault was not surprised to see the citizens; he knew the smell of blood would draw them like jackals, though they would not venture far while there was any danger. For a moment he thought he might ride out among them, see if there were any old soldiers he could appeal to. He could imagine them growing silent and turning their faces toward him, could hear his own voice shaping for the last time the deliverance, the sacrifice, the cause he represented. But that was as far as his vision would carry him now. It ended with the image of their mute faces turned upward in the sunlight, believing in the light, ignorant of the dark that was falling.

Gault spat the powder taste from his mouth and turned his back on the square. He pushed the horse through a ragged jumble of tents and shanties and found a group of women with their hands wrapped in their aprons, half-naked whelps clinging to their legs. Negroes stood among them, silent, watching toward the south. The negroes looked away as Gault passed. One of the women spoke a question, but Gault ignored her. In a moment, he was on the road that led to Holy Cross church, and here he met the new priest. The man was hurrying along, holding the skirts of his cassock out of the mud, his face glowing with an earnestness that Gault found absurd. "You're too late, Father," he said, pulling the horse crossway in the road. The priest stopped short and looked at him, blinking in the bright sun.

"Too late?"

"For martyrdom, I mean," said Gault. "It's all right, though. There's plenty about to cross over—maybe they'll let you hold their hands."

"Sir, let me pass," said the priest, his pale cheeks coloring.

"Sure," said Gault. "I need your help first, though. You know Judge Nathan Rhea?"

"I . . . yes, I know him. I just saw him, in fact."

"And where was that, Father?"

"Well, it was in Mister Carter's yard. He—"

"Thank you, sir," said Gault, and backed the horse out of the road so the priest could pass. The man hurried on without looking back. "Come up," said Gault to the horse, and pricked him with his spurs.

◆　　◆　　◆

AT THE SHIPWRIGHT house, Gawain found Morgan and Aunt Vassar in the dining room with the wounded. The women's faces were shiny with sweat as they moved among the men with a bucket of water and a dented tin dipper. Thomas told him later that the two women had volunteered to tear up their petticoats for bandages in the old Confederate way, but the surgeon assured them, with ponderous courtesy, that the Federal army was well supplied with bandages, and they could better serve by providing refreshment.

"I never thought I'd live to see the day," said Aunt Vassar. "Bringin water to the yankees, my God. Next thing, I'll be servin tea to the nigrahs. Morgan, honey, you go outside with Nephew and take the air—I'll linger among these handsome lads. Maybe one'll want me to write a letter for him after while."

"And maybe the surgeon has some laudanum," said Gawain when he and Morgan were in the hall. He shook his head. "My beloved aunt."

"Don't fault your good aunt," said Morgan.

"Never," Gawain said. "She has lived with my daddy all these years without killin him—she may have all the relief God can provide."

"Do you suppose it was God provided laudanum?" she asked.

"That is an excellent question," said Gawain. "I'll ask Harry, next time we are havin a discussion, and let you know."

They were about to pass through the door when old Mister Shipwright emerged from the parlor in a dressing gown and fez. "Excuse me," said the old man. "Do you have any word? Any word at all?"

"About what, sir?" asked Gawain.

"Ain't you heard?" said the old gentleman. "There has been a great cataclysm! Oh, a very great cataclysm!" He lowered his voice and grasped the sleeve of Gawain's coat. "You know, of course, Mrs. Shipwright has a nervous disposition—she believes it heralds the end of the world."

"Oh, *that*," said Gawain. "You may tell her that the Army of God has prevailed."

"Thank you," said Mister Shipwright, turning to the stairs. "That is exactly what *I* told her, but of course she won't listen!"

They passed through the open front door then. Gawain noticed for the first time that the oval pane of ruby glass was broken out, a mildewed shelter half tacked in its place. On the porch the wounded raiders lay, looking as wounded always did: numb, reeking, disheveled, strangely removed, as though they had crossed an invisible chasm. They waved at flies, picked at their clothes, muttered to themselves. Some groaned and writhed in pain; others, having arranged themselves for death, lay calmly and stared at nothing. Dozens of yellow butterflies danced among them, as if the wounded men were curious flowers opening.

Gawain took Morgan's arm, thinking to lead her past this wreckage, but she stopped him. Brushing Gawain's hand away, she approached the soldier on guard. "What are these poor devils doin here?" she asked. "Who is lookin after em?"

The soldier removed his cap. "The surgeon said they must wait, Miss."

"Blessed God," said Morgan. "Tell me, then—where are the ones who are already dead?"

The soldier pointed to the yard beyond the end of the gallery. Morgan passed down the steps, Gawain following.

✦　✦　✦

YOUNG ALEX RHEA had thought the war over. Now it seemed to have commenced again, and he and Beowulf spent the morning on the front gallery listening to the guns. He was forbidden to go into the yard, so he perched on the balustrade and tried to imagine the scene, as he had done before when there was fighting around Cumberland. His only reference were the engravings in *Harper's Weekly*, which his father had received in the post all the way up through the second year of the war, so he usually thought in terms of long lines of men dressed exactly alike, sweeping forward under little puffs of smoke. Somehow, though, that image did not suit his mind now. Since yesterday, he had gathered in his memory too many faces of men who had been to the places described in the magazine. These were not easily imposed on the faceless swarms in the engravings.

He had asked about his sister and was told that she was at the Harper house, visiting. His father had wanted to go fetch her, but Mother was in a terrible nervous state, so the Judge had shut himself in the room with her. That left only Cousin Carter to talk to, and Alex tried, but the old man thought the boy was Cousin Bushrod again and chastised him for letting the horses get loose, though they hadn't any horses that Alex knew about, except Zeke, who hadn't gone anywhere, and whom he had not yet been permitted to ride as Captain Stribling had promised. So he was sitting with Beowulf on the shady gallery, even after the firing had stopped, hoping he might see some soldiers, when the gentleman rode into the yard.

✦   ✦   ✦

THE DEAD REBELS were laid in a row in the sun, ankles crossed, hands on their breasts, in the way that Gawain knew so well. He estimated twenty-five, then counted thirteen. It did not surprise him: dead men always appeared more numerous than they really were. In fact, he thought, just one of them seemed like a lot. He watched Morgan move along the row, the hem of her dress brushing the muddy bare feet or broken-down brogans. She looked at each of their faces, even lifted the handkerchief that veiled the face of one. When she reached the end, she turned to Gawain. "Solomon Gault is not here," she said.

"I did not suppose he would be," said Gawain.

"No, of course he wouldn't," she said. She crossed her arms on her breast and looked around, as if she might find Gault standing in the yard. "The prisoners?" she said, walking back along the row of dead to the place where Gawain waited.

"They all down by the creek," said Gawain. "Harry and I looked already. He ain't there either."

Gawain put his arms about her and she pressed against him, though her arms were still crossed on her breast. "Where, then?" she said.

"Some of em got away," said Gawain. "Maybe he's gone back in the woods. Maybe he's on his way to Texas right now, or turned into a frog, or—"

"No," she said. She was tense, and Gawain could feel the muscles in her jaw working. He knew by instinct not to pet her, and understood that whatever he might say would only sound stupid. So he held on to her, just that, letting her have her own thoughts. In a moment, she relaxed a little; he could feel her playing with the beads around his neck.

Over the top of her head, Gawain could see the line of dead men, their pinched, twisted faces and motionless hands. He knew many of them: they were men with whom he'd watched the horses run on Wagner's Stretch, or coon hunted with, or bought corn whiskey from. One of them had been a stoker on the cars, another a noted cock fighter. That one yonder—a sleet storm had caught Gawain rabbit hunting once, and that one had taken him in, and his wife had fixed coffee and corn cakes for supper. Now they were dead, for reasons that none of them, perhaps, could have named. But *perhaps* only, Gawain thought, for they might have felt deeply, might have chosen gladly, and maybe dying in this muddy yard was not so bad an end. He wanted to say these things to Morgan, was already thinking how to frame them, when he felt her stiffen in his arms. She pushed away, her eyes suddenly quick with light.

"Papa!" she said.

✦   ✦   ✦

TIME MOVED DOWN its seamless corridor, away from the bruise of morning, and all persons followed as they must. After the fight, L. W. Thomas collapsed in the yard and, in a little while, woke dimly on the surgeon's table. "Ah, there you are," said the doctor, and slapped the ether pad over Thomas' nose. While Terence heated the ramrod, and the surgeon irrigated his wound, Thomas dreamed of fantastic illuminations, of landscapes rising against skies of impossible blue, of maidens dancing. At one point, an enormous flower of fire blossomed, and the sky turned orange and yellow and was filled with birds whose plumage were flames, and who cried in the pain of their burning. Then cool darkness dropped down like a curtain, and Thomas stood with his back to it, bowing, the audience rising and filling the hall with wild applause. Then he passed through, and found quiet streets where lamps flickered in a slick of rain.

Carl Nobles had surrendered his musket and accoutrements and was sitting against the wall of the old Brummett Livery with Marcus Peck and three Federal soldiers. They were watching the artillerymen secure their guns and limbers.

"I wisht them cavalry hadn't burned the Citadel," said one soldier. "I could surely use a cool jolt."

"That von Arnim done it," said another. "He is your pyrotechnic wonder."

"*Was,*" said the third man.

"Come again?"

The soldier, who had been standing near the gallery when the provost was killed, told the story.

"Well, I am sorry to hear it," said the first man. "I knowed him since Jeff Barracks, a long time ago."

They were silent for a moment, saying to themselves all the things it would sound so foolish to say aloud. Then the soldiers began to talk of the other men who had died that morning, raising their comrades' names to light for the last time, rounding out their lives and letting them go to catch up with the long, dusty column of the dead. Nobles and Peck listened, heard the names and marked them; it made no difference that they had no faces to go with them, nor voices, nor memories of brave or foolish or funny things the men had done in life. The names alone would do. Then, as the soldiers' talk moved to other things, Peck tapped Nobles on the leg.

"What you gon' do now, Carl?" he asked.

The other shook his head. "Damned if I know," he said. "Maybe I'll cull out one of these loose horses and go to Mexico."

"What's down there?" asked Peck.

Nobles shrugged. "Freedom, maybe."

"No," said Peck.

"No?"

"Nope," said Marcus Peck. "Either you got it, or you don't." He laughed then, and adjusted the stump of his leg. "If I went to Mexico, I'd have to take a steamboat, so I ain't goin."

"What you gon' do, then?"

Peck thought a moment. "Well, I might see if Thomas needs a partner. We might build a new tavern—a real one—and paint it blue." He looked at Nobles. "You think we might?"

"I wouldn't paint it blue," Nobles said.

While Nobles and Peck argued about the color of the new tavern, Craddock and Bloodworth were walking northward toward the square. They ignored the citizens streaming toward the scene of the fight and walked in silence until the wreck of the courthouse came into view. Then Bloodworth stopped and spoke.

"What?" asked Craddock. His ears were still ringing from the muzzle blast of the guns.

"I said I got to wash my hands!" shouted Bloodworth. "I can't stand it." He held up his hands, smeared with the dried blood of Bill Huff.

"What?" said Craddock.

They found the old watering trough still intact by the courthouse fence. It was filled with rainwater, leaves, tadpoles, and mosquito wigglers. While Bloodworth washed his hands, Craddock plunged his head into the water and stayed under nearly half a minute. He came up spluttering, tossing his head, the silver drops scattering in the sunlight.

"I'll be glad to get home," said Bloodworth, wiping his hands on his breeches. "No matter what."

"Ah, shit," said Craddock, laughing. "Let us go home then, and die like men." So they went on, and on the north side of the square they parted, each passing out of one dream and into another down the seamless corridor of time.

After his face was bandaged, Old Hundred-and-Eleven picked up a canteen of water and went hunting Molochi Fish. He found him in the grove across the road, sitting cross-legged on the soft ground, his back to the Shipwright house. His face was turned up to the dark canopy of the cedar trees. "You want some of this?" the old man said, and held out the canteen. Molochi took it and drank, the water running down his chin.

"Godfrey! I thought I was a goner!" exclaimed Old Hundred-and-Eleven, wanting to tell of his adventures, but Molochi made no reply. "Well," said the old man after a moment, "I reckon we never will catch old Solomon Gault now. He have slipped the traces. He have—"

"You see them?" asked Molochi, pointing upward.

"What?" said the old man.

"Them birds."

Old Hundred-and-Eleven searched the cedars, saw only a wren flitting nervously above them. "I see that little one yonder," he said.

Molochi stood up then. "I wisht I had a gun," he said.

"Well, they's a God's plenty back 'ere in the yard," said the other.

"Go fetch one," said Molochi Fish.

✦   ✦   ✦

THE SUN, FOLLOWING time, was climbing toward noon in a cloudless sky. No breeze shivered the leaves, and the rain and the cool night were a distant memory now. Only the hot sunlight remained, flat and bright, drying the mud, crusting the blood on wounds, glistening in the metallic bodies of flies.

Morgan Rhea was frantic. She had broken away from Gawain, seemed to have forgotten him, was running toward the road, shaking her hands as if they'd been stung. "He will go after Papa," she said to no one.

"How do you know that?" Gawain said, following along, thinking *That was stupid* because Solomon Gault was more alive to her than any who were standing visible in the sunlight, including Gawain himself, and so of course she knew. And so did he. Then he caught up with her, took her arm and jerked her to a halt. "We got to tell the Colonel," he said, and knew at once, even as he spoke, that he'd really made a mistake now, had misjudged her and dishonored himself. So he was not surprised, was almost grateful, when she spun on him, her eyes shining with anger, and slapped him so hard across the face that he reeled backward, shame bursting like a Congreve rocket in his head.

"*No!*" she cried, and pushed him so that he fell in the mud. Somewhere a man laughed. Gawain turned his head, caught sight of Old Hundred-and-Eleven humping across the road, carrying his Bible and a Short Enfield carbine, heading for the cedar grove. *Strange,* he thought, as if nothing else was happening. But Morgan was standing above him now, pointing her finger at his face. "No!" she said. "Who are you? You dared to come back here, *dared* to present yourself to me as a living man and damn you talk about *honor* damn you and you made a *bargain* damn you! You remember that? You made a bargain and now you must stand to it!"

"Morgan!" he said, struggling to his feet. But she was on him again, striking him.

"No!" she cried. "I want you to find him. Don't you see we got to find him before—"

Then Stribling was there, behind her, wrapping his arms around her and holding her wrists, saying Easy, easy, easy, and she drew her arms in tight and raised her face to the sweet blue sky. "Why can't he die!" she sobbed. "All you men, and he just goes on and goes on and goes on—"

"All right," said Stribling. "It's all right."

"That's a goddamned lie," she said, and twisted away, and stood between them with her teeth clenched, her fists raised as if she would strike the very air she breathed.

"Where?" said Stribling. "Where is Gault?"

"Judge Rhea," said Gawain, wiping his face on his sleeve.

"Of course," said Stribling. "Come quick."

Gawain took Morgan by the hand—she resisted, but only a little—and together they followed Harry Stribling toward the trees along Town Creek. They passed Professor Brown sitting in the shade, waving at flies with his straw hat. "Got to borrow your cart," said Stribling. Brown did not reply, only waved his hand in acknowledgment.

✦   ✦   ✦

A STILLNESS CAME with the gentleman. He rode a great brown horse, but the horse made no sound, not even a creak of leather. The trees in the yard seemed to bend toward him listening, and the insects were stilled, and the birds. Beowulf stirred on the porch, shook his jowls, but made no bark.

"Hidy," said Alex, and his voice sounded flat in the heat, the stillness. The gentleman nudged his horse closer. He was holding a rifle down along his right leg; the weapon was short and ugly, of a kind the boy had not seen before. The man watched for a moment, not moving his head but moving his eyes, from the boy to the dog to the windows of the house, his mouth pursed in contemplation. When he spoke at last, his voice was soft, pleasant. "I bet you are young Alex Rhea," he said.

"Yes, sir," said the boy. "Hot, ain't it?"

The man nodded. "Who's here with you?"

The boy shrugged. "Papa, Mama, Cousin Carter, Zeke, and Beowulf. And a cat somewheres."

"I see," said the man. "Who's Zeke?"

"A horse," said the boy.

"And Beowulf?"

"That's him yonder."

"Ah," said the man. "And your cousin—that would be old Tom Carter?"

"Yes, sir. He's in the back."

"Call your daddy," said the gentleman in his pleasant voice. "Tell him an old friend is here to see him. Tell him I have word from Lily."

"Oh," said the boy. "Ain't you heard? Aunt Lily is—"

"Just call your daddy," said the gentleman.

The boy backed away toward the door. The stillness seemed to follow him, push against him, as if it, too, wanted in the house. Then he heard the click of the latch behind him, and turned, and there was his father in his shirtsleeves, his eyeglasses perched on the end of his nose. "Solomon Gault," the old man said.

The gentleman bowed in the saddle.

"Alex, you get in the house—go in where your mama is," said the Judge.

"No," said the gentleman, bringing the ugly rifle into view. "I insist the boy stay." Then he laughed, and his voice was smooth and cool as pond-water. "If he moves, I'll kill him," he said.

✦   ✦   ✦

BEHIND THE CEDAR grove lay a patch of young corn, bright green in the sunlight, tall from the rain. From the center of it rose the chimney of a burned cabin, hump-shouldered and black, the corn rustling all around. Someone had driven spikes in the chimney and hung tin pans to scare the birds away; in a little breeze, the pans flashed in the sunlight and danced against the bricks: *clank, clank, clank.*

Sometimes, off in the night, Molochi Fish could hear the mill machinery on Mister Pershing's place. The mill itself had burned long ago, but the sound still lived in the air: the clanking and grinding, and the groan of the waterwheel, and sometimes even the hiss of the milled corn as it poured from the hopper. The rank, dark cabin would be filled with the sound, and Molochi would lie on his cot and wait for it to slow. That meant something was caught down in the shaft tunnel, down among the gears. But the wheel would keep on turning—the buckets going shush-shush-shush in the cool green water—and the white ducks in the grass, and the bloody corn.

Molochi and Old Hundred-and-Eleven moved through the corn, fol-lowing the birds who were not scared by the silver pans flashing, or the noise from the machinery. Molochi had no idea where they were going; he understood only that the Mover was guiding them, and all they had to do was follow. But there was something else now, something drawing, like leaves were drawn down the millrace. Molochi daubed his eyes against his sleeve and wished it was dark.

"Cassiopeia!" declared Old Hundred-and-Eleven. "Where you goin, anyhow?" But the other made no answer, only pushed through the rustling corn.

Old Hundred-and-Eleven had torn off the bandage on his cheek, with the result that he was pestered by gnats and horseflies and regular flies buzzing around his head. Moreover, the deep slice in his palm stung with sweat, and that hand was getting stiff. In his other hand, he carried the musket he had picked up in the yard near the artillery piece. His Bible was tucked under his arm. "You! Molochi Fish!" he said. "Where you goin?" But again no answer. The other man went on as if he hadn't heard a thing Old Hundred-and-Eleven was saying.

When they emerged from the corn, they found themselves behind the buildings on the south side of the square. From this side they looked all right, except you could see the sky through the back windows. "I never will get used to that," Old Hundred-and-Eleven said, but the other had already passed through an open door, and by the time the old man caught up, Molochi was halfway across the square. A good many people were gathered there, and they moved away as Molochi passed among them, and moved further still when Old Hundred-and-Eleven came stalking in his bare feet and frock coat and gun and Bible. They passed on through the hoots of children, through the stares and whispers of the citizens, and in a moment turned down the cemetery road.

✦   ✦   ✦

THE OLD MARE would trot, but she would not run. Stribling slapped her with the lines and used all the invective he thought Morgan could stand, but the animal was satisfied with its gait. "Well, it ain't far anyhow," said Gawain. "Let her jog as she will."

Morgan sat between them, staring over the horse's ears at the road. She would have willed the horse to fly if she could, but she couldn't, so she just sat and listened to the voices in her head. Maybe they should have told the soldiers after all. No, they would just fool around and have to get orders from this one or that one, and the day would come and go before they did anything. But now Gawain and Captain Stribling were going in harm's way. Well, they'd been there before, and anyhow, Gawain pledged his honor. Well, fine—but Saturday you told him— Well, that was Saturday. Well, but—

Shut up, she told herself. *Just shut up, can't you?* But, voices or not, the pictures remained. She saw herself by the gallery while Vassar Bishop fired her pistol into the melee. She had as much as promised Gawain—led him to believe, anyway—that she would keep his aunt safe, and herself as well. Then that business in the yard. She had slapped him, shamed him in front of all those men, said terrible things to him. *Well, you can't go back,* she told herself. *You were an ass then; don't be one now.*

She turned to Gawain and touched his arm. "Hey, you," she said. "You Gawain Harper."

"Yes'm?" said Gawain. He sat with the shotgun between his knees, smiling at her as if they were only driving out for a dove shoot.

"I am sorry," she said.

The wagon lurched then, and threw her against him. He put his arm about her and held her. She could smell the rank, sweaty wool of his coat, and the powder and tobacco and wood smoke on him.

"You all quit that," said Stribling. "I am tryin to drive."

"Drive on," said Gawain.

◆　　◆　　◆

HIS FATHER SMELT sour, like old milk, but the boy pressed his cheek into the broadcloth of the Judge's coat and looked through the open door behind them. The breath of the house was stale, as though of air pent up too long and drawn over and over through the same lungs. At the end of the long hall, the back door, too, was open, and Alex saw framed in it the green of the wild garden. He thought of rabbits shivering in their holes, peering out at a world of sunlight and grass where the birds sang.

No birds sang here, only the voice of the man Gault, too pleasant, too soft for the words it bore, and his father's coiled tight and barely heard at all.

"You sent a man to kill me," said Gault. "You should have come yourself."

"I sent no man," said the Judge.

Gault laughed. "Well, let's not quibble," he said. "I only have a minute before the hounds arrive. Are you armed?"

The Judge held up his hands. "You see I am not, sir."

"Well, of course you wouldn't be," said Gault. "Talk, lots and lots of talk and great debate, that's all you know to do." He motioned toward Alex with the carbine. "You come down here, boy. Or you can try and run away if you want to; the door's right there, wide open. Seems close, don't it?"

Alex looked up at the Judge, then moved away and down the steps, his eyes still on his father. He stopped at the horse's head and put his hand on the bit.

"That's good," said Gault. He leaned forward in the saddle and reached behind with his free hand into the tail pocket of his coat. After a moment of fumbling, he brought out a Colt pocket pistol. "Here," he said, and held it out butt-first to the boy. Alex took it, held it awkwardly by the grip.

"You know how to shoot that?" said Gault.

The boy shook his head.

"I swear," said Gault with a sigh. "We are raising little maidens. Look—you pull the hammer back—all the way, mind—then point it at what you want to shoot, then squeeze the trigger. Can you do that?"

"Yes, sir," said Alex.

"Well, do it then!" snapped Gault.

The boy put both thumbs on the hammer and eased it back until it clicked.

"Now put your finger down there—that's right." Gault tapped his chest. "Now point it here."

"Gault, for God's sake," said the Judge. "Let me—"

"Shut up," said Gault. "You had your chance. Now, boy, you point that goddamned pistol right here."

Alex raised the pistol, his hands trembling. He looked back at his father. "Papa?"

"None of that," said Gault. "Hold it steady and look at me, that's right. Now listen, boy—I killed your Aunt Lily. I split her head open like a mush-melon so her brains leaked out."

"No!" said the boy. He was crying now, holding the pistol with both hands.

"Oh, I killed her," said Gault, "and now I mean to kill your daddy, and maybe your sister, too, if I can find her. What do you think of that?"

"No," said the boy. "Papa?"

"What's that make you want to do, boy? Think about it—you have the means to stop me, just pull the trigger there. Your daddy couldn't do it, but maybe you can. Go ahead, show him how a *man* looks after his folks."

"Papa!" cried the boy. "What should I do, Papa?"

"Goddamn you, Gault," said the Judge.

"Go ahead, boy!" cried Gault. "Damn, if you'd of heard the sound it made—"

"No!" sobbed the old man, and moved, but too quick, his foot slipping over the edge of the step, and he was falling toward the brick walk then, heard the snap of his wrist when he hit and his own voice crying "Lily! Lily!"

Solomon Gault shook his head and sighed. "I swear," he said, and raised the Spencer, and drew back the big hammer, and squeezed the trigger.

✦　✦　✦

"PAPA!" WAILED MORGAN. She stood up on the seat and would have jumped had not Stribling snatched her down. Halfway up the lane, Gawain leapt from the cart with his shotgun and began to run.

✦　✦　✦

MOLOCHI FISH AND Old Hundred-and-Eleven came into the lane behind the studio wagon. They heard the sharp detonation of the rifle, heard the woman cry out and saw Gawain leap from the moving wagon, stumble, begin to run. Molochi raised his arm and pointed toward the Carter house.

"What?" said Old Hundred-and-Eleven.

"You wanted the son bitch," said Molochi. "Yonder he is."

The old man peered into the sunlight, slapping at the flies around his head. "Well, aye God," he said. He put the Bible in Molochi's hands. "You hold this," he said, and broke into a loping run, waving the Enfield carbine over his head.

Molochi watched him for a moment, then looked down at the book. He opened it. On the page was a picture of a woman with wings spread like a great bird's. Her dress flowed like water, and she hovered over two children sleeping in some hay. Behind the woman, veiled in feathery clouds, was a rising moon. Molochi stared at the picture. He touched the woman's face, but it was cold and hard like the one in the graveyard. He looked up then. He could hear the woman's voice. He kept the book open in his hand and started that way, opening and closing his mouth so the breath would come faster.

✦　✦　✦

WHEN JOE CREE yielded up the Spencer to Solomon Gault, way back in the morning by the Leaf River bridge, he failed to mention that its bore was jammed with mud. Cree knew it was, for he had watched the cavalryman fall, watched him pull the weapon out of the mud, then shot him and took it for himself. He was just starting to clean it when Gault came shoving up, putting out his hand like he thought Joe Cree had gone to all that trouble just for him. Joe Cree didn't say a word, but he had a thought: *Sure, Cap'n—you go ahead and take it, see what happens.* Poor Joe Cree wasn't thinking anything now, for he lay dead in the yard of the Shipwright house.

But if his spirit dawdled on the road a little, he might have had this to lay at the feet of the scowling saint who awaited him: the carbine acted just like Joe Cree knew it would when Gault pulled the trigger on Judge Rhea.

The late officer's gelding was a cavalry horse trained to stand fire, so he did not bolt when the carbine exploded in Gault's face. The horse stood with his feet planted solid; when he felt the weight leave his back, he turned his head to find Gault writhing on the ground, one foot caught in the stirrup. The man's face was blackened, and little beads of blood were already popping out of the powder burn.

Young Alex, still holding Gault's pistol, almost pulled the trigger when the breech of the carbine blew. He had no idea what happened, but the noise and the smoke and flame scared him so bad he wet his pants a little, though he never told that to anybody. Now the man Gault was clawing at his face, cursing and trying to loose his foot from the stirrup, and Alex stood with the pistol pointed at him crying "Papa! Papa!" Then his father was there, with his hand pressed against his belly, saying "Give it to me! Give it to me, boy!" and he took the pistol from Alex's hand.

Gault was trying to rise now, straining to reach his boot that had slipped all the way through the stirrup, but the horse kept sidestepping, dragging Gault along, until Alex finally took hold of the bit. Then it was not just his father, but Gawain Harper with a shotgun cradled under his arm, and Old Hundred-and-Eleven with a soldier's gun, the three of them standing in a row, watching. Then Morgan was there, and she came to the boy and caught him up, and it was her voice he heard, shouting at them: *Do it! Do it now! You would to a copperhead wouldn't you?* all the while squeezing the boy so tight he could hardly breathe. Then Gault, propped on his elbows, the blood running down his cheek and his eye swelling, watching them all, and his teeth clenched so his voice was not soft now: *Sure. Go ahead, Judge—it'll be easy now. Or maybe you still want Harper to do it for you, or this old freak.* And Morgan: *Give me one then! I will do it! I will!* And then sobbing, pressing the boy's head against her breast: *Damn you all! Damn your honor goddamn you!* until Gawain came and held out the shotgun. *All right, you do it then.* The boy cried *No,* but she pushed him away and took the shotgun and held it with the butt plate pressed right in the middle of her chest. Gawain said *No, like this* and put it against her shoulder. Then *You have to cock the hammers,* and she pulled them back, *click-clack.* Gault watched her with nothing in his face at all, and the men stood by silent while Morgan raised the barrels. The boy watched her finger where it pressed against the trigger; she had cut herself, it was bloody, and the nail was torn to the quick. Her hair had fallen down, and she flicked it out of her eyes, and the boy knew she was going to do it and turned his head. He saw a moth caught in a spiderweb on the porch. It fluttered, but the spider didn't come. The boy waited. At last he couldn't stand it and looked again, and found that another man had come into the yard. He was a country man, of the kind that sometimes brought wood to sell in winter, or game, and always to the back door. But Alex had never seen one like this, with skin raw and peeling under his straw hat, and his eyes leaking and blinking, and his mouth working like a fish's. They all watched him, even Solomon Gault. He had no gun, but a big open Bible in his hand, his palm under the spine. He moved stiffly, and as he came to where Morgan stood, he put his free hand out toward her face, as if he were trying to feel for her in the dark. *Molochi,* said Gawain, but the man came closer, and Alex thought perhaps he was going to take the gun away. Gawain must have thought so too, for he said *Molochi* again, sharper this time. But the man didn't want the gun; instead, he put out his hand, and with his blunt, dirty fingers he touched Morgan's cheek. She didn't flinch but only looked at him, as if she knew he was going to tell her something she needed to hear. He said, *I come all this way. I come all this way.* Then they all watched in amazement as he knelt down and pushed the hem of her dress aside and touched her foot.

Then it was over. The stillness went out of the morning, collapsed like a puffball. Alex heard a redbird in the trees. Morgan lowered the shotgun and turned her face away from all of them. Gawain came and took the gun, and Stribling raised the country man up by his elbow. Then the boy heard a *ping* and saw the glint of a gold coin spin in the air, saw Old Hundred-and-Eleven catch it in his palm again. Then the old man tossed it in the grass by Solomon Gault. *There ye go, Cap'n,* said Old Hundred-and-Eleven. *I reckon you're worth the whole twenty now.*

Colonel Burduck kept his promise, and in the twilight walked down the road to the ruins of the Citadel of Djibouti. He wore no coat, nor sword nor pistol, only a plain muslin shirt and enlisted man's blue trousers and Jefferson shoes. He did carry a stick for snakes, a fat cigar, and a few lucifer matches. Under his arm was a dispatch case bearing the memoirs of Solomon Gault.

Gault was brought in around noontime. Burduck and Captain Bloom were at the bridge, so Lieutenant Osgood received the prisoner. He told how the photographer's wagon rolled in out of nowhere, Stribling at the reins, Harper with a shotgun, Gault between them, his hands tied with a picket rope. Harper helped the prisoner out of the wagon, and the sergeant of the guard took him to the surgeon. Gault's saddlebags and a shattered Spencer carbine were in the wagon; Harper gave these to the Lieutenant, then he and Stribling led the horse and wagon into the shade and walked away together up the road toward the square. Neither man had spoken a word, and Osgood apologized to the Colonel for not detaining them so they could learn how the capture was made.

"No, no," said Burduck. "That's all right. I am not sure I want to know." He thought a moment. "We got the saddlebags and the Spencer," he said. "What about the horse?"

"Oh," said Osgood, his face coloring. "Sir, I never thought—"

"Never mind," said the Colonel. "We have too goddamned many horses anyhow."

Later, Burduck summoned the prisoner to his office. Gault stood in the center of the room, his face bandaged by the surgeon, in manacles now, hand and foot. He did not seem to be interested in his circumstances; in fact, he looked around the room once, then fixed his gaze on the window as if he thought he might take a turn in the yard after a while.

"Well, here we are again," said Burduck. "The victor and the vanquished. That was your phrase, as I recall."

Gault might have smiled.

The Colonel pushed Gault's last note across the table. "I am glad to
have this," he said. "I'll be sure to include it in my memoirs. Do you still
wish to discuss the subject of mortality—your own, I mean?"

Gault did smile this time, a little. Burduck tapped the note with his finger. "I infer from this that you spared my life last evening, though I might
have had more to say about losing it than you thought. In any event, you
understand that I cannot extend the same courtesy?"

Gault nodded slightly, the least inclination of his head. The smile
remained, faint, innocuous, not even insulting. Burduck leaned forward
then, hands together on the table. "You fancy yourself an officer," he said,
"yet you deserted your men, left them to take the consequences of your
own folly—no, stupidity—and not once, to my knowledge, have you asked
about their fate. How is that, sir?"

This time, Burduck was rewarded with a twitch in the other's face, and
a reply. "I did not desert," said Gault. "As for the others, they are not
important."

"I see," said Burduck, and leaned back in his chair again. "You can tell
that to Mister Huff—you and he will spend your last night together."

A movement then, unconscious but telling: a slight twisting of the
hands, a turning of the head. Burduck was gratified. "Sir," said Gault, "I
would prefer—"

"I do not care what you prefer," said the Colonel. "You caused a good
many men to die today, who might have preferred to live a while longer.
However, you did accomplish one useful thing—you killed yourself as well,
a great courtesy to the race, sir."

"Is that all, sir?" said Gault.

"If, at any time this evening, you should desire a minister—"

"No," said Gault.

"Very well," said Burduck, and called for the sergeant of the guard.
Burduck followed them through the parlor and out onto the gallery, empty
now except for L. W. Thomas, still groggy with ether, sitting in a rocking
chair. When Gault saw the man, he stopped and pulled away from the
sergeant, took a step toward Thomas. The other looked up dully, his jaw
slack. "Gault?" he said.

"I saw you in the fight today," said Gault. "Heroic behavior. Your
greatest role perhaps." He turned to the Colonel then. "Mister Thomas is
a great actor; he can be anything he chooses."

Burduck said nothing.

"Mister . . . Gault," said Thomas, struggling with his slurred speech. "If you have anything to say to me . . . I should be glad to call on you—"

"Don't bother yourself, sir," said Gault. "You know what you are." Then he turned for the last time to Burduck, and spat at his feet. "Victor and vanquished," he said. "You think you know which is which now, don't you?"

"Sergeant," said Burduck.

As Gault was led away, he watched over his shoulder as long as he could, his eyes never leaving the Colonel's face.

It rained that afternoon, a quick, intense shower that washed the blood from the ground and cooled the air for a little while. From his window, Burduck watched the soldiers; they did not seek their tents, but danced and capered in the rain like boys. Old Shipwright, in his fez and uniform coat, crept in and stood beside the Colonel, so close that Burduck could smell the aged wool of the coat, the tarnished buttons, the cedar shavings in the pockets. And something else, too, perhaps: youth, gallantry, fiddles at a dance, all gone the way of the old slavers on the African coast—but still there, the ghost of them, if you knew where to look.

"How are you doing, sir?" asked Burduck.

"Oh, just dandy," said the old man. "How 'bout you?"

"I am all right," said Burduck. "I suppose I am all right."

"That's good," said Mister Shipwright. "I want everbody to have a good time while they're here. Like those boys out there—ain't they havin a good time?"

"They are indeed," said the Colonel.

The old man mumbled to himself, then spoke again. "You know," he said, "ever time it rains like this, makes me want to drink coffee. Does it you?"

"Each and every time," said Burduck, and turned away from the window and called for the guard. In a moment, an orderly appeared with two tin cups of coffee from the cooking fire. Burduck took his to the window while the old man sat on the settee, his little claws wrapped around the steaming cup.

Burduck opened the window and let the smell of the rain come in, and the sounds of the men's voices. What did he expect from Gault? he thought, as he sipped at the vile coffee. An impassioned speech? Cowering in the face of death? No, Gault was his own explanation; what he said to Thomas applied to Solomon Gault more than any, and it was as close to a revelation as anyone was likely to get. As for cowering, Burduck confessed to himself that he was glad the man had not broken. Too many men had

died, and if their passing was to mean anything, then the evil they faced
had to be strong, sure of itself, convinced it was right. Otherwise, there
could be no victory. Burduck imagined Gault's face as it looked on the
gallery, and he raised his cup in salute. "Yes," he said aloud. "I do know
which is which."

"Beg pardon?" old Shipwright said.

Now it was twilight, the air still smelling of wet leaves, and a breeze
coming up from the river, and the sky a powdery blue and filled with chimney swifts. Burduck watched the birds and marveled at their speed as they
swirled overhead chattering to one another, or dove headlong into one of
the chimneys of old Frye's tavern. Between the chimneys, the ashes of the
Citadel of Djibouti still smoldered, even after the rain, sending aloft little
tendrils of smoke here and there.

Burduck felt all right standing in the road in the twilight, watching the
ashes. Once they would have saddened him, but now he thought they
might not be such a bad thing in the end. Like all the ashes strewn across
this country, they had to be there, needed to be there, if anything better
was to rise from them and take its shape against the stars. It was a hard
thing, but there it was. *I could have told you,* Burduck thought. *Maybe I
will tell you yet.*

And maybe Gault was right after all, though not in the way he intended.
Maybe what they had been trained to see as victory and defeat was neither
one in the end, but all part of the same turning. He thought of von Arnim,
dying on the porch after coming all that way, and the cavalrymen massacred on the road, and the soldiers and raiders shot down in the yard, and
Gault, who would die tomorrow. Win or lose, it was all the same to them
now, just as it was to the vast legions left behind in the war. *And to Colonel
Burduck, too,* he added, smiling to himself. He might call the morning's
fight a victory if he wanted, but it had been a soldier's fight and none of
his, and it should never have happened at all. Certainly General Washburn
would call it a victory, and see that the Northern press called it that, too.
Then, after a decent interval, Colonel Burduck would be called to
Memphis, as his brother had been summoned to Dakar. From there, a
Quartermaster's billet at some isolated post in the far West, among rocks
and sand hills far from the sea, where a failed soldier might be buried and
never mourned.

Burduck thought of the soldiers' graveyard above the camp, where yet
another grave had been dug that afternoon. That would be the last. There
had been enough burials there, too many caskets rotting in alien soil too
far from home. The bodies of von Arnim, the troopers, the soldiers—these
would go north on the same train with the prisoners—north to the fields

they had known once, to unburned towns waiting in the valleys among the corn. And he would see that the others were moved in time: back to Illinois, Ohio, Kentucky, Tennessee, anywhere but here in this place. He was still in command, and he would see to it. He would leave no bones behind.

In a little while, Burduck moved past the ashes and down to the creek. A cat emerged from the cedars and followed him, its tail in the air, complaining of neglect. On the creek bank, Burduck and the cat found a large negro woman fishing. She had a cane pole and a bobber made of a porcupine quill, on which a dragonfly perched. She sat on an empty whiskey keg and smoked a corncob pipe. When Burduck approached, she looked at him and scowled.

"Is you come to build it back?" she asked.

"Build what back, Auntie?"

"Why, all these here taverns, all that."

"No, not I," said Burduck. "But somebody will, I expect."

"I sho wish they'd get on with it," huffed the woman. "I get tired eatin with the soldiers."

The creek was shadowed by the trees and moved in a soft light, and from it rose streams of mist like smoke from the ashes. A little upstream, a heron stood motionless among the roots of a sycamore. The air hummed with mosquitoes.

The woman had a bucket with some fish, and the cat expressed an interest in it. The woman picked out a little perch the size of an oak leaf and gave it to the cat, who watched it flop around for a moment, then took it delicately between his teeth and marched off. Meanwhile, Burduck found a log to sit on and lit his cigar. He opened the dispatch case and propped the manuscript on his knee. He thought again of the man whose testimony it was, and wondered what he was thinking back there in the boxcar jail. Regret? Probably not. *You know what you are*, Burduck thought, and opened the manuscript to a random page, and read.

> I have heard it said—and from the pulpit, too—that God cursed Ham to eternal servitude & from that we are to deduce that the Negro race is doomed to slavery. What better argument than this for the Reformation, that every man might read & understand for himself the supposed Word, rather than hang his reason upon the mouthings of the Priest. For it was Noah, in the pangs of a "hangover," who cursed not Ham but Canaan, thus the ancients explained the profligacy of the Canaanites and justified their ruin at the hands of Israel. But as to the mythic curse—can they not see

that it lay, not upon the Sons of Ham, but the Sons of Adam—that
is, upon ourselves—a race of men chained to a System that
degrades, brutalizes—not the Negro, for what is he but a Beast?—
but the architects and stewards of a civilization that

Burduck raised his eyes from the fine, careful strokes of Solomon Gault's
pen. The negro woman was humming to herself; her cane pole made a
graceful arc over the water, and the dragonfly rose to the tip of it. The
heron was wading, lifting his long legs in the shallows. When he looked at
the manuscript again, Burduck found that he didn't want to read it after
all, not now, maybe not ever. He straightened the pages, spread his handkerchief on the log beside him and lay the manuscript upon it. He relit his
cigar and held the match for a moment, considering the flame as it burned
itself out, the last blue skein of smoke vanishing like an idle thought. He
had other matches, enough to—

But no, he wouldn't burn Gault's manuscript. Nothing would arise from
those ashes, once they drifted away over the moving water. He would keep
it, and some day by a winter sea, he would read it all—every word—and
hear once more the pleasant voice reply *As for the others, they are not
important.* Then, maybe then, he would build a fire of driftwood and be
rid of Gault forever.

"You are having some luck, Auntie," he said.

"Some," the old woman said, "but they's too much fresh water."

"So I've heard," said Burduck.

He took up his stick and drew idly in the mud: a crescent moon, a
comet, some stars. Then he watched the light change on the water, and let
his mind be still. The twilight had reached that fragile place where day and
night balance on the point of a single moment, when all things and all persons are hushed and motionless, and the world seems to lie behind a pane
of yellow glass. In such a moment, all that is touched by the light seems
already passing, already gone, so the heart perceives it as memory even as
the eye holds it fast. The mist, the trees brushed with gold, the moving
water dimpled with shadow and taking its color from the sky, the face of
the old woman burnished like copper—all these things Burduck watched,
held to as long as he could while they dissolved into yesterday down the
long corridor of time.

Yet in that moment something else took shape from the light, emerged
from it as though made of the light itself, insubstantial as light and just as
real, and just as likely to dissolve. Burduck turned his head. He had not
heard the horseman come, but there he was a little way up the slope,
watching.

"Well," said Burduck, "I didn't think any of you would come."

The horse pricked its ears at the sound of the Colonel's voice. The rider shifted in the saddle, rubbed his leg as if it pained him. Burduck heard the leather creak. Man and horse seemed to stand in a shadow of their own, but Burduck could see the rider's frock coat, the long curl of his hair, the watch chain gleaming faintly, and behind the saddle a bedroll tied, and a pair of saddlebags. Above him hung the lamp of the evening star.

"You didn't do so bad, your first day as sheriff," said Burduck. "No doubt you have found your calling."

The horseman laughed. "No, it is incompatible with that of a philosopher. Besides, I threw the badge away—and anyhow, I didn't do anything, just drove the wagon, is all."

"Well," said the Colonel, "I don't suppose you'd light and tell me about all that—what happened with Gault."

"No, sir," said the other. "I better go on. But I wanted to satisfy myself that you'd really come here like you said you would. And I wanted to tell you—"

He paused then, and in that moment the balance tilted, and it was night. Not dark yet, not for a while, but night just the same. Up the bank, the old woman laughed to herself and jiggled her line. The current made a black V around her quill bobber. The heron stretched his wings and lifted off, long legs dangling. Stately and silent he flew, and disappeared into the shadows of the trees. When Burduck looked at the horseman again, he seemed to have moved further back toward the road, though it might only have been a trick of light. "What would you tell me?" the Colonel said.

"I saw the ocean once," the horseman said. "Way off in Carolina, a long time ago. Maybe I'll see it again sometime."

"I hope so," said the Colonel.

"What about you, sir?"

Burduck thought a moment. A long way he'd come, following the old flag to this dim shore fading into night. He smiled then, and found it easy. "I expect I'll see it pretty soon," he said.

"That's good," said the horseman. "That's what I come to find out." Then, after a moment, he said, "I liked the sound of it—the ocean. I won't forget it."

"Nor will I," said the Colonel. "I promise."

"Good," said the horseman.

The old woman had gathered in her line now, and took up her bucket of fish. She was moving away up the bank, the cat following behind. Before she had gone too far, she stopped and turned, and though Burduck could barely see her face, he knew that she was smiling. "That's all right," she said. "Somebody burn it down, somebody build it back. That's all right."

"Yes," said Burduck, and raised his hand, and watched her pass on toward the Shipwright house where there would be a cooking fire, where the ground was washed clean of blood. Then the Colonel turned his face toward the road, saw the black rectangle of ashes between the chimneys, and the empty shadow. A long time he sat on the log beside the moving waters, slapping mosquitoes, the cigar cold in his fingers.

✦   ✦   ✦

THAT MORNING, AFTER Solomon Gault was taken away, Old Hundred-and-Eleven looked around for Molochi Fish. The man was gone, and nobody had seen him go. Then Old Hundred-and-Eleven unsaddled Gault's horse and tied him to the fence that ran along the side of the yard. Alex Rhea watched with interest.

"That's a big horse," said the boy. "He seems friendly, too."

"I bet you all got a currycomb somewheres," said the old man. "You fetch it, and I'll show you how to bresh him."

In a little while, the boy was combing the mud out of the gelding's tail. "I wonder if we get to keep him," he said. "I'd brush him every day if we did."

"Well," said the old man, "if it weren't for that 'ere U.S. mark on him."

"Oh, that means he belongs to *us*," said Alex. "Here's Sister. Morgan, can't we keep this horse?"

"Oh, why not," said Morgan. She was a mess, her hair straying in her eyes and her dress spotted with mud, her face streaked with powder and tears. "We'll keep him 'til they make us give him back, anyhow," she said, and tried to laugh, though it wasn't convincing.

Old Hundred-and-Eleven had swept off his straw hat and stood aside when Morgan approached. She looked at him now, her eyes narrowing. "What happened to your face?" she asked.

The old man swallowed and hunted his voice. "Face?" he bleated.

"Hah!" said Morgan as if she'd caught him in a lie. "And your hand— what about that? Let me see it."

Old Hundred-and-Eleven held out his good hand. "Not that one, the *other* one," Morgan said. So the old man produced his injured hand, and she held it open like a book and stared at the palm. "How'd you *do* this?" she asked.

Old Hundred-and-Eleven was shivering at the touch of her. "Oh, oh, it was for to seal a bargain," he stammered.

"Singular bargain," said Morgan. "It's cut to the hamstrings."

"It was with Molochi Fish," the old man said. "For to catch Solomon Gault that killed my niggers."

"He did *what*?"

So the old man told her the story of Dauncy and Jack.

She listened with her face turned away, so fearful was the gust of the old man's breath, but she kept hold of his hand. When he was done, Morgan looked him in the face again. "Who is this fellow Fish, anyhow?" she asked.

Again she turned her head as Old Hundred-and-Eleven told all the stories he knew about the strange man Molochi Fish. "I don't know why he done that this mornin," the old man said finally. " 'Twas Providence, sure. Agamemnon!"

"Well, you kept your bargain, the both of you," said Morgan. "Now you go and wash this—wash it good, mind. And tell Miss Ida we want some whiskey. I will fetch a needle and thread—maybe it's not too corrupted yet."

In a few moments, Old Hundred-and-Eleven sat in a kitchen chair, his hand open on the table. He refused a drink of liquor but took a tablespoon of paregoric. It made him sleepy, but not so much that he didn't cry out when Morgan poured the whiskey in his palm. The pain ran up his arm like a bolt of lightning, and all at once he was sick.

"Here's a bucket," Ida Rhea said calmly, and they waited until he was finished.

Morgan had a curved upholstery needle and a spool of black thread. He watched her thread the needle's eye, then turned his face away. It took all his will not to cry out when the needle went in, but though the pain was sharp and red, it didn't last long. The old man gathered up his courage and looked, and found the woman crying. She was steady, and her voice was even, but the tears ran down anyway, following the tracks of earlier ones in the grime on her face. "All right," she said. "It's too far gone. Mama, what shall we do?"

"There's the surgeon—don't the soldiers have one?"

"Hah," said Morgan. "He would take the hand."

"Or maybe this," Ida Rhea said. She lifted Old Hundred-and-Eleven by the arm and led him out of the kitchen, Morgan following. They shuffled along, for the old man was groggy and Ida Rhea just out of bed and trembling. They went around the front of the house where Gault's horse was tied.

"Now open your hand," Ida Rhea said. "There, hold it out. Let them come." And in a moment, the flies had come, and walked over the wound, and rubbed their feet in it, and laid their eggs.

They made a pallet for Old Hundred-and-Eleven next to Alex's in the upstairs bedroom. He was glad to take another dose of paregoric, for he liked the sweet, drowsy feeling it gave him. "Don't you dare say anything about this physic around Aunt Vassar Bishop," Morgan warned. "Now, you lay here and rest yourself."

The old man yawned. "Miss Morgan," he said. "I remember you when you was little."

"That was a long time ago," she said.

"Not so long. Miss Morgan?"

"Yes?"

"You like me, don't you?"

Morgan almost laughed, but stopped herself. "I don't stick needles in just anybody," she said, and smiled at him.

"I was jes studyin on it," he said. "You was always kind to me."

"Go to sleep, sir," Morgan said, and touched his shoulder. "I'll wake you for supper."

She left then, and the old man lay in silence. He had a new bandage on his cheek; he wanted badly to tear it off, but knew he better not. In the palm of his hand was another bandage, thick and damp, and he knew that soon they would waken under there, and the tiny jaws would set to work on the poisoned flesh. Maybe that way he could keep his hand.

The house murmured around him, unfamiliar sounds, and the way everything was so *close* seemed peculiar to Old Hundred-and-Eleven. Still, it was all very pleasant. A breeze moved the gauzy curtains, and sunlight played upon them, and the pallet seemed airy and light as the stuff of clouds. The room was perfumed with what Old Hundred-and-Eleven assumed were woman-smells: odors like flowers, like spring water and rain, that seemed to have colors to them, blues and whites. He was trying to imagine what those smells were attached to, and how they could have color, when a boy came out of the fireplace and stood looking down at the old man. He was barefoot and had his breeches legs rolled up, but he was no country lad: his shirt was good linen, and he wore a straw boater with a red band.

"Hey, there," said Old Hundred-and-Eleven. He knew the boy, but couldn't call his name to mind. That was a long time ago, just as Morgan had said, though he ought to remember a boy's name.

The lad put out his hand. Old Hundred-and-Eleven rose from the pallet and took it. Together they passed through the hall and down the stairs and out into the sunlight.

The old man wondered if he'd been sleeping a long time, into another day perhaps. The air of this one felt different, smelled different. It seemed to be high summertime, the sky pale blue and daubed here and there with journeying clouds whose shadows raced across the land. The roads were dry, and all that lay along the roads was coated with dust: leaves, the bloom-heavy crepe myrtles, grass in the ditches, the fronts of houses. The fences were sifted with dust, and the wild roses over them, and the honey-suckle. Grasshoppers buzzed in the heat.

They crossed the yard and went down the little lane to the cemetery road, then west toward the square. In the glebe of Holy Cross, Mister Garrison's milk cow grazed, her bell clanking, jaws working side to side. She looked up with her kind eyes as they passed. Almost to the square and another bell then: the deep tolling of the courthouse clock, and for counterpoint the tenor chimes of the Academy, and above them both the clangor of the dinner bell from the Planter's Hotel. Amid this carillon, then, the day traveled into noon and left the morning behind.

All persons, all things, woke to the bells from out the drowsy heat—woke as if summoned to the glory of the sun. Pigeons swirled from the courthouse cupola, doors opened and shutters closed, and well pulleys squeaked and squawked in their drawing. From the stores men came into the street, pulling on their coats, and above them others clumped along the galleries, leaving their offices behind. Tom Jenkins strode forth from his hardware, a straw hat tilted over one eye, and behind him a nervous, bespectacled clerk with a sheaf of papers, still talking. From the courthouse gallery, Sheriff Bomar watched the men spilling out the wide doors below: Judge Rhea and a brace of Memphis lawyers, Constable John Talbot and Ben Luker, Sam Hook with his hands in his pockets, a newspaper corre-spondent, twelve jurors all feeling important. All the while, old Doniphan's mute sister clanged and clanged the dinner bell from the porch of the Planter's Hotel.

The dusty square was full of children rolling hoops, tormenting ants, ignoring their mothers' cries and their nurses': *Marster Jack, you know you cain't be out here in the hot afternoon!* and *You all get home fo' the dogs get you!* The children laughed with high, clear voices. Under the trees, country men squatted on their heels and with their clasp knives carved at wedges of cheese, and before each one lay a square of muslin piled with biscuits or bread, and for each a tin of sardines with the top rolled back. Old Dan the Rag Man sat with his china cup rattling coins, while a black woman in a scarlet headrag moved through the shade, a basket on her arm, crying *Bla-a-a-ack berries! I got bla-a-a-ack berries! Blackberries!* Wagons drew up to the hitching rings, and beneath every tree, and by every water-ing trough of mossy wood, horses and mules switched their tails.

Then down the southerly road past Audley Brummett's livery where, in the feed lot, Audley and Mister Johnny Cross were discussing a mule. Houses now, windows thrown open, dogs lounging in the yards. Houses never seemed more content, more serene and eternal, than at a summer noontime when dinner was laid in the dining room and the doors thrown open to the breeze. At Shipwright's, two boys wrestled in the dust while a negro woman scowled at them from the gallery. A little farther then, and Frye's Tavern, swaybacked between its two chimneys, and on its rambling gallery a dozen men with their boots propped on the rail, waiting for Queenolia Divine to announce dinner. Then John Walker's, where a pair of colts stood tethered, and young Dauncy combing their tails, and a green parrot swinging from its perch on the gallery screeching *Damn the Whigs! Damn the Whigs!*

Through all these things Old Hundred-and-Eleven moved, following the boy, still clinging to his small, damp hand. He didn't bother to speak, for he knew somehow that his voice would not be heard, any more than he could feel the dust under his soles.

Then they left the southerly road and made their way up a sunken lane, once an Indian trail, now rutted by carts and wagons and bordered by worm fences. The heat was palpable here, and the air still and murmurous with insects. On either side, the corn grew tall, tasseling, and redwings perched on the stalks. The boy passed over a thick rattlesnake sunning in the lane, and Old Hundred-and-Eleven followed unafraid. In a little while they left even the sunken lane, and here was new ground dotted with stumps, then a pine thicket, then the slope of Carter's hill rising. The old man bent to the slope, following the boy.

At last, Old Hundred-and-Eleven found himself on the cleared knob of the hill, in a grassy place strewn with yellow, black-eyed flowers and clumps of blackberry vine. The old man was surprised to find the boy suddenly gone; he searched and found him sitting with his arms wrapped about his knees, his face toward the town and the hills beyond. *I thought I'd lost ye,* said the old man, but this time the lad gave no notice that he'd heard.

Old Hundred-and-Eleven stood quietly then, a little behind the boy, watching the wind ruffle his hair—and seeing all below just as the boy saw it, knowing it was for the last time. He looked over the canopy of trees, the cleared places where cabins and houses stood, the spires of churches and the cupola of the courthouse where the bright flag waved, and he somehow understood that he'd been given this moment to say goodbye. Not to life, not yet, though the old man would not have been afraid, nor very sorry, to give it up; but to the world down yonder that was gone, and to the boy who was gone, whose name he no longer knew. Old Hundred-and-

Eleven did not know why he was chosen. Certainly it was not to judge, not to weigh the decency and kindness against the cruelty, the greed, the niggers with welts on their backs. Old Hundred-and-Eleven would not judge, even if it had been offered him, but he was glad to see it all spread out below him one last time, falling toward the afternoon, the twilight, the darkness that must come. He put his hand on the boy's head, though he knew he wouldn't feel it, and spoke, though he knew the boy couldn't hear him now. *I thank ye,* he said. He turned to go then, went a little way down the hill toward where the pines were green and dark, then stopped and turned again. The boy still sat there with his knees drawn up, the sun high so that he made no shadow. *Don't grieve yourself,* said Old Hundred-and-Eleven. *It'll always be there, somewheres.* This time the boy looked up, but if he heard the old man, or saw him against the trees, he gave no sign.

A different light then, for the sun had long since passed over the house, and Morgan's voice, and the touch of her cool hand on his forehead. "You gon' sleep all the day?" she said. "It's suppertime, and—here now, what you got to be cryin about?"

✦　✦　✦

THEY HAD SUPPER in the yard, fireflies rising all around them, on a table spread with Irish linen. The cloth was yellow from years in a cedar chest, and the silver tarnished to the color of eggplant, and most of the china chipped around the edges as if mice had chewed it. But the candles burned bright, dancing their flames in the little breeze, never minding the twilight that lay golden on the grass.

"A waste of good tapers, you ask me," said old Frank Harper. He picked noisily at his teeth with the bone of a chicken Uncle Priam had stumbled upon in the road. The solitary bird had not gone far among so many, but the greens had, and the early peas.

"Nobody asked you, sir," said Aunt Vassar to the old man, and wiped his mouth with a handkerchief that had come from France.

Old Mister Carter regarded the table as if it were a lost city come to light again. He had not had the china and silver out of the sideboard, nor even seen the linen, in the twenty years he had been a widower. But now he remembered each piece, where it came from, what the weather was like and what his wife was wearing, and on and on, spinning hours and days from a teaspoon, a plate, a cruet etched with irises. All these things he told to Professor Brown and Uncle Priam as they sat under a leaning scuppernong arbor after supper. Uncle Priam, who had never been out of Cumberland County, tried to imagine the scenes the old man described. Professor Brown, who rarely spoke at any time, was a good and patient listener; he drowsed in his chair while the old man went on, nodding his head from time to time to the sound of carriage wheels on the Champs-Elysées.

The cavalry mount Gault had ridden was tied now in the shade of a hackberry tree, swishing his tail at the flies. Beowulf, having gleaned all he could from beneath the table, lay under the horse's feet. Young Alex Rhea was currying the horse for the third time that afternoon, running his hand along the shiny flanks and legs where not a speck of mud or dust remained.

"I swear, son," said Ida Rhea, "you are goin to wear that horse out combin him. He won't be any bigger'n a fyce dog, you keep on."

"Don't let him get behind that beast," warned Aunt Vassar. "He'll get knocked in the head, sure."

The two women sat at the table, resting, reluctant to clear it away. Mrs. Rhea was wrapped in a shawl despite the heat, while Aunt Vassar fanned herself. "You won't go to Brazil then?" Aunt Vassar asked.

"Oh, Lord," said Ida, "I don't want to hear mention of that place long as I live. I was *always* dead set against it, you know, but the Judge—well, he had this notion . . . oh, never mind. Now that Morgan is to marry again, he'll have to stay around so he can worry them to death. Talk about Providence!"

Aunt Vassar lifted her eyebrows at the mention of marriage. Apparently, Ida Rhea was privy to information that she, Vassar Bishop, was not—and her very nephew the groom! Presumably, anyway. Certainly. Now Ida was laying for her, consumed with the desire to press her wrinkled old hand to her breast and say *Oh, my dear—you didn't know?* Well, let her be consumed. "You know, I have been thinkin," said Aunt Vassar. "Have you ever been to the coast?" She was gratified by the slightest hint of pique in her old friend's eye.

"To—," Ida began, and drew her shawl around her. "Well, yes, I suppose I have—a long time ago."

"I have an old acquaintance in Pass Christian," Aunt Vassar said. "A Miz Necaise, a widow upon whom virtue sits lightly, though she has long since passed into the theoretical stage. I have a mind to visit her, as I used to in the old times. Come along."

"Oh, my," said Ida. "I don't know."

"Nonsense," said Vassar. "Don't stop to think about it, just say you will. We'll make the Judge come too, tedious as he is. A packet to New Orleans, a steamer to the Pass—it'll be lovely, won't it, to get the stink of ashes out of your nose?"

"But the expense! I—"

"Pah!" snorted Aunt Vassar. She leaned forward and touched her companion on the arm. "Come to think of it, let's leave the Judge home. Then we can flirt our way to heaven's gate."

"Vassar Marie!" cried Ida. She colored scarlet, and Aunt Vassar fanned her briskly. "I am too old for such foolishness," said Ida, "or even to think about it." Then, after a moment, "Do you really think we could?"

"Hah!" said Aunt Vassar. "Child's play."

Ida looked down and plucked at her shawl. "I always loved the sound the water made. I never forgot it, you know."

"One never does," said Vassar gently. A moment passed, while the old women listened to the sea. Then Vassar sat bolt upright and snapped her fan shut. "Now then," she said. "Tell me about this marriage."

On the back porch, Old Hundred-and-Eleven sat working up a new chaw of tobacco. It was some of the Judge's stock, and not bad for war times, but a little too sweet for Old Hundred-and-Eleven's taste. Still, he hadn't had a chaw in three days and was not about to find fault with this one.

Beside him sat a crystal goblet full of cool water. He could not remember the last time he'd drunk from a glass, and this particular glass, he'd discovered, rang like a bell when he tapped it. Next to the glass lay his Bible, open to the picture of the angel and the sleeping children. From time to time he would look at the picture, then steal a glance at Morgan where she sat on a garden bench with Gawain Harper. Every time he did so, a sigh would make its way out of his heart. Well, it was all right, as long as it wasn't that Stribling fellow. He wondered where Stribling had got to. He hadn't been at supper, and somebody had remarked that his horse was gone from the shed. No doubt he was off stirring up some more trouble for everybody.

As the twilight deepened, the old man found himself looking at all the people gathered in the yard, and listening to their voices as they talked quietly about this or that. The sight of them made him feel good, in spite of his broken heart, and he knew that what he said to the boy on Carter's hill was true. Then the thought of that made him sad, so that he felt sad and good at the same time, and he found others walking through his mind: General von Arnim, and Molochi Fish, and poor Dauncy and Jack who, this time yesterday, were playing marbles in the dirt, and now they were under the dirt themselves. He shook his head. "Pandemonium!" he said, and spat a stream of ambure into the yard. "Don't grieve yourself!" Then he tapped the glass with a horny nail and made it ring.

So the twilight grew, and the yard was full of fireflies, and chimney swifts twittered overhead, and the bullbats were coming out. The mosquitoes too, and Morgan felt them at her ankles, so she and Gawain rose from the bench and passed around the house to the front yard.

The oaks were solemn and full of shadows, their crowns brushed with the fire of the setting sun. Along the fence rows, where the good, sweet clover grew, a troop of rabbits inched along, grazing. Across the lane, in the glebe of Holy Cross, the priest swung at the tall weeds with a scythe. He made a mysterious figure there in the golden light, and the sound of the blade was soft and pretty—one of those sounds, Gawain remarked, that give comfort when you don't have to make it yourself.

Morgan laughed at that. She had gotten some better at laughing as the day wore along. She had slept awhile; then, though it was only Monday, she took a bath on the back porch, shielded by blankets hung all around. Now her hair was clean and pinned up, and she wore a soft cotton shift she had made from old sheets, and the violence of the morning seemed far away now, like a dream in chiaroscuro. But it was no dream, and when they came to the place where Gault had lain, Morgan turned and fisted her hand and pressed it to Gawain's chest. "You tell me somethin, you," she said.

"I'd be delighted," said Gawain, smiling. "Last night in the barn, I found your—"

"Hush!" she said, reddening. "I don't mean *that*. I mean—" She struck Gawain lightly with her fist. "I mean, why did you put that shotgun in my hands this mornin? Why did you do that to me, for God's sake?"

"Ah," he said. He blew out his breath and took her hand. He unfolded the fist and pressed her palm to his cheek.

"Was it to teach me a lesson?" she persisted.

"No," he said. "No, there ain't any lesson you could get from that, nor any I could teach you."

"What then?"

He thought a moment. His eyes strayed away, and the gesture was not lost on Morgan. "I am sorry for it," he said at last. "I wanted . . . I wanted the choice to be yours. I didn't trust the rest of us, but I trusted you, and I knew that whatever happened would be the right thing because you wouldn't do the wrong thing."

She bit her lip and nodded. "That is a smooth answer," she said.

"It's the only one I got."

"And if I'd pulled the trigger?" she asked.

"But you didn't," he said, and when she started to reply, he held up his hand. "You didn't, and if you want to go on wonderin, you may do so, but you didn't. That's all that matters."

"You think so," she said, and pulled her hand away.

A coolness passed between them then, and for a moment Gawain wished he were home in bed, or under it. "I don't know what to tell you," he said lamely.

"The truth," she said. "Why did you do it?"

"I *told* you—"

"You tell me what you think I want to hear," she said, and felt the hot tears rising. *I will not cry,* she thought. *I will not!*

"Now, darlin—," began Gawain.

"What if I'd blown that man's brains out!" she cried. "What kind of dreams would that make?"

"Oh, I could tell you all about that!" snapped Gawain Harper. "Where would you like me to start? How about Perryville? Did I ever tell you—"

"I'm sorry!" she said, so shrilly that the priest across the lane raised his head. Then, softer now: "I'm sorry. That was not fair. Let's forget it."

"Only you won't forget it," he said. "I don't see how you could."

"All right," she said, her voice pleading now. "Tell me why, then."

Gawain took a deep breath, let it out. "You were right the first time," he said. "I wanted to teach you a lesson."

"Damn!" she said. She crossed her arms and turned her back on him.

A long moment of silence passed, and Morgan began to think that he had gone away. She was about to turn when he spoke again, his voice soft and deeply tired.

"You were after blood," he said. "I couldn't blame you, but I was—am—sick of blood. I knew pretty soon that none of us would kill Gault, not like that—and I knew that you'd never forgive any of us if I didn't bring you into the circle. Don't you see? You had to find out for yourself what it means to make that kind of choice."

"Choice," she said.

"Yes. Your papa would say it was God's will you didn't shoot. I say God was holding his breath with the rest of us, hoping you wouldn't. I had to give you the choice, and you chose right. That's all I know to tell you."

She did not turn right away, though she knew he had told the truth now. Once more she heard the hammer's *click-clack,* and she shuddered. Perhaps one day, if he asked, she would tell him her own truth, but not now. The day had been long for Gawain Harper; he did not need to know how close she had come to ruining their lives forever. Then he surprised her. He took her by the shoulders and turned her.

"You came close, didn't you?" he said.

"Yes."

"Old Molochi helped you choose, didn't he?"

"Yes," she said.

"I love you, Morgan Rhea," he said, and kissed her, and took her hand.

They went along the fence row and tried to see how close they could get to the rabbits without them running. Morgan asked why they didn't have rabbit for supper tomorrow. Gawain pointed to a big buck. "See that one?" he said. "He's got a wolf. Look close."

She did, and recoiled at the thing growing from the creature's flank. "Lord," she said, "what is it?"

"It's like a botfly," said Gawain. "They get em in the summer, and the fever, too. You have to wait 'til winter if you want to eat rabbit for supper."

"My God," she said, and thought about all the rabbits she had eaten, and how she was unlikely to eat one again. A cart rattled by on the cemetery road, and to the north, a locomotive whistled for a crossing. Morgan pressed close to her companion as they walked, glad that he had told the truth, but still not sure what to think of it. If she had pulled the trigger—

She stopped suddenly and grasped his lapels. "What if I *hadn't* chosen right?" she asked. "What then?"

"I would still love thee," said Gawain. "And all else would be the same, except you would know yourself better."

"But, my God in heaven," she said, her voice growing loud again. "Gawain, all my life I'd of seen—"

"No, darlin," he said. "You almost did, but you didn't, and that is what you have to think on. Besides—" He grinned. "That shotgun wasn't loaded anyhow."

"What!"

"Empty as a jug."

"Gawain *Harper*!"

She sat down in the grass, and he knelt beside her. He did not speak, only watched her face, hoping she wouldn't slap him, though he wouldn't blame her if she did. Finally, she laid her hand on his knee.

"All right," she said. Then she looked him in the face. "I have only one thing to say to you, sir, and that will be an end on it. School is *out*. No more lessons."

"No more lessons," he said. He spit in his palm and held it out. She shook his hand like a man would, then pushed him over into the grass.

They strolled down to the lane and back. "Papa will holler pretty soon," she said. Then she stopped again. "Gawain, where is Captain Stribling? Why didn't he come to supper?"

Gawain surprised her again. He pulled away a little and shoved his hands in his pockets. She could barely see his face now, but she could sense the puzzlement in it, and what might have been anger or hurt, she couldn't say which. "What's wrong?" she asked.

"Oh, he is gone," he said, and in his voice was hurt and anger both. "Harry is gone."

"Gone? Gone where?"

Gawain shrugged. "Just gone."

"Tell me," she said.

"We left Shipwright's and walked home," he said. "We didn't talk much; my head was hurting pretty bad by then, and Harry . . . I don't know. Seems like he was locked up inside himself. Anyhow, we got home, and I laid down on the porch for a minute, and when I woke up three hours later, I found this."

Gawain fished in his waistcoat pocket and pulled out a folded sheet of paper. It had come from one of his sisters' letter stock and still smelled of the drawer where it had lain for a decade, and faintly of perfume. "I was goin to show you," said Gawain morosely.

"It's all right," said Morgan, and took the paper. She unfolded it and turned it to the light.

> Friend Gawain:
> Now you know what a coward I am, for if I was half a man, I would wake you and say goodbye. You can't raise the dead, Gawain, it is fatal to try. So don't try. Promise me that, when you are done being mad at me.
> I had a good time. I would stay if I could & steal Miss Morgan Ray away from you. Say goodbye to her and Aunt Vassar & all the rest. I will remember you always & hope you think kindly on
>
> Your Pard,
> Harry
>
> P.S.: Your daddy's pistol is right off the bank by a big willow tree. You could get a boy to dive for it for a dollar, I bet. If you find mine, you can have it. Leave the Henry where it lays.
>
> H.

Morgan folded the paper again and tucked it in Gawain's pocket. She daubed at her eyes and wondered how many more things she'd have to cry about before the day was over. But it was all right this time. It was better than not being able to. "I am sorry," she said. "Are you mad at him for goin?"

"Some," he said.

"How did he know that . . . about the pistol?"

Gawain shrugged again. "He knew a lot of things he oughtn't to," he said. Then he frowned. "Dern it," he said, "we might of had a nice time."

She held him then, pressing him close, listening to the watch ticking in his pocket. The rabbits were gone now, and the priest had quit his chopping for want of light. In a little while, they went back toward the house. The Judge was waiting on the gallery, his arm in a sling. "Morgan Rhea," he said, "do you realize what time it is?"

"Aw, Papa," she said. Then the whippoorwills began, and a solitary mockingbird, away off in the fields of night.

✦   ✦   ✦

HARRY STRIBLING WATCHED from the shadows of the cemetery road. He could see them walking among the oaks, could hear their voices rise and fall. When they started for the house, he almost called to them, but it wasn't any use; by now, they could not have heard him anyway. *Just as well,* he thought, and knew it for a lie, and made himself believe it just the same. Then they were gone, and the yard was left to the fireflies. "Come up, Zeke," he said, and turned the horse's head eastward. He looked one last time at the house, watched the windows light one by one. Then he looked no more.

At the cemetery gate, he reined up again. Molochi Fish was sitting with his back against one of the brick pillars. "How is it with you, old Molochi?" Stribling asked. Molochi looked at him and blinked. "You been here all day?"

"I run off from all them people," said Molochi.

"What about *them* people?" the horseman asked. He waved his hand toward the cemetery where the grave markers gleamed against the dark grass. He saw the stone maiden there, her hand outstretched as if she would catch a firefly rising. She might have moved, or the breeze moved in her gown, or her eyes raised to them—but the horseman knew that was only the light, beguiling.

"They ain't but the dead ones here," said Molochi.

"Hmmm," said Stribling. He reached back and unbuckled his saddlebag and rummaged around in it until he found his pipe and tobacco. He loaded the pipe and stoked it with a lucifer. "Now, Molochi," he said through a cloud of blue smoke, "what about all that business with Miss Morgan?"

Molochi hawked and spat into the grass. "What bidness is that?" he said.

"You will surely try a man's patience," said Stribling. "But I am inclined to be charitable, and offer you the consolation of my philosophy. You see those birds yonder?"

Molochi peered into the dusky burying ground and saw the dark birds—more than he'd ever seen before—gathered on the stones and huddled in the branches of the trees. They were restless, preening and ruffling, muttering to one another. "I see em," he said. "I *been* seein em all my—" Then he stopped and looked again. He thought he saw the old woman, hunched over, wringing her hands, her mouth moving without sound. And the Indian woman, and the pale fog that meant the dogs were moving yonder in the far trees. Molochi had never seen them away from the cabin, and now here they were in town. He made a mewling sound in his throat and gathered his shirtfront in his hands. The rotten material tore under his fingers.

"What's the matter?" asked Stribling. "You said yourself there wasn't any but dead people out here."

"But not them," said Molochi. "They don't belong here."

"Sure they do," said Stribling. "They don't belong anywhere else. Now go on home. Leave it to em."

"They'll stay here?" asked Molochi.

"I guarantee it," said Stribling.

"All right," said Molochi.

"Well, goodbye," said the horseman.

Molochi Fish, who had never been said goodbye to before, only looked at the man, at his shape against the sky. He saw him go, the horse's hooves making no sound, then rose and stood watching in the road until he could see the horseman no more. Then came a rustling in the graveyard. Molochi looked and saw the birds, hundreds of them, in a black cloud flying toward the night. He watched until the last one disappeared in the darkening east, then he turned and made his way toward home.

✦   ✦   ✦

A HALF MILE down the road, Harry Stribling came to a ridge. There he stopped again and turned in the saddle. Behind him lay the pale ribbon of the road, the twinkling fields and the dark shadows of the trees. He could see no lights of houses, nor anything of Cumberland now. He supposed that if he were to feel regret, this would be the time, for the last gate was closing, and there would be no returning. He waited, wondering which of his many wrong turnings would come to mock him this side of the bourne. Certainly they were all out there in the darkness; having pursued him this far, they might well pursue him yet.

But the starlit road was empty; the shadows harbored no sins, and the only voices were the katydids and the frogs in the bottom. Then Stribling knew that he had outrun them at last: the guilt and shame, the little cruelties and the secret moments of cowardice, the gossip, the pettiness and envy. All these passed away into Time where they belonged, and they left no ashes behind.

He rode a long time in the darkness, and at last drowsed in the saddle, as in the old times on campaign. Sometimes he would wake to fields opening away on either side, and sometimes to the deep woods, the trees meeting overhead and hiding the stars. Zeke moved steadily, plodding along at a slow walk, for he knew they were in no hurry. When the moon rose, dim and waning now, it cast among the trees a yellow light of no more luminance than a candle.

When at last Zeke stopped, Stribling woke in confusion. His first thought was that the column had halted and the infantry were clogging the road again like so many sheep. Then he came to himself, and remembered that he was alone. Looking around, he felt the solitude close in on him, and he shivered with a sudden panic. Then he discovered he was not alone after all.

The road fell away to a creek bottom here, and a bridge, then curved into the deep shadows of a cedar grove. A man sat on the plank rail of the bridge, holding the reins of his horse. His face was round and jovial; he wore a forage cap pushed back on his head, and a frock coat with a high collar. The heels of his boots were hooked over the bottom rail, and his spurs gleamed in the starlight. "Well, Harry," he said. "You been a long time comin."

Stribling pushed closer. "Major?" he said. "Major Cross?"

The man stood up then and stretched himself. He grinned at Stribling. "The same," he said. He came and took hold of Zeke's bit and rubbed the horse's nose. "I am glad to see you," he said to Stribling. "The last time was Nashville—the Granny White Pike, as I recall."

"Yes," said Stribling. "It was a gallant charge we made, wasn't it?"

The Major laughed. "Mighty gallant," he said. "I am sure it saved the army." He yawned then, and consulted his watch. "Well, all that was a long time ago, and best forgotten, though I don't suppose we ever will, eh?"

Stribling yawned in sympathy and rubbed his neck. "No, sir," he said, "I wouldn't know how to forget it. I am obliged you'd wait for me."

The Major smiled. He patted Zeke's neck in the unconscious way that horsemen have, then moved back across the bridge. His boots made no sound on the planking, but when he mounted, the leather of his saddle creaked. He looked up the road a moment, then turned to Stribling. "I wish it could have been different," he said.

Stribling nodded. "It's all right," he said.

"You're not scared, are you, after all our adventures?"

"A little," said Stribling. He lifted his face to the stars, saw that they had shifted in the night's passage. It was late, and the morning could not be far away. He looked at the Major again. "I was always scared a little," he said.

The Major nodded. "I know," he said. "Well, come along. It ain't far now."

"Where we goin?" asked Stribling.

The Major laughed. "Why, we are goin home," he said, and turned his horse.

Stribling took one more look at the stars. They were diminished now, and the whippoorwills had hushed, and a little breeze was stirring in the trees. When he looked down again, he could see the Major waiting for him down the road, one leg cocked up on the pommel of his saddle. Stribling was about to move onto the bridge when he discovered it was not empty; a boy stood there, steadying himself against the low rail, his blind eyes turned toward the sound of Stribling's horse.

"Well," said Stribling, "you have come a long way too, I reckon."

The boy nodded. Stribling eased forward. The boy put out his arms, and Stribling lifted him up, settled him behind on the rolled blanket. Then Harry Stribling touched Zeke lightly with the spurs. They caught up with the Major just beyond the bridge, and together they rode into the cedars.